Full Exposure

'Gianfranco, you can't use this office anymore,' said Professor di' Bianchi. 'Do you understand? You barged in just when I was . . . when I was getting changed.'

'Of course, *signora. Mi dispiace*,' said the young Italian with a shy smile, withdrawing the key from his pocket.

The smile lit up his face, and suddenly Donatella didn't want him to go. 'Stay there,' she said, and pulled up a chair to sit close to him. She nonchalantly loosened one of her recently refastened buttons, allowing the young man a further glimpse of the swell of her breasts.

The lust that filled her so unexpectedly surfaced unbidden. She felt a needy urge to seduce this young man on the spot; to unzip his fly and fondle his cock. And how sweet he smelled. She bent forward and inhaled his scent; his lightly tanned skin was redolent of satsumas.

Donatella looked at her companion and saw that he sensed her desire. She touched Gianfranco's hand to take the proferred key and held it longer than necessary.

With her other hand she was reaching for the remaining buttons on her blouse when reality returned like a douche of cold water on Donatella's erotic aberration. The moment was lost.

What the hell was she playing at? What was wrong with her? She'd been seized by a desire to have sex with two complete strangers in as many days.

Full Exposure
Robyn Russell

BLACK LACE

Black Lace books contain sexual fantasies.
In real life, always practise safe sex.

First published in 2002 by
Black Lace
Thames Wharf Studios
Rainville Road
London W6 9HA

Design by Smith & Gilmour, London
Printed and bound by Mackays of Chatham PLC

ISBN 0 352 33688 9

For Russ, Gloria and Siena Bear

Contents

Prologue

The hour was late, well past midnight, and the warm wind of early summer blew softly up the Valdichiana, ruffling the hair of the tall slender man standing on the high terrace. He leaned over the ornamental iron balustrade, and the breeze brought the scent of honeysuckle to his nostrils, the same fragrance he remembered from his first summer in Tuscany, ten years ago.

Enjoying the aura of affluence surrounding him, the man gazed thoughtfully into the street below, mulling over the decade. The ten years had been a productive time for him, enabling him to consolidate his domain until it was akin to a private fiefdom.

But now he was troubled. An unknown quantity had invaded his finely tuned world.

Some snooty bitch was coming to investigate. Who put the Americans onto his trail he didn't know, but he'd make it his business to find out. The meddling party was arriving soon, but he'd see to it that she didn't stay around long.

The breeze tugged at the hem of his loose robe, billowing it gently away from his body. Beneath the silk he was naked and his penis slowly stiffened at the thought of punishing the interloper. He'd get pleasure from silencing her before she had the chance to mess things up. With a cruel smile he imagined his victim stripped and tied to a chair; or better yet, splayed out on a bed, bound hand and foot, thighs wide apart. Then the real fun could begin.

This prospect brought to mind other, more immediate delights that lay in store for him tonight.

The man fondled his cock, now fully erect in the moonlight, and ran his free hand over his torso. His body still felt firm and supple and the fine lines around his mouth and eyes could be attributed to years of living through hot Tuscan summers. His skin was free of tan lines; he received his full dose of rays from hours spent lying naked up here on the secluded terrace, free from prying eyes.

He had chosen this house carefully. It provided him with the best of both worlds: the privacy of his own space coupled with the accessibility and anonymity of the city immediately beyond his walls. He enjoyed living up here, high above the press of the vulgar crowds. Even in the early hours of the morning, young people continued to stroll in the streets below, moving languidly from bar to bar, finding the few that stayed open this late on the weekend. Now, as many of the walkers nuzzled and kissed, the man imagined arm-in-arm lovers bringing their ritual courtship closer to a night of sex.

Often the man spied from above on those who couldn't wait. He guessed that if he peered tonight into the lurking shadows of the alley that slid past the side of his building, he would see one or more pairs of lovers fucking against the wall. Their urgent thrusting and squealing was so crude, so wanton, so exciting, but so lacking in style. His aristocratic features creased into a grimace of lust mingled with distaste.

He worked in the city during the day. Sometimes it pleased him to be like the common masses, become one of them, to blend in and disguise his true nature. Down there he often met women to satisfy his casual lusts. He'd fuck the women he chose and feed from their affection.

But he didn't invite the common hoi-polloi up here. None of his colleagues knew this hideaway; it was owned by an anonymous company he'd set up as a business front several years ago. Only a select few, their silence bought and paid for, entered this private sanctum, which was specially chosen and cultivated for his esoteric pleasures. His mind wandered as he enjoyed memories of flagrant scenes the lofty vaulted space had witnessed.

With a rude 'beep' the mobile phone in the pocket of his robe punctured the night-time sounds of the city and his sexual reverie. With a flash of anger, he felt like flinging the offending gadget from the balcony but, controlling himself, flipped it open with a shake of his wrist. *'Pronto!'* His speech was impatient.

He listened for a moment, then he spoke urgently. 'Yes, I understand, I understand perfectly well. But you know not to call at this time.' Irritation lined his face as he listened to the caller's explanation, and his reply was tinged with real anger. 'Yes, yes. I've told you how to deal with them, how to make sure they stay silent!' Another pause.

'Do I have to do everything in this fucking deal? What the fuck do I pay you for? Our partners in Rome won't be pleased about this! As if I didn't have enough trouble . . .' His voice tailed off. He listened some more.

'No!' he resumed with irritation. 'No, I can't come; I'm expecting visitors . . . Who? None of your business. You deal with your fuck-up and I'll call you in the morning. You've been here as long as I have. You know the ropes. I expect to hear it's all taken care of. *Capisce?*' Without saying goodbye, the man snapped the phone shut.

He stepped back from the balustrade and lay on a small patio couch, seething with animosity. He inhaled deeply, allowing the subtle scents of the potted lavender and roses lining the terrace to fill his lungs. Slowly letting go of his anger, he savoured each moment before filing the information away for future use. Other aromas, of rosemary and other lush greenery that filled the private patio, helped to calm him.

He reached into the drawer of a small table and withdrew a long silver box, from which he selected a Cuban cigar, neatly clipping the end with the little guillotine he kept for that purpose. The flare of the lighter illuminated the line of his jaw as he transferred the flame to the rolled end of the densely packed leaves. Drawing deeply on the tobacco, he exhaled slowly, adding another scent to the perfumed air.

His cock had grown limp when the phone call had diverted his thoughts, but now his hand returned to fondle himself. His cock, impressively long even in its detumescence, rose as he drew the foreskin back, massaging his shaft between thumb and two fingers.

His own familiar sexual touch soothed him as he gleefully planned the interfering bitch's downfall. Perhaps he'd bring her up here. The walls were solid stone and the windows triple glazed. No one would hear her cries as he shackled her hand and foot and intimidated her. At this thought his cock stood ramrod stiff in the moonlight, the pale beams lightly brushing the curls of his pubic hair with silver.

A low but piercing whistle, audible from the street below, was repeated three times. To the unsuspecting bystander it could have been the tuneless melody of a young drunk. But the man understood a more personal signal.

In one fluid motion he stood up and strode to the railing, momentarily exposing himself to those he knew were waiting below. He had perfected this pose: a lone virile figure silhouetted against a full moon, like some priapic classical god.

Giving his visitors a few minutes to climb the winding alley that led through the urban maze behind his house, he pressed a button on a small remote control resting on the table. Beyond his sight, far below, a tall wooden door slid silently open, admitting his guests into the rear of the house. On a closed-circuit TV screen he watched the two young figures step into the lighted hallway.

The hidden camera revealed a pair of beautiful teenagers, bathed in the glow of cleverly recessed lighting. The lens followed the young couple to a narrow hardwood staircase, up which they slowly climbed, gripping hands tightly. The stair gave direct access to his luxuriously appointed bedroom; the coverlet was turned down, exposing black silk sheets.

The man waited for their arrival and slid open the door from the terrace. 'Hello, my beauties,' he murmured, stretching his lips to a mirthless smile. He let his thin robe fall to the tiled floor. '*Come stai?*'

'*Molto bene, grazie, signore,*' the two youngsters chimed in unison but without meeting their host's eyes. They undressed without ceremony, knowing from previous visits where to fold and hang their clothes.

They lay naked, side by side on the bed. The boy fondled his cock, urging it to firmness, lubricating it slightly with one of the extensive range of sensual products lining the night stand.

Aware that their patron liked him and his young female companion to be ready, he passed the lotion to the girl, watching as she gently massaged herself, sliding first one, then two fingers inside her cunt. She smiled shyly under the gaze of the two males, pouting her lips as she'd seen actresses do in the pornographic movies the trio sometimes watched.

This intimate sight roused the boy to full hardness, and he quickly lubricated his anus in preparation for what was to come. He leaned across and anointed the girl's tight little arsehole, gently easing his slick finger inside. A low moan, which could have been pleasure or trepidation, escaped her lips.

Both heads jerked around at the slight sound of the lock on the bedroom door. Above their prone bodies stood the man who had ultimate power over them. His penis stood out before him, a full eight inches of firm flesh. In one hand he held a long ornately decorated dildo; in the other a length of silken rope.

'*Buona sera, i miei regazzi,*' he purred, enjoying the sight of their sexual readiness and submission to his desires. The bruises from their last session had nearly faded. 'Shall we begin?'

1 *Il Sesso alla Leveta del Sole* (Sex at Sunrise)

'You should be a sculptor,' the young woman said, 'the way you're exploring my body.' Though her comment was flippant, her voice was coloured with arousal.

The sleepy young man in the bed beside her said nothing. He communicated only with his hands, which travelled slowly across the contours of female flesh, climbing the gentle mounds of small firm breasts, lingering at the hard *picci* of the woman's nipples before exploring the flatlands of her firm abdomen and probing the forested depths of her dark red bush.

The young redhead obligingly spread her thighs, allowing the explorer's fingers to continue their progress into the liquid cavern contained there. The first pale ray of the morning summer sun found its way through the heavy wooden shutters, across the terracotta tiled floor and slanted across the rumpled sheets, highlighting the movement of the man's fingers. His thumb nuzzled the precious little cairn of the woman's clitoris.

Kiki Lee studied the motion of the man's hand between her legs, as his fingers curled in her cunt. Always looking for new images to shock her art professor, she wished she had a camera to capture the erotic composition. But the camera was in the next room and she didn't want to interrupt the ripples of pleasure beginning to tweak her. Allowing her academic ambitions to be diverted, she lay back and enjoyed a slow rhythmic finger-fucking. Closing her eyes, she drifted into a sensual reverie, enjoying the residual spicy scent of her companion's cologne. As her concerns for the day slipped back into her subconscious, she welcomed the pleasure.

A moment or two later, Kiki returned to full wakefulness. Her lover's fingers had ceased their delicate investigations and now rested, unmoving, inside her. With a grunt of annoyance she shifted position, rising on one elbow to stare irritably at her partner, now fallen back to sleep. As she moved, the boy's fingers, slick with juice, slid from her cunt and made a damp mark on the sheet.

Kiki's eyes fell to her partner's semi-erect penis, draped invitingly across his thigh. His handsome face reminded her why she had picked him out of the crowd at Bar Sandy last night. His big cock had been a welcome bonus, ascertained by early groping in the shadows in the Via Brancusi outside the bar. She'd unzipped his fly and virtually led him by his cock all the way back to the small villa she shared with another young woman on the hill above the town centre.

Kiki struggled to remember the boy's name but couldn't retrieve it from the slurred memories that swirled around in the bottom of her mind. It had been quite a wild evening at Bar Sandy, with a lot of wine and ribald conversation. On the bedside table stood an opened bottle of red wine from the nearby Rendola vineyard, only half consumed. The remains of a shared joint combined with little piles of ash, burn marks on the wood, and the unfinished wine composed a slightly seedy tableau. She and her new friend had drunk this fine merlot straight from the bottle, not bothering with glasses. Kiki shuddered at her uncouth behaviour.

Instead of dwelling on last night's debauchery, she struck a match, lit the joint and took a hit. Marijuana always made her feel horny and, after another deep toke, she stubbed out the roach and reached for the young man's cock. Her dark carmine fingernails, cut short to facilitate her work in the studio, matched the tint of her lover's cockhead. Unable to resist the appetizing morsel, she took the velvet tip between her lips, tasting their mingled juices from the last few hours of hectic sex. Kiki remembered the taste of his come, but what *was* his name?

Catching sight of herself in the bedside mirror, she watched her reflection suck avidly on the cock with no name. Her short red hair, its spiky cut enhanced by the dishevelment of rolling round her bed all night, framed a pale and delicate face, out of which stared a pair of pretty dark-green eyes. As she crouched, her small breasts hung in shallow arcs below her slight figure. Her silver nose ring glinted in a morning sunbeam as her head bobbed up and down on the ever-stiffening shaft. There was another photograph begging to be recorded for posterity.

The boy stirred and gave a shuddering groan, and his penis jerked in Kiki's mouth. She moved her lips away but she was too late; her lover's cock erupted and coated her cheeks and chin with warm salty semen.

'*Bastardo!*' growled the redhead, slapping her companion across his thigh. She was annoyed that the tingling between her legs wasn't going to be satisfied in the way she wanted. 'Claudio!' she cried, remembering the cocky bastard's name! 'You selfish jerk!' She wiped the come from her face and smeared it across the boy's lips in a none-too-gentle gesture.

A smirk of satisfaction lit the young Italian's face, only to vanish as Kiki pushed him onto the floor in an unflattering sprawl of limbs.

'Hey,' he complained with a yelp, scrambling to his hands and knees on the thick lambskin rug, a gift from one of Kiki's former lovers.

'Out, Claudio. *Via! Se ne vada!*'

'What's your hurry, *la mi'amora*?' Though slightly bearded in the morning light, his expression was that of an immature little boy.

'I've got things to do,' she said. Right on cue the alarm issued its clarion call.

The young man started, but Kiki jumped out of bed to silence it with some relief. At least she hadn't been too drunk or stoned last night to forget setting the clock.

Claudio pouted, looking longingly at the young red-head standing by the bed. Kiki stretched her sleek body to its full five foot three inches; the nipples on her firm little breasts jutted upward provocatively as she raised her arms above her head. Reawakening lust shone through Claudio's eyes as he surveyed the woman's uninhibited nakedness from his lowly position on the rug at her feet.

'There's something you should know, smart-ass,' Kiki said crossly, her fluent Italian marred only by a strong Midwestern American accent. '*Gentlemen* don't come in a girl's mouth unless she asks! Got it?' Despite her annoyance, her dark green eyes twinkled with ironic humour. 'Anyway, *I've* gotta work, lover boy.' She pointed to her naked chest. '*Il l-a-v-o-r-o,*' she said for further emphasis. 'You, Claudio, go home, *vai a casa.*' The young woman emphasised her command with several prods of her toe.

He reached for her ankle but, quickly eluding his grasp, Kiki gathered the young man's clothes from the piles strewn across the floor, and tossed the bundle at his chest. 'You can shower back at your place. I'm in a hurry. It's been great. Bye.'

'But . . .' Scrambling to grab his clothing, Claudio tried to salvage some dignity from his abrupt dismissal.

'I'll call *you*,' she said, just to make sure he got the message.

'We can do this again sometime, can't we, *la mia cara*?' he pleaded. He was still on his knees, holding his dick with one hand, his clothes with the other.

'Yeah, sometime,' Kiki replied noncommittally, 'but now you get dressed.' She hustled her hapless companion into his clothes. Moments later, she pushed him unceremoniously from her bedroom and out of her front door. 'I'll see you round town,' she added, tossing the poor lad a bone of future possibility.

Still naked, Kiki stood framed in the front doorway to watch him leave. The cool moist morning air prickled her skin as she watched the half-dressed young man slouch grumpily down the flight of steps that separated her little villa from the small piazza crowning the hilltop. He looked around in puzzlement. As if reading his mind, Kiki reminded him, 'You left your scooter down at the bar. It'll be OK. No one would want to steal that heap of junk!' She gentled her harsh words with the ghost of a smile, shut the door on last night's boytoy distraction, and faced the surfacing worries of her working day.

Kiki tiptoed to the room occupied by her housemate, Francesca Antinori, and paused. All was quiet within. She opened the door softly and peeked inside. Francesca was sleeping soundly, alone and peaceful, her naked body splayed across the bed as if waiting for her dream lover. A vibrator lay discarded amidst the wrinkled sheets.

From the doorway, the slim redhead admired her friend's sensual curves and the sexy fullness of her breasts. Not making a sound, Kiki stepped to the bedside and leaned over the reclining Francesca to brush one nipple with her lips. With just a touch of envy at her companion's beauty, she retreated to the bathroom.

After a shower and a brisk breakfast, Kiki ran a brush through her hair, darkened her eyes with kohl, threw on some bicycle shorts and a tank top, not bothering with a bra, and ran down the hill towards the small unmanned train station of Bucine. The early commuter train from Florence would get her to the main line Arezzo station just in time to meet the first express of the day from Rome. Kiki was determined to meet the new arrival, Dr di'Bianchi, before anybody else could talk to her. She wanted the new professor from America to hear the truth about what had been going on at the college.

The small *locale*, covered in graffiti, pulled into the platform just as Kiki pounded up the station steps. She flung herself into a seat and slammed the door behind her with a sigh of relief.

Her satchel bulged with essays by freshman art history students she'd graded for Professor Stewart Temple-Clarke, the Director of *Il Collegio Toscana's* School of Visual Art, a foreign studies facility shared by a consortium of universities in Boston, Massachusetts, in the US. Kiki had been working as Temple-Clarke's graduate assistant for six months, glad of the extra money that helped pay the rent on the little house in Bucine.

Sitting in the deserted carriage, Kiki pondered her situation, musing about life in Arezzo and Bucine. The sex was wonderful here; Italian men were suckers for her aggressive American attitude. In many ways Tuscany was a great place for her. Arezzo was a beautiful small city, relatively uncluttered by tourists, and life in the nearby town of Bucine was pleasant, with fine local wines and fresh farmers' produce available at the little street market below her house.

As her train rattled through a series of tunnels and stopped interminably at the small towns of Laterina and Indicatore on its way into Arezzo, Kiki didn't notice the beautiful landscape. She was lost in her own fears and hopes. She scowled at thoughts about the mediocre education she was receiving; despite her provocative lifestyle she considered herself to be a serious student. Over the last month, when her discontent concerning the quality of the department had boiled over into anger, she had led several student demonstrations, gaining the attention of the local media.

This had infuriated Temple-Clarke, who had summoned Kiki to his office, admonishing her not to interfere in college business if she wanted to stay in the programme. Ever since, he'd loaded her down with more and more work, leaving her little time for protest activities. She certainly didn't trust Temple-Clarke but, in truth, she was a little frightened of him, although she'd never admit it to her peers.

Kiki's thoughts returned to the present when the station sign announcing Arezzo appeared in her peripheral vision and the train clattered round the last curve and stopped with a screech of brakes. Kiki hopped off, anxiously looking at the station clock. The Bucine train had arrived late and there was only a moment before the Eurocity from Rome arrived for its brief stop in Arezzo.

Breathlessly, Kiki ran along the station underpass leading to platform four. As she reached the platform, the sleek express glided into the station with barely a whistle from the overhead electric wires. Kiki was immediately surrounded by a flood of disembarking passengers hurrying to work in the city. Prepared for this eventuality, the redhead scanned the crowd anxiously for someone who looked like an academic type while she held aloft a sheet of paper on which she'd written 'la dottoressa di'Bianchi,' in big block letters.

2 *L'Espozione* (The Exhibition)

As Kiki's train trundled through the fertile hills of the Valdarno, her housemate Francesca Antinori was just waking. A chorus of songbirds announced the arrival of the *International Herald Tribune*, a special delivery by one of the beautiful *Italiana's* many local lovers.

At the sound of the rolled newspaper hitting the slate flagstones outside her bedroom window, Francesca smiled, opened her eyes and stretched. No one else got their morning paper delivered in the town, let alone a foreign edition.

Francesca enjoyed reading the English-language *Tribune*, which helped her with her English. The ginger-blonde woman rose naked and swung open the casement windows of her bedroom, letting in the cool morning air. Francesca gazed over the small piazza and peered down the narrow lane leading to the town centre. Lights illuminated bedrooms and kitchens as her neighbours started the day, adding a faint wash of amber across the beige and grey paving slabs that reflected the strengthening sun. Beyond the piazza, on the next ridge, vineyards and olive orchards were brushed with fresh green from the weekend of gentle but persistent rain.

Well aware that she was fully visible from the waist up, Francesca faced a wall of windows in the apartment house across the piazza, leaned over the window sill and cupped her prominent breasts, caressing herself so that the peaks of her nipples grew rigid. Overt about her femininity, the young Italian knew that someone across the square would be watching, and the thought made her grow excited. She relished nudity, and found regular employment as a life-drawing model at the *Collegio Toscana* in Arezzo. Often her desires were too strong to be satisfied by this relatively decorous display, and early in the mornings she frequently flaunted her uninhibited self to the neighbours.

The morning newspaper lay on the courtyard, a few feet away from where she stood. Francesca opened the door and brazenly descended the steps, her bare feet toughened to the stone paving. Sauntering to the spot where the rolled-up *Tribune* lay, she heard the bell of the farmer's young milkman behind her. She looked back and saw his bicycle turn into the piazza, bouncing over the stones.

She cried out to him, waving. '*Buon giorno, Ambrogio!* You're early today!'

With a screech the young man brought his bicycle to a halt, making the milk bottles rattle precariously in their carrier. Spellbound, the boy stared at the beautiful naked woman standing alone in the piazza in the morning light.

Making no effort to cover her nakedness, Francesca walked towards the boy, her long hair curling around her shoulders. She enjoyed his expression as he straddled his bike, licking his lips as his eyes roved across her large bouncing breasts and down her belly until his vision locked on the precise 'v' shape of her pale-gold pubic curls.

She cocked one hip with a teasing invitation. 'Do you have any milk for me?' she asked coyly.

'*Si, signorina!*' The boy stumbled off his bike and grabbed a bottle from the rickety basket. He walked awkwardly in a futile effort to hide his erection, and held out the milk bottle. '*Il vostro l ... l ... latte, signorina Antinori,*' he managed to stammer. His eyes couldn't leave her body.

'*Grazie tante, Ambrogio,*' she replied, grasping the bottle with one hand. 'It won't be long now, Ambrogio,' she teased him, enjoying the boy's arousal and confusion. Looking at his penis through the thin cloth of his trousers, she said, 'Oh, yes. That cute little dick of yours will be big enough for me soon!'

She pivoted gracefully and strolled back inside. 'That's enough for you today, *il mio regazzo*!' she said with a laugh and a wave goodbye to the awe-struck teenager. Not everyone had their milk brought to their door but even bottled water was delivered, with no objections, to this address. And the farmer himself brought fresh cream three times a week. Francesca's liberal nudity, while scandalising the neighbourhood, guaranteed personal household service for the two unrestrained young women living in the tiny villa.

Francesca stepped back inside the warmth of the room and shut the front door, her nipples still erect with the cool air and her exhibitionist excitement. What a rush, she thought, calling to mind an American phrase she had learned recently. Feeling that young boy's eyes upon her body was almost as good as having sex! Well, almost.

She waltzed into the simple cosy kitchen at the back of the house. Kiki had left her breakfast dishes to dry in the drainer, but there was still warm coffee in the pot. Francesca put the milk in the fridge and spread the newspaper across the table. Without a glance towards the unshuttered window in the kitchen, she filled a mug with coffee and sipped it black as she scanned the headlines of the *International Herald Tribune*. She liked to impress Kiki with her knowledge of world affairs. She might not have fancy academic degrees like her friend, and some townsfolk might regard her as the local slut, but Francesca knew she had a good mind. Untutored, but good.

The memory of young Ambrogio's penis, as hard as a little rod in his trousers, brought a smile to her face. He must be fourteen or so. Not too young for sex, she thought. After all she'd lost her virginity at about that age, with an older man who'd taught her to survive on the streets of Florence, even as he broke both Italian law and moral taboos by fucking her nearly every night.

Succumbing to her sexual memories, the naked girl leaned back, parted her pubic hair, and played with herself softly, delicately, sliding one finger and then two inside herself. She was very wet. Francesca blithely licked her fingers, tasting her own musk. She slid them back between her legs, eager to feel their familiar touch on her swollen clit.

At a slight noise, she turned and glanced out the window behind her. Nico, a neighbour who worked for the local telephone company, was staring in at her from the back porch that looked over a lush back garden, eagerly devouring the sight of the beautiful naked woman, a stupid grin on his face.

'Oh!' she said with a note of mock alarm. 'Nico, what are you looking at?' She moved her hands and put her legs together but made no move to cover her nakedness. Nico had come to her window a few times before, usually with some lame excuse, hoping to catch her naked. On the days he did, Francesca indulged his transparent desire, gently teasing him with her body, keeping the window open but the door locked.

'Are you feeling horny again, Nico?' she asked. 'Isn't Berzitta treating you right?'

Francesca noted a small consistent movement of his right arm as he watched, his hand invisible below the window sill.

'Nico, are you playing with your cock again?' she scolded with playful severity. 'Last time you did that, Berzitta got very angry!'

Berzitta, Nico's girlfriend, was parsimonious with her sexual favours. Francesca thought it only fair for the poor man to get some relief from his prudish girlfriend's attitudes. Though funny looking at her window, with his mouth gaping wide and eyes bulging at the sight of her, Nico was trim and fit, tanned from his daily work in the Tuscan countryside laying and repairing telephone cables. Although not the swiftest of intellects, he had the reputation of being a hard worker, and the sympathy of many local men for being engaged to Berzitta.

'Signorina Francesca, Le sta proprio molto bene!'

Francesca laughed at Nico's compliment about her beauty and stood facing him, hands on hips, flaunting her nudity for her visitor's enjoyment. She laughed again when he gestured that he'd like to come inside. 'Oh, Nico!' she said, shaking her finger at him. 'Naughty, naughty. You know Berzitta doesn't like you visiting other women!'

But today the hot eyes of the man seemed to bore right into her body. The young *Italiana* found herself warming to the rustic appeal of *l'uomo di telefono*, and she felt her horniness ratchet up a few notches. Besides his attraction as a means of appeasing her desire, she wondered if a tumble with the telephone man might get her and Kiki the new line for the computer they wanted so badly. Nico could be a very practical friend to have.

Her mind made up, Francesca stepped nimbly to the kitchen door and opened it wide. With a wicked grin on her face, she gestured for Nico to enter. *'Vuole entrare un attimo?'* she asked the excited man.

The expression on his face made Francesca laugh out

loud. She leaned forward and repeated more softly, 'Come on in, Nico. Berzitta need never know.' She reached for his cock, which stuck out of his open fly and pulled him through the doorway. 'Come here, Nico,' she said. Holding his cock with one hand, she wrapped her other arm around him and kissed him long and hard. Under a thin T-shirt, the man's body was firm and well muscled.

Francesca slid her hand along his shaft and glanced at it admiringly. That stupid bitch Berzitta didn't know what she was missing! She stroked Nico's penis gently, rolling back the foreskin to expose the rich purple head, already moist from wanking at the window.

As she slowly pumped his cock to emphasize her words, Francesca said, 'Do you want to fuck me?'

Nico nodded urgently.

'Will you do something for me in return?'

Nico swallowed hard and found his voice. 'Anything you ask, *Signorina Francesca*. Anything!' The desire in the man's eyes was pathetic in its intensity. His cock pulsed in Francesca's hand.

'Here's the deal, Nico.' She reached further down to cup his balls; they were big and heavy in her palm and full of come. She squeezed them gently. Nico moaned and closed his eyes.

'If I let you fuck me, Nico, will you rig up a new phone line for us?' she asked plainly. 'A line we can use for the computer? One that won't take six months to get approved?' With each question, Francesca dragged her fingernails along the vein on the underside of his shaft, feeling herself get wetter by the minute at the thought of having that long dick inside her.

'*Signorina Francesca*, if you let me fuck you, I promise you'll have a new line by the end of the week. I'll see to it personally! Is there anything else . . .?'

His promise was stifled by Francesca's lips as she

kissed him deeply, probing his mouth with her tongue. He tasted of peppermint toothpaste. 'I'll let you know, Nico,' she said as she drew back and led him into the bedroom.

Nico needed no further encouragement. Within a moment he had stripped off his shirt and lowered his trousers and underpants. Before he could untie his heavy work boots, Francesca pushed him onto the bed, where he lay with his dick sticking straight up. She eagerly straddled him, taking his cock deep within her mouth, and offering her cunt to his straining tongue.

To Francesca's delight, Nico was clearly no slouch in bed despite being severely rationed by Berzitta. His tongue found its way directly into her slick crevices and circled the little bud of her clitoris. As she pressed her cunt into his face, feeling his nose, tongue and chin explore her juicy lips, her delight at this easy conquest of a new lover and the taste of his lovely cock in her mouth stimulated her own pleasure, and she felt her desire building inside her.

'OK, Nico, you asked for it!' Francesca said. 'Here's your reward – and mine.'

Nimbly shifting her position, Francesca impaled herself onto Nico's cock, feeling the long thick shaft fill and stretch her. Rubbing herself as she rode him, she ground herself against his body and climaxed quickly, her juices flowing over the tops of his thighs. A moment later she felt his hot gush inside her and laughed out loud with pleasure.

'Oh, Nico! Does Berzitta know you fuck like that?'

Nico blushed, embarrassed now his passion was spent. 'We don't do it much.'

Francesca smiled. 'I can tell. The amount you pumped inside me, I think you've been saving it up for weeks!' She slid off his cock, now soft but slick and shining with juices.

She could have basked for another hour in sexual contentment, but her new lover was eager to leave. He put his clothes back on. 'I must go now,' he said, shyly. '*Mille grazie*, Francesca, for ... for ...'

'For the sex, Nico?'

He nodded. Blushing, and avoiding Francesca's coolly affectionate gaze – one she might bestow on a well-trained pet – Nico quickly changed the subject as he walked into the kitchen. 'I'll run a new phone line to your house tomorrow or the next day from the box down the street. I'll make sure everything is in order.'

'Thank you, Nico. You are so kind ... and such a good fuck!' Francesca kissed the man lightly on his lips as he stepped out of the back door. 'Come back after you've fixed the line and we'll celebrate.' She caressed a nipple as she spoke, just to make sure he got the message.

Nico blushed, but his eyes shone at the prospect. With a slow smile he shuffled quickly down the steps, climbed over the garden fence and vanished in the trees. Francesca picked up the paper again, poured some fresh coffee and sighed contentedly. She wished every morning could begin with a good fuck like that.

3 *Il Arrivo* (The Arrival)

From her well-cushioned seat on the Eurocity express from Rome, Dr Donatella di'Bianchi came fully awake to the sound of a conversation in Italian. Shaking herself free of a dream, she opened her eyes to see a man and a woman standing silhouetted against the opposite window.

'*Hai visto la casa nuova di Rosanna?*'

'*Si, l'ho vista. E bella, vero?*'

'*Hai visto le camera da letto . . . ?*'

Dr di'Bianchi smiled, taking pleasure in her returning fluency in Italian. She wondered vaguely what the bedrooms in the unknown Rosanna's beautiful new house were like, but the chatting couple moved on, taking their suitcases and their conversation with them.

Dr di'Bianchi sat up tall in her seat, straightened her neat linen suit and gazed at the distant view. The train was slowing and from the window she could see the fortress of an ancient terracotta city, poised on a hill and ringed by a medieval wall. Arezzo! She was there!

The elegantly dressed American, her senses heightened by excitement, deciphered the mundane chatter of her fellow passengers all around as they prepared to leave the train. Few were watching the city glide into full view, but Donatella was entranced by the spire of *il duomo* dominating the skyline, framed by taller ridges of *le Alpe di Poti* in the background.

The train rolled through the outskirts of the city, entering the modern industrial suburbs that stretched into the fertile plain around the historic settlement. A moment later, the professor glimpsed a station sign, in big white letters on its blue field, that announced her destination.

Her trip from Rome had been fast, under two hours, and she had dozed fitfully after an unusually early start. Here she was in Arezzo already, and it was not yet eight in the morning. The train glided to a stop.

Dr di'Bianchi, though pale from the long Boston winter, was a dark-haired woman who looked native in the Tuscan environment. Rising to her feet, she fastened her grey linen jacket across her chest and brushed the matching skirt flat over her hips. Tucking a stray wisp of dark brown hair back into its neat bun and checking the safety of her passport and wallet, the tall brunette adjusted her deep blue silk blouse to show just a hint of cleavage, and picked up her briefcase and single suitcase.

As she stepped down from her first-class carriage onto the noisy crowded platform, Dr di'Bianchi thirstily assessed her new surroundings. She looked at the softly coloured medieval walls in the background, and at the bustling early morning crowd of good-humoured passengers. Yes, Italy. Yes, Arezzo. Setting down her two bags, she surveyed the platform and pursed her lips. Where was her welcoming committee? As she examined the thinning crowds for someone resembling the image of Stewart Temple-Clarke from his file photo back in Boston, she saw no likely candidates.

Not that she'd *be* very welcome, she thought. Much as she loved Italy, the tall professor found herself wondering why she'd accepted this assignment to investigate the academic standards and financial operation of the art programme at *Il Collegio Toscana*. This job could be a rough ride to nowhere. She would certainly make few friends, if any. What if she became entangled in some sordid web of academic intrigue? Donatella shook her head at these negative thoughts and reminded herself that if she did her job properly, quickly and thoroughly, it would be a big feather in her cap. It would even put her in line for the coveted Associate Provost's position back home.

The platform was emptying rapidly and, except for one small slight young woman, everybody was moving briskly towards the exits. Donatella banished her doubts and fastened her wide-set, clear grey eyes on the girl, who was looking about her with a look of growing puzzlement and disappointment.

Donatella recognised her own name on a hand-lettered sign the girl carried, almost forgotten in her hand. Walking up behind her, she alerted the young redhead with a gentle cough.

The girl's head whipped around and her eyes widened, surprise clearly registering on her features. Professor di'Bianchi studied her one-person reception committee, a pretty punkish, arty-looking girl, about twenty pounds lighter and about ten years younger than herself.

Donatella appraised the girl's outfit and her figure beneath it. She was wearing a loose-fitting black tank top, thin bicycle shorts, black socks and lace-up boots. Donatella's immediate reaction was disapproval. The overall ensemble clearly identified the young woman as a graduate art student, a type with whom Donatella was well acquainted and not particularly enamoured. But they were not usually this attractive, thought Donatella, trying not to notice the clear outline of the younger woman's breasts through the thin cotton top. Despite the obligatory nose ring glinting from one nostril, the face, a pleasant intelligent oval with a pointed chin, had a pale complexion and deep-set green eyes.

'D ... Dott ... Dottoressa di'B ... Bianchi?' stuttered the young woman.

Donatella's eyes held the younger woman's own in a piercing gaze. 'And whom were you expecting, young lady?' she said with barely concealed irony. 'Some wizened academic crone perhaps?'

'No. Er ...' A smile. 'Um, yes, actually.'

'Are you the welcoming committee?' Donatella asked briskly, secretly amused.

'Yes. Er ... no.'

'Which is it?' Donatella asked, 'No or yes? If no, why are you here? If yes, why did you say no?' She paused and noted with some satisfaction the shifting emotions evident on the redhead's face. There was never a bad time to teach students the need for clear, rational expression.

'N ... No ... *dottoressa*,' fumbled the younger woman, trying unsuccessfully to cover her evident embarrassment. 'It's just that I was expecting someone ... not as ... well, someone older, and not as ... well, beautiful.'

Donatella's eyebrows lifted sharply in inquisition. She wanted to say, 'You could be beautiful, too! Without those shabby clothes and that ridiculous spiky red hair,' but she said nothing. Despite the hair and the overdone eye makeup, the girl was quite cute, even sexy.

'I *am* from the *Collegio Toscana*,' the girl continued, 'but I'm here unofficially.'

Donatella noticed the girl's apprehensive look and filed it away for future reference. 'Professor Temple-Clarke didn't send you?' she asked, surprised and angered by the college's lack of official welcome.

'The director doesn't know I'm here,' said the girl.

By now the long platform was deserted save for a few railway workers. With hydraulic precision the carriage doors hissed shut, and a single blare on the horn announced the sleek train's otherwise silent departure. The acceleration of the Eurocity blasted a breeze through the hair of the two women, untidying Donatella's smooth dark chignon, and soon they found themselves alone on platform four. Donatella pursed her lips in irritation.

'And who are you?' she asked bluntly. 'You're American, aren't you?'

Her young companion rushed to explain. 'Yes, I am. My name is Kiki Lee,' she said. 'I'm a graduate student in the photography department. Let's have a coffee and I'll try to explain.' Taking a deep breath, she stuffed the hand-lettered sign bearing Donatella's name into a trash bin. 'Here, let me carry one of your bags.'

Hefting the weight of her single suitcase easily, Donatella handed her sleek Roman briefcase to Kiki and followed her new acquaintance down the stairs and up again, to emerge into the station's main booking hall. The pair found space in the café off to one side. Kiki ordered *due cappuccini* at the counter and carried the steaming coffees to a small highset table.

Setting down the cups and saucers, the student spoke urgently. 'Dr di'Bianchi, I was hoping to have a word with you privately before you got to the college and met the faculty.'

Donatella's finely groomed eyebrows came together in a frown. 'But you're a student, are you not? What could you tell me that the faculty wouldn't know? Something that you don't want them to hear?' She asked the questions severely. 'What exactly is going on here?'

Kiki blinked rapidly at the tall domineering brunette. 'Oh, dear,' she replied. 'I'm being clumsy about this. Please forgive me, Dr di'Bianchi.'

The strong milky coffee lifted Donatella's incipient

bad mood a little, and she relaxed her shoulders to sit more comfortably. She stirred three spoonfuls of sugar into her cup. Though still stern, she injected a slight note of warmth into her voice. 'Now, Ms Lee,' she said. 'Start over and tell me what all this is about. Please explain why you're here "unofficially", and why there is no proper welcome from the college.'

'I'm here,' the student replied, gesturing around the small coffee bar, 'because no one else is coming.'

Donatella watched her acquaintance's face grow more animated as her deep green eyes lit up with passion. The girl leaned forward and locked her earnest gaze with Donatella's. 'I'll be frank, Dr di'Bianchi. I'm very worried about the *Collegio*. The place isn't being run properly, the facilities aren't well maintained, most of the faculty don't do a good job, and there's no money for materials, visiting lecturers, field trips or *anything*! I've approached Dr Temple-Clarke but he just dismisses my complaints. The faculty are the same; they're all in the director's pocket.' Kiki's words were tumbling out.

As suited her professorial detachment, Donatella remained silent, absorbing this new information carefully. Assessing her companion, Donatella adjusted her initial opinion of the girl, from ditzy art student to someone with more depth. At first glance Ms Kiki Lee did fit certain stereotypes of graduate students but possibly this was a young woman with a good mind as well as being cute.

'Several graduate students organised a protest petition and a demonstration, but neither got us anywhere,' her youthful acquaintance continued. 'The director fobbed us off. He says budgets are tight and there isn't enough money coming from the States. I don't believe it for a moment. The real problem is

Temple-Clarke. He's ruining everything!' The younger woman paused, as if to gauge the effect of her words on Donatella.

Silent, too, for a moment, Donatella wondered whether this student had been the source of the detailed e-mail correspondence that had alarmed her superiors in Boston enough to send her to Arezzo, post-haste. If so, Kiki Lee would be an important part of the investigation. She smiled to put her companion at ease. 'I'm here, Ms Lee, to conduct a full investigation. You can be sure of that.'

Her compatriot looked relieved. 'I'm glad,' she said. 'I hope you will listen to what I have to tell you.' Now that she was more relaxed, Kiki leaned eagerly towards Donatella, not seeming to notice that her skimpy top fell forward to reveal her breasts to Donatella's gaze.

Donatella schooled herself to avoid the pleasant view of her young companion's breasts and tried to stay focused. But with the practiced eye of someone who had spent years in rigorous academic study of figure drawing, the professor couldn't help but notice the unforced naturalness of the young woman's good posture, not to mention Kiki Lee's complete lack of concern that her pert nipples were clearly visible.

Donatella wondered if the aura of Tuscany, the place where she had spent happy and productive times as a graduate student, was already reworking its magic on her. With a rush, Donatella remembered the many passionate love affairs and sexual couplings that felt so exotic at that time, and that later seemed so silly and jejune in the context of her ever-so-proper academic career in Boston.

Letting her tired mind ramble, Donatella felt her senses expand to the fullness of the atmosphere: the flowers, the coffee, the tactile sense of old stones, the honking scooters and the quiet of the little café. She remembered them now, the sensations of Tuscany. Part of her mind still equated them with her sexual coming of age.

Maybe it was jet lag that made her want to say, 'Kiki, your little breasts are like rich cream and apricots, your nipples like ripened cherries,' and 'That boy in the corner got a hard-on the moment we walked in the door.'

But instead Dr di'Bianchi said aloud, 'I want to hear everything you have to tell me. Are there other students I should talk to? Are there any faculty who would speak freely about the situation at the school?' She stirred her coffee, dropping her eyes to the table to give the younger woman time to collect her thoughts. And adjust her top. The young man at the doorway was now staring at Kiki Lee with intent recognition.

But Kiki was momentarily oblivious. 'There are several students,' she replied, 'and perhaps one member of the faculty who ... oh, shit. Oh, fuck!'

4 *L'Impressioni Primi (First Impressions)*

Donatella's head shot up at the expletives and the annoyance in Kiki's voice, half expecting to see Stewart Temple-Clarke bearing down on them like a thundercloud. But instead she saw the young Italian man who'd been watching them approach their table. She observed Kiki Lee hitch up her tank top and square her shoulders as if for some confrontation, which had the effect of outlining her breasts and nipples even more prominently.

Donatella sucked in her breath excitedly, half-expecting the boy to reach forward and fondle the inviting softness of the young woman's breasts. Instead he put his hand on Kiki's shoulder and faced Donatella. *'Buon giorno, signora. Il mio nome e Claudio Pozzi,'* he said by way of introduction. *'Mi scusi, per favore,'* he added and refocused his attention on Kiki.

Though the fellow had a certain charm, Kiki Lee seemed angry and she shrugged off his proprietorial hand, speaking fiercely to him in a whispered undertone of fluent Italian. Whatever Kiki had to say evidently didn't please the young man, who strengthened his grip on her arm only to have it removed with surprising ease by the slight young woman.

'Excuse me, Dr di'Bianchi,' said Kiki, clearly embarrassed and annoyed by the unwelcome attentions of her new companion. She slid off her stool and turned to face the American professor. 'Claudio is a . . . a friend of mine. We have a little disagreement over something. Can you give me a moment to sort it out? I'll be right back.'

'Of course,' said Donatella, feeling the weariness of jet lag sinking in. She watched the couple walk to a distant corner.

There an animated tableau unfolded. Claudio gesticulated urgently and tried to hold Kiki's arms and kiss her, but was firmly rejected. Nevertheless he persisted loudly, attracting the attention of the few café patrons and the worried stare of the proprietor. Kiki, having none of it, surprised him by bending back his fingers painfully. Lithely dodging Claudio's angry but clumsy advances, Kiki twirled round and twisted his arm, drawing a shout of rage and pain from her baffled adversary. Consolidating her advantage, the little redhead propelled the young man to the café door, where she gave his bottom a hard dismissive slap, and shooed him away.

'*Vaffanculo, Claudio!*' she yelled. 'I'm not your fucking property! Leave me alone. You hear?' She thrust her face into his, daring him to contradict her.

'*Va' a farti fottere, Americana* bitch! I don't take that from any woman!' the infuriated paramour yelled, and tried to grab Kiki by the shoulders. As she dodged him the young man instead grabbed the neck of her tank top and ripped the thin cotton, fully exposing her breasts.

'Jesus! You stupid bastard!' swore Kiki. With an explosive force that surprised Claudio – and the crowd of attentive onlookers – she pivoted expertly on one leg and slammed her other booted foot into his belly so hard it left stud marks on his shirt.

All was quiet for a moment as the surprised and humiliated Claudio lay sprawled on the floor for the second time that morning. The barman was the first to move, pulling the angry young man to his feet and hustling him away, doubled over in pain, before he could damage the morning trade any further.

'You bitch!' gasped the humiliated suitor as he lurched towards his scooter. 'I'll get you for this!'

Kiki, bare to the waist and framed in the doorway, stood with her arms akimbo, watching him depart. 'Not very original, Claudio,' she mocked. 'I can take you anytime. Don't you forget it!'

Donatella quickly opened her suitcase and found a Spandex and cotton T-shirt that fitted her snugly; it wouldn't be too big for her half-naked comrade. She stood behind Kiki and thrust the garment into the arms of the young woman. 'Here, take this.'

Kiki nodded her thanks and pulled the small garment over her firm pointed breasts. Donatella stood back and studied her new acquaintance with a more discerning eye. She noted the developed biceps, a feature that had escaped her initial appraisal. Her eyes travelled down Kiki's body, taking in her trim thighs and powerful leg muscles. Here was a young woman who worked out regularly and obviously could take care of herself.

'Is this sort of activity an everyday event?' Donatella asked with a stern expression. 'Or do you put on special shows for visiting professors?'

Kiki blushed. 'Gosh, I'm so sorry, Dr di'Bianchi. Whatever must you think of me? This is *not* the kind of impression I wanted to make! That was just some creep of a boyfriend who wouldn't take no for an answer,' she added by way of explanation. 'Oh, and, er . . . thanks for the loan of the T-shirt.'

Donatella refused to allow herself to smile. 'Ms Lee,' she said brusquely, 'why don't you get freshened up in the ladies' room and then we can go to the college.'

Kiki nodded acquiescence. Donatella, bedecked in

expensive suit and jewellery, watched the petite martial arts practitioner stride into the ladies' room, turning men's heads as she went. Donatella mentally compared her own physique to the ample display she'd just had of her new companion's body. Although she was confident that her own abs and thighs were well toned from hours spent at Boston's La Sylphide gymnasium, and rowing in the women's coxless fours on the Charles River, she nevertheless felt a twinge of envy at the young woman's comfort with her body and sexuality.

Donatella firmly checked her intuitive desire to respond to this attractive young woman as a new friend. She recognised long-buried but unmistakable feelings that stirred within her at Kiki Lee's uninhibited attitudes to sex and life in general. Her jet-lagged mind wandered to the last time she had had sex with her lover, Henry Fogg. Why wasn't she more excited at the thought? Was it because the sex was so average?

With a start, she realized that Kiki Lee, recombed, refreshed and completely unflustered, had returned to their table and was looking at her expectantly.

Donatella smiled briefly, making a determined effort to be more friendly. 'Sorry,' she said. 'Jet lag getting to me, I think. Everything all right?'

Kiki nodded. 'Yes. Sorry again about that scene.'

Donatella asked, 'A student boyfriend?'

Kiki laughed with a harsh little bark. 'Claudio, a student! Ha! No, not Claudio; the only school where our Claudio studies is the School for Dickheads,' she said, her words tinged with bitterness. 'You fuck them once and they think they own you! Oh! sorry, Dr di'Bianchi, I didn't . . .' She blushed at her direct language, obviously worried that she'd upset her visitor.

Donatella frowned but temporarily pushed the matter away with a wave of her hand. 'Your relationships are your own business. We need to talk about academic matters. You were going to tell me about other students and faculty.'

'Yes,' replied Kiki eagerly. 'I'll introduce you to some of the students. As for the professors, well, the only one I think is worth meeting is Ian Ramsey, an Englishman who teaches ceramics and helps out with a photography class, even though that's not his speciality.'

'Isn't that a bit of a stretch?' asked Donatella. 'Ceramics to photography?'

'That's typical of the *Collegio*,' said Kiki, annoyance peppering her tone. 'Nothing against Ian ... Professor Ramsey; he does a good job, but we should have more faculty, experts in their fields, if this graduate programme is going to live up to its potential. Temple-Clarke says there isn't enough money to hire the people we need.'

Donatella avoided comment. 'I'll talk to Professor Ramsey soon,' she said. 'Meanwhile, I'd like to get to the college. Can you show me around? I want to see Professor Temple-Clarke and find out why he didn't send someone to meet me!'

Her redheaded guide paid for the coffees and led Donatella outside, carrying the suitcase with ease despite her slight frame. 'It's only ten minutes up the hill, Dr di'Bianchi,' she said, 'over by the Piazza Grande. Shall we walk?'

Donatella nodded and the pair set off at a brisk pace. The sun was climbing in the sky and the day threatened to be a hot one but, at nine in the morning, pleasantly cool shade lined the narrow streets. The women passed through a portal of the medieval walls and climbed up the Corso Italia. In a few minutes Kiki turned right into the great sloping town square, dominated by Giorgio Vasari's *Loggia*, a many-arched building that ran the full length of the northern edge of the piazza.

'Lovely!' Donatella said and paused to admire the great façade. Amid the pleasant sounds of cutlery and china, and the smell of more good coffee, she turned to follow Kiki along a small side-street that led up a steep incline adjacent to the star-shaped Medici fortress. Several *palazzi* were built into the remains of the medieval wall, and Kiki stopped at one of them, a tall narrow structure on four floors, with carved shields decorating the wide stone doorway.

'Here we are,' Kiki said with a grin. 'Abandon hope, all ye who enter!' she added, paraphrasing Dante. But Donatella wasn't laughing. Instead she was gazing thoughtfully up at the building, as if pondering its secrets.

'Take me to Professor Temple-Clarke's office, please,' she said, keeping all emotion from her voice. 'Will you be able to show me around the building when I've finished?'

'Sure,' Kiki said and led Donatella to the second floor. In a pleasant sunlit office overlooking a courtyard full of riotous colour, two secretaries were pretending to work when Kiki knocked and Donatella stepped inside.

Beyond the enclosure of the room, Donatella glimpsed the smooth green lawn of an open park, and beyond that the great walls of the *fortezza Medicea*, its masonry worn smooth with time. Suppressing an exclamation of awe, she said, '*Buon giorno. Sono dottoressa Donatella di'Bianchi. Sono venuta a vedere il professor Temple-Clarke,*' in stiff but correct Italian.

A glance that Donatella couldn't interpret passed between the two young women.

'*Mi dispiace, dottoressa di'Bianchi,*' said the nearer of the two. '*E non possibile. Il professore e uscito.*'

'Gone?' Donatella asked, astounded. 'Why? *Perche? Per quanto tempo? Per amor di Dio!*' She raised her hands in a gesture of annoyance.

'*Non so fino a quando,*' the receptionist shrugged.

Donatella turned to Kiki with irritation. 'Would you believe it! He's gone out. But he knew what time I was arriving!'

Her young companion faced the receptionist and spoke swiftly in Italian so fluent that Donatella couldn't follow it at first. After a moment Kiki took Donatella aside and explained. 'Gina says that Temple-Clarke left half an hour ago. He didn't say where he was going or when he would be back. That isn't unusual, apparently. Gina saw your name in his diary for today, but no other information. She doesn't know where you'll be staying. She says nobody made any arrangements for a hotel.' Kiki looked a little embarrassed. 'Sorry about this. It's typical of the kind of run-around you get here!' she added bitterly.

Donatella turned back to the receptionist and tried asking about a hotel. '*Puo dirmi Lei dov'e un albergo?*'

The girl shrugged again. She was filing her nails, Donatella noticed.

'Don't worry,' said Kiki, intervening before Donatella could get angry. 'I know a little hotel where you can stay until this gets sorted out. Look, why don't you leave your bags in my studio? I'll show you round the building and then we can go to the hotel.'

Donatella was relieved but tried not to show it. 'Thank you, Ms ... er ... Kiki. That's very kind of you.' She turned to Gina the receptionist and picked up a pen and some paper from the desk. She scrawled across it, 'Have arrived. Will be back in the college this afternoon at 3 p.m.,' and signed her name with a flourish. She handed the note to the girl, who was now applying nail varnish '*Sono le tre*,' she added and tapped her watch, pointing to three o'clock.

The receptionist nodded noncommittally.

Donatella shook her head and walked out.

Kiki followed her through the door, after depositing her bundle of graded papers on the desk. '*Ciao, Gina. Ciao, Sophia*,' she called back over her shoulder.

'*Ciao, Kiki*,' they replied in unison.

Donatella followed Kiki to her studio without saying a word, but as soon as they were safe behind closed doors she gave vent to her feelings. 'Why were those two secretaries so friendly to you, yet didn't give me the time of day?' she demanded.

Kiki shrugged. 'I've known them for over a year. We've ... shared some boyfriends. They trust me. They don't know you and Temple-Clarke's probably told them you're a bitch. They're afraid of him and don't want to do anything that will annoy him.'

Donatella wondered fleetingly just how intimately Kiki and the other young women had 'shared' their boyfriends but pushed the errant thought to the back of her mind. 'OK,' she said, resignedly. 'No one said this would be easy.'

She looked around Kiki's studio, which had large windows facing north over the park. Surprisingly most of the artwork was turned to the walls. As if reading Donatella's mind Kiki explained, 'I like to surprise myself each time I come in the studio. Most of the pieces are photographic prints that I'm manipulating and collaging in different ways and, when I turn them around after not seeing them for a while, sometimes I get inspiration or a new idea. I don't let people see them until they're ready,' she added, almost apologetically.

Donatella nodded and turned her attention to some

photographic portrait nudes that were lying on a desk. 'May I look at these?' she asked.

'Of course,' said Kiki. 'That's my housemate, Francesca. She's a life-drawing model here at the college. I'm sure you'll meet her soon.'

Donatella picked up the prints to find a cheerful young woman in a variety of suggestive poses – some of them blatantly sexual – smiling back at her from the hard-edged black-and-white images.

'These are very ... interesting,' said Donatella, trying to hide her incipient sense of arousal behind a mask of disapproval. 'But these can't be typical poses for life-drawing classes,' she added, tapping one particularly erotic shot of Francesca in an odalesque pose reminiscent of Giorgione's *Sleeping Venus*. However, where the late Renaissance painter had laid the recumbent woman's hand gently in her crotch, Kiki's portrait of Francesca showed the nubile young woman openly masturbating.

Kiki was unfazed. 'Oh, no,' she replied, straight faced, matching the older woman's disapproval with irony. 'The students would never be able to concentrate once Francesca gets going. These are for my photography class with Ian Ramsey.'

Donatella's eyebrows shot up but she decided not to pursue for the moment the issue of near-pornographic subject matter in graduate classwork. Instead, she laid the photographs back on the desk with their pictures downwards. 'Let's get on with the tour,' she said, striving for neutrality and achieving only primness. Kiki's answering smile made Donatella wonder in alarm whether her internal struggle between professorial demeanour and reawakening interest in sex was visible on her face.

Trying to push this concern along with the images of the attractive Francesca out of her mind, Donatella trailed behind Kiki for the next two hours as the girl led her around the college building. The old *palazzo* had clearly been altered many times over the years since its origins in the *Cinquecento*. Plaster crumbled from the walls in many places, and there were few signs of tender loving care lavished on the old building, but overall the structure seemed in fairly good shape. Bigger than it looked from the outside, it penetrated through the old medieval wall, spreading sideways behind the adjacent buildings.

Many rooms overlooked the park Donatella had glimpsed from the secretaries' office. Donatella's casual glance from a window revealed some people practising soccer on the grass, including a tall handsome man in a black-and-white striped jersey with what appeared to be a beer advertisement on the front. He was shouting instructions and shooting soccer balls at an agile young woman who leaped around between some goalposts, catching and beating the shots away. Very few got past her.

'That's Ian Ramsey,' said Kiki as she joined Donatella in her scrutiny of the pair. 'My photography professor. I'll introduce you to him later. Better not interrupt their soccer practice. He and Jennifer –' she indicated the athletic goalkeeper, '– take their practice very seriously! They're at it every day.'

Something in the younger woman's tone made Donatella look round sharply, but Kiki's face was devoid of expression. Donatella changed the subject. 'Are there any empty rooms on this side of the building?' she asked. 'I'll need an office and, if Temple-Clarke can't even book me a hotel, I doubt if he's assigned me somewhere to work. If there's a spare room that's decent, I'll simply claim it and argue later.'

Kiki thought momentarily and then nodded. 'Yes,' she said. 'When the last photography professor left, the position was never refilled. Ian's got his own office, so that space has been empty ever since. It's just down the hall and my studio is around the corner; that means we can be near each other and out of Temple-Clarke's hair. He rarely comes back here into this old part of the building. It's like a rabbit warren back here.' Kiki smiled encouragingly at the new professor.

Donatella was not in the mood for sharing confidences or forming alliances yet. She merely nodded.

Kiki's smile dimmed but didn't vanish altogether. With a wave of her hand she set off down the corridor. 'Wait here and I'll get the key from the front office. I'll be right back.'

Donatella's gaze returned to the view out the window. The newly identified Professor Ramsey had his arm around the shoulders of his goalkeeping protégé, apparently congratulating her on her performance. Donatella's eyes widened in shock as the man's hand slid down the girl's back and inside her shorts, cupping her buttocks in a frankly sexual gesture. In response the girl jabbed her companion playfully in the stomach and, with a quick glance over her shoulder, reached for his cock and gave it a squeeze through the black nylon material of his shorts. Arm-in-arm, the pair hurried from the field and out of Donatella's sight.

Kiki Lee returned a moment later and clearly hadn't witnessed the sexual vignette. Donatella had never approved of faculty having sex with students; at the politically correct Charlestown University where she taught, it was one of the few justifications for dismissing tenured professors.

Broaching the subject hesitantly, Donatella asked her companion, 'Are Professor Ramsey and ... Jennifer ...?' She paused, not knowing how to phrase the question.

Kiki lifted her eyebrows quizzically. 'You mean are they lovers?' she asked, a rueful grin playing with the corners of her mouth. 'You bet! If you want my considered, objective and totally unbiased opinion, Ian Ramsey and Jennifer Wrenn fuck like bunnies!'

Before Donatella could reply, Kiki turned and pranced down the hall. 'Come on,' she called to Donatella, 'Let's get you settled in your new office. I think you'll like it. It has nearly the same view over the park. If you're lucky, you'll get to watch Ian and Jennifer every day!'

Donatella didn't miss the bittersweet tinge in her young compatriot's voice, but let it pass for the moment. Her job was to investigate malfeasance at the college, not get involved in petty sexual rivalries. She walked into a tall, well-lit room through a door unlocked by Kiki and suppressed an exhalation of wonder at the view of the park, the ancient battlements and the Tuscan hills beyond.

Before her, Kiki made a deliberately mocking bow, sweeping her arms low in a parody of Renaissance courtly manners.

'Welcome to your home away from home, *dottoressa* di'Bianchi. A room with a view!' she said with a gently sardonic tone.

5 *La Testa alla Testa* (Head to Head)

After a brief lunch with the new professor at a small café in Vasari's great *Loggia*, Kiki excused herself to run some errands. 'How about meeting me in my studio about four o'clock?' she asked. 'Then I'll take you to the hotel.'

Nodding her thanks, Donatella watched the young student stride across the piazza and disappear up one of the many narrow side-streets. It was nearly time for her three o'clock appointment with Stewart Temple-Clarke. Fortified by her glass of Chianti, Donatella made sure her appearance was crisp and professional and headed back to the college.

As she climbed to the top of the stairs, Donatella heard the voices of the two secretaries inside the director's office, interrupted by a deeper baritone. She stopped momentarily to breathe deeply and reminded herself sternly that she was backed by the authority of the American Board of Trustees for the college; she was *not* going to be intimidated by somebody she had never met!

Without knocking on the partially open door, Donatella strode into the outer office. Inside the spacious room Gina and Sophia were chatting with a tall elegant man with long dark-blond hair and chiselled features. He broke off his conversation with the two women and appraised Donatella coolly, his eyes seeming to mock her just as they had from the photograph in his file back in Boston.

'Can I help you?' he said, his tone conveying that any such action would be very low on his list of priorities.

Donatella plunged ahead. 'Professor Temple-Clarke, I'm sure you know who I am: Donatella di'Bianchi, from Boston. And I'm sure you know why I'm here.' She forced a smile. 'I'm glad you could be here to meet me.' She managed to keep most of the sarcasm out of her tone but some slipped through.

There was no answering smile from Temple-Clarke, just a brisk jerk of his head. 'Follow me,' he said curtly and led the way to an inner office, where he closed the door behind them. The director sat behind his desk but made no move to offer Donatella a chair. Unfazed by his rudeness, Donatella claimed the seat nearest to the desk and tried to look relaxed. She glanced around the walls, taking in the studied minimalism of the surroundings. A couple of decent engravings by Piranesi, a copy of a woodcut by Dürer showing a technique of perspective drawing, and what looked to be a contemporary black-and-white photograph of the Piazza Grande hung on simple white walls. There was no colour except the green of the trees visible in the courtyard outside. With few personal effects on display, the environment revealed little about its occupant. Although no ashtrays were visible, an odour of cigar tobacco hung in the air.

'Seen enough, have you?' Temple-Clarke's sneering question refocused Donatella's attention on the person sitting opposite her. At first glance Temple-Clarke seemed to match the room. He was dressed simply in a pressed white linen shirt, open at the neck, and crisp khaki slacks. His hands, large with slender fingers, lay quietly on his lap as he leaned back in his chair, his expression a studied mask of apparent boredom. His long face, tanned and creased with the first lines of middle-age, remained handsome. Donatella's first impression was of Peter O'Toole as Lawrence of Arabia but with longer hair.

With a heavily ironic sigh Temple-Clarke acknowledged the appraisal and slowly sat upright, staring directly at Donatella. His piercing gaze belied his indifferent manner. Donatella felt herself stiffen involuntarily under the probing assessment of his startling, almost colourless eyes.

'Yes,' he said, in a neutral voice that didn't match the hostility of his stare. 'I know who you are, Professor. And I know why you're here. Let me tell you straight away,' he continued, 'you're wasting your time, and the Trustees' money. There is nothing for you to find here; no scandals, no corruption, no conspiracy. Just a small art school trying to provide a decent education for our students on limited resources. We can't boast American *luxuries –*' he emphasised the word with a slight sneer '– but on the whole we manage pretty well.'

Donatella remained silent.

'I know some of our American students have complained,' the director continued, with another slight but unmistakable emphasis on 'American', 'but, frankly, this isn't the US, and what might be normal in your country doesn't always apply here, in the Old World.'

Temple-Clarke's overpronounced English accent irritated Donatella as much as his words in its casual assumption of cultural superiority, but she controlled her annoyance and put her smile back in place.

'Professor Temple-Clarke,' she said politely, 'you know as well as I that the Boston authorities have sent me here to conduct an investigation into allegations about falling academic standards and financial mismanagement of this programme. They are not satisfied with your general assurances and neither am I. I have clear instructions from our superiors to examine all aspects of the academic and financial status of the college and its operations. They, and I, naturally expect you to cooperate fully in this process.'

She paused, but the director said nothing.

'Of course,' continued Donatella, 'I shall need to interview faculty, staff and students, and have unedited access to all documents.'

Temple-Clarke sighed, a picture of injured resignation.

'And,' Donatella pressed on, 'I shall be here for some time. I have already selected my office and I'm booking into a local hotel for as long as I need.'

Temple-Clarke stared lazily at Donatella, as if daring her to mention his lack of hospitality. 'As you will,' he said. 'Personally, I doubt if you'll be staying as long as you think.'

'That depends on several things,' said Donatella, with a studied calm she didn't feel. 'I must be allowed to do my job ... unimpeded.' She leaned back and crossed her legs, matching the director's apparent lack of concern. 'Frankly the more difficult the investigation, the longer I'll be around.' She raised her eyes, forcing Temple-Clarke to return her steady gaze, trying to put him on the defensive. Mutual hostility crackled in the room.

The temporary impasse was broken by Gina, who tapped on the door and looked around nervously. '*Mi dispiace, professor* Temple-Clarke, but *il professor* Ramsey wants to see you. He is outside.' Donatella was startled by Gina's decent English, and glowered at the girl for pretending otherwise that morning.

'*Grazie*, Gina,' replied Temple-Clarke. 'Please ask him to wait a moment. I won't be long.' The director glanced pointedly at Donatella. Gina vanished.

Donatella managed a level tone with great effort. 'Professor Temple-Clarke,' she said. 'I shall call a meeting of the faculty to introduce myself and my mission here. You may resent my presence but, remember, my visit has the full backing of the Trustees, over your objections, I might remind you. The Chairman of the Board told me you were unhelpful during their preliminary enquiries. I'm here to find out what's really happening. We can work together or not – as you wish – but you can be sure that I shall submit a full and detailed report to the authorities in Boston.'

Temple-Clarke clapped his hands lazily. 'Bravo, *dottoressa*,' he mocked. 'A fine speech. I'm sure my colleagues will be impressed.' He yawned ostentatiously. 'When did you say you propose to start this great inquisition of yours?'

'I've already started,' replied Donatella tartly. 'I've begun interviewing graduate students,' she added with some exaggeration, and instantly regretted it.

For the first time anger shone in Temple-Clarke's pale eyes, but it was instantly dampened. 'Oh, yes,' he said, 'Kiki Lee. My girls next door told me she was with you when you arrived earlier. She's a disappointing student, unreliable.' He shook his head with what Donatella interpreted as mock sadness. 'If she applied herself half as much to her work as she does to stirring up trouble, she could be a good photographer. But there have been numerous complaints about her.'

He paused, inviting Donatella to fill in the implicit question. When his guest remained silent Temple-Clarke continued anyway. 'Oh, yes, complaints aplenty. Not just about her trouble making, that's bad enough – ask the faculty – but about her art as well. I've had to talk to her about it. There *is* a difference between art and pornography, but Ms Lee doesn't seem to understand that. Her judgement is lacking, I'm afraid, and what there is of it is perverse. Several students have objected about the blatant sexual nature of her work.

They think it casts our college in a bad light with the local people here in Arezzo. In fact the city council complained about one exhibition of photographs she put up in town recently. We had to close it down and issue a public apology.'

Temple-Clarke stood up and looked sternly down at Donatella.

She sat as tall as possible.

'I'm afraid Ms Lee has developed a sense of persecution over this,' he said, 'with me as the focus of her anger. She has elaborated some of our minor difficulties –' he shrugged with a dismissive little gesture '– into some grand conspiracy and intrigue, or web of incompetence. The story changes every week,' he added with another shake of his head. The director looked at Donatella with a martyred expression. 'I'm afraid you need to be careful with her. You mustn't believe everything she says!'

Temple-Clarke's words gave Donatella pause. They certainly rang true with some of the things she had noticed about Kiki in their short acquaintance. The kind of student described by Temple-Clarke had crossed her path more than once and it was always bad news. But Donatella didn't want to discount her personal intuition. Despite Kiki's clearly problematic personal life, she felt a nascent regard for the younger woman, even though her casual attitude to sex made Donatella uncomfortable.

'She is my teaching assistant, but her work has been so poor these last few weeks that I'm about to fire her,' continued the director. 'If you take my advice, Professor di'Bianchi, you'll have nothing to do with that foolish young woman.'

In a flash Donatella's intuition triumphed over caution. 'That's very convenient,' she retorted, 'because I've asked Ms Lee to be my assistant. She has willingly agreed.' As soon as the words were out of her mouth, Donatella wondered if she'd just made a fool of herself. What if Kiki rejected the offer, now so publicly made? And without even asking her first!

Temple-Clarke seemed to divine her sudden doubt, for he smiled mockingly. 'In that case, my dear *dottoressa*, you will have your hands full. Apparently my advice comes too late. Well, on your head be it. You can't say I didn't warn you.' He waved his hand vaguely in the air. 'Now if you'll excuse me, I have a college to run. I'll tell Gina and Sophia to give you access to the college files,' he added dismissively, as if the matter was of no importance. He walked to the door and held it open. 'I'm sure you have more important things to do than talk to me,' he said sardonically. 'I bid you good day.'

Donatella rose and walked slowly past him, retaining as much poise as she could from the man's dismissal. She nodded curtly, thinking that their first round of combat had ended about even, but she wasn't sure. She'd made a potentially rash decision simply on the unproven grounds that an enemy of Temple-Clarke's was likely to be a friend of hers.

Her chain of thought was broken by the tableau that confronted her in the secretaries' office, where a tall athletic man she recognised immediately as the soccer-playing Ian Ramsey was blatantly trying to look down the front of Sophia's dress, much to the young woman's amusement and that of her companion.

Sophia playfully swatted the man's face away from her breasts.

He straightened gracefully, casting his eyes deliberately over Donatella as she emerged from Temple-Clarke's sanctum, apparently unfazed at being observed at what was juvenile behaviour at best and sexual harassment at worst.

'Well,' he said in a northern English accent Donatella found hard to place. 'This must be the great Doctor Donatella I've been hearing so much about. You know,' he said to Sophia in a theatrical aside, 'we were expecting some wizened old Boston bluestocking. Those Americans didn't say they were sending over a raven-haired beauty!' The pleasant smile that enlivened his English good looks took the sarcastic sting out of Ramsey's words, and he stepped forward to take Donatella's hand in his own. 'Welcome, Donatella,' he said, squeezing her hand gently. His hazel eyes locked onto hers. 'Ian Ramsey at your service. You bring a ray of sunshine into the musty old corners of this decrepit old place!'

Ramsey held on to her hand longer than a casual greeting demanded and, when he released his grip, Donatella felt his fingers rake the inside of her wrist.

She met his eyes as he reached up to brush a lock of long unruly brown hair from his forehead. My God, she thought. Temple-Clarke looks like Peter O'Toole; now this guy Ramsey does his Hugh Grant impression.

But the touch of this sexy-looking stranger did something to her. Her mind said this was a man who had sex with his students, and was probably a rogue and a reprobate, but the sensation between her legs urged her to a very different conclusion. Feelings of pure lust that had been long buried flashed into her consciousness. Here was someone she wanted to bed, the sooner the better.

Shocked by her carnal craving from nowhere, Donatella blushed and stuttered a greeting, walking quickly out of the room before she did something that disgraced herself. From the hallway she heard muffled giggles from the women and a mellow laugh from Ramsey, until both were cut off by a peremptory command from Temple-Clarke and the closing of a door.

Covered in confusion Donatella walked the hallways looking for Kiki's studio. The corridors were busy with students returning to late afternoon classes after the midday siesta, and Donatella was soon lost. She stopped a tall gangly student to ask for directions. To her surprise the young man blushed at the mention of Kiki's name, but led the professor to the studio, turning, almost running away when they neared the door.

Donatella shook her head at further evidence of the strange effect Kiki Lee seemed to have on men. She sincerely hoped that her spontaneous plan for the graduate art student to become her assistant would not backfire.

The studio door was shut but Kiki's voice yelled a welcome in reply to Donatella's knock. Inside the student was at work on a large table, cutting and pasting from a stack of photographic fragments. She looked up at Donatella's entry, wiping her hands on a stained denim apron that only partially covered her bare torso. She wore the same bicycle shorts and heavy boots, making the overall ensemble look strange, to say the least.

'Excuse the costume,' Kiki said, interpreting Donatella's gaze correctly. With a grin the girl tugged the small bib of the apron to conceal her nipples. 'I didn't want to get glue and paint on that sexy T-shirt you loaned me.' She pointed to a small closet in the corner where Donatella's simple garment was hung with care. 'How did it go with T-C?' the young student asked eagerly. 'Isn't he a creep? Doesn't he just weird you out?'

'Kiki,' said Donatella sternly, 'one of my tasks is to make up my own mind about the situation here, not to adopt ready-made opinions.'

Kiki's face fell, and Donatella immediately felt guilty.

The young student didn't deserve to bear the brunt of her own confusion.

'Let's just say,' the professor continued in a softer tone, 'there's good news and bad news as far as you're concerned . . . although I don't know if you'll see it that way.'

Kiki shot Donatella a guarded look. 'What do you mean?' she asked suspiciously.

'The bad news is that Professor Temple-Clarke has fired you as his graduate assistant,' replied Donatella. 'The good news, if indeed you think it's good, is for you to be *my* personal assistant. I can pay you a stipend,' she added hopefully, 'to make up for losing your teaching position.'

Mixed emotions crossed Kiki's face. 'The bastard!' she exclaimed. 'Did he say why? Oh, never mind, we can talk about that later,' she continued before Donatella could speak. 'It's good news and good news as far as I'm concerned. I hated working for Temple-Clarke anyway. I would much rather work for you and help nail the bastard!'

'Kiki, please remember, my task isn't to "nail the bastard," as you indelicately put it, but to write a detailed, objective report about what's going on at the college. Unless you accept that, we can't work together.'

Kiki, hands on hips, was unfazed. 'But if you do find out that the director's the cause of the problems, you will say so, won't you?' she rejoined. 'You won't just sweep it under the carpet, will you?'

'Certainly not,' replied Donatella. 'The Boston Trustees have given me *carte blanche* to handle this inquiry and the funds to back me up. They take your complaints very seriously. They *were* your e-mails, weren't they?' She asked, playing her hunch.

Kiki nodded. 'Yes. And everything I wrote there is

true!' she added defiantly. She paused. 'Did the bas—did Professor Temple-Clarke say why he fired me?'

'He said you are incompetent, untrustworthy, a pornographer and a troublemaker. That you have a persecution complex about him and are incapable of sound judgement.' Donatella made a pretence of trying to remember any other items on the list. 'I think that was all.'

Kiki was furious. 'The lying, conniving bastard,' she said through gritted teeth. 'I'm going to make him eat his words,' she growled and headed directly towards the door. Donatella grabbed her arm and held on as Kiki tried, not very hard, to shake free.

'If you do that,' snapped Donatella, trying to ignore the girl's breasts that jiggled into full view, 'you'll be demonstrating the bad judgement Temple-Clarke is accusing you of. You'll be playing right into his hands.' Donatella released Kiki's arm and stepped back.

Kiki pulled the loop of the apron over her head and peeled the bib downwards, exposing her breasts completely. She licked her fingers and rubbed off a smudge of ink close to her right breast. Her expression remained defiant.

Donatella waited until she had the younger woman's full attention. 'Now listen. Just because Temple-Clarke says those things about you doesn't mean I believe him. If I did, why would I want you as my assistant?'

Kiki looked chagrined. 'Sorry,' she said, 'I wasn't thinking straight.' She dropped her hands and turned to face Donatella. Her small breasts bounced provocatively as she became animated. 'You're right, of course. But it's so damned unfair. He can say whatever he likes about me, and I can't get back at him.'

'That's where you're wrong,' replied Donatella. 'If my investigation finds evidence of wrongdoing by the director, my report can finish him here at the college. Are you willing to help me?'

'You bet!' said Kiki. Untying the apron and removing it from around her waist, she hung it on a nail by the door. 'When can I start? What do you want me to do?' Now she wore only her bicycle shorts and heavy boots.

'Assuming up front you're *not* incompetent, give me your side of the story.'

Kiki leaned against the wall, looking at her and, to Donatella's surprise, remained bare breasted.

'What do you say to his charges that you're an untrustworthy troublemaker, and a pornographer?' Donatella asked.

Folding her arms beneath her breasts, Kiki smiled wryly. 'That last one's easy. I deal with sexual themes – particularly women's sexuality – in a lot of my work. It's a legitimate subject, Dr di'Bianchi, and deserves to be treated frankly.'

Donatella was surprised that the redhead still made no move to cover herself, even while she lectured on a topic she was obviously quite passionate about. This was the second time the professor had been treated to a sight of her assistant's breasts and, while the first was accidental, there was no doubt that this second instance was deliberate on Kiki's part. Donatella kept her poise with some difficulty, determined not to communicate the nascent arousal she was feeling.

'For years we've swept women's sexuality under the carpet,' Kiki continued. 'Male masturbation is a well-documented topic, but women pleasuring themselves is still taboo in the minds of many people.' She moved to the table and reached to pick up the photographs of the naked Francesca. 'These are the sort of thing that Temple-Clarke censored. Do you think they're pornographic?'

'No, personally, I don't. But it's a close call. Let's face it, Kiki, pictures of women with –' Donatella blushed at the effort to speak directly on the subject, especially while the girl before her was half-naked. '– their fingers inside themselves are going to shock a lot of people.'

'So what? People masturbate, but they're too shy to talk about it. I masturbate. Francesca masturbates. I bet even ...' Kiki broke off and quickly rephrased her statement. 'I know not just young people masturbate. It's a perfectly normal activity, for men *and* women. Why do we have to hide it, deny it? But you see,' she added diffidently, 'the reaction of a liberated, educated woman like yourself to these photographs illustrates my point. You're disturbed by them. And I bet it's difficult for you to say "cunt" out loud.'

Donatella made a face. 'You're right, of course,' she admitted, but she stopped herself owning up to anything else. It was difficult enough talking about sex with a half-naked, sexually alluring and probably available student, let alone getting personal.

'Do you find them arousing?' Kiki asked, tapping the photographs.

Donatella blushed again. 'Yes. Yes I do.'

'What about my tits?' To Donatella's dismay Kiki caressed her bare breasts provocatively.

'Yes, they're very pretty,' said Donatella. 'But I'm not a lesbian,' she added hurriedly.

Kiki laughed. 'I didn't for one moment think you were, Professor di'Bianchi. Look, we're standing here alone and you haven't reacted at all. If you were queer, I would have picked it up by now.' She smiled at Donatella's third blush of the afternoon. 'Tell you what. Why don't I get some clothes on and get you booked into the hotel? Then we can go for a drink and talk about this some more. Is that OK?'

At Donatella's agreement Kiki crossed the studio.

Donatella let her eyes follow her companion, appreciating again her attractive, compact body as she slipped on the Spandex T-shirt. So sexy and cute! She stopped her train of thought abruptly. She'd never had sex with a woman and saw no reason to start now. Lusting after Ian Ramsey was going to cause enough complications.

6 *Il Disegno dal Vero* (Life Drawing)

Two afternoons later, Donatella was working with Kiki Lee in the room overlooking the park that had become her new office. Thankful that her new assistant now remained fully dressed in her presence, Donatella looked up from one of the stacks. 'Kiki, what are you working on at the moment?'

Kiki lifted her head from her own pile of documents gathered from the college archives. 'I'm trying to square last year's budget figures with every receipt Gina and Sophia could find,' she said. 'So far I'm not having much luck. It looks more like very sloppy bookkeeping than fraud. How about you?'

'Not too good,' said the soberly dressed Donatella. The professor sighed and pushed aside several stacks of files and other papers piled on her desk. 'These documents are about academic matters. I'm wading through the teaching goals and objectives for the college. It's pretty standard material.'

'What exactly are you looking for?' Kiki asked.

'For a clear sense of academic priorities, at least on paper, so I can relate them to resources and budget figures,' Donatella said and crossed her long legs. 'If I find a pattern of expenditures I might be able to spot irregularities more easily.'

Kiki nodded. 'I see.'

'I also want to check files of student work against the syllabi to see if educational goals are being met,'

Donatella explained. 'Does the college keep archives of past work?'

'Sure,' said Kiki. 'But it is not exhaustive.' She paused, mulling it over. 'A couple of years ago, we digitised a bunch of stuff and e-mailed it back to Boston as part of an overall accreditation process for the programme. I could book some time in the lab and print it out in hard copy.' Kiki looked at her new professor. 'You know, Dr di'Bianchi, I don't think we're going to find anything interesting in these files.'

'Because Temple-Clarke gave them to us too readily?'

'Yes. If he doesn't mind us looking at them, they can't contain any compromising material. Oh, I meant to ask, how did the faculty meeting go today? And is the hotel working out OK?'

Donatella scowled. 'The hotel's OK, but the faculty meeting was awful. You could have cut the hostility with a knife! You were right; they're all under his thumb. Listening to their excuses, I found myself doodling the faculty as a flock of sheep, with Temple-Clarke as the shepherd!'

Kiki grinned at the analogy.

Donatella continued, 'He calls the tune and they shamble off and do his bidding, just like you said. He'd obviously told them not to say anything to me this morning that could be construed in any way as coop-erative for my – our – investigation!'

Kiki smiled grimly. 'Was anybody helpful? A black sheep, say?'

Donatella nodded. 'The only person who came across as helpful was your friend Ian Ramsey. He seems to hold himself apart from the others,' she said. 'At times he seemed to be sneering at them.' Hiding her ambiva-lent sexual thoughts about the Englishman, Donatella turned back to her stack of papers.

But Kiki pursued the subject. 'Really? That's strange. Nobody else was helpful?'

'No, not really,' said Donatella. 'I'll interview them individually, of course. That might shake something loose. I can huff and puff and threaten them with all sorts of things; see if anybody starts to wilt.'

When Kiki didn't answer, Donatella glanced at the student. 'I was particularly disappointed by the women professors. I hoped I could bond with them, sisters against male incompetence, that sort of thing.'

Kiki rolled her eyes.

Donatella grinned ruefully, 'I hoped to find a feminist spark I could work with. But there was nothing there.'

Kiki shrugged. 'I know. Sometimes I think it's hopeless.'

Donatella shook her head. 'The main thing to remember, Kiki, is not to get discouraged if we don't find anything at first. This might take us several weeks. Frankly,' she continued, 'I don't think the faculty will be much help. Even precious Professor Ramsey. My hunch is that we'll find the key by carefully sifting through papers and finding little bits of information that don't quite add up.'

'You're good at that, aren't you?' Kiki said.

'What makes you say that?' Donatella asked, surprised.

'I found you on the Charlestown University website and went to your web page. Then I looked up some of your books, particularly the one on Caravaggio, and read some of the reviews. One said something like: "Doctor di'Bianchi excels in historical detective work. Her meticulous research enables her to piece together disparate facts and inferences that other scholars have missed." I was impressed. Made me want to go out and buy the book.'

Donatella flushed with pleasure. 'You know,' she said, 'You may have put your finger on something. I wondered why the Trustees chose me to do this investigation. I was too excited about coming back to Italy to think about it much, but perhaps they saw that this task needed rigorous research rather than a frontal assault on Temple-Clarke's little fiefdom!'

Kiki nodded, as if to congratulate a classmate on good logic.

Donatella smiled at the younger woman. She got the sense that the student liked working with her; they'd developed an instant rapport, more like partners with a mission than professor and assistant. 'We might make a good team, Kiki,' she said. 'I'll do the patient detective work and, if that fails, you can kick down Temple-Clarke's door with your *jujitsu*!'

Kiki laughed. 'Maybe I'll go on a little mission now,' she said and stood up.

'What's that?' Donatella said.

'To infiltrate the computer database. Maybe I can find those archives of student work.' She paused beside the door. 'By the way,' she added with a smile. 'I practice *tae kwan do*, not *jujitsu*.' The girl turned. 'I'll see you later. I might spend a little time in my studio, if you don't mind.'

'That's fine,' said Donatella. 'I have plenty to do here. Then I'm going over to the gym you showed me by the old amphitheatre.' She patted the gym bag beside her. 'Just let me know what you find. Oh, and lock the door on your way out. I don't want to be disturbed.'

After her young companion left, Donatella worked conscientiously through a large stack of paper, making copious notes. It was late afternoon before she finally took a break to change clothes for the gym.

Standing and stretching, she unbuttoned her grey silk blouse, removed it and draped it over the back of her chair. Looking out of the open window, Donatella reached behind to unfasten the hooks of her stiff bra and, with a sigh of relief, unclasped and slipped it off and laid it across the blouse.

But instead of changing clothes right away, the professor deliberately left her breasts bare and ignored her exercise bag for the moment. She luxuriated in the feeling of the fresh air playing gently across her flesh. She took her full breasts in her hands, slowly rolling her nipples between her fingers. She couldn't help comparing them with Kiki's smaller ones and considered – with what she hoped was academic detachment – her growing interest in her assistant's – no, her friend's – sexy little body. Her nipples sent her little tingling messages of arousal that surprised her.

She leaned forward over the sill to gaze down on the deep green grass of the park. Donatella felt her heart give a leap when she saw Ian Ramsey, dressed again for soccer, run onto the grass, followed shortly by the blonde girl named Jennifer Wrenn, resplendent in full goalkeeping kit of yellow jersey and black shorts. Thoughts of Kiki Lee were banished, to be replaced by more familiar feelings of lust for a handsome man.

Absorbed by curiosity, she watched as the Englishman smiled and blew the tall blonde girl a kiss. The thought of this pair being lovers annoyed Donatella, yet it also aroused her. She squirmed, realising that her displeasure had less to do with the inappropriateness of a professor having sex with a student than a feeling of envy that someone else was fucking the Englishman.

With her blouse off and bare breasted, she realised she was in full view; if the players looked up they'd see her standing wantonly exposed in the open window. Donatella stepped back hastily, feeling like a spy, her semi-nakedness disturbing yet exciting.

Turning to her exercise bag, Donatella extracted her sports bra and T-shirt, but feeling so aroused by her state of undress, she hesitated to pull them on. Instead, she walked over to her beige designer suit jacket hanging behind the door and withdrew a black, executive Mont Blanc pen from an inside pocket.

The art historian quickly pulled her chair over to the window and, keeping Ramsey in view, settled just out of sight with a pad of paper across her knees. Entranced by the activities below, Donatella unscrewed the thick top from the shaft and applied the gold nib expertly to a clean page. Many years' experience of life drawing enabled her to render the human form quickly and effectively; with swift economical movements she captured the essence of the man's physique in a few strong lines. As Ramsey moved, Donatella held that motion in her mind's eye and transferred it unerringly in ink to the paper.

Using up several A4 sheets from the ream that Kiki had liberated from the college storeroom, she sat high in the window of her new office, drawing study after study of the Englishman playing football below. Donatella relished the sensation of being warmed and ripened by the sun, and her sketches became more and more sensual in character.

When the sound of Jennifer's laughter drifted through the open window, Donatella did a quick drawing of the young American woman, too, as the girl retrieved the ball from the net and threw it smartly overarm back to her professor. The tanned student's blonde pony-tail bounced merrily across her shoulders.

'You can't win them all, Jenny!' Donatella heard Ramsey shout, his accent pleasant to her ears. 'I've got to slip one in there a few times!'

Donatella heard the girl giggle and call, 'OK, *Professor*

Ramsey, we both know you're very good at slipping one in. But just wait till it's my turn to –' A gust of wind blew away the end of the sentence.

Donatella watched Ramsey turn quickly and hammer the ball towards the top corner of the goal. This time the girl excelled herself and, with acrobatics worthy of a gymnast, flew through the air to tip the ball over the crossbar.

'Well done, Jenny!' Donatella heard Ramsey shout as he ran across the penalty area to haul the grinning woman to her feet. Beneath Donatella's gaze, the couple's sporting hug turned into a more passionate embrace. As Jennifer pinned her teacher in her arms and treated him to a long sensual kiss, his arms snaked up inside her goalkeeper's jersey. Donatella had a sudden idea of the good-looking man modelling for her in the nude. Focussing on her fantasy, she completed another vivid sketch – this time of Ramsey naked, with an erect penis – and tossed it on the pile with the others.

Thoughts of Ramsey posing for her made Donatella remember her last weekend with her Boston boyfriend Henry Fogg, a colleague at the university. Henry had refused Donatella's requests to pose, embarrassed at the thought of being naked in the daytime. On the occasions they made love, it was always in the dark, to suit Henry's modesty. While Donatella had become accustomed to this low-key and undemanding relationship that fitted occasional lovemaking into her busy work schedule back home, here in the warm Tuscan sun she wanted more than the distant Henry could provide. She wanted to fuck now. To fuck Ian Ramsey.

Awash with new desire and feeling a pleasant wetness between her legs, Donatella stopped drawing, put down her pen and eased off her expensive leather shoes. She reached beneath her skirt to pull off her tights and stuffed them in her gym bag. Released from these constraints, she stretched out her long slim legs with a low sigh of pleasure. Except for her skirt, she was now naked.

Squirming with the desire to touch herself, Donatella ran her hands over her body. Rubbing the peaks of her naked breasts, her nipples stiffened and she murmured to herself, 'I want to fuck the Englishman . . .' Repeating the phrase over and over in her mind, she pressed her bared breasts forward as if presenting them to the man below and imagined him standing naked in front of her, the tip of his penis rubbing against her nipples. She gently eased a finger between her thighs to enjoy the slick moisture of her pussy and felt the wetness pooling there. Donatella lightly massaged her clit, heightening her arousal. This was the first time in weeks that she had touched herself. Giving in to the desire to masturbate, she pulled her skirt up around her waist and slid two fingers deep inside her. Closing her eyes, she rubbed herself eagerly, imagining Ramsey naked in front of her

A loud peel of bells from the *duomo* chiming across the fields broke Donatella's erotic reverie. As her eyes flew open, she saw that the dulcet tones issuing from the church had also brought an end to the football practice. Donatella regretfully stopped masturbating and watched as Ramsey and Jennifer Wrenn looped arms and walked off the pitch. Pausing, the girl turned up her face and received a lengthy deep kiss from her mentor.

Frustrated from being aroused but unfulfilled, goose-pimples arose on Donatella's naked flesh and she shivered with desire when she saw Ramsey wipe his lips with relish, his eyes alight with desire, and heard him speaking to his partner. 'Let's run,' he urged. 'We've got time for a quickie!'

Donatella's eyes followed the handsome man as he picked up the ball and loped after the young blonde who dashed for the back entrance of the college and disappeared beneath the cypress trees that ringed the base of the old building. Her fantasy object was gone.

Cooling slowly after her heated arousal, Donatella withdrew her fingers and sucked them, enjoying the half-forgotten taste of her own juices. She patted herself dry between her legs with a hankie, smoothed down her skirt and slipped her arms through the sleeves of her discarded blouse. She left the thin garment unbuttoned, tying the tails of the fluttering silk beneath her breasts.

Trying to breathe normally, she leaned forward and cranked the window shut, and turned back to her suite of recent drawings. They were definitely good, she thought. Getting horny did wonders for her technique! Sitting back, Donatella wondered where Ian Ramsey and the girl student would fuck. But she didn't have much time to mull over that student/teacher relationship, or to fantasise her way to orgasm, for the sound of a key turning the lock of her newly claimed office door froze her partially clad figure to her seat in alarm.

7 *La Guardona* (The Voyeur)

The door swung open to reveal the figure of the tall long-limbed student who had directed Donatella to Kiki's studio on her first day at the college. He had his arms full of books and, stooping to retrieve the key from the lock, he didn't initially register Donatella's presence. The young man stepped inside and stopped short at the sight of the scantily clad woman in the room, his eyes wide and his mouth agape. A book slid off the stack in his arms and hit the floor with a loud thud. Donatella automatically noted it was photographs of Paris by the great French photographer Eugène Atget.

Donatella clasped her open blouse together in one hand and stared at the intruder. He looked harmless, she thought, but one couldn't be too careful. 'Who are you?' she demanded. 'Why are you in my office?'

Her unwanted guest was still rooted to the spot, so Donatella spoke again, this time in Italian. The young man tried to answer but still no sound came out. He moved towards the door, but Donatella spoke quickly. 'Stop! Put those books down,' she ordered. 'Tell me who you are and why you are here.'

Her visitor meekly put his books on the desk Kiki was using, averting his eyes, his cheeks crimson with embarrassment.

'Now sit down, please, and explain what is going on,' Donatella said.

In his haste the youth tripped over the book on the floor and stumbled into a chair, arms and legs flailing to keep his balance. He looked so funny that Donatella couldn't keep from laughing, as her concern transformed into amusement at the young man's awkwardness. She buttoned her blouse lightly and stood before the clumsy youth, who looked confused and scared. His face was flushed and he tried to look away, but his eyes kept sliding back to Donatella's breasts, still visible in part beneath the thin garment.

'M ... mi d ... dispiace, signora!' he stuttered at last. 'M ... mi chiamo Gianfranco della Parigi. S ... sono studente. Sei Americana?'

Donatella nodded, trying to sound cool and casual. 'Yes, I'm American. Mi chiamo dottoressa di'Bianchi. This is my office. I arrived a few days ago,' she added by way of explanation.

Gianfranco wrung his hands in embarrassment. 'Mi scusi, per favore, dottoressa! I didn't know the office was occupied,' he explained. 'It's been empty for several months. I've been using it as a quiet place to study. Nobody ever comes here.'

'But how did you get a key?' Donatella asked.

'I was the student assistant for the old photography professor,' replied the young Italian. 'This was his office and he gave me a key. I never gave it back after he retired. No one ever asked for it,' he added defensively.

Donatella held out her hand. 'I'm afraid you'll have to give me the key now,' she said. 'Signor della Parigi ... Gianfranco, you can't use this office anymore. Do you understand? You barged in just when I was ... when I was getting changed, so I was alarmed.'

'Of course, signora. Mi dispiace,' said the young Italian with a shy smile, withdrawing the key from his pocket.

The smile lit up his face and suddenly Donatella di'Bianchi didn't want the young man to go. 'Stay there,' she said and pulled up a chair to sit close to him.

When he smiled, Donatella thought, he was quite handsome in a cute, nerdish sort of way. His thick-lashed brown eyes were beautiful, open and honest.

The professor was amused when another expression of alarm flashed across Gianfranco's face, closely followed by a hungry doe-eyed look as he registered Donatella's scantily clad body close to his. Donatella nonchalantly loosened one of her recently refastened buttons, allowing the young man a further glimpse of the swell of her breasts.

The lust that filled her so unexpectedly at the sight of Ian Ramsey resurfaced unbidden; Donatella felt a needy urge to seduce this young man on the spot, to unzip his fly and fondle his cock. And how sweet he smelled. She bent forward and inhaled his scent; his lightly tanned skin was redolent of satsumas.

Donatella looked at her companion and saw that he sensed her desire. She followed his eyes as they took in the bra casually draped over a chair and one of her drawings lying on the floor, depicting a nude man with a large cock. With a start she noticed the boy's own penis in front of her was mimicking the drawing; a very large erection was burgeoning beneath the thin material of his lightweight summer slacks. Donatella wanted nothing more at that moment than to take that big young dick in her mouth and savour the kid's arousal. She could almost taste him. Her nipples tightened with desire, standing taut through their flimsy silk covering, and juices once more moistened her sex lips.

She touched Gianfranco's hand to take the proffered key and held it longer than necessary. With her other hand she was reaching for the remaining buttons on her blouse when reality returned like a shower of cold water on Donatella's erotic aberration. The moment was lost.

Guilt and confusion flooded into the void where lust had been a moment before. What the hell was she playing at? What was wrong with her? She'd been seized by a desire to have sex with two complete strangers in as many days! Alarmed at her behaviour Donatella sat up straight, and the fingers that a moment ago had been about to undo her blouse to reveal her breasts now buttoned up the garment fully.

Confused by the sudden turn of events, the young Italian nonetheless seemed to realise that whatever the moment might have been, it had passed as quickly as it came. He rose, blushing again, to take his leave. Standing up beside him and smoothing her skirt, Donatella fumbled for the right words.

'Er ... what happened here was clearly a simple misunderstanding, *signor della Parigi*,' she said, resorting to formality to hide her own embarrassment. 'I'll forget it ever happened, but this room is off limits. Now, if you'll excuse me,' she concluded, turning away to her desk, 'I've got some work to finish. It was ... nice meeting you.'

Gianfranco took his cue. '*Piacere, dottoressa di'Bianchi*,' he murmured shyly. '*Arrivederci ... grazie...*' He looked as if he wanted to say more, but instead lowered his eyes, picked up his books and shuffled out of the room.

Sitting at her desk, Donatella found her hands shaking. She could barely believe what she had so nearly done. Tenured women professors most certainly did not go round giving blow jobs to students they had only just met! Nor should they *think* about doing so, even if they were rather cute! Blushing, hot and humiliated by her frustrated desire for sex, she gathered her belongings and stuffed her various pieces of underwear in her gym bag. Grabbing her briefcase and opening the door of her office, Donatella peeped into the hallway to make sure Gianfranco was nowhere in sight.

The coast was clear; she fled her office and headed for Kiki's studio. But the work space was empty. Disappointed, Donatella walked on, looking for the computer room. At this time of the afternoon the building was empty and, with no one around to point her in the right direction, she soon found herself in an unfamiliar corridor. Kiki had fittingly likened the old *palazzo* to a rabbit warren, and Donatella realised she must have taken a wrong turn amidst the dark winding passages. Now she was lost.

Turning a corner, she came upon a stairway leading downwards and gingerly descended into the gloom below, her suede pumps making little sound on the worn wooden treads. She hoped she could find an exit on the ground floor, but two flights below only revealed another dingy, unused corridor.

Dust lay undisturbed on old furniture piled against a wall and cobwebs were draped densely over the clutter. Donatella was on the point of climbing back up when she heard muffled sounds coming from a bend in the passageway. Human voices. A man and a woman murmuring and giggling.

Listening closely, Donatella held her breath. Cautious but unafraid, she crept to the corner and peeked from behind a pile of old broken chairs. When her eyes adjusted to the dimly lit space, Donatella had to stifle a gasp of surprise. Fifty feet down the musty corridor, a female figure was illuminated by the dim light of a small dusty window. Except for football boots and socks, the young woman, her long blonde hair clasped into a pony-tail, was completely naked. As Donatella stared, the girl, whom she recognised as Jennifer Wrenn, moved to a kneeling position as a naked and erect Ian Ramsey stepped from the shadows.

As Donatella watched, stunned by the erotic tableau, Ian Ramsey grabbed the girl's blond head and pressed her face into his groin. Without hesitation, Jennifer Wrenn opened her mouth and eagerly sucked the Englishman's cock, rewarding her football coach for the tutorial.

Awestruck, Donatella observed Ramsey ease his cock from his girlfriend's mouth after a few moments and masturbate slowly while the girl scrambled to change position, turning her golden body so that a pair of rounded, upturned buttocks faced Ramsey's ramrod erection.

God, it was a huge penis! Donatella shuddered at the sight as Ramsey grasped the eager girl from behind. She watched the girl pitch forward, bracing her hands flat against the wall as Ramsey thrust his long cock, slick from oral caresses, into the girl's cunt.

Donatella stared fixedly as her colleague slid in and out with a slow patient rhythm, his fingers finding the girl's clit with casual expertise. Jennifer squealed and wiggled with abandon, thrusting her arse hard against her lover's groin, taking every inch of his cock inside her. The raw animal lust of the duo's rough coupling struck Donatella to the depth of her womb, where she felt the tingle of delicious, resonating arousal. At first fearful of being observed, Donatella soon realised that the couple was blind to all but their own lust.

Donatella stayed hidden in the gloom. How she longed for the touch of such a man between her legs! In the dusty quiet she heard the slurping sound of the Englishman's cock plunging into the girl's warm, wet tunnel and the slapping of his balls against her bottom. To quell the growing, insistent throbbing in her loins, Donatella slid her hand under her skirt and sought her renewed wetness. All pretense at academic propriety was shredded as she slipped her fingers between her legs for the second time that afternoon. She shivered with the intensity of her furtive desire and felt her clit throb under her increasing pressure. She moaned with an involuntary spasm.

Quivering at the sight and sound of Ramsey fucking Jennifer, Donatella could think of nothing beyond frantically furthering her own pleasure and releasing the frustrations of the afternoon. She moved her hand ever more urgently, her clothes awry and hair falling in long tendrils from her chignon. Observing the increasing force of Ramsey's rhythmic humping, and fascinated by the sight of his long cock sliding in and out, Donatella felt herself pulse over the edge. She came with a tremor. Her moan of surrender to ecstasy was drowned only by Jennifer Wrenn's squealing climax, followed by a series of low shuddering grunts by Ramsey as he pumped his come deep inside his student lover.

Opening her eyes and gasping for breath, Donatella saw the naked couple's final breathless collapse over each other. Within a moment or two the pair eased themselves apart and pulled on their clothes. Donatella's eyes locked onto Ramsey's glistening dick until the very last moment it disappeared inside his shorts. A little unsteadily the lovers walked away down the corridor and disappeared from sight, the clack of their boot studs on the tiles fading from earshot.

Donatella's fingers were so wet she had to dry them on her handkerchief, still damp from her earlier escapade and then dab the dripping juices from her pussy. She eased down her skirt and, seeking the light, walked towards the small window that had illuminated the scene so effectively. She extracted her compact from her briefcase and, opening it, stared at her reflection in the mirror. Her eyes were unusually bright. Her cheeks were crimson. Normally so well groomed, her tidy chignon was now disheveled. She usually wore her long sable-coloured hair tightly wound, precisely to look more distinguished and academic. Now clusters of silken tendrils trailed across her face and neck. With trembling hands she unpinned her hair and let her locks tumble to her shoulders. She shook her curls loose, letting her hair regain its natural flowing lines, feeling some of her professorial demeanour slip away as she did so. Three times aroused, no wonder she had come like that!

Feelings of guilt about her sluttish behaviour filled her mind, and Donatella walked distractedly along the passageway until she found the doorway by which the lovers must have exited the building. Opening the door gingerly, she found herself in a deserted alley that led downhill from the park to the city centre. Two blocks away she glimpsed the Piazza Grande. Craving a strong drink to calm her nerves, Donatella shouldered her briefcase and exercise bag and walked slowly towards the town square. She still felt moisture seeping between her thighs.

8 *Le Amice Nouve*
(New Friends)

Kiki and Francesca sipped tall Peroni beers, relaxing at their favourite table at La Taverna Vasari inside the arcaded *Loggia*. They looked out over the Piazza Grande, which sloped dramatically away before them, and enjoyed watching the last of the vendors of the craft market clearing away their stalls and unsold wares after a long hot day in the sun. The two women lounged in their chairs in the shade, under the light breeze from an overhead fan.

'Hey, Francesca,' shouted a boy riding past on a bike. Francesca waved to him.

'Who's that?' asked Kiki.

'Milk boy,' said Francesca.

'He's just a kid,' said Kiki. 'Surely you ... haven't fucked him?'

'Not yet.' Francesca, just finished modelling for a life-drawing class, was dressed simply in a beaded denim jacket – buttoned once across her otherwise uncovered breasts – and an Indian print skirt with a ruffled hem. There was little evidence of any underwear. Kiki wore a variation on her usual uniform: the ubiquitous bicycle shorts and boots, complemented this time by a black lambskin camisole that zipped up the back. For the umpteenth time she glanced at Francesca's feminine curves, seductively revealed beneath her partially open jacket, and wished she was as generously endowed as her friend.

Kiki knew she was by no means the only one studying Francesca's body. Several of the market-stall holders lingered in their tasks to observe the beautiful ginger blonde, and waiters clustered close by their table. When Francesca nonchalantly crossed one leg over the other, her hem rode up nearly to her crotch and the waiters stopped in their tracks.

Kiki smiled and took advantage of one of their favourite *camerieri* to order a snack. '*Benito, qualcosa da mangiare, per favore ... Un panino al fromaggio per me, e una pizzetta per Francesca.*'

'*Bene, Kiki. Qual cosa da bere?*'

'*Si, grazie, Benito, due per favore...*' Kiki paused, thinking she saw a familiar figure wandering in the crowd. She stood up, slightly puzzled, then smiled and waved energetically. '*Dottoressa* di'Bianchi! Over here!' She turned to the waiter. '*Scusi, Benito, ci porte un altro Peroni, per favore.*' The waiter reluctantly tore his eyes away from Francesca's cleavage and loped away.

'Who's that?' asked Francesca, craning her neck to observe a tall dark-haired woman walking towards them.

'She's the new professor, the one I'm working for,' explained Kiki, waving a welcome as the long-legged American's tense expression changed to one of pleasurable relief.

'*Molta bella!*' Francesca said as the professor approached their table. 'Mmmm, and sexy,' she added. 'I like her hair.'

'It's the first time I've seen her wearing it down,' said Kiki. 'I wasn't sure it was her at first in the piazza. Normally she wears it wound up tight, in a chignon. Attractive but very professorial. I like it better this way.'

Kiki stood to welcome Donatella, and Francesca did likewise, depriving several nearby men of a delicious glimpse between her thighs.

'Kiki! What a relief to see you! I was afraid I'd missed you!' The student could hear the tension in her professor's voice.

'Is anything wrong?' asked Kiki with concern. 'You looked a bit worried, if you don't mind my saying so. 'Oh,' she added, 'you haven't met my friend Francesca Antinori.'

'Hello,' said Donatella, and the pair shook hands, smiling at each other. Kiki waited for an answer to her question but none was forthcoming.

Instead Francesca picked up the conversation. 'Kiki told me about you, *professoressa*,' she chided, 'but she didn't say you were such a beautiful woman!'

The sophisticated American laughed at the compliment. 'You flatter me.'

'But no!' said Francesca, gesturing for Donatella to take a seat beside her.

Donatella smiled at her new acquaintance. 'You're very kind, Francesca,' she said, sitting down. 'But I have the advantage of you; I already knew you were beautiful.'

Francesca's eyebrows rose as she resettled in her chair. 'And how was this?' She looked at her housemate. 'Kiki?'

But Donatella spoke. 'Kiki didn't have to say anything. I saw your photographs.'

Kiki, sitting on Donatella's other side, explained to her housemate. '*Dottoressa* di'Bianchi saw the photos I took of you after class last week for Ian's seminar.'

'The ones where I was playing with myself?' Francesca covered her mouth with one small well-manicured hand and giggled.

Benito nearly dropped the cheese sandwich in Kiki's lap as he overheard the last fragment of conversation. He hastily placed the food and drink on the table and retreated, but not too far.

Francesca laughed again. 'Now Benito will think of me this evening when he plays with himself!'

Donatella joined in the laughter and Kiki observed the remaining tension ease from her face. The older woman picked up the beer. 'Is this for me?'

Kiki nodded to her mentor. 'You looked hot and bothered, *dottoressa*,' she said, dropping another hint for Donatella to unburden herself. 'I thought you might like a long cool one. And you've let your hair down,' she added. 'Looks good.'

'Thank you, Kiki,' Donatella said, taking a hearty swallow. 'That hits the spot.' She put down the beer and ran her fingers through her long silky tresses. 'I might keep it this way,' she mused. 'It seems more fitting for this place ... more relaxed.'

Kiki nodded enthusiastically.

'It's time to drop this "*dottoressa*" formality,' said the older woman, smiling at her companions. 'Kiki, you must call me Donatella. You too, Francesca.'

The young Italian raised her glass. '*Sì.* I propose a toast,' she announced dramatically. '*Le amice nouve!* New friends!'

The trio clinked glasses.

'Do you two live together? asked Donatella.

Kiki nodded. 'We rent a little villa in the centre of Bucine, half an hour away on the train. Here,' she added, reaching into her bag for a notebook and pen, 'let me give you the address and phone number.' She wrote down the information, tore out the page and handed it to Donatella.

'Thank you,' said Donatella, tucking the note into her briefcase. 'Perhaps I could drop by and visit some time?'

Kiki nodded eagerly. 'That would be great. How was the gym, by the way?' she asked, changing the subject.

Donatella evaded the question. 'I think I need something stronger to drink!' she said. 'All this tension at the college gets to me.' She turned to the hovering Benito, whose ears were flapping for more juicy tidbits. 'Vodka-Martini, *per favore*.'

'You need to talk to some of the graduate students,' said Kiki, 'such as Jennifer Wrenn. Get a different perspective. Jen was a protester too; she and I could get a small group together,' she explained.

At the mention of Jennifer's name, Kiki noted that Donatella's colour deepened and she took a long sip of the cocktail that Benito had magically placed in front of her.

'Is something wrong?' Kiki asked. 'Did some guy hit on you at the gym?'

Donatella shook her head. 'I didn't get to the gym,' she said. She sipped her drink again and then seemed to make up her mind about something. 'Oh, hell!' she said. 'I shouldn't tell you this but I can't get it out of my mind.'

Startled by Donatella's tone, Kiki and Francesca leaned forward attentively. Benito, surreptitiously rubbing his cock beneath tight black trousers, edged closer to the women's table.

'After you left my office, Kiki,' Donatella began, 'two rather disturbing things happened.'

Kiki nodded encouragingly.

Donatella said, 'It was hot in my office and I was ... changing clothes, when in walked this strange student. I'm there with my bra off and blouse undone, and a tall gangly guy is staring at me!'

Kiki exchanged looks with Francesca.

'His name is Gianfranco something or other,' Donatella continued. 'Do you know him?'

Both women grinned. 'Yes,' they chimed, 'indeed we know him. I'm afraid we tease him a lot, but he's a harmless nerdy kind of guy really,' Kiki elaborated. 'He used to be a seminary student but he rebelled against his strict parents and switched to art – partly to piss them off. He's quite a good photographer,' she said. 'Poor guy!' The young American shook her head rue-fully. 'He's still a virgin, you see.'

Francesca's peal of laughter interrupted the explanation.

Kiki continued, 'Those Jesuits mess with your mind. Gianfranco's a bit confused about sex and he is very shy with women.' She smiled broadly. 'It must have been a big shock to him: entering the room and seeing a beautiful woman flashing her tits.'

It was Donatella's turn to laugh. 'I was hardly "flash-ing my tits,"' she protested. 'I was changing clothes. He was shocked. I'm afraid I chewed him out for being there.'

The three women sipped their drinks in silence for a moment.

'You said two things upset you,' prompted Kiki. 'What was the other one?' She noted that Donatella wasn't wearing a bra and that her breasts were free beneath the silk blouse.

Donatella hesitated. 'You'll think I'm fixated on sex,' she said slowly.

'That's OK,' interrupted Francesca. 'We are, too!'

The older woman smiled. 'All right, but this is a confession,' she demurred. 'Please don't tell anyone.' Leaning forward on her elbows, Donatella sipped her martini. 'I got lost when I left my office,' she explained. 'I found an old staircase that I thought would bring me out somewhere. When I got to the bottom it was very dark, and I heard voices. I peeked around the corner, and I saw Ian Ramsey ... er, with Jennifer Wrenn. Right there in the corridor!'

'What were they doing?' demanded Francesca.

'Well, having sex,' stated Donatella, averting her eyes under the enquiring gaze of her two companions.

'We want details!' said Francesca.

'I didn't look closely,' said Donatella primly, but this remark met a skeptical silence.

Then Kiki said, 'But you looked a bit.'

'Well, yes.'

'And . . .?'

'Well, Jennifer was naked and leaning against the wall, and Ramsey was . . . taking her from behind. They both had their soccer boots on,' she added inconsequentially.

Francesca nodded sagely. 'That sounds like something Ian would do,' she affirmed. 'He likes doggy-style.'

Donatella's eyes widened. 'Do you mean that you . . . that he's . . . that you and he . . .'

Francesca grinned. 'Do you mean have I fucked *il professore magnifico*?' she asked. 'Oh, yes, but only once. He insisted on doing it from behind. I think he wanted to put his dick up my arse, but I wouldn't let him.' She jabbed Kiki in the ribs, 'Kiki here is jealous because she hasn't had him yet!'

'I'm not jealous,' Kiki shot back. 'I just said it would be nice to share.'

While Donatella gaped, Francesca appeared to consider the idea. 'Well, that should be easy enough,' she said. 'I doubt if *il signor* Ian would say no to two such sexy women. His *cazzo* is plenty big and juicy enough to go round,' she added casually. 'Perhaps we can arrange something.'

To Donatella's shock, Kiki nodded. 'Yes,' she said, 'I'd love the chance to fuck Ian Ramsey.' She winked wickedly at Donatella and added, 'It's almost a point of personal pride not to play second fiddle to Jennifer Wrenn.' But her smile vanished when she saw how much the sexual banter had embarrassed Donatella.

The professor was looking at them unbelievingly. 'Did I hear what I thought I heard?' she said in a slightly shaky voice. 'The two of you planning three-way sex with Professor Ramsey?'

'Oops!' said Kiki. 'Dr di'Bianchi, we meant no offence. We shouldn't presume to display our petty lusts in front of you. I'm afraid we're just a couple of horny gals who can't keep our minds off sex,' she said self-deprecatingly, dropping her gaze.

'No, no,' said Donatella. 'That's not it. I'm not offended by talking about sex. In fact,' she blushed slightly, 'I . . . rather enjoy it. It's just that I'm not used to people being so frank about it. And, students with faculty – well, it's not done in Boston. And, well, Henry and I, Henry's my . . . friend in Boston,' she explained. 'We haven't . . . done that sort of thing for a long time.'

Kiki opened her mouth to speak, but Francesca beat her to it. 'What sort of "thing," Donatella? Talking about sex, or having sex?'

For a moment the muscles around Donatella's mouth clenched, but the irritation was quickly replaced by melancholy humour. 'Good question, Francesca!' Donatella replied dryly. Turning to Kiki with a frank gaze she said, 'I'm envious of you two. Your attitude about sex is so carefree. I've made love – had sex – once in the last two months! It's hard for me to talk about sex now. Words like . . . cock and . . . fuck seem like a foreign language.'

'I don't believe this Henry appreciates you,' said Francesca. 'Maybe you need a new lover.'

Donatella shook her head. 'No. It's not all Henry's fault,' she admitted. 'I've been wrapped up in work, I don't have the time or energy for sex anymore. I think about sex but that's as far as it seems to go.'

Kiki was surprised at the change between the brilliant, sometimes intimidating academic and the diffident and insecure woman who sat at their table. She surmised that Donatella had left things unsaid regarding the incident with Ian Ramsey and Jennifer Wrenn. But she also realised that now might not be the time to press the issue further. Instead she said, 'I have an idea.'

Donatella looked up.

'We're friends, right?' Kiki said with a smile.

Donatella nodded. 'New friends. Yes, I hope so.'

'I propose a bargain. I know there's one hell of a lot I can learn about the history of art from you. You're an expert in your field and I'm very interested. I've got Francesca interested, too. Isn't that right Fran?'

Fran nodded eagerly.

'It's only fair,' continued Kiki, 'that we teach you something in return. This is the deal: you educate us about art history and Francesca and I will be your tutors in a post-graduate seminar on sex. All you have to do for the first lesson is watch what we do. OK? Is that a deal?'

Donatella laughed. 'You make me feel like a teenager again,' she said.

'That's OK,' said Francesca, standing. 'I learned a lot of things when I was a teenager.'

Kiki paid their bill, tipping the eavesdropping Benito generously.

Dropping her voice, Francesca said wickedly, 'Donatella, what shall we do about poor old Benito? He got a hard-on just listening to us talk.'

To Kiki's amusement and Donatella's startled delight, Francesca sidled past Benito as the trio left their table, her hand deliberately brushing his cock. It was clearly as hard as a rock. The wanton blonde gave it a gentle squeeze and rubbed his shaft.

'Have a good wank tonight, Benito,' she said in a seductive *sotto voce*. 'Think of coming all over my tits,' she whispered slyly. Then in a normal voice she added, *'Ciao, Benito. A domani!'* With a parting wave, the *Italiana* led the trio down the few steps into the piazza and into the crowds of the evening's *passeggiata*.

9 *Le Difficolta Doppia* (Double Trouble)

'*Buona notte*, Donatella,' said Kiki and Francesca, as the trio stood in the quiet Piazza San Domenico. 'We're driving home tonight.'

'Not riding the train?'

'Not tonight.' Kiki said, 'I drove the car to carry in some photo equipment to the studio.'

'Well, good night!' Waving to her two new friends as they turned to walk towards the public car park, Donatella heard Francesca's high-pitched laughter. She watched the pretty pair walk away, swaying arm-in-arm through the San Biagio gate in the medieval wall and vanishing from sight.

The tall American strolled the short distance towards her hotel. She felt happier than she had for several days, even weeks. The irreverent good humour of the two younger women lifted her spirits. She could probably tell them the truth about her lascivious afternoon's activities and all they would do is laugh, or even approve of her flagrant behaviour. Her guilt began to recede, to be replaced by warm memories of her first orgasm in a long time and the delightful anticipation of more to come.

Arriving at her own doorstep. Donatella was surprised to find the front door of the *pensione* in the Via delle Paniere open. Normally it was closed and guests let themselves in with keys. Alarmed that anybody could just walk in, Donatella looked around before entering the small foyer, but the deeply shaded street was deserted this time of the evening.

Inside the front door of the *pensione*, Donatella found the front desk deserted, too, but that was not unusual in this little establishment. Two lamps lit the flight of stairs as Donatella walked up to her room. On the landing she stopped, her heart pounding in her chest. The door to her room was also unlocked and standing ajar.

She listened intently, but all was silent. Taking a deep breath she pulled the door fully open, and then froze on the threshold. Her room was in chaos, furniture tipped over, her suitcase ripped apart and her pillows slashed. She felt a surge of anger at this despoilation of her tiny refuge, but her anger turned to fear as she saw what lay on the bed. The few clothes she had brought with her had been deliberately cut into pieces and arranged in a macabre jigsaw of a human figure lying on the bedspread.

Fragments of bras and panties had been mounded to form breasts and a compact triangle in the figure's groin. Shredded remnants of other clothes, skirts, jackets and blouses made up the body of the figure. Even her two extra pairs of shoes had been ruined and placed carefully at the foot of the bed.

Keeping a sense of rising panic under control, Donatella forced herself to check the tiny bathroom. What met her eyes there was just as bad: a crude cartoon drawn on the mirror in lipstick depicted a kneeling, naked woman, bound hand and foot and being sprayed with urine or semen from half a dozen disembodied penises. Toiletries, slashed open, were trodden into the floor tiles. Nothing seemed to have escaped the attention of the vandals.

Beneath her state of agitation, one part of Donatella's brain recorded the scene for future reference.

Those coolly dispassionate brain cells registered that the ugly cartoon was actually well drawn. In another context the female figure could be part of a respectable composition, erotic certainly, but not terrifying of itself. But the trashed room and the brutal invasion of her private world made the drawing terribly menacing. Even the horrific collage on the bed had the proper proportions of limbs and torso. In a wild moment Donatella thought this might an unbalanced attempt at installation art, but she quickly realised her foolishness. The smashed chairs and complete destruction of the room was far more serious than an art prank.

Racing downstairs she found the proprietor in the kitchen.

'*Signor* Simonini!' she gasped. 'Someone has broken into my room! Come quickly, please!'

The elderly owner looked startled and annoyed at the interruption. '*Ma che! Impossibile! Non faccia lo stupido!*'

Donatella bridled. 'I'm not being stupid. We must report this to the police. *Subito!*' She took the proprietor by the arm and assisted him upstairs.

The horrified *signor* Simonini took one look at the desecrated bedroom and let out a wail of complaint. '*Non va! Non si fa cosi!* What madman did this? What have you brought to my hotel?' he demanded of a startled Donatella. 'I have never had a problem with a single guest in thirty years. You've been here three days and it is wrecked!'

Donatella's fear turned quickly to anger at the old man's tone. 'This isn't my fault. *Sono innocente!* You should provide security in this hotel. My belongings are ruined!'

Signor Simonini pointed to the bed and the lipstick drawing in the bathroom. 'This is not natural,' he exclaimed. 'This is the work of a pervert. This is someone who knows you!' He wagged a furious finger in her face.

Donatella blanched. That thought had not occurred to her, but it made a certain sense. She had little of value to steal in the room, and burglary didn't seem to be the primary motive of the intruder. Her PowerBook, purse and passport were (thankfully) in her briefcase, still over her shoulder. She gripped the strap tightly. Was this indeed some grotesque attack on her personally? But who? And why?

Frightened as well as angry, Donatella left the unhelpful proprietor bemoaning the mess and hurried out of the building, heading for the police station in the Via Garibaldi.

The bored-looking policeman on duty duly listened to Donatella's complaint and filled in a lengthy report form. 'I'll send an officer as soon as possible, *dottoressa*,' he said politely. 'But we have extra guard duty today for an important visitor. All my colleagues are out ... and as you are not hurt ...' The policeman spread his hands as if to show how helpless he was in this situation. 'Will you be there this evening?' he asked.

Donatella didn't want to set foot in that crummy little *pensione* again. 'No,' she said on impulse. 'I'll be staying with friends ... in Bucine,' she added, dictating the phone number and address from the piece of paper that Kiki had written for her only an hour earlier.

'*Bene, dottoressa*. Please call back in the morning and another officer will help you.'

Donatella doubted that, but she didn't want to argue. She wanted to be out of Arezzo and with friends. She doubted Kiki and Francesca would be home yet, but called their number anyway. There was no answer and no voice mail. Frustrated, she headed for the train station, redialing every five minutes but to no avail.

Bucine was a small town. How hard could it be to find Kiki and Francesca's little villa?

The train station at Bucine was deserted when Donatella descended from the last *locale* of the evening. It was now dark as the diesel sounded its muted horn and rolled slowly away from the platform. The train soon vanished into a tunnel beneath the hills that marked this section of the roundabout branch line between Arezzo and Florence.

Rather than taking the underground passage beneath the tracks, Donatella ignored the warning signs and scampered across the rails on a causeway of sleepers. A small sign outside the station pointing up a steep hill read 'Il Centro', and Donatella glumly climbed the sloping street that twisted its way between small houses and apartment buildings. At the top of the hill she entered what was evidently the main street of the little town, with a bank, some shops and a bar at the far end. An illuminated orange sign over the door announced that Bar Sandy was open and the only activity in sight.

Donatella stepped through the beaded curtain into a smoke-filled interior. Several elderly men were sitting at tables and from a back room came the click and clatter of balls on a pool table. Smiling bravely at the suddenly silent men, Donatella made her way to the bar. Behind the counter a middle-aged man regarded her appraisingly.

'Mi scusi, per favore,' ventured Donatella. 'Non so dove mi trovo. Sto cercando il mia amica Francesca Antinori, in piazza...,' she consulted her diary, 'Piazzetta Cavour. In che direzione devo andare?'

At the mention of Francesca's name, the *barista* smiled broadly. 'Ah, si, si. La bella Francesca!' Donatella heard several chuckles from her audience. The barman gave Donatella a little wink. *'Sei una buon'amica, un'amica speciale di Francesca?'* This question brought ribald laughter from the old men, and several youths stopped their game of pool to smile and watch the proceedings.

Donatella was not in the mood for riddles. 'What do you mean, *a special friend?*' she asked. 'Look, I don't mean to be rude, but it's late. I'm tired and I need to get to Francesca's house. Can you direct me there?'

The barman made a gesture to some patrons behind Donatella, which elicited a round of sniggering, and turned back to her, leering lewdly. *'Con piacere, Signorina! Naturalmente!'* He led Donatella to the doorway and pointed up the street opposite. *'Sempre dirrito, la via Brancusi, Signorina, e la prima strada a destra.'*

'Grazie,' said Donatella coldly and deliberately turned to the watching men in the little bar. *'Buona notte, signori,'* she said with mocking politeness, and a saccharin smile that didn't touch her eyes. Tossing her bags over her shoulder, she strode out of Bar Sandy and marched up the hill.

'Fuck you, *cogglionazzi!*' she said to herself under her breath.

It was only a short walk up the hill to what was the highest point of the small town. Only a few street lights cast a glimmer on the flagstones and, above, the sky had turned a deep indigo filled with jewelled stars. Donatella allowed herself a calming moment to savour their beauty. She never saw stars like this in the light-polluted environment of Boston.

She turned right as directed and found herself in a small stone-paved square. There were no street signs, but this was surely the Piazzetta Cavour. She looked for house numbers, but in the darkness none were visible. The longer side of the square was formed by a row of apartment buildings, and on the other a few small houses stood slightly apart from each other. Most were dark, but one was ablaze with light from high windows. Donatella made her way towards this structure and climbed the dozen steps from the pavement and rapped on the oak door.

'Who the fuck's that?' Kiki's alarmed voice came from within.

'Kiki, it's me, Donatella. Let me in!'

After a few seconds filled with the sounds of heavy bolts being drawn back, the door flew open and an agitated Kiki stood backlit in the doorway wearing only a thin slip, almost transparent from Donatella's point of view. 'Donatella!' she cried. 'How did you know? How did you get here? Come in!' and the young American unexpectedly threw her arms around Donatella and hugged the older woman tightly. 'It's so good to see you. God, I was so scared!'

Donatella felt Kiki's firm young body trembling in her arms and automatically stroked her back with the fingers of one hand, while the other reached up to caress the woman's spiky red hair. It felt surprisingly soft to the touch and smelled freshly washed with a delicate apple fragrance. She kissed Kiki's hair lightly. 'It's OK, Kiki,' she murmured. 'It's OK. I'm here. Tell me what happened. What frightened you?'

Kiki stood back and looked at her friend. 'You mean you don't know? I thought somebody must have told you. Why are you here, then?' Her green eyes widened. 'Is something wrong in Arezzo?'

'Yes, but we can talk about that later. First, I want to hear what's happened to you. Is Francesca here?'

An answering shout came from another room to announce that the young Florentine was indeed at home. 'I'm here, Donatella. I had to have a shower, I was so dirty. God, it was awful!' Francesca opened the door to what looked like her bedroom and came forward, her hair still wet, wearing a minuscule silver thong. Her round breasts swung beneath a thin vest in the glare of the hall light. 'Come in,' she said with a friendly gesture. 'We all could do with a drink. I've got a bottle of Rendola open in the kitchen.' She led the other two women to the back of the house.

Donatella noticed Francesca walked with a limp and her thighs and lower back were covered in scratches. She started to ask about the injuries when Francesca thrust a glass of wine in her hand and motioned her to sit. Soon all three were sitting around the kitchen table and Donatella's questions came tumbling out.

'What happened?' she demanded. 'What were you so upset about when I arrived? And why has Francesca got cuts all over her legs?'

'She's not the only one,' said Kiki, and lifted the hem of her silk slip, revealing a series of ugly purple marks and red scratches on her body that matched her friend's. 'We were in a car crash earlier, just after we left you. Some bastard ran us off the road between here and Levane, and we went over the edge into a bunch of olive trees,' she said, dropping the hem to cover her wounds. 'The car's a complete write-off.'

'Oh, my God, that's awful!' exclaimed Donatella. 'Did the other driver stop?'

'Hell, no!' exploded Kiki. 'And it *wasn't* an accident! This big old Mercedes was following us all the way home, and just where the road curves and narrows – before you cross over the river – the bastard came right up alongside and sideswiped us! Bam! My poor little Fiat crumpled like a piece of tin and over we went.'

'Thank God you weren't badly hurt!' exclaimed Donatella. 'It must have been awful. You could have been killed! Are you very sore?'

'A bit' admitted Kiki. 'These bruises will hurt like hell in the morning. It was a pretty close thing; another few yards round the bend the land drops very steeply down to some rocks. If we'd gone over there we probably wouldn't be here to talk about it. As it was the bastard misjudged it, and we landed in the olive trees instead.'

'Are you sure it was deliberate?' asked Donatella. 'Did you see who was driving?'

Francesca and Kiki shook their heads in unison. 'No,' replied the Italian. 'The windows were heavily tinted. I think there were two men inside, but I could only see their outlines. And yes, I'm sure it was deliberate. It was attempted murder!'

'A licence plate?'

'No,' admitted Francesca. 'The police asked us all these same questions and we couldn't tell them anything. It was just a dark-coloured Mercedes, probably about ten years old. Beaten up and dirty. That's all I can remember. The stupid *polizia stradale* think it was a hit-and-run accident. They don't believe anyone tried to kill us.'

Donatella sat white-faced as she listened to her friends' terrible tale. It seemed so far-fetched. Why would anybody deliberately try to kill Kiki and Francesca? Why would anybody ritually slash her clothes and lay them out like a corpse on her hotel bed? She hadn't thought about that interpretation to the macabre figure in her room until now. Her friends' life-threatening experience put a different light on these strange occurrences. She poured them all another glass of the delicious local red wine and drank hers down quickly.

'I'm afraid I have bad news of my own,' she said. The tone in her voice made her companions stare in apprehension. 'Someone broke into my hotel room this afternoon and trashed everything, all my clothes and personal items. Luckily I had my PowerBook and purse with me, but everything else has been destroyed.'

'Passport?' queried Kiki, immediately.

'I have it, thank God,' said Donatella. 'I always carry it with me. But I haven't told you the scariest part,' she continued. 'My clothes – blouses, skirts, underwear – were sliced up and the pieces laid out on my bed in the form of a body! I couldn't stay there another night. That's why I'm here, to ask you to take me in, at least for a day or two.'

Francesca gasped. 'This can't be a coincidence.'

Donatella didn't want to think about that possibility. 'We can't say that for sure, Francesca. We have no evidence.'

Kiki demurred. 'It seems more likely to me that these two acts of violence *are* connected than not,' she said. 'After all, what are the odds against two completely random acts on the same day? It makes more sense if they're part of a pattern.'

'But who?' demanded Donatella. 'Who on earth would go to these lengths to scare and injure *us*? What have we done to provoke this violence?'

Kiki gave Donatella a cautious stare. 'You'll think this is all part of my "persecution complex" that I'm alleged to have about Temple-Clarke, but in my book he's the number one candidate for this. He doesn't want you here and he knows I'm helping you. He's the only thread that links this stuff together.'

'I can't believe it,' argued Donatella. 'It's one thing to be scheming and incompetent, but quite another to threaten people and try to kill them!'

Kiki shrugged. 'I know I can't prove it. It's only a theory, but whoever is behind this, we've got to take it seriously. We need to be very careful.'

'What should we do to protect ourselves?' asked Donatella. 'The police in Arezzo didn't seem to take my complaint very seriously, and the local cops dismissed your attack as an accident. Who can we turn to?'

Francesca grinned. 'I can help there,' she said. 'I've already called my friend Salvatore Provenza. He's a *capitano* in the *carabinieri*,' she explained to Donatella. 'He'll come around first thing in the morning, after he gets off his special security duty for some visiting politician. In the meantime he told us to stay inside and keep the windows and doors locked. A patrol car will cruise by a couple of times in the night.'

Donatella yawned, aware of her growing fatigue. 'May I stay here tonight?' she asked.

'Of course, Donatella,' Kiki replied. 'Francesca and I were talking about this on the way home, even before all this happened. Why don't you move in with us? We have a spare room. It's not prepared, but we can see to that tomorrow. It's Saturday and we can drive ...' She stopped, her shoulders slumping. 'Oh, stupid me. We don't have a car anymore! I was going to say we could drive over to the Iper-coop in Montevarchi and get some basic furniture and more bedding. And some clothes for you. They won't measure up to your designer togs, though. A bit more like Wal-Mart!'

'I have an idea,' Francesca piped up. 'I'll go down to Marcellino's garage in the morning. He usually has an old car or two in the shop. He can probably loan us one. He owes me a favour or two,' she said with a smile.

Kiki grinned. 'Or if he doesn't he soon will,' she teased her friend.

Donatella looked at the two young women doubt-fully. Was Francesca suggesting exchanging sex for a car? Surely not! She must have misunderstood. She glanced at the young Italian, still unselfconsciously semi-naked at the table, her attractive breasts prominent beneath her vest as she leaned forward on her elbows.

Kiki interrupted her train of thought. 'How about it, Donatella? Would you like to live here? You're very welcome.'

Francesca agreed. '*Si, la mia cara*. It will be fun having you here!' She reached over and caressed the older woman's forearm. Despite her fatigue, Donatella felt a little shiver of pleasure at her touch.

'There's no other place I'd rather be right now than with the two of you,' Donatella replied. She smiled at the free-spirited young women. Even in her worried state she still felt comforted by their presence and stimulated by their unorthodox approach to sex and life. 'I'd love it, Kiki,' she replied. 'Thank you, Francesca. We can sort out the details over the next few days. I insist on paying a third of the rent and household expenses.'

Francesca waved the details away. '*Domani*,' she said. 'We'll talk about all that tomorrow. It's the weekend, so we have plenty of time.'

Donatella looked about her. 'Where can I sleep this evening?' she asked.

'You can sleep in my room,' offered Kiki. 'I changed the sheets today. It's pretty comfortable.'

'Oh, I couldn't,' protested Donatella. 'Where would you sleep?'

'With me,' said Francesca casually. 'It's a big bed. OK, Kiki?'

Kiki grinned. 'It's fine,' she assured the doubtful Donatella.

Donatella was too tired to argue. Kiki showed her where she could hang her clothes and loaned her some toiletries.

'We'll go shopping in the morning,' she said. 'While

Francesca's giving Marcellino his blow job, we'll go to the market.' She laughed at the expression on Donatella's face. 'Don't worry, Donatella, we're not quite as crazy as we seem. It'll be good having you here.' The petite woman gave her friend a big hug and a kiss on the cheek. 'Good night. See you in the morning.'

Donatella quickly took off her clothes and lay naked on the bed. Kiki's sheets had a pleasant, freshly washed scent of apples, and she soon fell asleep to the sound of murmuring voices across the hall.

A bad dream of being chased by Temple-Clarke and Henry Fogg woke Donatella, sweating, in the middle of the night, and she rose to pad to the kitchen for a drink of iced water. On her way back to bed, on impulse she noiselessly opened Francesca's bedroom door. There on the large bed Francesca and Kiki lay entwined, their naked bodies curled around each other in slumber. Kiki's thigh rested between Francesca's open legs, and one hand lay gently on the Italian's breasts.

The older woman gazed at her two young friends, noting their pleasured abandon. So that's what that creep in the bar meant by a 'special friend', thought Donatella. He thought I was a lesbian! Smiling, she gently eased the door closed. She shook her head at the half-formed thoughts creeping into her mind. It's all the stress, she told herself sternly. I'm just not thinking right.

Interlude

The young girl moaned on cue as she felt the boy's cock move deep inside her. His smooth hairless body knelt over her own as he thrust into her. We're getting better at this, she thought dispassionately.

Her opinion was shared by the third person in the room. The flash of a digital camera illuminated the scene in harsh contrast. 'Excellent, Anna! Excellent.' The man's voice was thick with arousal.

From her prone position, Anna Gentileschi watched the man put the camera on a dressing table and walk over to her. He straddled her lithe young body, and she could see the well-toned muscles of his arse tighten as he thrust his cock into the compliant mouth of the boy who was fucking her. Looking upwards, she saw the older man's heavy balls swing as he moved his hips, bent his knees and thrust forward.

'Suck my cock, Leo,' he demanded, grabbing the boy's hair. 'You know how I like it!'

The obedient young man swallowed several inches of flesh inside his mouth. Anna could see his cheeks contract as he sucked, and watched his lips as they embraced the thick shaft. His head bobbed forward and back, and she felt the rhythm of his fucking falter as he transferred his attention to pleasing his master.

Despite the regular routine of their copulation, Anna found herself aroused by the sight of the two men above her; one a teenager like herself, and the other their domineering lover and patron, the source of their adolescent wealth. How many sixteen year olds in

Arezzo had their own apartment, all the cool clothes they could wear, the latest stereo and video equipment, and enough spending money to make other teenagers very envious?

A shiver of pleasure rippled through her as Leo regained his rhythm and his penis probed deep into her. She reached down and rubbed her clit, the little bud standing up stiffly amidst the pink folds of her naked pussy, shaved clean of pubic hair by order of *il padrone*.

Anna tensed as she watched the man's cock spasm into Leo's mouth. Semen dribbled from the boy's lips and dropped on her breasts. It was already cool, and she rubbed it into her nipples. She opened her mouth as Leo released the man's cock and leaned down to kiss her, transferring his come onto her tongue. She knew this routine well. She let their mouths mingle and felt the sperm ooze down her chin. She moaned and wrapped her legs around Leo's buttocks, drawing him deep inside her as the older man stepped quickly aside. The camera flashed again several times.

Anna could feel Leo's excitement peak; he was getting off on it today. Her own arousal increased but, before she could come, the boy's dick jerked and spurted deep inside, filling her up with his youthful seed. She tried to fake it, but the older man was not fooled.

'You selfish oaf, Leo!' chided the man severely, slapping the boy hard. He reinforced his displeasure with another series of stinging slaps on Leo's arse that left red hand prints. Anna knew from experience that he spanked hard.

She felt Leo's cock slide out of her. She lay prone, not knowing what was coming next as her young companion rolled off and lay beside her on his stomach, the cheeks of his arse still red. Her clit was buzzing; she wanted very much to rub herself to a climax and her fingers played tentatively with the tender flesh.

The man had other ideas. 'Stop it, Anna!' he commanded. At that moment his cell phone warbled from the floor near the futon. He bent to pick it up and looked at the digital display. 'Don't move, either of you!' he ordered. 'I must take this call.'

Anna watched the man who held so much sway over her and Leo walk to the other end of the studio. As he moved, his semi-erect penis, still slick from his come and Leo's saliva, bobbed in front of him. Switching to English, he spoke urgently into the phone. Anna's limited grasp of the language barred her from understanding much of the conversation; all she could make out were disjointed phrases about getting rid of the car and something about a hotel.

Anna turned her attention back to Leo, who was looking sullen now, his dick soft and his arse sore. 'Leo,' she said, stroking his hair gently, 'Are you OK?'

Leo grunted. 'Yeah,' he mumbled. 'But I wish he didn't hit so hard.'

'Why don't you just leave if you don't like it?'

'Why don't you?' the boy retorted. 'You stay because you like the clothes he buys you. You like the new DVD player he bought you last week. He said he'll buy us cars when we can drive. I like those things, too. I guess an occasional bruise or two isn't so bad.'

'What do you think our friends think of us?' Anna asked.

'I don't know. I haven't really thought about it,' Leo said and shrugged. 'They're probably jealous,' he said. 'They'd love to have the things we have and live where we live. They don't know about any of ... this. I never mention it.'

'Don't your parents ever wonder about us living together in the apartment?'

'No.' Leo was dismissive. 'I told them it was like a dormitory, where apprentices live. They never come down here from Urbino. I'm out of their hair and earning good money. That's all they care about. I haven't even spoken to them in six months.'

'Mine neither,' said Anna, although the boy hadn't asked. 'My mother and stepdad are glad to be rid of me. When I was little, my stepdad used to creep into my bedroom and watch me undress. I told my mother, but all she did was slap me and call me a dirty-minded little bitch!'

'Are they in Turin?'

'Yes, and good riddance as far as I'm concerned. I have an uncle here in Arezzo I haven't seen for a couple of years. I think he's some sort of cop, so I stay away from him. There's also a cousin who's a bit older than me. Sometimes Gina and I go shopping. She's nice; I like her. She has a boyfriend who's always feeling her up as they walk down the street and who fucks her in his car.' Anna giggled. 'She thinks I don't know much about sex. She'd be shocked if she knew the money I spend comes from lying on my back with you and him!' She jerked her head at the distant figure, still naked, still talking on the phone.

From the futon on the studio floor, she could see racks of nearly completed ceramic figurines awaiting their finishing touches before shipment to Rome. They lined two walls behind the man who now paced back and forth, becoming more agitated. A few moments later Anna watched him put down the phone and stride back towards them.

'Fun's over, *mi regazzi*,' murmured *il padrone* as he stood over them. 'Time to get back to work.' His voice was sharper, authoritative. 'Leo, leave us. Go next door and fire up the kiln. Then mix up some of that antique glaze. The people in Rome are getting impatient.'

Leo scrambled to his feet and Anna made to follow, but her employer held her down. 'Not you, Anna. Not just yet,' he barked. 'You and I have a little unfinished business.'

The man's dick was hanging semi-erect in front of him but, ignoring it, he knelt over Anna and plunged his tongue deep into her pussy, licking her juices and lapping at her clitoris. A little bolt of electricity jolted through her and Anna swung her legs up over the man's shoulders, opening herself up to him, urging him deeper, faster.

A lubricated finger found her anus and eased inside; her muscles were used to this intrusion. This time her moans of pleasure were not faked. Anna bucked her hips and came within minutes under the stimulus of the man's tongue, yelling her pleasure with uninhibited gusto.

'You like that, don't you?' he murmured. The man leaned back, gently massaging her clit. 'You always were a noisy little cat,' he said. 'I liked that about you the first time I fucked you.'

Anna groaned with unabated lust. 'More,' she pleaded. 'Again.'

'If you insist,' the man laughed. 'I like to keep my horny little bitch satisfied. A happy worker is a good worker, and I always demand good work!'

Effortlessly he slid his cock, now as long and hard as before, inside her. To Anna it felt completely different from Leo's: broader, longer and filling her completely. In her young life, this was the only man who'd fucked her – little Leo didn't count in her mind – but this older man had tutored her slim body to appreciate sensual perfection. A few moments of his expert handling brought her back to her peak, about to slide into bliss, but the malicious skill of her older lover kept her there, tantalisingly on the edge until she was begging for release. With a cruel little laugh he obliged at last.

Anna's young body shuddered with joy. At that moment nothing else mattered. She'd do anything to be fucked like that. Even though she knew he was an unpleasant character.

10 *Il Tormento di Gianfranco* (Teasing Gianfranco)

The following morning, Francesca walked into Donatella's temporary bedroom on the excuse of loaning her some underwear. Finding Donatella totally naked and focused in the yoga 'bridge' position, Francesca spent a moment admiring the older woman's trim muscles, tight arse, dense bush of tight brown curls and nicely rounded breasts.

'Breakfast in ten minutes,' she said, jolting Donatella out of her concentration. The professor collapsed on the carpet and made instinctive motions to cover her nakedness. Then she relaxed and with a wry smile took the skimpy garments that Francesca held out to her.

'Thank you.'

'Don't mind thongs, do you?' asked Francesca.

Donatella shook her head. 'No, but it's been a while . . .'

Standing up, the American slipped into the tiny silk panties and examined herself in the full-length mirror.

'Not bad,' said Francesca appreciatively, admiring anew Donatella's well-honed figure.

The object of her regard smiled shyly. 'I'll just need a few minutes,' she said.

A little while later, the three new housemates were sitting around the breakfast table, enjoying *panini* and coffee. Francesca and Kiki wore very little, and Donatella noticed that yesterday's bruises showed up vividly on their bodies.

'Salvatore isn't coming over until after lunch,' Francesca said. 'He phoned while you two were having your showers. I told him about both incidents. He sounded quite concerned but he has to escort that visiting politician to Florence airport this morning. They're afraid of a Mafia hit or something. Of course, he's very contemptuous about the *polizia stradale*,' she added.

'The *carabinieri* think all other police forces are incompetent by definition,' Kiki informed Donatella with a grin. 'Especially the traffic cops.'

'How did you meet Salvatore?' Donatella asked Kiki.

Francesca looked at Kiki. How much should she tell her new friend? Kiki nodded imperceptibly and Francesca decided that the older woman should know the truth. 'He took care of me when I came out of jail,' she said.

Donatella's mouth fell open. *'Jail?'*

Francesca smiled ruefully.

'What did you do?' Donatella asked.

'Oh several things,' the *Italiana* said with a shrug. 'I'd been in and out of reform school a few times, and so when I was caught breaking into a computer store I was sent to prison. I served six months and was then released on probation. Because there's no full-time probation office in Arezzo, my file wound up on Salvatore's desk by default. We became friendly after a while and, you know, one thing led to another.'

Donatella was all concern. 'What about your parents?' she asked. 'Where are they?'

'Dead. A long time ago. I've been an orphan since I was ten. I grew up on the streets of Florence, ripping off tourists for a living. You see these?' She fondled her breasts and pointed her nipples in Donatella's direction. 'As a young girl, I let men play with my tits and feel me up for a few hundred lire. Then I found I could screw men for money and what I needed to get by.' She looked into Donatella's eyes, seeking understanding. 'It was a rotten life and prison was worse. It shook me up and I determined never to go back. When I met Salvatore, he was kind and helped me straighten myself out. I paid him back the only way I knew, but with him sex was fun.'

Donatella said, 'My God! You did incredibly well to survive that ordeal.'

Francesca laughed to lighten the mood. 'What the hell, sex for me was always fun! But now, I fuck guys because I want to, not because I have to. There's a big difference. Then, of course, I met Kiki, who's been my best friend ever since.' Francesca leaned over to ruffle the petite woman's red hair and received a grin in return. 'She taught me English and a lot about art. I've even started taking classes at the college, unofficially. That's how I met Ian Ramsey.' She trailed off, feeling she'd said enough.

Kiki quietly sipped her coffee.

Donatella broke the silence. 'What you've described would have broken most people, but you've turned out remarkably normal.'

Francesca laughed. 'Apart from being an exhibitionist nymphomaniac?'

Donatella waved away the surprisingly bitter irony. 'Let's just say you're a little more highly sexed than most women,' she said, smiling at Francesca. 'But you're not a nymphomaniac. Deep down they don't like sex or themselves,' she explained. 'I used to date a psychologist. He said nymphomaniacs often use sex as a way of demeaning themselves, to compound their low self-esteem. You, however, seem to revel in sex, to enjoy it immensely.'

Francesca laughed. 'Now I do,' she said. 'Speaking of which,' she added, 'it's about time I went down to see Marcellino. We need a new car.'

'Are you really going to ... give him a blow job?' asked Donatella.

'Depends what the car's like,' responded Francesca, enjoying her new friend's blush. 'Donatella, you really need to loosen up about sex! You have a great body – I know, I checked it out earlier.'

Donatella looked down at the tabletop, saying nothing.

'To my mind,' Francesca continued, 'your problem is simple. All you have to do is get comfortable with your obvious sensuality; it's so tightly controlled!'

'And does the solution also appear simple?' asked Donatella.

'Sure,' replied the Italian girl, 'you just need to get laid!'

'And you're determined to assist in this project?'

'Yes! Want to come with me to the garage?' she teased. 'Marcellino's not bad looking, and mechanics are very good with their hands.'

To Francesca's pleasure, Donatella laughed, humour winning over embarrassment. 'No,' she said. 'Not this time. I'll leave those ... delicate negotiations to you. But,' she added with a sly look on her face, 'perhaps you can give me a ... blow-by-blow account later?'

With a smile, Francesca put the dishes in the sink and dressed quickly in a light summer frock that showed plenty of cleavage. She'd found a longer skirt and a white silk shirt to fit the taller woman and accompanied the two Americans down the hill to the market in the main street. She herself continued up past the pharmacy and the bakery till she came to Marcellino's small workshop, tucked between two taller buildings.

That Saturday morning the proprietor was the only person in evidence. The tall angular man in his thirties smiled with pleasure at Francesca's arrival. He leaned over to kiss her, keeping his greasy hands well away from the girl's pretty frock, and Francesca noted the man's eyes linger on her breasts.

'Go and wash your hands, Marcellino,' she said with a grin, 'and you can do more than look!'

Within a moment the mechanic was back, smelling of soap and arousal. He threw his overalls across the bonnet of a car, and Francesca saw the outline of his dick poking up in his trousers. Francesca put her arms around her friend and rubbed her thigh against his erection.

Marcellino looked down at her with a grin on his face. His warm hands caressed her breasts. 'My little Francesca,' he purred. 'To what do I owe this pleasure? Have you finally realised that I am the man of your dreams and you can't live without me?'

Francesca laughed in return. Marcellino was indeed an attractive man, but for the moment her longer term plans focused on *capitano* Salvatore Provenza. 'One day, Marcellino, one day. My friends and I need to borrow a car, and I wondered if we might come to a little arrangement?' Her voice lifted suggestively and she sighed as his thumbs buffed her nipples.

Marcellino's grin widened. 'We're not taking about money here?'

Francesca moved her thigh from the mechanic's crotch and replaced it with her hand. 'No, my love,' she purred and pulled down the zip of his jeans. She massaged the warm flesh of his penis and felt it expand between her fingers. He groaned appreciatively.

'Darling Marcellino, do you still have that old Peugeot?'

'Ah, yes,' he moaned, thrusting his hips forward to grind his cock into Francesca's hand.

'Might you rent it out to damsels in distress for a . . . small consideration?'

He seemed to nod.

She quickly knelt down and took the tip of his cock in her mouth, running her tongue around the ridge of the head. She massaged his balls and pumped the shaft gently. She felt Marcellino tug urgently at her hair. 'Come into the office,' he said.

On the rack over the desk were several car keys. The proprietor took one and handed it to Francesca. 'Here's the Peugeot,' he said. 'It's out the back. You can borrow it for a few weeks. I don't need it. Will you come by every Saturday morning and ... pay the rent?'

Francesca smiled. 'It will be a pleasure, Marcellino,' she said. 'Here's the first week in advance.' She pushed her eager partner back onto the big oak desk and straddled him backwards, taking his cock deep inside her mouth. In return she hiked up her frock to expose her bare arse and cunt lips, lowering them onto the man's face.

Marcellino's expert tongue set to work on Francesca's clit, sending shivers of delight through her. Who was paying whom? she wondered with a moan of pleasure. Flicking out her tongue, she licked the garage owner's cock; it tasted of musk but smelled like soap. Obviously he had washed more than his hands after her arrival. She pumped his shaft hard, tasting the pre-come that oozed from his slit.

His tongue lapped her clit and delved deep into her. His thrusts became more urgent and Francesca felt his body buck beneath her; then with a shuddering moan he exploded in her mouth. Francesca swallowed the flood of come and pumped Marcellino's cock till every last drop was spent. She kept her lover pinned to the desk until she reached a satisfying climax, pressing herself hard into his face and letting her juices flow into his greedy mouth.

The bargain sealed, Francesca clambered off the table

and straightened her dress. She picked up the key and bent one more time to kiss Marcellino's flaccid penis. 'See you next Saturday!' she said. '*Ciao!*'

Later that day, Francesca drove the threesome back to the villa after a long lunchtime conversation between themselves and her policeman lover, followed by a shopping trip to Montevarchi. Besides a new futon for Donatella, extra bedding and basic clothing for a few days, at Salvatore's suggestion they had all purchased new cell phones from the electronics department at the *Iper-Coop* hypermarket. The three women also carried pepper spray self-defence canisters in their purses and piercing sound alarms on their key chains.

Salvatore followed up on the partial description of the old Mercedes but found no leads; neither he nor the women were hopeful of locating the relatively commonplace and inconspicuous vehicle. In the farming district around Bucine most cars bore dents and scratches from their everyday use. A new car might have stood out, but not an old workhorse like the Merc.

'I think we should coordinate our schedules,' Francesca said to her companions, as she steered the old Peugeot through the narrow lanes taking them past the Rendola vineyards. As they drove down the hill past Mercatale Valdarno and into Bucine, fields of sunflowers stretched before them, ablaze with cadmium yellow. But the women hadn't come this way for the view; none of them wanted to drive the Levane road today. 'If we can stay together most of the time, we'll be safer,' said Francesca. 'We shouldn't be alone for any length of time if we can help it.'

Kiki nodded. 'Good idea, Fran,' she said.

Francesca liked it when Kiki called her Fran. It made her feel American. 'You know, Kiki,' the Italian woman continued, 'even though Salvatore believed us about the car crash not being an accident, I don't think he bought your idea about Temple-Clarke being behind it.'

Kiki shook her head. 'No. Nor that the two attacks are related.'

'Perhaps we can persuade him this evening,' Francesca offered. 'He's going to be staying at the villa. In fact, he suggested spending his off-duty nights there. That way he says he can protect us and sleep with me. What do you call that in America?'

'A win-win situation?' offered Donatella.

'*Si*. A win-win. I thought I might let him stay for a few nights, if that's all right with you. I like having him around.'

Francesca saw Kiki and Donatella exchange looks. 'Yes, I know he looks a bit silly in that tight-fitting uniform with his white sash and funny peaked cap, but he's a decent man, and he's great in bed!'

'I thought that was a given,' said Kiki.

The weekend passed uneventfully and on Monday, after Salvatore went back to work, Francesca drove the trio into Arezzo and parked in a different car park, out by the old hospital. Walking into the city, Francesca had an idea.

'We've been so serious this weekend,' she said. 'Perhaps we should have some fun, take our minds off things.'

'I didn't see you being very serious with Salvatore!' exclaimed Donatella.

'Yeah, it's hard to be serious when you don't have clothes on,' added Kiki with a straight face.

Francesca pouted. 'Well, if you don't want to hear my idea . . .'

Kiki laughed. 'Of course we do, We're just giving you a hard time. You rolled around in bed with your lover all weekend. Donatella and I didn't have a man between us!'

'I did get horny thinking about Ian Ramsey,' admitted Donatella.

'Doesn't count,' said Kiki as she led the group around the corner from via Colcitrone and up the hill of the via Pellicceria, taking a short cut to the college. 'Doesn't count, even if you masturbate.'

Francesca caught the fleeting expression on the older American's face. 'Kiki,' she cried, 'I do believe Donatella's been getting off by fantasising about Ian Ramsey!' Laughing, she turned to her friend. 'Admit it!'

Donatella coloured. 'OK! OK! It's not such a big deal! It's just that I can't seem to get him out of my mind. He's the only member of the faculty who's been pleasant to me and since I saw him and Jennifer ... doing it in the hallway ...' Her sentence trailed off.

'I know,' said Francesca, 'you keep thinking about his beautiful dick. I do, too,' she added smugly.

'Stop gloating!' chimed in Kiki. 'Just because you've fucked Mister-I'm-such-a-great-lover-Ramsey doesn't mean you get to lord it over the rest of us. Now, tell us your idea.'

'It's about Gianfranco,' said Francesca.

'Yes?'

'Well, I model for that life-drawing class this morning.'

Her two companions nodded.

Francesca said, 'Gianfranco is in that class and he always gets a hard-on looking at me. He tries to hide it, but everybody knows. Anyway, I thought that after class is over, we might ... give him a bit of extra instruction.'

'Count me out,' said Donatella with a slightly regretful smile. 'After nearly stripping for that young man in my office I don't think it would be a good idea for me to be there!' she said. 'Anyway, a senior professor could never condone such sexual antics!'

The two young women smiled at each other.

'Oh, you two go ahead,' said Donatella. 'Just remember that you never mentioned anything about it to me. I hope someone has some fun this morning,' she added glumly as they entered the *Collegio*. 'I have more interviews with the faculty. That's going to be as pleasant as going to the dentist.' With a rueful smile she left her young friends and climbed the stairs to her office. 'See you at lunch.'

Kiki arrived to help her housemate clean up after the life-drawing class with *il professor* Sanzio. The professor always had some pretext for not clearing away.

'What's his excuse today?' Kiki asked the scantily clad Francesca.

'Today *il professore meraviglioso* has an urgent lunch meeting with the director,' said Francesca, rolling her amber eyes. The Italian wore nothing but a model's robe over a long T-shirt.

'I see our boy is here,' said Kiki in an undertone as she nodded towards the storage units where Gianfranco was putting away his charcoal and conté crayons.

'Come on,' said Francesca, taking Kiki's arm. She sidled over to the boy and spoke softly behind him. 'Gianfranco, stay with us and talk awhile ...'

Gianfranco jumped in shock. 'Oh! Signorina Francesca,' he said, turning around quickly. 'I ... I have to go,' he apologised.

'What's your hurry, Gianfranco?' asked Kiki. 'Wouldn't you rather stay to look at my friend's tits some more? Make some more drawings? Get real close-ups?'

'Yes ... but ... I mean no!' yelped the tall youth,

staring goggle-eyed at Francesca's nipples showing through the thin cotton top.

'Oh, come on, Gianfranco,' cooed Kiki stroking her fingers along his forearm. 'All good artists need practice. Francesca and I thought we might give you a few extra lessons.' She stared pointedly at the boy's raging erection bulging in his trousers.

Francesca removed her model's robe and pranced around him, making it amply clear she wore nothing beneath the thin T-shirt. Her blond pubic hair was visible.

'Holy Mother of God . . .,' muttered Gianfranco.

'It's a pity,' Kiki complained sarcastically, 'that you don't know what to do with that big dick of yours.'

Involuntarily Gianfranco looked down at his crotch.

'Oh, yes. That's a very impressive erection you've got there,' Kiki teased mercilessly. 'We feminists refer to a cock like yours as the phallo-centric fixation of men's lust . . .' Pausing for emphasis, she asked, 'Do you lust after me, too, Gianfranco? Or just Francesca? Or perhaps –' she smiled wickedly '– after *la dottoressa* di'Bianchi? She told me you saw her tits the other day.'

The young Italian gulped. 'I . . . I . . . I didn't mean to,' he blurted out. He turned crimson as Francesca came near and stood in front of him. She didn't think the poor youth could blush any deeper, but his complexion turned nearly beetroot. He remained silent and averted his eyes.

Both young women admired the length of his dick as it pressed against his trousers.

'Did you show this dick to *la dottoressa*?' asked Kiki, delicately stroking his erection with a fingernail. 'Did you take it out and wank in front of her?'

'No! No!' pleaded Gianfranco. 'I never . . .'

'Oh, I see,' continued Kiki. 'You waited until you

were in the darkroom, then you took out this lovely cock of yours and wanked it till your come flowed all over your fingers.'

'Ha!' Francesca exclaimed triumphantly. 'That's just what you did, you naughty boy. You went into the darkroom and played with your big fat dick.'

'Play with it now, Gianfranco,' she ordered, and removed her thin T-shirt, swaying seductively in front of him. 'Play with yourself and suck my nipples.'

'Wait a minute, *la mi'amica*,' Kiki said. Emboldened by her companion's brazen actions and nudity, Kiki quickly unzipped the fly of Gianfranco's bulging trousers. The boy was frozen by a mixture of fear and lust; he looked down as the petite redhead took out his cock.

'Mmmm,' said Kiki. She gripped its full impressive girth firmly in her palm and masturbated the youth slowly. 'Real men know how to make love to a woman,' she murmured teasingly, close to his ear, 'All you know about is wanking in the darkroom.'

'We could teach him more. A lot more,' said Francesca, and she knelt between Gianfranco's legs and pressed her bare breasts towards his dick. 'Wouldn't you like to come on my tits, Gianfranco?' she urged.

Kiki pumped the boy's dick harder, her hand a blur of motion.

With a strangled cry, Gianfranco twisted out of Kiki's grasp but not before a thick jet of come spurted from his cock, splashing across Kiki's forearm and onto Francesca's shoulders. Frantically stuffing his penis back into his trousers, the red-faced youth stumbled out of the door, scattering his drawing supplies across the floor.

Wiping themselves dry with a couple of paper towels from the studio sink, the two women listened to his frantic footsteps pound along the corridors until out of earshot. Kiki and Francesca looked guiltily at themselves and burst into laughter.

'*Che peccato!* Oh dear!' said Francesca. 'Do you think we went a bit too far?'

11 *L'Ossessione* (The Obsession)

Early in the morning two days later, Donatella and Kiki were munching *panini e cappuccini* in a small bakery halfway up the Corso Italia on the way to the college. Donatella, casually but elegantly 'dressed down' in an Iper-Coop outfit of cotton T-shirt, short summer skirt and delicately strapped sandals, was eager to gain a summer Tuscan tan.

Kiki completed her uniform of loose tank top cropped to expose her midriff and black bicycle shorts, with black running shoes and thick black socks. As usual, the skinny redhead's nipples were clearly visible through the skimpy cotton tank, attracting the notice of several male customers.

Now that Donatella lived at the villa, the young women's states of partial undress had begun to seem commonplace to her. At the moment, however, her mind was on other matters.

'Just as I predicted,' grumbled the American professor. 'In all the interviews over the last two days, nobody's offered any useful information. Some teachers have been actively hostile. You'd think they would at least try to be polite! I could be damning in my report and they could lose their jobs. Strictly speaking all of them serve at the pleasure of the university trustees, but they act as if Temple-Clarke is a god. It's maddening!' Donatella pulled off a bite of her roll and chewed furiously.

Kiki looked thoughtful. 'I've been working on my theory,' she said. 'Salvatore and the *polizia* may not believe it, but I think your break-in was a deliberate attempt to scare you off. And the more I think about our "accident", the more I think the driver knew exactly what he was doing. He timed it to push us into the trees. It was all so planned. If he'd waited another two seconds he could have pushed us over the steep cliff.'

'OK, but that doesn't mean they are connected.'

'Come on, Donatella.' Kiki said with annoyance. 'Don't be obtuse! Temple-Clarke's furious with me for being the whistle-blower. He'd love to get rid of me!'

'That doesn't mean he'd try to kill you,' argued Donatella. 'It couldn't have been him in the Mercedes. A couple of the faculty saw him at a reception in town when it happened. And he was in class the afternoon my room was ransacked.'

Kiki was dismissive. 'It didn't have to be him driving the car or breaking into your room. He could have paid someone to do it for him. And if I'm right, he didn't plan to kill me, just frighten me enough to back off this investigation.'

Donatella was still skeptical. 'You're saying that Temple-Clarke hired professional hit men and burglars to frighten us? I can't believe it! The man's an art historian, for God's sake!'

Unconvinced by this flimsy reasoning, her companion snorted. 'Temple-Clarke's an evil, wily bastard,' she said. 'He's been here a while and knows all sorts of people. I wouldn't put anything past him. We must be very careful.'

Donatella nodded in final agreement. 'If only there were more faculty like Ian Ramsey. I saw him yesterday. He was pottering around in the file room behind the office yesterday, looking for something when I went in there. I'm afraid I startled him; he looked guilty, like some kid caught with his hand in the cookie jar. But he was very friendly.' Donatella didn't add that she had been tempted to push the Englishman into a corner and grab his cock while they were alone in that small space. She dismissed the tantalising image from her mind and focused on more professional thoughts.

When Kiki said nothing, the elegant professor continued, 'I don't understand where the money goes! That's the heart of the issue. I have the budget numbers from Boston, but I don't have enough information. There wasn't anything incriminating in last year's figures you checked, so I'd like you to do more digging this morning. See if you can find details of the budgets for the last five years, and we'll go over them together later. I want everything – especially anything Temple-Clarke doesn't want us to see.'

'I'll talk to Gina and Sophia,' said Kiki. 'They'll know where all that stuff is. It might still be kept in the file room you mentioned. I'll get on it as soon as I've finished this. What will you be doing after I've gone?'

A smile crept over Donatella's face. 'I'm going to interview Ian,' she said, 'to see if he can help me.' In more ways than one, she added to herself. Her mind filled with the memory of seeing Ramsey's big cock pumping in and out of Jennifer Wrenn, and of imagining what it would be like to have that long thick cock filling *her*. A tingle of pure lust shuddered through her groin.

'Do you remember Jennifer Wrenn?' broke in Kiki with uncanny serendipity.

Donatella nodded, uncertain whether her friend had read her mind.

'Well, I've fixed up a meeting with her and some other grad students for tomorrow afternoon. Is that OK?'

Donatella was relieved. 'Fine. Are they men or women?'

'Mostly women, why?'

With a flash of jealousy Donatella wondered how many of the female grad students had fucked the handsome Englishman. 'Oh, nothing,' she said casually. 'It's not important.'

'If you're going to ask Ian out for a drink,' said Kiki, with a glint in her eye, 'why not invite him back to the villa? We wouldn't mind!'

'I'm sure you wouldn't,' said Donatella with a laugh. 'He's a very popular guy. But what makes you think I'll ask him out?'

Now it was the younger girl's turn to laugh. 'Remember,' she said teasingly, 'we've established that you masturbate thinking about him! What's the next logical step, Professor di'Bianchi?'

Donatella had to smile. Just a week ago she would have been mortified by such a conversation. Now, here in Tuscany, with Kiki and Francesca around, it seemed almost normal to talk about masturbating and wanting to fuck this handsome colleague.

And want to fuck him she did, Donatella admitted. Her loyalty to Henry Fogg back in Boston faded in response to her increasingly urgent desire. Her fantasies were becoming more and more explicit; last night she had brought herself to a better orgasm than Henry had ever provided. In the large bedroom mirror, she'd watched her reflection rubbing her clit in a frenzy while sliding up and down on one of Francesca's many dildos. Donatella was stimulated by this new image of herself; all the picture needed was the real Ian Ramsey, naked in bed beneath her, his cock inside her instead of the dildo.

'Having a sexy little daydream, are we?' asked Kiki in an innocent voice, breaking the fantasy. 'Don't deny it!' she warned her friend as Donatella opened her mouth to do just that. 'You're talking to an expert here! I know that look when I see it. You were thinking of having Ian's cock inside you, filling you up, making you come! It's nothing to be ashamed of,' she added. 'I make up fantasies like that all the time, sometimes even when I'm fucking some other guy. It's natural!'

Donatella wanted to say, Yes, that's it! I was playing with myself while riding his cock! But she couldn't. Not even to Kiki. Not yet.

Later that morning Donatella was disturbed by a knock on her office door. She looked up in irritation, then realized it was already 11.30 a.m., time for Ian Ramsey's interview. She'd planned to do her hair and makeup before he arrived and put on a more sophisticated blouse she'd brought with her. Quickly improvising an alternative plan, Donatella reached inside her T-shirt, unfastened her bra, shook herself free of the straps and stuffed the garment in her desk drawer. She jiggled her breasts as they swung free and pinched her nipples till they stood up, clearly visible. Ian couldn't miss the signal. 'Come in!' she called.

Ramsey sauntered into her office with studied casualness, a pleasant smile on his face. He sat down and swung one leg over the other in an exaggerated gesture of relaxation, leaning back with his hands behind his head. Donatella watched his eyes rake her chest. His smile widened. She felt an answering ripple deep inside her.

'Fire away, *dottoressa*,' he said. 'I'm all yours.' He looked at his watch. 'For the next half an hour, at least. I have a lunchtime engagement just after noon.'

Plenty of time for a quickie, thought Donatella, imagining the man across her desk with his dick standing stiff inside her. With an effort she brought her thoughts to the matters at hand. 'Professor Ramsey, I . . .'

'Call me Ian, please. May I call you Donatella?'

'Thank you . . . Ian. May I ask, what part of England are you from? I can't place the accent.'

Ramsey smiled. 'It's nice to know the accent's still there, after living here for so many years,' he said. 'I'm from Newcastle; it's a Geordie accent.'

'Oh, you've lived in Italy a while,' said Donatella. 'I didn't know that. How's your Italian?'

'Pretty good. Yours is excellent, by the way.'

'Thanks,' said Donatella, glancing at her notes. 'You've been at the college, what, three years?'

Ramsey nodded. 'I worked in Florence and Siena before that,' he said, 'and in Cortona with the University of Georgia's programme. But I chose a long time ago to live in Arezzo. It suits me; I like living quietly. The town's not so crammed with tourists. All those Brits and Americans on holiday get me down!'

Donatella laughed. 'So what are your opinions about the *Collegio*,' she asked. 'Why did you come here?'

'Temple-Clarke offered me a job, simple as that. I thought it would be more convenient, less travelling, that sort of thing. I think the college has a lot of potential.'

'But not realised?'

'Frankly, no. I think we could – perhaps even should – be doing more. But I'm afraid I don't get to decide that sort of thing. I'm just a lowly studio professor; turn up, teach my class. Stewart more or less runs the show.'

'Have you known Temple-Clarke long?'

'Our paths have crossed over the years. Two English ceramic artists working in the same part of Tuscany are bound to get to know each other.'

'What's your impression of him? Do you think he does a good job here?

If Ramsey objected to this inquisition he gave no sign. 'He's a bit pompous, if you want my honest opinion. A good teacher, but not one the students really warm up to.'

Not like you, thought Donatella. I bet Jennifer Wrenn finds your cock very warming! Instead she asked, 'Do you have the resources you need for your classes?'

'That's a funny thing,' said Ramsey. 'Money's always a bit tight. Stewart blames the folks in Boston, says they don't understand what it takes to keep this programme going, exchange rates, local costs, whatever. I do what I can with what I've got, but we really need a new kiln in the ceramics department. They cost millions of lire.' He flashed a smile. 'I'm not much good with numbers,' he said. 'I'm afraid I'm not being very helpful, am I?'

Donatella leaned back and pushed her chair away from the desk. Her T-shirt rose to expose her navel and her nipples sprang to attention through the thin material. She relished Ramsey's appreciative gaze.

Casually crossing her legs, she let the hem of her skirt ride up to expose an expanse of trim, sleek-muscled thigh. 'Everything helps me form a picture of what's going on here,' she said casually. She felt sexy just sitting there, showing off her body for the handsome Englishman. 'I'm eager to understand the finances of the college and Temple-Clarke isn't being much help. Actually you're one of the few people here who'll talk to me politely. Good at numbers or not, I'd like to talk some more later –' Donatella paused, and took the plunge, slipping from business to her personal agenda '– perhaps over a glass of wine this evening. We could . . . spend some more time together.'

Ramsey looked apologetic. 'That would be nice, but this evening's booked, I'm afraid.'

'Oh . . . Well, another evening, then?'

'I'll look in my calendar; see when I'm free. Let me get back to you.'

'Sure,' said Donatella, but the tone of Ramsey's voice had changed, become flatter. She could tell that he had no intention of getting back to her and her spirits sank. Damn! she thought. She'd hinted pretty clearly that she wanted him, but his only response was a polite brush-off.

Taking refuge in her brisk professorial manner, Donatella said, 'I'm sure I'll need to talk to you again, when I have specific questions about the programme. I'll let you know when that will be.' Without waiting for a reply, she stood up to indicate the interview was at an end. 'Now,' she continued in a more confident voice. 'Don't let me keep you from your lunchtime appointment.' Her traitorous nipples still betrayed her sexual desire but she squashed her impulse and extended her hand. 'I'll see you in a few days, Professor Ramsey.'

'It will be a pleasure, Donatella,' replied the Englishman, taking her hand and holding it gently for a moment longer than politeness required. His fingers brushed her palm as he let go.

Despite her annoyance Donatella's heart jumped as her brain registered this conflicting signal. One minute the guy was giving her the brush-off, the next sending electric charges across the surface of her skin. She was still in a quandary when Ramsey slipped out the door without a further word.

'Damn! Damn! Damn!' she exploded, left to herself in the empty room. 'Shit! Fuck!' she added, in a most unprofessorial outburst. She quickly picked up her briefcase and left the office, determined to see where Ramsey was headed. She came to an abrupt halt when she saw her quarry leave the building with the director, deep in conversation. Were they talking about her?

Following at a discreet distance, Donatella saw the pair enter a small *trattoria* with the clear intention of having lunch. Glancing in the window as she strolled oh-so-casually past, she saw the little restaurant was too small to provide cover for eavesdropping; she had no option but to leave the two Englishmen to their private conversation. Annoyed, Donatella stomped off to find Kiki.

Back at the college, Donatella found her assistant sharing *insalata caprese* and a bottle of Chianti Classico with Gina and Sophia. 'While the cat's away . . .' said Kiki with a grin. 'Temple-Clarke will be out for a while. Want some?' Without waiting for an answer she found a clean glass and poured a healthy measure of the rich red vino.

Donatella watched Kiki pile several slices of tomato on a plate, add a hunk of mozzarella cheese and decorate the impromptu platter with a couple of basil leaves and some olive oil, and realised she was ravenous.

'Help yourself to bread,' Kiki invited, indicating a still-warm *ciabata*.

'Find anything?' Donatella asked, before Kiki could interrogate her about Ramsey.

Kiki preened theatrically. 'With the help of my trusted assistants here,' she said, acknowledging the two Italian girls with a sweep of her arm, 'I've found some things that *il dottor* Temple-Clarke would rather we didn't know. We haven't just been feeding our faces since the boss left for lunch,' she added proudly. 'Earlier this morning Gina looked for the stuff you asked for. She couldn't find it but in the process of searching found some other budget files that were mislabelled, intentionally I think, to hide them. You know, like Edgar Allen Poe's *Purloined Letter*.'

'Hidden in plain sight, you mean?'

'Right! If Gina hadn't been looking so carefully she'd have skipped right by them.'

Donatella looked suitably impressed, and Kiki added,

'As soon as Temple-Clarke left, Sophia made copies of everything and we've put the files back exactly where they were before, so nobody will know we've found them.'

'What do the files show?' asked Donatella eagerly.

'I only had a few minutes to look but, from a quick overview, they seemed to indicate that a couple of years ago lots of money started going to a company in Rome for unspecified "artistic services and equipment". If we can find out what these services and equipment are or, more importantly, if they even exist, then we might be a bit further along. Now we've got something specific to look for. It makes things easier.'

Donatella agreed. 'Great work, Kiki!' she exclaimed. '*Grazie, Gina, e tu, Sophia!*

'You're welcome, Donatella,' replied the two secretaries in English, laughing in unison. Donatella raised her eyebrows in surprise.

'I've told them you're one of the good guys,' said Kiki with a grin. 'Now you're in with the "A" team.'

Donatella smiled. 'It's an honour,' she said.

The four women passed a pleasant half hour engaged in college gossip. Donatella learned that shortly after several long-term teachers had retired a couple of years before, Temple-Clarke had instituted a new budget procedure that minimised faculty input. He had justified it on the grounds of more efficient management; the new faculty, all of whom he had appointed, had not felt inclined to object. Kiki and Donatella shared a meaningful glance at the potential importance of this information.

'Let's go to the office,' said Donatella, briskly. 'I want to look over those new files. *Ciao, Gina! Ciao, Sophia. Tante grazie!*'

'*Prego, Donatella. Ciao, Kiki.*' The two secretaries were all smiles as the Americans left.

Two hours later Kiki and Donatella had carpeted the floor of their workspace with sheets of typed figures, arranged by date and partly cross-referenced by category. 'What a fucking shambles,' swore Kiki, on her knees amid the paper explosion. 'Where's a damn Excel spreadsheet when we need one?'

'Be patient,' censured her older companion gently, sitting at her desk and typing quickly. 'Now that we have a list of payments made to this Rome company, some of the answers might be here. If receipts to support these expenditures don't exist, we're on to something. Funny you should mention the spreadsheet,' she added. 'While you've been crawling on the floor with those papers, I've summarised these figures in my PowerBook. They'll be easier to analyse here than scrabbling about on our hands and knees! I'll make you a copy.'

As Kiki moved gratefully to stand up, she caught sight of something dangling from a drawer in Donatella's desk. With a big grin on her face, she extracted her friend's bra and held it up by one finger. 'And what do we have here?' she demanded in mock accusation. 'More striptease in the office?'

Donatella thought about fibbing, but opted for the truth. 'I took it off just before Ian Ramsey came for his interview,' she admitted. 'I thought...' What had she thought?

'You thought that jiggling your tits at Ian would get him into bed!' said Kiki, divining Donatella's ambition most accurately. 'Did it work? Are you meeting him tonight?'

'Absolutely not!' complained Donatella. 'He was pleasant enough until I mentioned going out for a drink...'

'Just a drink?'

'Well, a drink first, and then perhaps ... take your clothes off and fuck me,' admitted Donatella. 'I didn't *say* that, of course, but I made my intentions fairly clear.'

'And he just said no?'

'As good as. He said he was booked this evening and, when I suggested another time, he clammed up. Maybe I'm simply not his type. Maybe I'm too old. I don't know!' Donatella's voice grew increasingly anguished. 'I think I'm in pretty good shape, don't you? There's nothing wrong with me, is there?' Donatella heard herself whining like some pimply adolescent. She looked at Kiki helplessly.

Kiki rushed to reassure her friend. 'You look great!' she insisted quietly. 'A knockout, in fact. Having your hair down makes you look very sexy. Any guy would be a fool not to go out with you. Francesca was saying as much the other day. She said she was tempted to seduce you herself!'

Donatella blushed. 'Are you and she ... Do you and she ...'

'Are we lovers? Are we queer? Are we bisexual? Which question do you want?'

'Any,' said Donatella, shyly.

'Yes, occasionally. No, definitely. Yes, I suppose we must be. In that order,' replied the little redhead frankly. 'Franny started going with girls in prison. I guess that's inevitable, a survival instinct, you might say. As for me, I was strictly hetero until I moved in with Fran. She's beautiful and oozes sex without even trying. It's like a gift. We got high one night and tumbled into bed. The next thing I knew I was having one of the best times of my life. Fran's a talented young woman. And the only woman I've been with,' Kiki added. 'I'd miss cock if I didn't fuck on a regular basis but, after making such a disastrous mistake with that creep Claudio, I wonder if I should lay off men for a while!'

Any response to these disclosures was stifled in Donatella's throat when the office door swung open with a crash and a thunderous Temple-Clarke stood on the threshold. He strode into the room, all traces of his previous bored hostility replaced by vivid anger.

'What the hell's this?' he demanded, pointing to the papers that covered the floor. Stooping he snatched up a handful, disrupting Kiki's embryonic ordering system. 'Where did you get these?'

'I found them,' said Kiki, eyes blazing defiance, 'in the college files.'

'On my orders,' interposed Donatella quietly, before Kiki could say something she might regret, and to protect Gina and Sophia from this man's wrath. 'Do you have a problem with that?' The steel in her voice made Temple-Clarke look up sharply.

'You have no right!' he blustered. 'These are private papers. I insist that you give them back to me. Now!'

'Like hell we will!' shouted Kiki. 'The evidence is here that you've been ripping off the college, screwing up our education. We'll find it and expose you, you fucking old fraud!'

Temple-Clarke turned on the young woman. 'Get out!' he roared, 'Get out of this room! Get out of my college!' He raised his hand as if to strike her.

Kiki dropped immediately into a martial arts stance; her single silver nose ring caught the light as she danced out of range.

Donatella took advantage of the momentary space between the two adversaries to interpose her body between them. She fixed the tall professor with her sternest gaze, usually reserved for the most recalcitrant students. 'Listen up, *Mister* Temple-Clarke, the only person who's going anywhere is you,' she said quietly, her voice cutting through the tense silence like a knife. 'Get out of my office this minute. Now!' she barked.

The lean Englishman stepped back in temporary confusion.

Donatella followed up quickly. 'Let's get a few things straight, you pathetic bully. You do not order my assistant around. You certainly *never* raise your hand to her. She works for me, and for the Boston authorities. *I* have seniority here. This is *not* your college.'

There was utter silence as Temple-Clarke's mouth moved like a fish gasping for air. Donatella smelled alcohol on his breath.

'You're merely a paid employee,' she continued, hostility icing her voice. 'And a lousy one at that. One more display of violence like this and I will have your contract yanked so fast you won't know what hit you! You'll be out of your office with the locks changed, your belongings in the street and a lawsuit slapped up your ass! Do you understand?'

No words came out of the director's mouth despite another series of facial contortions.

'The answer, Mr Temple-Clarke, is "Yes, I understand, Doctor di'Bianchi." Can you say that?'

'You fucking bitch! You fucking American bitch!' screamed Temple-Clarke, finding his voice at last. His handsome chiselled features were twisted in rage. 'Nobody speaks to me like that. I'll shut that stupid mouth of yours and your precious little slut of an assistant!'

A low growl indicated that Kiki was about launch herself at the tall Englishman. Although Donatella had little doubt that the young woman had the fighting skill to flatten her larger opponent, she threw out her arm, warning her young friend to stay back.

'That's it!' Donatella said, tension lending her words

a venom that surprised her. 'Consider yourself suspended as of this moment, professor, pending a formal enquiry. I'm e-mailing Boston right away and calling them first thing tomorrow. I have the authority to suspend you.' Donatella wasn't sure she did, but she wasn't going to let a technicality stand in her way. 'Leave this building at once!' She held open the door.

'You stupid bitch,' hissed Temple-Clarke. 'You don't know what you're saying. You don't know who you're dealing with!' He bent quickly and grabbed handfuls of paper, ripping them into shreds and flinging them to the ground. Taking a lighter from the pocket of his sports coat, he ignited the end of a page remaining in his hand and tossed the burning paper to the floor. Flames spread quickly and, as Donatella and Kiki frantically tried to stamp them out, Temple-Clarke dashed into the hallway, vanishing with one last menacing threat. 'Watch your backs, you stupid cunts!' he snarled. 'Watch your backs!'

A frantic war dance by the two women failed to put out all the flames, so Donatella whipped off her T-shirt and beat the series of small fires into submission with hefty strokes. Kiki quickly stomped on any embers before they could ignite the remaining fuel supply that lay strewn around. Coughing from the haze of smoke, Donatella opened the window once she was sure no more sparks remained and gulped in the fresh air. 'Close the door, Kiki,' she commanded.

The pair slumped in their chairs and surveyed the mess. Sweat ran down between Donatella's breasts.

'I could have handled him!' protested Kiki, annoyance evident in her tone.

'I know you could,' said Donatella. 'He'd be in the hospital now, and you'd be in jail on assault charges. I don't want either of those things. Understand?'

Kiki nodded.

'Good. Now, quickly, we have to move fast. I'll tidy up here. You go to Gina and Sophia and get them to print up several notices announcing that Temple-Clarke has been suspended and that there will be an emergency faculty meeting at noon tomorrow. Post them around the building. I'm afraid our meeting with the grad students will have to be postponed. I'll see you in the general office or, if I miss you, at the station for the 7.45 p.m. Bucine train. OK?'

The tension slowly eased out of the young redhead. She nodded. 'Nice tits, by the way,' she said and left on her errand, grinning from ear to ear.

Donatella turned her attention to her physical attire. Her sandals were scorched; her feet stung from the bite of the flames, although her skin was not burned. Her T-shirt, however, was ruined and she had a momentary flash of panic before she remembered the sexy top she had brought with her this morning to wear during Ramsey's interview. With a little sigh of relief, she pulled it over her head and stuffed her bra in her briefcase.

As she cleared up the damaged papers, Donatella saw that the relative isolation of her office had worked to their advantage. No one seemed to have heard their dramatic fracas. She stacked the papers on her desk, checked her computer, took out the disk and slipped it into her briefcase. Then for good measure she made other digital copies and slipped them in Kiki's satchel.

She opened her e-mail connection and sent a stinging report to her employers in Boston, detailing Temple-Clarke's behaviour and her actions. She emphasised the man's physical threats to the two women. In the politically correct campus atmosphere of Charlestown University, such behaviour would never be condoned. She felt on safe ground there.

Fluffing her hair, she turned to the open window,

from which familiar sounds and voices intruded on her reverie. She felt very sexy in the revealing copper V-neck top. It showed off the swell of her breasts nicely, and her nipples were clearly prominent.

In the park below, Ian Ramsey and Jennifer Wrenn were at their damn soccer practice. The banality of their activity, in comparison to the drama just played out in her office, struck Donatella as childish. The Englishman seemed obsessive in his silly little routines. But then another thought struck her. Was he going to follow the same routine after soccer practice? Would he and his companion fuck in the corridor again?

And would she watch again? She knew the answer was yes, even as she tried to argue herself out of her growing obsession with Ian Ramsey.

With a note to Kiki confirming she'd meet her at the train station, Donatella grabbed her briefcase and hurried along the corridor and down the old staircase. This time she carefully found the perfect hiding place: a disused broom closet thirty feet from the spot that Ramsey and Wrenn had chosen for their last escapade. The old wooden doors were split and warped and even when closed there were gaps wide enough to peek through but not too wide to reveal her presence.

Inside the small space Donatella listened for footsteps. She knew the pair practiced on the field for about thirty minutes and by her watch that left fifteen minutes to go. Deliberately she reached up under her skirt and pulled off her panties, pushing them into her briefcase to accompany her bra. She placed a finger lightly between her sex lips and, to her delight, she was already wet and tingling with anticipation. After all those times she'd had to rely on the memory of Ramsey's cock to get off, now she was going to see it again in full fleshy glory. Her nipples peaked with frustrated desire, and she caressed herself eagerly.

Ten minutes later Donatella began to feel ridiculous, like some spy lurking in a closet in a bad 'B' movie. Inwardly she scorned her obsessive behaviour and was just about to give up in mortified embarrassment when she heard the sounds she'd been avidly listening for: the scraping and clatter of boot studs on the old tile floor.

12 *L'Imboscata* (The Ambush)

Donatella held her breath, eyes glued to the cracks in the woodwork. By the time Ramsey and the girl came round the corner, Jennifer, apart from socks and boots, was already naked.

Despite a flare of renewed jealousy, Donatella appreciated the beauty of the young woman's body: well-shaped small breasts, a slender waist, tightly muscled buttocks and long lithe legs that had obviously benefited from dedicated hours of training. Her pubic hair was thick and bushy, a slightly darker tint than her long blonde hair. Donatella's feelings of lust intensified at the sight of Ramsey's cock emerging from his shorts; it appeared every bit as desirable as the last time she saw it, long, thick and hard, with a full purple tip.

Near the same window that had illuminated the scene of their last coupling, the pair stopped. After a quick look round the girl caressed Ramsey's balls and played with his shaft, pumping it gently.

In turn he fondled her breasts and reached between her legs. 'You juicy bitch. You're already wet,' purred Ramsey.

Exploring her own sex lips, Donatella enjoyed the same sensation from her hiding place. She watched one of Ramsey's finger's disappear inside the dense mat of hair that guarded the entrance to Jennifer's cunt and followed suit with a finger in her own pussy. She couldn't imagine that the young soccer player was any wetter than she was!

The young woman bent over to pull off Ramsey's

black shorts and his Newcastle shirt, and Donatella appreciated again his fully nude body. A sheen of brown hair covered his muscular chest and back. His buttocks were trim, and only the slightest hint of excess flab around his stomach betrayed the approach of his middle years. Donatella was more than willing to forgive that slight paunch in the context of the man's glorious cock.

That glorious cock had now almost fully disappeared inside Jennifer Wrenn's mouth as she did a creditable impression of a sword swallower, taking several inches down her throat, her mouth moving avidly up and down the shaft.

'I want to taste you, too,' said Ramsey. 'Come here.'

As Jennifer released him from her oral caress, the tall Englishman lifted the young woman off her feet and swung her upside down with her legs around his neck. Her cunt was open to his tongue, and he plunged it inside her. The agile girl hastily resumed her fellatio from her inverted position, wrapping her arms around Ramsey's waist.

Donatella was transfixed. She had certainly never witnessed sex like this. The missionary position preferred by Henry Fogg seemed unbearably tame by comparison. Donatella's breathing became more ragged as she brought herself to a level of excitement that outmatched even her recent solo session with Francesca's dildo. She thought she might even get to come first.

But Jennifer Wrenn beat her to it. The powerful slurping and suckling of Ramsey's tongue on her clit, combined with deep probes into her pussy, took the young athlete over the top. She shuddered and shouted, letting Ramsey's cock slide from her lips in the process.

'Jesus! Sweet Jesus! God, Ramsey, that's good!' she yelled. 'That tongue of yours is as good as your dick!'

'No way, sweetheart,' chuckled Ramsey. 'That was merely the warm-up act. Are you ready for the big show?'

'Fuck, yes!' whispered Jennifer, breathing hard as her lover swung her back to the ground, on her knees and facing away from him. 'Give it to me all the way!'

'My pleasure!' said Ramsey. He pulled a small sachet from his shorts as they lay on the floor. Donatella watched him tear it open and squeeze a generous blob onto his fingers. 'Open up,' he growled, and eased a finger and then two inside Jennifer's anus.

A low moan escaped the girl as she thrust her buttocks back onto Ramsey's hand. 'Fuck me, you bastard. Fuck me!' she groaned.

Donatella's vision blurred as the force of her first orgasm swept through her. She pressed her mouth into a hard, thin line to keep quiet. When her vision cleared, Ramsey's cock was pounding Jennifer's arse, while the young woman reached between her legs to pleasure herself.

Donatella's skirt was now around her waist and her pelvis wantonly thrust forward, the fingers of her right hand massaging her little bud with furious strokes. She came again as she watched and was unable to suppress a moan, but the couple was too enrapt in their own sensations to notice. Jennifer cried out once more and Ramsey slid his cock out of her arse at the very moment of ejaculation, spraying the full length of the young woman's back and into her hair.

Ramsey scooped his come from the naked girl's back and rubbed it into her nipples. They locked arms together in a sweaty union, both breathing in short gasps. Donatella fancied she could smell the spicy odour of Ramsey's come from her hiding place. She pushed two fingers deep inside herself and rubbed her clit urgently with her thumb. Her pussy spasmed one final time and she slumped against the back wall of the closet, exhausted.

Donatella watched fixedly as Ramsey and Jennifer unwound themselves, rubbing each other's bodies and kissing passionately, their tongues down each other's throats. As the statuesque pair rotated slowly, like dancers in slow motion, Donatella stayed as still as a sculpture, scarcely breathing until the lovers had departed.

It was a full five minutes before Donatella crept gingerly from her hiding place. Her legs were no longer shaking and her pulse had settled back nearly to normal, but she still felt her juices running down the inside of her thighs. She felt wild and stirred up inside to a level of wantonness she hadn't known for years. With a new sense of abandon she left her panties and bra in her briefcase and walked slowly through the back door and into the town.

For the second time since an unrestrained affair in graduate school she was walking in public with nothing between her juicy pussy and the big wide world. Back then she and her lover had fucked on a deserted downtown street corner, daring somebody to discover them. Now her short skirt flared as she walked, and she fantasized about the hem lifting sufficiently for some handsome stranger to catch a glimpse of her wet pussy.

Stalling for time before heading to the station, Donatella stopped at a small bar off the Piazza San Agostino. She stood at the counter, sipping an *Amaretto di Saronno*. She felt the eyes of the men in the room roam over her body, noting the absence of a bra. She surmised they were probably speculating about whether she was wearing panties. Where once she would have found this objectionable, she now enjoyed it, feeling her nipples tighten. She wanted to flaunt her sexuality,

137

to find an outlet from her obsessive focus on Ian Ramsey. She wondered if she could emulate Kiki and Francesca: pick up a likely-looking man and fuck him for the sheer personal gratification of the act, to feel a warm cock deep inside her. She juiced up again at the thought. If it wasn't going to be Ramsey, then it could be a total stranger; in fact it would be better if it *was* someone she didn't know and wouldn't see again.

She cast her eyes around the bar. Most of the older men glanced quickly away, but a younger one sitting alone in the corner matched her gaze. His expression gave nothing away. Their eyes locked for several seconds.

Unsure whether she could go through with it, but with a reckless desire building in her groin, Donatella swallowed the last drop of her Amaretto, tossed some notes on the bar and walked nonchalantly towards the ladies' room at the back, brushing past the stranger's table and climbing the few stairs to a half-landing. A short corridor branched off, obscuring any view from the bar.

Hesitating outside the door to the ladies' room, Donatella heard a soft step behind her and she turned to see the tall young man standing a few feet away. He stared at her, saying nothing. In his hand was a single condom package.

Donatella slowly pulled her top clear from the waistband of her skirt. Pulse racing, she deliberately allowed the man a glimpse of her bare skin. She backed towards the door to the bathroom and tested the handle. It gave freely and she slipped inside, holding it open in silent invitation.

In seconds the stranger was with her, his hand closing the lock with a snap. Inside the small space Donatella grabbed his body and scrabbled his shirt buttons open. She felt his hands slide up beneath her top and cup her breasts. Fingers found her nipples and she stiffened as a jolt of pleasure shuddered through her body.

Unlike Henry Fogg's straggly chest curls, this young man's torso was nearly hairless, and Donatella's hands quickly moved to unbuckle her partner's belt and slide his trousers and underpants to the floor. His long thin cock sprang to life, curving up towards his stomach. She grabbed the shaft and pumped it experimentally, enjoying the sensation of a man's dick in her hand. Her fingers reached to cup his balls. The man groaned with pleasure and moved to kiss her, but Donatella turned her face and clamped her teeth into his neck. She wanted an anonymous fuck, on her terms.

Holding her partner by his cock, Donatella backed to the toilet and sat on the low cistern. The porcelain was cold to her arse, but her cunt was on fire. Letting go of his cock, she spread her legs and lifted her skirt, sliding two fingers between her legs and transferring her juice to the little knob of her clitoris. '*Lecca la fica!*' she ordered, speaking the first words between them, a phrase she'd learned from Francesca. 'Lick the fig!'

Without further invitation the young man straddled the toilet seat and plunged his tongue into Donatella's pussy. She quivered with pleasure at the touch of someone other than herself. It wasn't Ian Ramsey but it was a good-looking guy with his face buried in her. At that moment it was all that mattered. Donatella grabbed his hair and pulled his face tight into her groin, bucking her hips to increase the pressure and friction. She came moments later, a swift, delicious current from her clit to her fingers and toes.

Before the ripples had subsided the stranger had opened the condom package. Donatella slid down onto the toilet seat and presented her wide-open lips to her anonymous lover. She hooked her legs over his shoulders and drew him towards her, guiding his cock inside her with one fluid motion. Leaning back, Donatella used all the power in her thighs to hold her lover captive, unmoving, while his dick filled her passage and his pubic bone crushed her clit. Years of dedicated rowing on the Charles River had toned her muscles to perfection, and the young man wriggled once or twice, but soon abandoned himself to Donatella's vice-like grip, slumping against her body.

Releasing him slightly, Donatella allowed the man to thrust himself a little way in and out, gradually relaxing her hold until the long cock was ramming her like a piston. She slipped her fingers around her little bud, playing with herself in time to the man's thrusts.

'Più forte! E bello il cazzo!' she grunted. 'Harder! Your cock's beautiful!' As the young man ground into her she came again, a medley of half-forgotten sensations pulsing through her loins. Donatella sensed her partner's approaching climax.

He spurted inside her; she wriggled away and he withdrew, quickly tossing the used condom and flushing it away.

Time seemed to stop as Donatella stood up and straightened her skirt. She watched the young man move in slow motion to pull up his trousers and stuff his dick back in his briefs. With the thinnest of smiles and minimal eye contact, Donatella opened the bathroom door and slipped out, giving the half-dressed man no time to follow her. As she walked through the main room of the bar, the buzz of conversation died, and she felt again the eyes of all the men on her. She tossed her hair and strode out the door without looking left or right. Inwardly amazed at her behaviour she laughed out loud as she strode across the piazza and into the evening shadows of a narrow side-street, heading for the train station.

Donatella walked downhill towards the *anfiteatro Romano*, the remains of an old Roman coliseum, slowly coming back to reality. She could hardly believe what she had just done and imagined she could smell the urgent lust of her nameless lover upon her skin.

Although shocked by her lewd behaviour, Donatella felt a weight lifted from her shoulders. Part of her still wished the cock sliding inside her had been Ramsey's, but now she had a new sexual experience to help erase the Englishman's lurking presence in her fantasies. Donatella was replaying these newly wrought memories and images in her mind when a shadow blocked her path.

'*Scusi*,' she said and stepped aside.

But the shadow followed her.

She looked up and her heart turned to ice. A tall figure stood in front of her, wearing a black ski mask; except for two eyeholes and an opening for his lips, his face was covered. Donatella started to scream, when a pair of hands belonging to a second person closed over her mouth from behind. She struggled fiercely but the figure in front grabbed her and pulled up her silk shirt to expose her breasts to his greedy stare. One hand mauled her nipple while the other reached between her legs and found her damp triangle, still bare and exposed. With little difficulty, the masked man pushed two fingers inside.

'*Puttana! Whore!*' he hissed. 'The *Americana* is like a bitch in heat!'

'*Di cosa stai parlando?*' asked his companion.

'She's as wet as a little *puttana*!'

Donatella gathered her wits and her strength to push the attacker's fingers free from her with a stiff jab of her knee against his forearm. As the other man's fingers shifted their grip on her face, she bit hard on a digit that strayed towards her mouth, her teeth digging into the flesh and clamping on the bone. She tasted the salty flavour of blood on her tongue.

'*Cazzo!* Fuck!' shrieked her hidden assailant and let go, snatching his bleeding finger from Donatella's mouth.

Twisting free from his grasp, Donatella fumbled in her purse and found her pepper spray canister. Before either man could pin her arms, Donatella blinded the first attacker with a blast full in the face, and he reeled away against the wall. The second man struck the spray from her hand, but in the struggle she managed to butt him across the bridge of his nose as their heads clashed. As the man fell back clutching his face, Donatella scooped up the pepper spray from the cobbles and deliberately aimed a burst into his eyes. The man screamed again and fell on his backside.

Furious at the attack, Donatella jabbed her foot into his groin and ground his balls under her heel. She was rewarded with another screech of agony and, with a swift pull, she ripped the mask from her attacker's face. She received a shock for her trouble.

'Claudio!' she cried, in utter confusion. 'What the hell are you doing here?'

Though twisted in agony, there was no mistaking those handsome pouty features, but Donatella couldn't fathom why Kiki's ex-boyfriend would attack her so viciously. However she had no time to question him as the taller man had partly recovered and was groping his way towards her. His eyes must have been streaming with tears, but his manner was still full of menace. With a deadly click, a knife blade glinted in his hand.

'I'm going to slash your pretty face for this,' he gasped, and lunged at Donatella.

Donatella screamed and sprayed another burst of pepper in his direction, then took off down the street with all the speed her legs could muster. Behind her the threats of her attacker turned to sobs and retching as the pepper seared his eyes, but Donatella didn't stop until, gasping for breath, she reached the train station and the safety of its brightly lit concourse. To her immense relief she saw Kiki lounging against the newspaper stand, thumbing through a magazine.

The look of alarm in Kiki's face alerted Donatella to her appearance. A glance in the café window illustrated why other passengers edged away from the wild-eyed woman, her shirt untidily bunched around her breasts, hair askew, blood on her lips and a can of pepper spray in her hand. Hysterical laughter bubbled up from within her, and Donatella collapsed on a bench before her manic laughter turned to tears.

She felt Kiki's arms around her, clasping her tightly, one hand stroking her hair and pulling her clothing into some semblance of order.

'Donatella, *la mia cara*,' she said softly, urgently. 'What's the matter? Whatever has happened?' She prised apart her friend's fingers and eased out the pepper spray. 'God! You've used nearly all of this up! Were you attacked? Who was it? Are you hurt?'

Donatella shook her head. Speech was momentarily beyond her.

'You don't know who it was? Or you don't know if you're hurt?'

The alarm and concern in Kiki's voice stirred Donatella to reply more coherently. 'I'm not hurt, just shaken up. Yes, I was attacked, over by the amphitheatre in a little side street, but I got away. One of them was Claudio!'

'What?' Kiki was incredulous. 'That little creep? Are you sure?'

'Absolutely,' Donatella said. 'He was masked but I

143

pulled it off his face. There was another guy, bigger, but I didn't see his face. He had a knife.' She shuddered at the memory.

'It's OK now,' said Kiki, smoothing Donatella's hair. She placed a light kiss on the top of her head, and Donatella gratefully leaned into her young friend's comforting embrace. From the corner of her eye she saw two youths leaning against a pillar watching them and snickering.

'*Due lesbiche!*' said one, and dug his giggling friend in the ribs.

'Go fuck yourself!' snarled Kiki, and stared them down. She stood up and gently shepherded Donatella down the steps into the subway and under the track to platform four. The battered little *locale* was waiting, and Donatella relaxed into her seat with a sigh of relief. Kiki glanced warily out the open window.

'No sign of Claudio,' she said. 'You must have fixed him good!'

Donatella smiled weakly, watching Kiki rummage in her satchel for her little *telefonino*. She pressed one of the speed dial buttons.

'Salvatore? Thank God you're on duty! Can you meet us at the villa? Donatella's been attacked ... No, she isn't hurt, just shaken up, but we know one of the attackers. It was Claudio Pozzi, a little jerk I dated once ... No, I don't know where he lives. He came to my place ... No, just the once. Short, chunky, good looking in a baby-faced sort of way. Brown hair, clean shaven. Got it? We'll be in Bucine in thirty minutes. The train's just leaving Arezzo. Great! Thanks. See you there. *Ciao.*'

Kiki turned to Donatella. 'He said he'll meet us at the station. We can try and sort this all out when we get home.'

Donatella nodded and felt the train shudder into life. Slowly the platform slid past them and they watched the unappealing industrial suburbs of the city drift by in the failing evening light. She nestled in her seat; they were safe now the train was moving. She smiled at her friend sitting opposite, her red hair blowing in the draught of the open windows.

Donatella slung one leg over the other and lay back, eyes closed, completely exhausted. Evidently this position gave her young companion an unexpected view, judging by her quickly indrawn breath.

'Donatella, you're not wearing any underwear!' exclaimed Kiki. 'What have you been doing?'

Too fatigued to care and too tired to move her legs, Dr Donatella di'Bianchi, tenured professor and renowned art historian, mumbled her reply. 'I fucked some guy in a bathroom,' she said and fell asleep.

13 *I Carabinieri Provocanti* (The Sexy Policemen)

Preparing supper in the kitchen, Francesca wore only a linen apron to protect herself from the sizzling olive oil. She was thinking about Nico the telephone man. He'd been a good fuck and that afternoon's escapade was still fresh in her mind.

A faint tingle emanating from her little bud fleetingly revived the sensations of the electrician's large cock inside her and of Nico's eager, untutored fingers on her clit. Nico was a fast learner and Francesca had enjoyed his body. And now their computer was nicely set up with its own phone line.

When the two urgent phone calls came in, first from Salvatore, then from Kiki, Francesca detoured into her bedroom to dress, slipping on a scoop-necked silk top and tiny shorts. Her friends' tense conversations gave her pause; Donatella sounded in serious trouble. Francesca decided that the first item on the agenda was a good supper; then they could face the world.

Back in the kitchen she added some extra pieces of chicken to the hot oil. She chopped more garlic, onions and fresh rosemary, preparing enough food for the trio of housemates, plus Salvatore and a colleague he was bringing along from work, Sandro Tirabosco, whom she hadn't met.

She glanced at the wall clock. The train was due in ten minutes and it would take only a moment for the two policemen to drive Kiki and Donatella up the hill in Salvatore's patrol car.

Francesca turned up the heat under the sauté pan and added the freshly chopped garlic and onions to the browning meat. She poured some more olive oil to the pan of warming water ready for the pasta, which she set aside ready for when the others arrived.

With everything under control, she poured a hefty portion of white Vernaccia wine from nearby San Gimignano into a glass before setting two extra bottles to cool in the refrigerator. She swigged the wine appreciatively and on impulse added most of her glass to the sauce that was thickening around the chicken. Next to fucking, Francesca loved to cook, but she hated recipes. Kiki teased her that nothing ever tasted the same twice.

Moments later Francesca heard the police car screech to a halt in the piazza outside and she quickly put the *focaccia* in the oven. She raced to the door just as Donatella opened it and led the procession into the house.

If Francesca had dreaded seeing a sad and dishevelled Donatella, her spirits were lifted. Her friend looked almost her normal self; only some tension lines around the woman's lips betrayed her anxiety.

'Are you all right?' she demanded. Not to lose the opportunity for a dramatic welcome, Francesca threw her arms around the older women and hugged her tightly, kissing her on the lips and smoothing down her hair. 'Did they hurt you?'

'No,' said Donatella with a little smile. 'No, I'm OK, Fran. I had a little nap in the train. I feel better now. As the expression goes, you should see the other guys!'

Kiki elaborated. 'Donatella got them with the pepper spray,' she said admiringly. 'One was that dickhead Claudio, but we don't know the other guy. Salvatore alerted the local hospital in case someone goes to the emergency room with pepper-sprayed eyes.'

Salvatore stepped forward and kissed Francesca. 'My darling, now we are here, everything is all right.' His hands automatically strayed to her breasts, which were clearly outlined under her top. 'Supper smells perfect! Is there enough for Sandro? He is my new partner. The others have met him; now I want you to meet him.'

Francesca reluctantly released herself from her lover's embrace and smiled at the newcomer. The second *carabiniere* stepped into the light. Tall and slender, with dark curly hair, the handsome man looked at the scantily clad blonde, bowed, and kissed Francesca's hand with impeccable manners. 'My pleasure, *signorina*,' he said quietly. 'I have heard a lot about you.'

Francesca liked what she saw. She gave him a big wink and asked playfully, 'Has Salvatore told you everything?'

'Only as much as he thinks I can handle,' replied Sandro, keeping a straight face.

'As much as you can handle without getting hard and embarrassing yourself in the patrol car?' asked Kiki with a cheeky grin.

Sandro blushed but his eyes were taking full inventory of the three women who had burst out laughing.

Tensions eased, Donatella nodded towards the bathroom. 'I'm just going to have a quick shower and change,' she said. 'Can supper wait five minutes, Fran?'

'Yes, but no longer. I'm about to put the pasta in the water.'

Francesca noticed how Sandro avidly studied Donatella's retreating figure, a smile playing on his lips. Salvatore gave his colleague a playful slap on the shoulder. 'You should get yourself a good woman, Sandro. Francesca here makes me feel like a new man every morning!'

Francesca settled the two policemen in the living-room with glasses of wine and returned to the kitchen to put in the linguine when she was interrupted by a grinning Kiki.

'Fran,' the redhead said breathlessly, 'you'll never guess what Donatella got up to!'

'What? When?'

'This evening! Before the attack. She went into some bar and fucked a guy in the women's toilet! She wasn't wearing any panties on the train. I saw her! Who ever would have guessed? I thought she wanted Ian Ramsey.'

Francesca stared at her, then dropped the pasta into the boiling water, fanning the steam towards the open window. 'Good for her,' she said. 'Donatella's needed a good fuck. I'm glad it wasn't Ian. I fucked him that one time but I don't like him very much. Donatella could do better.'

'Yeah, but some guy in a bar?'

'Don't you go judging her choice,' admonished Francesca. 'Remember, you picked up Claudio.'

'Yeah,' said Kiki, 'and now that asshole is mixed into this whole mess!'

Francesca stirred the pasta. 'Sometimes it's just important to fuck,' she said. 'It doesn't necessarily matter who it is. Her boyfriend in Boston seems pretty useless. I thought American men liked sex.'

'Oh!' said Kiki. 'I completely forgot. A letter came for her this afternoon from the US. From Boston.'

'From the university?'

'No, I don't think so. It didn't have an official-looking envelope or anything. Just a blue airmail. Do you think it's a letter from Henry? Jesus! Now how will she feel? She screws some stranger and then gets a letter from her boyfriend!'

'We'll deal with that after supper,' said Francesca

firmly, pushing Kiki out of the door. 'You'd better go out there before they drink all the wine. Here, open another bottle. The pasta will be ready in two minutes.'

At that moment Donatella, freshly bathed, entered the kitchen. Her hair was still damp and hung loose around her face and she looked refreshed. Francesca smiled. She noted the older woman hadn't bothered with a bra beneath a simple sleeveless top.

Donatella read her thoughts and grinned. 'I *am* wearing panties,' she said. 'I'm sure Kiki wasted no time in telling you what happened *before* I was attacked.'

Kiki blushed, but Francesca grinned back. 'I hope it was fun,' she said. Opening the door to the dining room, she leaned close to Donatella and whispered, 'If there ever was a woman who needed a good fuck, it was you!' Her words were audible to those in the dining room.

Sandro's ears pricked up. 'Excuse me,' he said. 'Someone needs a good fuck?'

Francesca set the food on the table and turned to the policeman. 'We all need a good fuck, Sandro,' the Italian said softly with a grin, 'and I'd love to fuck you, but Salvatore might object. Something tells me it's Donatella who might be interested.'

Her friend overheard the remark and blushed, but Francesca noticed the older woman didn't demur. She was sure Sandro had noticed, too. 'Donatella,' she said more loudly, 'you look stunning.'

Both men stared appreciatively.

'A toast to Donatella,' said Salvatore. '*Salute! La professoressa bellissima in Toscana!*'

Donatella looked pleased at the compliment. Indeed, Francesca thought, far from being cowed by her attack, her friend was clearly invigorated by her plucky defence.

'Sit down everybody.' Francesca ordered. 'Donatella,

sit next to Sandro. Kiki, go down the other end; and Salvatore, stay here so you can help.' She patted the chair next to her.

Francesca was relieved that supper turned out to everyone's satisfaction. During the meal the young Italian woman found it hard to concentrate on the food as Salvatore's hand kept sliding up her thigh, into her shorts, and nestling between her legs. In return she felt his cock hard beneath his uniform trousers. She leaned over and gave her lover a garlicky kiss. 'I won't taste of garlic down there,' she whispered.

Much as she was enrapt with her own foreplay, she noticed when Sandro edged his chair closer to Donatella. Casually dropping her napkin on the floor, Francesca stooped down to catch sight of Sandro's hand nestling between Donatella's thighs. Her American friend seemed pleased with the arrangement.

After supper and another bottle of wine, Francesca and Kiki cleared away and the group settled down for some serious conversation. Salvatore took charge. Sitting next to him, Francesca admired her lover's crisp authority. The girl from Florence wondered how much of her new American friend's adventure would come to light under this policeman's gentle probing.

'Tell me everything about the attack, Donatella,' he said. 'Sandro, take notes.'

Salvatore's partner reluctantly took his hand away from Donatella's thigh and sat up straighter in his chair. He flipped open his notebook and mimed licking his pencil. 'Don't speak too fast, Donatella,' he said. 'My English isn't as good as Salvatore's.'

Donatella laughed and gave her new acquaintance's thigh a gentle squeeze. 'We can speak in Italian, if you like,' she said.

The group listened intently as Donatella retold the

circumstances of the attack in fine detail. Sandro's pencil raced over the page, jotting down the salient points.

'Was this your usual route to the station?' asked Salvatore.

Donatella blushed. 'No. it wasn't,' admitted the American. 'I stopped at a bar to . . . well . . .'

'And that was unusual for you?' interjected Salvatore.

'Well, yes. The whole evening was unusual for me. Why? Does it matter?' she asked.

'If it was your normal route, they might have laid in wait for you,' explained Salvatore. 'If you were off your regular path, they might have followed you from the *Collegio*.'

Donatella nodded in understanding. 'When I left the bar, I took the quickest route to the station.'

'You're sure your attackers knew it was you? That it wasn't just an attempted rape of a pretty woman? These things happen all too often, unfortunately.'

'They didn't call me by name,' she said firmly. 'But they didn't attempt to steal my purse and run. They intended to hurt me. I'm sure they knew who I was. One of them called me "the American bitch."'

'I see. And Claudio?'

'He knew,' said Donatella.

Francesca was impressed by Donatella's calmness in the face of danger and felt a protective urge to take care of her new friend. 'When I see that little bugger Claudio Pozzi,' she said, 'I'll cut his tiny balls off!'

Donatella responded with a thin smile. 'I rather hope it won't come to that,' she demurred. 'It was the other guy, the tall one, who really scared me.'

'We must assume they will try again, Donatella,' said Salvatore. 'Next time you may not be so lucky. You were brave, very brave indeed, but next time they will be better prepared. From now on I insist that Sandro accompany you whenever possible. If for any reason he can't, Kiki or Francesca must be with you. Do you agree?'

Donatella was about to argue but Francesca butted in. 'You are quite right, Salvatore,' she affirmed, giving Donatella a firm glance that brooked no argument. 'Sandro should accompany Donatella at *all* times. They probably know where we live. They could attack us here at the villa!'

The others exchanged glances. Donatella said quietly, 'I'm sure I can work something out with Sandro.'

Francesca laughed at the transparent lust on the policeman's face. She was about to make a ribald remark when Kiki interrupted her.

'It's not like me to change the subject from sex,' said the little redhead, 'but aren't we missing something here? We know Claudio was one of the attackers. I bet the other was Temple-Clarke! He's been behind this all along.'

Salvatore was again all business. 'Can you identify the other man, Donatella – the one who attacked you with a knife? You said he spoke to you. Was it Temple-Clarke?'

Donatella hesitated. 'He was the right build,' she said, 'and he spoke in English. But to be honest, it didn't sound like him.'

Kiki refused to budge. 'He could easily disguise his voice, speak in a different accent from his lah-di-dah British sneering. I've heard him do that in art history lectures. If he's discussing a famous artist, he'll take on the character of the person, make the students feel that Rembrandt or Michelangelo is in the room with them. He's very good at that...' She stuttered to a halt, aware that she'd just paid her nemesis a compliment. 'You know what I mean,' she continued, fiercely.

'Temple-Clarke may be a good teacher, but that doesn't stop him from being an evil conniving bastard!'

'I want to believe that the second man was Temple-Clarke,' said Donatella. 'If it wasn't Temple-Clarke, who the hell was it and why were they out to get me?' She turned to the two *carabinieri*. 'Can you catch Claudio? Surely he'd tell you.'

Sandro looked up from his urgent scribbling and nodded. 'We hope so. We're searching for him now; he's not at his apartment and his flatmate says his Vespa is gone. It looks as if he grabbed some things and left town. We've alerted all police between Florence and Rome to be on the lookout for him. He can't get far.'

Francesca looked enquiringly at Salvatore. 'Is there anything else you can do this evening?' she asked.

Her lover shook his head. 'We can't arrest Temple-Clarke just because we would like to think he was one of the attackers. We have no evidence to connect him with the attack. In the morning we'll question him and all the other men at the college, and check their alibis. Then we might know more. Perhaps we will give the precious *il dirretor* Temple-Clarke an early wake-up call. If he's not fully alert he might let something slip.'

'Right!' Francesca announced, standing straight and stretching her arms over her head. Four pairs of eyes watched as her flimsy top struggled to keep her breasts covered. 'Time to wash up. Salvatore, come and help me in the kitchen.' With a careless gesture Francesca slid her top off her body and tossed it over a chair. She enjoyed the startled gaze of her companions as she shook her hair and ran her hands over her breasts.

'If I'm going to do the washing-up,' she explained coyly, 'I don't want that lovely silk to get wet.' Taking her lover's hand, she looked at Salvatore's bulge already evident in his tight trousers. 'I think we should take off your uniform, too, sweetheart. We wouldn't want to get it stained. Come with me.' She led the policeman into the kitchen and closed the door behind her.

Inside the kitchen it took only moments for Francesca to get Salvatore's uniform off and carefully draped over a kitchen chair, and his heavy automatic pistol in its shiny black holster laid on the seat. The policeman's underwear soon followed; his long cock stood to attention, rigid in front of him. Francesca cooed with desire and dropped to her knees, taking several inches of hard flesh between her lips.

Groans emanated from her lover's lips as Francesca expertly licked the ridge of his glans and the sensitive veins along the shaft of his cock. Salvatore's familiar musky scent and the taste of his flesh in her mouth made Francesca wet with lust, and she shrugged down her shorts, sliding a finger between the lips of her pussy, gently moistening her clitoris. It responded as she rubbed it, gently at first, but increasing the fervour of her strokes in time with the rhythm of Salvatore's cock as she sucked him.

Francesca could hear voices from the living-room, but paid them little heed as she sensed Salvatore's approaching climax. Foregoing her pleasure for a moment, she gripped his balls with one hand and the shaft of his dick with the other, releasing his cock from her mouth till just the tip remained nudging her lips. She tasted the first of her lover's pre-come and pumped his dick faster.

'Open your eyes, Salvatore. Look at me,' she breathed.

She locked her eyes on his and watched his pupils dilate and glow with lust as she pumped him to his climax, feeling the jets of come splash over her face and run down her lips.

Standing quickly Francesca embraced her lover, her

pulse racing as she kissed him long and hard. Before Salvatore could relax, she guided his hand to her clitoris.

'You little slut,' he said appreciatively. 'You're dripping wet!'

'Now it's your turn,' ordered Francesca, leading Salvatore to the large kitchen table. She lay back on the polished pine and spread her thighs wide.

'Eat me, baby. Make me come.'

Within seconds she felt her lover's tongue deep in her pussy, lapping her juices. Then Salvatore settled into a rhythm on her clit, hard, insistent, the day-old bristles on his chin adding friction as his face bobbed up and down urgently between her legs. As her climax approached Francesca contracted her thigh muscles and clamped her lover's head to her. Waves of pleasure took her over and she bucked on the tabletop, twisting and turning her pelvis and thrashing her arms. Shrieks of delight escaped her lips. A saucepan clattered to the floor like a timpani, announcing her orgasm.

In the living-room Donatella was moving more slowly towards a new sexual encounter. Talking quietly with Kiki and Sandro, her thoughts of having sex with two different men in one day distracted her from the airmail letter that lay discarded in a crumpled ball at her feet.

'Did you love him?' Kiki asked.

Donatella thought for several moments. 'I don't know. I thought I did at one time,' she replied.

'This Henry Fogg, he was your *amante*, your lover, yes?' said Sandro, hesitantly.

'More than that; we were thinking about getting engaged.'

'Are you ... sad?' Sandro asked.

'No, I'm glad he broke it off.' Donatella gave a funny

little laugh. 'Now I don't have to dump him!' She shook her head. 'I'm disappointed that he fell for a student. What a cliché!'

'So, all is over between you?' queried Sandro, a guileless look on his face.

Donatella wasn't fooled for a moment. She had no doubt this handsome Italian desired her. Without a boyfriend, it was a given. With increasing fervour she wanted to return the compliment. 'Yes, it seems that way,' she said with a little peek at Kiki, who was beaming. 'I can't blame him for being unfaithful; I've had sex with another man since I've been in Tuscany. And,' she added, looking straight at Sandro, 'I think I'm going to have sex with someone else tonight.'

'I rather think that's my cue to depart,' said Kiki with a laugh. With a wink and a wave to her friend, the young American retired to her own bedroom.

Donatella and Sandro looked up as delighted shrieks of pleasure emanated from the kitchen. They smiled at each other. Donatella glowed inside. Tomorrow the disciplined historian might be troubled by her wanton aggressiveness; but this evening the woman whose sexual repression had finally dissipated just wanted to act out her desires to their natural conclusion. Tonight, she wanted this handsome Italian's dick pushing deep inside her.

Following Francesca's example, she slipped off her thin top, allowing Sandro full sight of her breasts, firm and round. Her nipples stood out from large warm brown areolas. She leaned forward to kiss her newly appointed bodyguard on the lips. He tasted slightly of spearmint, and the subtle tangy scent of lime cologne pleased her nostrils. The policeman's hands moved upwards to fondle her breasts. She felt her nipples tighten with pleasure and quickly stripped off her skirt and panties.

Horny and wet, the American professor quickly freed Sandro's cock from his uniform trousers. It was an impressive sight, fully hard with the foreskin pulled back, a deep rich purple. It had been several years since Donatella had played with a cock that was uncircumcised – not since a nice English exchange student in grad school – and she traced her fingertips along its length and girth, exploring her new toy. Experimentally she licked the purple tip, and then took it inside her mouth. With her other hand she gently fondled herself.

The shrill ringing of the telephone next to Donatella's elbow interrupted their foreplay.

'Ignore it,' said Sandro.

Donatella hesitated but then sat up and shook her head. 'No. It might be important. Perhaps they've caught Claudio.' Keeping the fingers of one hand slowly circling her clit, Donatella raised the receiver to her ear. '*Pronto!*'

'American bitch, you won't get away next time. Next time we'll find ways to make sure you won't escape so easily. Next time we'll have you begging for mercy!' The English words were spoken in heavily accented Italian.

'Who is this?' demanded Donatella. Sandro's presence at her side emboldened her. 'You don't frighten me,' she said, 'whoever you are.'

Sandro immediately sat up and made urgent gestures for Donatella to hand him the telephone. The naked woman shook her head and put her hand over the mouthpiece. 'It's OK' she whispered. 'I can handle it. Just listen.' She held the phone an inch away from her ear so that Sandro could lean close and hear the conversation.

The caller spoke again; the malice in his electronic

sneer was clear even through the small handset. 'You have no business here, *dottoressa*,' the voice said. 'My associates and I know how to deal with an interfering bitch like yourself. And your meddling little friends. What do you think it will feel like to be naked and blindfolded in a cold little cell, when the only time you'll see anybody is when we come to use you? To do what we want with you when we feel like it.'

Donatella was furious. Not only had they called at a highly inappropriate time, they were threatening to undermine her professionally. Would they make such threats to a male professor? She doubted it very much. OK, she thought. I'll play them at their own sordid game.

'Talking like that just turns me on,' she taunted with more than a hint of irony in her voice. 'It makes me wet just listening to you.'

'This isn't some academic game, *dottoressa*,' responded her caller, asperity creeping into his voice. 'We're experts, my associates and myself. We will not hesitate to use violence if we have to ... and we may even enjoy hurting you.'

Sandro could keep quiet no longer and grabbed the phone from Donatella's hand. 'This is *Tenente* Sandro Tirabosco of the *carabinieri*. We are recording this call,' he barked in his most official manner. 'Be advised that making threats of this nature is a federal crime...' Before he could finish, however, the line went dead.

'Do you know who that was?' he asked.

'No, I didn't recognise the voice,' said Donatella, 'but it was either one of the men who attacked me this evening, or one of their gang. He kept referring to his "associates."'

'How do you know it was related to the attack?'

'The caller knew details,' she explained. 'He made

that clear before you started to listen. But I don't think the caller was Italian,' she added. 'I thought the accent was fake.'

'Like an Englishman trying to sound Italian?' asked Sandro, pointedly.

Donatella's eyes glinted. 'Exactly!' she said.

The couple looked at each other for a moment, the beautiful professor naked, the *carabiniere* still in his uniform, but with a semi-tumescent dick poking from his open fly. Donatella stroked the man's penis affectionately. 'We should do something about this,' she said.

With the handsome policeman at her side, lusting after her body, she felt more aroused right now. With her other hand she explored herself between her legs. She was still wet.

Sandro's eyes glinted. 'You are so brave! I was watching you as you were listening to those bastards and you looked angry rather than scared. You even continued playing with yourself when they threatened you!' he said. 'You're a dirty little slut,' he whispered lasciviously. 'You're still playing with yourself. Are you turned on by talking dirty, by danger? Do you want me to tie you up and teach you a lesson?'

The thought made Donatella's pulse race, but two men in one day was probably enough for now. 'Tonight I just want you to fuck me,' she said, feeling Sandro's dick growing rock hard in her hand.

Sandro shuddered with appreciation. He took off his gun, then boots, socks, and jacket but kept the rest of his uniform on. He looked magnificent.

'Lie down,' commanded Donatella. Without waiting for her partner to argue, she straddled his thighs, but facing away from her lover, still coveting some degree of anonymity. She was so wet, Sandro slid inside easily, filling her to perfection. She leaned back against his chest and reached between her thighs to fondle her clit. Rubbing herself while her lover's cock filled her made her juices flow anew. She felt sorry for poor, pathetic Henry and his little student; then she felt angry for all the years of lacklustre sex she had accepted from him. She was going to make up for lost time.

'Fuck me, Sandro!' she commanded. 'Fuck me slowly. Grind your cock into me!'

Her lover's strong hands gripped her waist and lifted her till his cockhead barely touched the lips of her pussy.

'Ooh!' Donatella gasped with anticipation, and Sandro lowered her slowly till every inch of him was inside her. She felt the pressure of his pubic bone against her clit. 'Oh, Jesus! Do that again. Over and over.' Bracing herself with her hands on Sandro's thighs, Donatella let her weight fall back into her bodyguard's hands.

Sandro's throaty chuckle signalled his compliance with the scheme, and he began to buck his hips in time with Donatella's movements, thrusting upwards as he brought Donatella's juicy sex lips grinding down onto his groin. Her muscles clenched hard around the long thick cock inside her. Her tension grew and, balancing herself with one arm she rubbed herself, transferring some of the juice that was flowing from her onto her little bud.

Within moments she came, a quake that shook her rigid and left her trembling from head to toe. She gripped Sandro's thighs tight and pushed her arse towards him, milking his cock for all it was worth till the policeman could hold out no longer. Donatella felt him spurt deep into her, pulsing and twitching as he came. She shuddered with delight at her wanton behaviour. This really was a new beginning.

Dozing on the couch in the afterglow of their coupling, the pair barely noticed the naked figures of

Francesca and Salvatore as the Italian woman led her lover to her bedroom. Nearly an hour passed before Donatella allowed herself to focus on the less pleasant aspects of the evening.

'What are we going to do about the phone call?' she asked, lying naked in her lover's arms. 'Do you agree that it might have been an Englishman faking an Italian accent?'

Sandro nodded. 'Yes,' he said. 'Or American. It didn't sound right. The pronunciation was a little too forced, like something you'd hear in a movie.'

'Hmmm,' said Donatella. 'Like Nicolas Cage in *Captain Corelli's Mandolin?*'

Sandro laughed. 'I haven't seen the movie, but I can imagine.' Then he became serious. 'I'm suspicious enough that I want to know what Temple-Clarke's been doing this evening. I'll make sure Salvatore remembers that he and I are going to visit him very early tomorrow morning. We'll hammer on the Englishman's door before dawn and catch him unaware.' The policeman glanced towards Francesca's bedroom. 'I'll wait a bit before reminding him though,' he added with a smile. 'I'm sure he's very busy!'

Donatella felt compelled to point out a flaw in Sandro's reasoning. 'Whoever made the call knows now that the *carabinieri* are involved,' she said. 'If it was Temple-Clarke, he probably won't be surprised to see you, however early.'

Sandro nodded. 'But if he's not at home, that will look suspicious. Why would he suddenly go away? Either way he's got some questions to answer.'

Donatella nodded. 'But that's still several hours away,' she said, her lust reawakening. Gripping her lover's cock, she played with it gently. 'I think we have some unfinished business,' she said. 'Let's go to my room.'

14 *Il Sesso di Telefono* (Phone Sex)

Kiki Lee stepped out of the shower and grabbed a big towel, rubbing herself vigorously. Leaving her hair to dry naturally, she picked up the collection of short stories she had been reading and stretched out naked on her duvet, propped on her elbows. The author, an American woman, wove a series of sensual portraits of lust and heartbreak that appealed to Kiki's mood of the moment. She felt stupid and embarrassed about letting Claudio Pozzi into her life, however briefly, and wondered whether she had let her standards slide in an unthinking quest for a different man each week. She stopped reading and sat up to look at herself in the mirror. The movement knocked Portia, her small white teddy bear, onto the floor. Kiki picked her up and regarded her small companion seriously.

'Do you think I should just go out and get laid tonight?' she asked. 'Put it all behind me and get on with my life?'

The bear was silent.

'No? Should I stay in? That's what Salvatore would say,' she admitted. 'He'd say we should all be together for our own safety.' She stroked the bear's fur.

'Yes, I know,' she continued, as if the bear had offered a comment. 'But it's all right for him; he's in Francesca's bed having the living daylights fucked out of him.'

Portia was unshockable.

'And Donatella,' grumbled Kiki. 'She's out there with Sandro. That's the second time she's been fucked today! What about me? I'm here all alone and haven't had any cock since Claudio.'

Kiki read a quizzical look into Portia's normally inscrutable expression. 'Well, that's not entirely true, I admit,' she said. 'I did play with Gianfranco a couple of days ago.' The young woman grinned at the memory. 'He's not such a bad-looking guy,' she confided to Portia. 'He's quite cute really. I really shouldn't tease him. It's a bit mean of me but he's such an easy target.' She heard the muted ringing of a phone and immediately reached for her small chartreuse *telefonino*, but realised it was another phone elsewhere in the house.

If it was for her, someone would yell. She placed Portia back on her pillow.

'Jesus!' she muttered. 'My friends are getting all the sex they want tonight, and here I am talking to a teddy bear.'

She heard muted voices from the living-room but nothing to announce the call was for her. Disappointed she picked up a bottle of body oil from the bedside, a lush product she'd borrowed from Donatella, and to soothe herself she lubricated her breasts, thighs and belly with the scented emollient. The fragrant sweet almond emulsion emanated with the heat of her body, and she thought about the amazing transformation the day had wrought in her friend. The *dottoressa* had indeed fully 'let her hair down.'

All in the one day the tall American woman had had sex with a strange man in a bar, fought off frightening attackers and, tonight, was getting laid by an attractive *carabiniere*! Instead of bringing on hysterics, recriminations or tears, these acts seemed to have triggered the rebirth of a personality Kiki guessed had been long repressed. For the first time in her brief but intense acquaintance with Donatella, Kiki saw a match between the combative, hard-hitting academic and the fully sexual woman whose seductive persona had been hidden beneath a prim patina of proper professionalism. Donatella had even dismissed the news of her boyfriend's break-up as almost irrelevant! It was as if she had sloughed off her past life like a snake shedding a skin. Kiki, who regarded herself as a tough, self-reliant young woman, was very impressed.

Kiki heard moans and grunts of pleasure from the living-room, and deduced that the pair of lovers couldn't wait till they got to the bedroom. As Kiki listened, she parted her lush pubic hair and gently stroked herself. But the images that came unbidden into her mind were of Gianfranco della Parigi.

She remembered the feel of his long hard cock in her hand, heavy and thick, his balls full of come. It was indeed the most handsome penis Kiki had ever seen; how ironic that it belonged to a guy who didn't know how to use it! Kiki imagined Gianfranco at home, or in the toilets at the college, wanking all alone, jetting his jizz in long arcs.

That image excited her and she felt the first ripples of pleasure spread through her groin as her expert fingers played avidly with her little bud. One part of her mind laughed at herself: Kiki Lee, an experienced, sexually aggressive young woman, with dozens of lovers filed away in her memory, getting off on images of a boy's virgin cock!

Kiki had to admit that the young man was an unlikely source of sexual fantasy for someone like herself. He was tall, gangly and serious, with 'nerd' written all over him – shy, reserved and focused on his studies. But Kiki imagined that if he combed his hair differently, dressed more sharply and carried himself more confidently, he could cut a handsome figure. In many ways he was rather sweet. She knew he was in great physical shape; she often saw him running, practicing for the long distance races he favoured.

She smiled ironically to herself as she circled her clit with her finger. She was talking about a major personality make-over here, the sort of thing she normally avoided like the plague with boyfriends. Why, then, was she still thinking of him of all people as she lay on her comfy bed, naked and wanking? She slipped a finger between her moist lips. Perhaps she should phone him and apologise, or ... Or what? She reached into her bedside drawer and took out her favourite vibrator, a slightly curved seven-inch shaft covered in lavender jelly rubber.

Giving in to her impulse, she picked up the phone and the student telephone directory. She saw that Gianfranco lived in San Leo, a small town on the western edge of Arezzo, and punched his number. Only when it was ringing did she realise it was nearly midnight.

Gianfranco stopped masturbating and caught the phone on the second ring. He was panting slightly when he answered with a grunt, *'Pronto!'*

'Gianfranco, is that you? I'm sorry to call so late.'

'Si, sono io. Chi è? Who is this?'

'Gianfranco, this is Kiki. Kiki Lee. Have you been running?'

'No. Why?'

'Oh, you just sounded slightly out of breath.'

Gianfranco didn't reply immediately. He swallowed hard and found his voice. 'Ki ... Kiki? What's happened? Is anything wrong?'

'No, nothing's wrong. I just wanted ... to apologise for the other day. It was rotten of us to tease you like that.'

'Oh.' Gianfranco didn't know what to say. 'I ... I'm

sorry I ran away,' he said eventually. 'You must think I'm a fool.'

'No,' Kiki replied. 'I don't think that at all. You're just shy. Gianfranco, hasn't a woman ever told you what a beautiful dick you have?'

'You're teasing me again! Stop it!'

'No, no! Gianfranco, I'm not teasing you! I mean it. Haven't you had a girlfriend admire that lovely cock of yours? Surely I'm not the first one!'

'No.' Gianfranco found to his surprise that talking to the sexy redhead on the phone, rather than in person, gave him greater confidence. He was still holding his penis. As they talked, he stroked and fondled his beautifully long and thick erection.

'No? That's it? Just no? Come on, tell me about it. Who was this woman?'

'I can't.' He stroked his rigid cock, enjoying the secret thrill of playing with himself while talking to a beautiful girl.

'Oh, Gianfranco, you can tell me. Look, I may have been mean to tease you the other day, but I got a big kick out of jerking you off.'

Gianfranco couldn't speak. His mind filled with images of Francesca and Kiki. He pumped his hand faster and moaned slightly with pleasure.

'Gianfranco?' There was a pause on the line, then Kiki said accusingly, with laughter evident in her voice, 'Are you pumping that lovely long cock of yours?'

The young man couldn't reply.

'Gianfranco, tell me,' cajoled Kiki. 'Are your balls full of come like last time?'

Gianfranco couldn't stand it any longer. 'Yes, oh, yes!'

'Come on Gianfranco, tell me about this other woman. Tell me what she did to you! I'm wet now just thinking about that dick of yours. Let's talk dirty over the phone, Gianfranco! Tell me what you're doing now, and what you did with this other woman!'

'I've never told anyone about it.'

'You can tell me while I slide my fingers into my pussy, and think about your big cock inside me. Who was she?'

'Are you masturbating, too?' Gianfranco was incredulous.

'I'm lying naked on my bed thinking about your sweet cock, and I'm very wet.'

'Are you're fingers inside you? Inside your . . . pussy?'

'Yes!'

'What are you doing with your fingers?'

'I'm rubbing my clit, Gianfranco. What are you doing?'

'I'm pumping my cock, thinking of you, Kiki. What colour is your . . . pubic hair? Is it red, like your hair?'

'Yes. It's red hair. It's thick and curly. Are you naked?'

'Yes.'

'And now, Gianfranco, I'm sliding a vibrator inside. It's making me quiver. Oh, please tell me about this other woman.'

'There's not much to tell.'

'Come on, you cute little shy boy! Don't be coy. I want to know all about that gorgeous dick of yours!'

Gianfranco screwed up his courage and finally spoke. 'I had an affair with an older woman. But, technically, I'm still a virgin.' He paused. 'God, I've never told anybody this. Why am I telling you?' Gianfranco felt close to tears.

'Gianfranco, sweetheart,' cooed Kiki. 'It's good to tell somebody. I promise I won't tell anybody. This is just between us.'

The young man gave vent to his frustration. 'Why are you phoning me?' he demanded. 'You can fuck anybody you want in the college! All the boys want to sleep with you. You're so cute and sexy in those little punk outfits you wear. I can see your nipples every time I pass you in the corridor. I just want to reach out and touch them!'

To his surprise the young woman on the other end of the phone sounded both apologetic and eager. 'Gianfranco,' she said, 'listen. I promise, next time you can run your hands all over my tits. You can suck my nipples as much as you want. I would like that. Perhaps I can make up for being so mean to you the other day. Do you forgive me for that?'

'Oh, yes! I enjoyed it really. But I felt so shy. I thought you and Francesca were laughing at me.'

Kiki sounded contrite. 'Well, we were a little bit. But it was wrong of us. I'm not laughing at you now, though,' she added urgently. 'Gianfranco, do you believe that?'

'Yes, I do.'

'Tell me about the other woman.'

'She was . . . the wife of a professor,' Gianfranco said at length, his voice soft and hesitant. 'Her husband was away on a fellowship in America. I had just moved to the area and was doing odd jobs around her house and the garden to earn extra money for college.'

'Was this local? Here in Arezzo?'

'No. Over in Siena. It was last year.'

'Well? What happened?' Kiki asked.

'Véronique was her name, from Paris originally – we said that was funny, my name being della Parigi and all – Véronique was really sexy and beautiful, and she was . . . lonely. She thought her husband might be having an affair and she started to flirt with me.'

'Go on,' said Kiki, and Gianfranco wondered whether he heard breathlessness in the girl's voice this time.

'Are . . . are you still masturbating?' he asked.

'Oh, God yes! Just talking with you over the phone is

making me so horny. I've got the vibrator up high, and my pussy's tingling. But I'd rather it was your dick!'

Gianfranco was stunned. It was as if his favourite fantasy was coming true. Kiki had to prompt him to continue his story.

'Oh, yes. Well, she was a bit strange. She thought her husband was cheating on her, but she didn't want to be "as bad as he was" as she put it. She said an affair without being consummated didn't really count; she could swear to her husband that she hadn't had sex with another man . . .' His voice drained away.

Kiki burst out laughing. 'A bit strange? She sounds really screwed up. So what *did* you do?'

Gianfranco was silent for a moment. Then he said, 'She taught me to masturbate her.'

'Just finger fucking?'

He was silent again for a moment, remembering. 'We got naked and she let me put my finger inside her. Only one, never two or three. And then, I had to rub her until she came.'

'Jesus.' Kiki sounded incredulous. 'So you never fucked? Even with that beautiful dick of yours? Are you really still a virgin? What did she do with your cock? Did she suck you off?'

'That was the other part. She wouldn't touch my cock, or let me put it in her mouth. She just told me to stand in front of her and masturbate while she watched and played with herself. I had to come on a towel, never on her.'

'How long did this go on?' said Kiki, concern evident in her voice.

'Every day for three weeks. Then the husband came back unexpectedly. She fired me. I haven't seen her since. I did hear she left her husband and went back to Paris.'

'My God, said Kiki, 'no wonder you're shy around

women after that experience! Gianfranco,' she continued huskily, 'I think you need a new lesson. I need to put you straight about what women really like! Are you still masturbating that lovely cock?'

'Yes.'

'If we had an affair I'd want that lovely cock inside me all the time!'

It took Gianfranco a moment to register what he had just heard. 'Could we really have an affair? You and me?'

'I don't see why not,' Kiki said. 'Would you like that?'

'Can I come to your studio now?' As soon as the words were out of his mouth, Gianfranco cursed himself for being a fool. He sounded so pathetically eager. And, of course, Kiki was probably at home, not in her studio at all this time of night.

'No, you silly boy,' replied the young woman. 'Meet me after school tomorrow. At The Speakeasy. You know it. I've seen you there.'

'Si. I go there sometimes.' The Speakeasy was a fanciful Italian version of an American prohibition-era bar, except that the waitresses wore micro-skirts and minuscule tops. It was a renowned pick-up joint where guys hung out to watch the waitresses, and girls hung out to study the available young men. Gianfranco had seen Kiki there many times and watched her pair off with some handsome guy or other.

'What time?' asked Gianfranco, trying to sound casual.

'How about 7.30?' she said. 'Let's have a few drinks and then go on ... somewhere else.'

'Can I see you naked? Can I play with your tits? Oh, God! Can we go to bed together?'

Kiki laughed. 'Sure,' she said. 'I promised, didn't I? I said you could fondle my tits. And,' she added, 'we can fuck. Would you like that?'

Gianfranco could only groan with delight. He pumped his cock as fast as he could.

'Gianfranco, don't come yet. Please.'

Her words brought Gianfranco up short. 'Are you still masturbating?' he asked.

'Oh, yes. I'm sliding the vibe gently in and out of my wet hole. I've been doing that all the time we've been talking.'

'Are you ready to come?'

'Yes,' said Kiki. 'Listen.'

There was a loud buzz on the phone. 'Gianfranco, can you hear that? The phone's between my legs. That's a vibrator buzzing. It's where your dick should be. Would you like to have your cock there, in my hot wet pussy?'

This was enough to send Gianfranco over the edge. 'Oh, yes! Oh God, Kiki! I'm going to come! Oh! Yes!' The young man's hand pumped frantically until an eruption of come burst from the tip, shooting high into the air, with other smaller fountains trickling down over his fingers like white lava.

'Do you have come all over your fingers?' Kiki asked, her voice a sexy whisper.

For the first time Gianfranco laughed. 'Oh, yes! Everywhere! All over the sheets. Some even landed on my face. I haven't *ever* come like that.'

'Now lick your fingers. Swallow it and tell me what it tastes like.'

'I've never done that.'

'Come on, do it for me. Tomorrow you can lick my cunt juice. Then you can compare the tastes.'

Gianfranco followed her instructions. 'It's cool now. It tastes a little salty. It burns the back of my throat a little when I swallow.'

'Ummm,' purred Kiki. 'I can't wait to taste it myself. Play with yourself and tell me what you're doing while I come,' she ordered.

'I'm still quite stiff,' said Gianfranco, all his earlier shyness gone. 'There's some come still on the tip.' He licked it off his fingers. 'My cock is about four or five inches long, even when it's soft,' he added proudly.

There was more loud buzzing in Gianfranco's ear, accompanied by a series of sharp cries and moans. A breathless Kiki spoke again after a few moments. 'Gianfranco, are you still there?'

'Yes, are you OK, Kiki? What happened?'

'I came, you silly boy!' said Kiki with a laugh. 'I came like a fucking express train, just thinking about that juicy cock of yours!'

15 *Il Occhio al Occhio (Eye to Eye)*

Riding with her housemates on the train into Arezzo the following morning, Donatella refused to be drawn into a discussion of her nighttime sexual adventures, however hard Francesca tried. Kiki was a little withdrawn; smiling, but saying little.

'Well,' said Francesca loudly, frustrated by her lack of success. 'All I can say, Donatella, is that anybody can tell from a hundred metres away that you got laid last night! Probably everybody in this carriage can see it!'

Two dozen heads swivelled in Donatella's direction. 'Now they can,' commented Kiki dryly, as Donatella blushed under the scrutiny of her fellow passengers and kicked Francesca under the table. Francesca just grinned in response.

'What are you going to do about Temple-Clarke if he shows up this morning?' Kiki asked, changing the subject.

'Make sure he stays out of the college,' replied Donatella firmly. 'After what happened yesterday, he has no business there. Maybe Salvatore and Sandro will lock him up,' she added hopefully.

This hope was dashed as the trio entered the college; the tall figure of the director, wearing large sunglasses, was in the lobby. Her heart pounded in her ribs but Donatella forced herself to remain calm. 'Something wrong with your eyes, Mr Temple-Clarke?' she asked pointedly.

'I have allergies,' the director snapped back. 'What the hell's it to you?'

'Sudden, wasn't it?' persisted Donatella. 'Your eyes were fine yesterday, as I recall. Unless, of course –' her voice dropped to an angry hiss '– something got sprayed into them.'

The director's hand dived into his pocket, and the three women flinched involuntarily, but all he produced was a bottle of pills. 'Here,' he said angrily, brandishing them in Donatella's face. 'See these? I told your precious policemen I got these from the *farmacia* last night. It wasn't me who roughed you up!'

Donatella stepped back, pondering the truth of this assertion.

'Oh, I know all about what happened,' snapped Temple-Clarke. 'Those two bullies from the *carabinieri* more or less accused me of trying to kill you when they dragged me out of bed this morning like a couple of Mussolini's bloody blackshirts!'

'That's because you did it, you evil bastard!' yelled Kiki.

The tall Englishman rounded on the petite American. 'You think you're so bloody clever, don't you, Miss Lee?' he replied. 'Your stupid martial arts games and your ridiculous tough-guy punk outfits don't impress me one little bit. Why do you think the *carabinieri* released me? Because I didn't do it, and neither you nor they can prove I did.'

Kiki's silver nose ring flashed as her right arm flew up towards Temple-Clarke's face. He quailed back, but not before the young woman had snatched the dark glasses from his face to reveal a pair of puffy red-rimmed eyes. Temple-Clarke blinked and screwed up his eyes in the bright sunlight.

'Give them back!' he yelled, but Kiki stepped aside quickly as his arm swung in a wild arc.

Donatella regarded the flailing man coldly. 'That's a very bad allergic reaction,' she said sarcastically. 'What a convenient coincidence that it should come on last night.' She stared directly into the director's irritated and tear-stained eyes. 'I think it *was* you who attacked me last night,' she said, emboldened by the presence of her friends. 'I'm going to prove it and get you locked up for a long, long time. You can count on it. And until that day comes, you are banned from this building. Your office is closed and your belongings impounded for my investigation into your corruption and misman-agement of the college.'

Temple-Clarke let out something akin to a sob. His face was white with rage. 'I'll tell you what, bitch,' he snarled. 'It wasn't me who attacked you, but whoever it was ... I wish they had finished the job!' Turning, he made a grab for his glasses, but Kiki stepped aside and dropped them to the stone floor. With slow delibera-tion, she stepped on them and ground them into small pieces on the flagstones.

'Oh, dear,' she said. '*Peccato!* What a shame!'

Temple-Clarke stood blinking, his hand over his eyes.

'Now get out!' said Donatella, 'or I'll call *il capitano* Provenza and he'll take you in for more questioning.'

Temple-Clarke stumbled out into the street, his inflamed eyes scrunched up against the glare. 'Next time, di'Bianchi,' he hissed, 'next time it *will* be me!'

The emergency faculty meeting went briskly. All the professors except Ramsey seemed now to be in awe of Donatella, a feeling she secretly enjoyed. She had dressed for the part, wearing one of several new outfits that she'd bought at a wonderful small boutique on the Piazza San Francesca. For today's cooler weather, she'd chosen a soft black lightweight cashmere pullover with a deeply scooped V-neck and short sleeves to go with black and gold paisley side-zip trousers that hugged her trim thighs and fitted over the top of high-heeled black suede boots. An antique pendant necklace from a little jewellery store fitted neatly in her cleavage.

Dressed provocatively but without being too revealing, Donatella radiated power and authority. She felt secure knowing Kiki and Francesca were working in a room down the hall in case she needed them. She had called Salvatore and reported Temple-Clarke's threats. The Englishman was back in custody for further questioning.

'The former director, Mr Temple-Clarke, is officially suspended from all duties as of today,' she declared, 'and the Trustees in Boston have appointed me acting director.' She waved a printed e-mail. 'This confirmation came this morning. Any questions?'

'Will we continue with classes as usual?' asked an elderly Italian professor. 'Who will cover the dir ... ah, Professor Temple-Clarke's classes?'

Donatella regarded the group. 'Everything should proceed on the same schedule,' she affirmed, 'but whether you all proceed "as usual" remains to be seen.'

Anxious glances skittered around the table. 'What do you mean?' asked one of the women artists.

'I have been authorised by the Trustees to make an evaluation of everybody's performance,' replied Donatella. 'Over the next few weeks I shall be visiting your classes and monitoring your teaching methods and their effectiveness.' The tall professor enjoyed the swift intakes of breath from several of her new colleagues. 'At the end of the month I shall draw up next year's teaching plan ... and place whatever advertisements for replacement faculty that might be necessary in the appropriate European and American academic journals.'

Donatella stared hard at her colleagues, holding each

of them in eye contact as her gaze swept across the table. 'I'm sure you will all cooperate fully,' she said, 'and that individually you will work hard to demonstrate why you should continue as a member of this teaching team. Those of you who do remain...' she paused for emphasis, 'will find things very different around here. I hope we can work together to raise the standards of this institution; it is long overdue. In relation to Temple-Clarke's art history classes,' she added, 'I shall cover those for the remainder of the term. Any questions?'

'Just one, Donatella.' Ramsey's pleasant voice and the use of her first name cut through Donatella's academic detachment.

'Yes ... Professor Ramsey?'

'How long will you be acting director, and what are your plans for a permanent appointment?'

'I'll be acting director as long as it takes to get this college functioning properly,' she replied. 'I'm not prepared to put a firm time on that until I know more. As for a replacement, the Trustees will of course advertise in the normal way when that becomes appropriate.'

Ramsey nodded, rubbing his eyes, apparently satisfied, and Donatella hustled the meeting through other, more mundane matters for another half an hour. When dismissed, the faculty duly rose and filed out to their classes but Ramsey dawdled behind, clearly wanting to speak to Donatella privately. She tensed inwardly as the tall Englishman approached.

'You know,' he said casually, 'I'd be interested in the director's position. I've been thinking that it's about time I gave something back to this place, help you turn it around, that sort of thing.'

Donatella was surprised and it evidently showed on her face.

Ramsey laughed, running his fingers through his

hair. 'I know you don't know much about me, but before I came to Tuscany I ran the graduate art programme at one of the colleges in Newcastle. I can do this job.' He rubbed his eye again in an absent-minded gesture.

Donatella was tempted to embrace the friendly Englishman as an ally, but some innate caution held her back. 'I'm sure you could put together an impressive resumé ... Ian,' she said, guardedly. 'I would be interested to see it.'

'I'd like to show it to you ... along with some other things that would help you to get to know me better,' Ramsey said smoothly, flashing a broad smile that illuminated his *double-entendre*.

Donatella's heart did a little flip. Images of Ramsey's body flashed into her mind. 'I'm sure we could make an appointment ...' she faltered.

Ramsey took her hand, and Donatella didn't remove it from his gentle grasp. 'I was wondering, if you like what you see ...?' he said. Just the barest of suggestive pauses was enough to send a vibration all the way to Donatella's womb.

'Perhaps,' continued Ramsey, stroking her wrist, 'you might be impressed enough with my ... credentials that we could dispense with any lengthy search process.' Tightening his grip slightly, the man led Donatella's hand downward towards the fly of his trousers. 'I'm sure the Trustees would pay serious attention to any recommendation you make. You could present them with a neat package of reforms *and* a new director. That would leave us time to, well, time to get to know each other better.' He held her hand close to his crotch, where a bulge was now clearly discernible.

Regaining control just in time, Donatella shook her head to clear the mists of arousal swirling in her mind and snatched her hand from Ramsey's grasp. The gall of the man! She stepped back to put some space between them. There was a palpable silence, broken eventually by Donatella's cool anger.

'Yesterday you gave me the brush-off,' she said. 'But now that you've decided you want the director's position, you're offering to fuck me to get the job. Is that the plan?'

Ramsey shrugged and smiled cockily. 'The offer's on the table. Don't say you haven't thought about it.'

When he smiled it was difficult for Donatella to stay focused. 'Yesterday . . .,' she began, starting to say she had craved that very thing, but in the amazing twenty-four hours since her clumsy attempt at seduction, she had fucked two different men and rediscovered a part of her personality long and deeply buried. She found her voice and looked the Englishman straight in the eye. 'Yesterday was yesterday,' she said. 'Today is different. I'm not interested in having sex with you today. Or tomorrow, or the day after that,' she added, feeling released from her former obsession with this smooth rogue standing seductively in front of her.

He shrugged again, still looking eager to fuck her.

'I'm sure you have plenty of . . . er, hidden talents, Professor Ramsey,' Donatella said coolly. 'I will give your resumé my attention at the proper time. But I'm sure you understand that in a situation like this, there is no alternative to a full and complete search process for a new director. There can be no short cuts . . . however they may be presented.'

Ramsey's smile fleetingly vanished, but his expression quickly returned to one of friendly indifference. If Donatella hadn't been watching closely, she'd have missed the flash of anger in his red-rimmed hazel eyes. 'Oh well,' he said, with a casual air. 'Just thought I'd mention it. Open up new possibilities if you were interested, that sort of thing. Offer still stands, if you change your mind. You'll find I don't give up easily.' He held Donatella's eyes for a moment, and she glimpsed an intensity of purpose that momentarily gave her pause. Before she could respond, the tall professor slipped from the room with a dismissive nod of farewell.

The remainder of Donatella's day was taken up by a series of meetings with anxious faculty members, all wanting to explain their unique importance to the college; a meeting with a group of graduate students that was a lot more fun, but which produced little in the way of concrete assistance; and several hours spent with Kiki going over the files that chronicled Temple-Clarke's relationship with the company in Rome. To their growing excitement the two women uncovered several discrepancies between the content of invoices and equipment that was nowhere to be found in the college.

'These documents look OK at first glance,' said Kiki. 'To an outsider, this could seem like business as usual. There are lots of unspecified services and maintenance items that eat up large amounts of money. But without more information from Temple-Clarke, it's going to be hard to find out where this went.'

'The Rome company should be able to provide us with some details,' said Donatella.

'But if they're part of the scam, they won't say anything,' countered Kiki. 'In fact, if we start asking a lot of questions, they'll know we're on to them.'

'If they're in cahoots with Temple-Clarke, he's probably warned them already,' said Donatella, glumly. 'We're making progress here, but I think perhaps Salvatore should get a colleague in Rome to pay this company a visit.' She tapped the paper on her desk with her pen for emphasis. 'That may be more effective than two American women turning up on their doorstep demanding answers.'

Their conversation was interrupted by Francesca, who poked her head round the door. 'Sandro's outside,' she said. 'He's ready to take us back to Bucine.'

Kiki looked up startled. 'Oh! I forgot, I ... I have a date tonight. I'll catch the late train, or call if I stay the night.'

Donatella thought her friend appeared uncharacteristically reticent and felt the need to ask some questions. 'Don't you think we should stay together, especially in the evenings?' she said. 'Is your date a good idea? I don't want to be nosy, but are you sure you'll be all right?'

Francesca was more direct. 'Who is it?' she demanded. 'Anyone we know?'

Kiki blushed. 'Just some guy,' she said, avoiding the women's eyes. 'I'll be fine. He's quite harmless. If it gets late I'll stay at his place.'

Donatella and Francesca gave their friend quizzical looks, but Kiki seemed determined to offer no more information.

Francesca quickly lost patience. 'OK,' she said, a little huffily. 'If you're sure you'll be safe, we'll be on our way. Just keep in touch.' She took Donatella's arm and led the American from the room. Kiki smiled and waved goodbye.

Francesca's good mood returned as soon as they were outside. She grinned at Donatella as they walked to the car. 'Sandro says he's staying the night again, orders from Salvatore.' The Italian looked at her friend innocently. 'That OK with you, Donatella?' she asked. 'Something tells me he's got big plans for tonight.'

Donatella laughed. 'I hope so,' she said. 'So do I.'

16 *La Conquista di Kiki* (Kiki's Conquest)

After Donatella and Francesca had left, Kiki cursed herself for being a fool. First, she had committed to a date with Gianfranco, which now didn't seem like such a good idea; and now she'd lost her nerve in front of her friends, too embarrassed to admit her stirrings of interest in the tall Italian boy. She looked at her watch; still two hours before she was due to meet Gianfranco at The Speakeasy. She tried to settle back to work but was too distracted. She put on her denim jacket, but realised that she shouldn't wander the streets on her own.

'Shit!' she said out loud to herself. 'This isn't like me! Kiki Lee, you're acting like a stupid teenager. Get a grip!'

She dug deep in her pack and removed a battered tin containing a small amount of weed and some rolling papers. With nimble fingers she quickly rolled a joint and, after striking a match, took a deep hit. Belatedly realising she was in Donatella's office, she opened the window and fanned away the smoke. Standing to one side she glanced outside, half expecting to see Ian Ramsey and Jennifer Wrenn playing below, but the only people in the park were some young children and their parents. A knock on the door startled her and she quickly crushed out the half-finished joint.

'Yes? Who is it?' she called.

'It's Jennifer.'

'Oh, hi! Come in!' said Kiki, laughing at her false alarm. 'I was just thinking about you!'

The door opened and the athletic girl sauntered in, dressed in paint-spattered T-shirt and tight jeans. She sniffed the air and closed the door quickly. 'Any left?' she asked.

Kiki sheepishly retrieved the joint and relit it, taking a toke and passing it to her friend. 'Are you looking for me or Donatella?' she asked.

Jennifer inhaled deeply and expelled the smoke from her lungs in a long, drawn-out breath. She coughed slightly and grinned. 'Out of practice,' she said, passing back the joint. 'Boy, that's good stuff. Where do you get this?'

Kiki wasn't about to reveal her source, one of Francesca's former lovers. At one point her housemate had a steady line of supply going, but once the relationship with Salvatore became serious, she had curtailed the habit drastically. 'Oh, just some guy I know in town,' she said, noncommittally.

Jennifer took the hint. 'I was looking for you, actually,' she said. 'I couldn't find you in your studio, so I thought you might be here. I wanted to ask you something about Ian.'

'Ian Ramsey?' asked Kiki in surprise, taking another drag.

Jennifer nodded, then hesitated. 'You probably know that Ian and I are lovers.'

Kiki nodded, suppressing a grin. 'I heard something to that effect,' she replied, with masterful understatement.

'You still have class with him every week?'

Kiki nodded again, wondering where this was leading.

'Does he seem the same to you?' asked Jennifer.

'Have you noticed anything different about him recently?'

'Like what?'

'Oh, I don't know. More distant, distracted. Do you know of anything that could be worrying him?'

'I doubt if he'd confide in me,' said Kiki. 'Most of the faculty regard me as the enemy because I work for Donatella.'

'Do you know if he's seeing anyone else?'

Kiki shook her head. 'No. Last I heard you and he were an item. Big time.'

This brought a fleeting smile to Jennifer's face. 'Yes, he can be a lot of fun,' she said but then became serious again. 'I know he went with your friend Francesca a couple of times.'

'Once, I think, but that's over as far as I know,' said Kiki.

Relief was evident on Jennifer's face. Kiki nodded, reading her mind. 'Yeah, Fran can be stiff competition,' she said. 'But not with Ian. Why do you ask? Do you think he's set his sights on someone else? Here, want the last toke?'

Jennifer accepted gratefully then returned to her problem. 'When we make love now, he just goes through the motions. He doesn't seem there half the time, as if his mind's on something else. Or someone else. I thought perhaps you might know . . .' Her voice trailed off.

'Maybe he's worried about what's happening here at the college,' Kiki suggested. 'Donatella's going to shake everything up; he may not have a job next semester.'

'He's a good teacher,' argued Jennifer. 'He should stay. Some of them could leave and we'd be better off, but not Ian.'

'I agree, but it's not up to me. Donatella's in charge.'

The two women fell silent. 'What's his place like?' asked Kiki, more to make conversation than any real interest.

'That's odd, too,' replied Jennifer. 'In all the weeks we've been going together, he's never taken me there. We always ... do it at my place, or somewhere exciting, somewhere we might be seen. He gets off on that ... or he used to. Once we fucked in the Piazza Grande at two in the morning!'

Kiki was impressed. 'Does he still come round to your place?' Jennifer nodded. 'About two or three times a week. It used to be every day. I could never get rid of the smell of those cigars he smokes. At least I don't have that problem now.'

'He smokes after sex?'

'Yeah, he has this kind of ritual. I thought it was a little weird but I never complained. I was usually lying there in bed so satisfied it seemed persnickety to make a fuss.'

'What kind of ritual?' Kiki was more interested now.

'Well, he always had a cigar with him. Once we'd finished he'd clip the end with his little penknife. It seemed a little creepy, like ritual circumcision. But then he'd lie back and fondle his dick while he smoked. Sometimes he'd ask me to play with myself so he could watch.' Jennifer coloured. 'Oh my gosh! Why am I telling you this? I'm so embarrassed!'

Kiki laughed. 'Don't be,' she said. 'It's just girl talk. I enjoy it. And about Ian, I wouldn't worry. Everybody's got their own little kinks. If he prefers sex in public places, maybe he keeps his privacy at home as some form of compensation. He's never played rough, has he?'

Jennifer appeared somewhat mollified. 'No, never,' she said. 'His lovemaking is very intense – at least it used to be – but never violent. It's delicious. That's why

I'd really miss him if he leaves.' She was quiet for a while. Kiki rolled another joint, lit it and passed it over. Jennifer took several big hits before returning it.

'What's it like living with Francesca?' Jennifer asked, changing the subject abruptly. 'When she's modelling in life-drawing sometimes she'll deliberately play with herself when the studio professor isn't looking.' She laughed. 'It drives the guys crazy. They all get instant hard-ons. I heard talk that she runs around naked all the time at home.'

Kiki smiled. 'Only half the time,' she said. 'You've just got to take Franny as you find her. You get used to her nudity; it's no big deal; she's got a great body. She's a real nice girl who's crazy about sex, the more the merrier as far as she's concerned. But she's a good friend. I like her a lot. So does Donatella.' She passed the joint back to her friend.

'Does she . . . does she do it with girls?'

'Why? You interested?' asked Kiki.

Jennifer blushed again. 'N . . . no. I was just curious.'

Kiki grinned. 'What would you do if a girl came on to you, Jen?'

'I don't know. I've never done anything like that. Wh . . . what's it like?'

'I'd love to show you,' Kiki teased, 'but I've got a date. With a guy. Come on, meet me downstairs. I'll buy you a beer on the way.' She carefully squeezed the remains of the joint between her fingers and put the roach in her tin. A couple of joints and the talk about sex had made her feel quite horny. Jennifer was very attractive and perhaps making a shy kind of come-on. Impulsively she pulled her friend's face down to hers and gave her an unambiguous kiss, full on the lips. Jennifer didn't pull away before Kiki stepped back.

'You should see the expression on your face!' Kiki said with a laugh. 'Don't worry, girl, I've got my mind on someone's big dick right now.' Her doubts about meeting Gianfranco had dissipated. Now she wanted him, just like last night. 'A gorgeous big cock is hard to beat.'

Jennifer giggled. 'I agree,' she said. 'But it's nice to know there are some options.' She held Kiki's gaze for a moment before stepping out the door. 'Wait for me in the lobby,' she said. 'I'll just be a moment. I'd like to take you up on that beer.'

The bar was crowded and Kiki found it hard to concentrate. Jennifer soon found a couple of friends and waved goodbye. 'Have a great evening, Kiki,' she said, with a knowing smile.

Kiki forced a grin and waved back. Her glass of Peroni held little attraction for her this evening and the atmosphere of the noisy, smoky room – something she normally liked – didn't suit her mood. She was prevaricating again about her date with Gianfranco. It had seemed like such a fun idea in the midst of the erotic phone call, imagining him pumping his cock and spurting everywhere. Now, in the dispassionate light of a cool, rainy evening she wondered if she was just being silly. What was it she saw in the lanky Italian youth?

She glanced at herself in the mirror behind the bar. Her everyday reflection stared back; her standard attire of black tank top, shorts and boots seemed trite and predictable. What was Gianfranco expecting this evening, she wondered. Probably to fuck a 'cute sexy punk,' to use his own words. Am I that easily pigeon-holed? she asked herself. What do I want?

In one sense the thought of the Italian boy was appealing. After all, it had been over a week since she'd actually fucked a guy, the unpleasant Claudio Pozzi. Since then, one night with Francesca and her phone sex episode with Gianfranco were all she could notch up for the past several days. A familiar desire tingled deep in her loins and, with a small smile, the little redhead made up her mind and shrugged on her denim jacket. She tossed back her beer and wandered into the street, an unusual thought forming in her mind. It would be amusing to give Gianfranco a big surprise, to shock him out of his expectations. It would also be fun to buy some new clothes, something she rarely did.

Several stores were still open and she glanced at the fashionable window displays. Something caught her eye and she stopped outside a trendy little boutique on the via dei Pileati. In the minimally elegant window display were several sexy summer dresses and a few expensive-looking shoes.

Checking her wallet for her Visa card, the young American entered the shop and perused the racks. A waif-thin assistant watched from a distance, appraising Kiki's lithe body with frank interest. Kiki smiled an acknowledgement to the girl and thumbed through the racks of the petite sizes, selecting several chic little dresses, holding them up and studying herself in the mirror.

'*Posso provarlo?*' she asked the assistant.

The girl motioned to the fitting rooms and held open a long curtain, letting it fall behind Kiki. Inside the small space Kiki quickly stripped and tried on the dresses. One in particular appealed to her, a short dark floral Lagerfeld made of a sexy silken diaphanous fabric, looking like a *peignoir*. The frock would have seemed innocent were it not for the bodice that drooped so low a good portion of her breasts were revealed, bouncing freely under the thin fabric. She twirled in front of the mirror, checking the transparency. She reckoned she could go without underwear. There was just enough pattern to hide her bush, but also little enough that most men would look twice.

'*Perfetto!*' said Kiki to herself with a smile.

She brushed the curtain aside and found the assistant waiting. The girl's lazy stare took in all the salient details. A smile brushed the corners of her mouth. 'Very nice,' she said. 'Very sexy.'

'*Lo prendo,*' said Kiki. 'I'll take it.' She hadn't even looked at the price. '*Quanto costa?*'

'Six hundred thousand lire,' said the girl. Her eyebrows twitched with the slightest of questions.

Kiki gulped. She had never paid $400 for a dress. But it was too late now. She had to have it. Her plan for Gianfranco's seduction depended on it.

'*Acceta carte di credito?*' she asked.

The girl nodded.

'And I'll need some shoes,' added Kiki. 'I saw a pair in the window . . .'

Ten minutes later a very different young woman emerged from the shop into the evening *passeggiata*. Despite the thin drizzle Kiki cut a startling figure, wearing her denim jacket over the shimmering fabric of her new dress. Her breasts were freely visible, just the nipples being covered by the neckline, and her shapely legs were accentuated by the black and silver high-heeled sandals that had put another major dent in her credit card. A large shiny boutique shopping bag contained her boots, pack and other clothes. She glanced at her watch; her shopping had made her late, but she was sure Gianfranco would wait. As she walked, men's heads turned in lustful admiration, and more than a few women glanced in envy. Kiki gave the best-looking men flirtatious smiles and strode confidently down the hill towards The Speakeasy and her prey for the evening.

Gianfranco was horny and anxious. He had arrived at the bar a full hour early, too nervous to stay home, and was now on his third *vermut* of the evening. He looked at his watch again. Two minutes had passed since the last time, but Kiki was now twenty minutes late for their date. What if she stood him up?

After being teased so often, he wondered morosely if this was just another game. Perhaps Kiki was drinking with some friends right now, laughing and telling them about this big dumb Italian who was waiting for her in a bar across town. Or, even worse, perhaps she was already in bed with a new boyfriend! His cock twitched in his pants and he groaned inwardly. His unrequited lust for Kiki Lee made him feel such a fool!

His cock got big and heavy as he watched the Speak-easy waitresses whisk past him in their brief tops, serving others. By eight o'clock he had polished off his third cold *vermut* and was dreaming of fucking one of these sexy women. Lifting his glass, he tried unsuccessfully to catch the eye of Anna-Maria, one of the sexiest servers, a gorgeous brunette who looked like one of the big-breasted girls in his girlie magazines. He let one hand fall under the table and surreptitiously felt the full length of his cock beneath the denim. If all else failed perhaps he could find one of the prostitutes who waited for their lonely customers in the street behind the train station.

This gloomy thought was dispelled by the sudden shock of another hand between his legs, shamelessly squeezing his dick. 'I think that's mine tonight,' said Kiki Lee.

Gianfranco whirled round on his stool and gaped with amazement at the beautiful girl who stood before him, shaking raindrops out of her familiar short red hair. But that was all he recognised. This girl was dressed to kill in a dress that had obviously cost a bomb. Her tits were nearly falling out of the low neckline and he had to look twice to determine if she was wearing any underwear. He concluded, with a quickened pulse rate, that the dark triangle just visible between the girl's legs was not panties. He noticed other men staring at his companion, their open mouths suggesting that they had come to the same conclusion.

Kiki was watching him with a small smile on her lips. 'Aren't you going to say hello, Gianfranco?' she teased. 'I can tell you're pleased to see me.' She slid onto the barstool beside him and traced the outline of his dick with her fingernails, scratching along the material of his jeans.

'Oh, Kiki! I'm so sorry! I didn't see you come in.' Gianfranco couldn't apologise fast enough. 'I ... I thought you might not be coming,' he added lamely.

Kiki laughed. 'So you were amusing yourself by staring at the girls with the biggest tits,' she said. 'Don't deny it! I was watching you when I came in. What were you going to do then? Jerk off under the table, or try to get one of them to give you a blow-job in the toilets? Wouldn't be the first time that's happened,' she added, looking around the bar.

Gianfranco felt himself redden at the young woman's unrelenting teasing, but at least she was here, sitting right beside him and looking very seductive indeed. He covered his confusion by catching the barman's eye. 'What would you like to drink, Kiki?' he asked.

'What are you drinking?' Kiki looked at the empties in front of him.

'*Vermut.*'

'Isn't three drinks a lot for a former seminarian?' she asked, eyes twinkling. She turned to the barman. '*Desidero una aqua minerale con gas, e con limone, per favore.*'

Gianfranco raised his glass. '*Un'altro vermut, per favore,*' he said.

'Don't drink too much,' chided Kiki. 'You've got a lot of performing to do this evening!'

Gianfranco felt himself respond physically to her close proximity with a renewed throbbing in his groin. Despite Kiki's teasing and flirting, he realised she was all he desired. He forgot the waitresses with the big tits. He forgot the older woman who'd seduced him last year. He forgot every woman except Kiki. He closed his eyes for a moment, and inhaled her delicious scent.

When he opened his eyes he saw his companion's gaze fixed on his face, the ever-present small mocking smile on her lips.

'You look gorgeous,' he said. 'Is that a new dress?'

'Oh, no, not really,' replied Kiki. 'I just thought I'd wear it for a change.'

'It suits you,' blurted Gianfranco, 'You can see . . .' he trailed off before he said the wrong thing.

'You can see my tits?' asked Kiki, leaning forward so the young man had a perfect view down the front of her dress. Her small breasts were smooth and round, her nipples were standing up like little acorns from large pink and brown areolas. Gianfranco wanted to reach out and touch them.

'They're not as big as the ones you were looking at earlier,' she said.

Gianfranco shook his head. 'I think they're perfect.'

'What else can you see?' asked Kiki, still teasing.

This time Gianfranco was ready. 'I can see your bush,' he said boldly. 'I can see through your dress to those dense little pubic curls you told me about last night.'

Kiki sat up straight and crossed her legs, pulling up the hem of her short dress to expose her thigh almost as far as her arse. 'Good boy!' she said approvingly, sipping her drink. 'I like a man with discerning vision, someone who can see clearly what he wants. Do you know what you want, Gianfranco?' She leaned closer, letting one of the spaghetti straps of her dress fall down over her shoulder. She smiled invitingly.

The young Italian felt her eyes heavy on him and felt the heat of her body. He could almost smell the musk of her arousal. 'I want to fuck you, Kiki Lee,' he said slowly. 'I want to fuck you all night long.' For a few seconds the pair stared hungrily at each other.

'Let's go for a walk,' said Kiki.

In the streets outside the rain had cleared and the pale evening sun tinted the very tops of the church towers as it slipped behind the surrounding hills. Gianfranco hesitantly took Kiki's hand and, when she didn't draw it away, he pulled her close. Arm-in-arm they strolled up the hill towards the cathedral. They stopped at the edge of the square, gazing across the paved space in the fading evening light. Neither spoke. Gianfranco felt his heart pounding in his chest.

With a motion that appeared accidental, Kiki brushed one of her breasts against his arm. Her nipple, as hard and pointed as a nut, grazed him through the thin silk. 'Excuse me,' he said, involuntarily, not knowing whether to move his arm away.

Kiki laughed at his flustered reaction. 'No, excuse *me*,' she said in a mocking tone, leaving her breasts pressed teasingly, maddeningly, close against his arm. 'Do you still think my tits are perfect?' she asked innocently.

'Of course I do,' he said.

'Then look. And touch.' She turned to face him.

Gianfranco felt an aching mixture of lust, embarrassment and the confusing feeling that he needed to protect this wild and sexy girl. But mostly he felt unqualified desire.

'Touch them,' she ordered him again. She lingered in the shadow of a building and arched her back so that her nipples projected invitingly in the evening air. Kiki raised his hands to her body and he found her flesh, bare and yielding beneath his palms.

'Oh, God!' he crooned as he massaged her pointed breasts, cupping them completely out of her dress. Kiki moaned with pleasure. 'Am I doing it OK?' he asked.

'Just keep doing what you're doing,' said Kiki. 'I like your hands. I want them all over my body.' She smiled up at him and pressed against his prick.

Still playing with one nipple, Gianfranco placing his other hand on Kiki's buttocks and raised her skirt. He gasped as the young woman's bare bottom was fully revealed. He stroked the tight curves and slid his fingers along the cleft of her cheeks.

Footsteps on the cobblestones broke into their reverie. Gianfranco looked up and saw a policeman approaching. He quickly withdrew his hand from Kiki's bum and let her dress fall down to cover her naked flesh.

'We'd better go,' said Kiki, turning quickly and pulling her dress over her nipples. 'Come on, lover boy.'

She walked across the piazza, her barely concealed breasts and pointed nipples attracting the attention of other men. Gianfranco didn't know whether to be proud this sexy woman was with him, or mortified at the lustful gazes she was receiving from all and sundry. He thrilled at the thought that under that fabulous sexy dress Kiki Lee was completely naked for their date. But he wanted this gorgeous woman just for himself. He didn't want half of Arezzo staring at her tits. He ran across the square after her, to join her and walk together into the shadow of the cathedral.

'Where are we going?' he asked.

'Where do you want to go?'

'Somewhere we can have sex!'

'We can have sex here,' she teased. 'Right here,

against the wall of the *duomo*.' She sat down on the wide stone ledge that ran around the base of the building.

'No! Somewhere it's just you and me.'

Kiki stopped and regarded the young man quizzically, the same half-mocking smile playing on her lips. 'Gianfranco,' she said. 'Would you like to be my sex slave? Do anything I wanted, anytime I wanted?'

'Yes! Oh, yes!"

'If I wanted you to fuck me here, right now, would you do it?'

'Y . . . Yes!'

'No hesitation?'

'No.'

'All right. Let's do it. Take out your dick.'

Gianfranco faltered. 'You mean it?' he asked.

Kiki nodded severely. 'You're my slave. You accepted the job. You pleasure me anytime I want, anywhere I want.'

Gianfranco looked over his shoulder. The nearest pedestrians were at least fifty metres away and it was getting dark rapidly. He unzipped his fly and presented the contents to his temptress, standing close to hide his cock from public view.

The mischievous redhead pulled up the hem of her already brief skirt, baring more of her delicious creamy skin. She licked a finger and spread her thighs. 'Look at me,' she murmured teasingly. 'Gianfranco, don't you want to look?'

With his penis sticking out like a pikestaff in front of him, still untouched, Gianfranco looked. The brazen girl, sitting on the edge of the public square, slowly spread her legs wider and fully revealed her cluster of mysterious downy hair between her legs. He stared, transfixed at the red curls forming a tidy mat of soft, alluring fuzz. Tiny twirls embellished Kiki's lips and, as

Gianfranco gazed in wonder, she parted them and inserted one finger, revolving it between her glistening lips.

'You said you wanted to fuck me,' she whispered. 'What are you waiting for?'

Glancing one more time over his shoulder and seeing no one was near, Gianfranco bent forward and slowly, ever so slowly, pushed his long cock into the girl's moist tunnel. She was wet and warm; he slid in easily.

He had to call on all his reserves of willpower not to shoot his load on the spot. He watched in awe as Kiki played with herself as he slid his cock in and out of her.

'Don't mind me, Gianfranco,' she said breathlessly. 'I just want to come, too.'

It was all too much for the young man. With a groan he shuddered and clenched his buttocks as he erupted inside her. Fountains of come flowed from his dick.

'Oh, I'm sorry!' he blurted.

'Don't worry,' said Kiki and fingered herself even faster. 'Just stay there. Don't move!' Gianfranco watched with mingled joy and shame as the young woman brought herself off with his half-hard dick still inside her. In a few moments she came with a shuddering sigh, and the young man felt the gush of juice flow over his dick.

'Will you teach me how to make you come like that?' he asked.

Kiki looked up into his eyes. 'Most definitely,' she said. 'After all, you're my sex slave. You'll do everything I say.' She sat up and Gianfranco slid out of her, still semi-tumescent. The girl fondled his cock appreciatively and pulled her dress down. 'Put it away, for now,' she said. 'Is your car here?'

'Yes. Why?'

'I thought we might go to your place,' she said. 'It's still early, and there are lots of lessons for you to learn.'

It was only a short drive to San Leo, a few miles west of Arezzo, where Gianfranco had a small apartment in an old converted farmhouse. On the drive Kiki raised the hem of her dress and started to play with herself again. Gianfranco nearly drove off the road.

'Why should I fuck you when I can pleasure myself?' she asked, putting her feet up on the dashboard. She slid two fingers deep into herself.

'Holy Mother of God!' said Gianfranco, stopping the car.

'Do you have an answer?'

'Because a cock can give you … greater … satisfaction,' he gulped.

'Is that so?' she said. 'How come I had to bring myself off earlier?' Her tone was mocking once more, and Gianfranco coloured in shame.

'I'll get better,' he said. 'That was my first time …'

Kiki looked at him. 'I fuck a lot of men precisely because I don't want to settle on anyone,' she said. 'I don't want to become anybody's property. Does that bother you?'

'No,' he lied. 'I don't mind if you don't want to be involved. I just want to fuck you!'

She studied him silently.

'Let's go,' he urged.

'On my terms?'

'Yes, let's go.'

'No commitments?'

'As you wish,' he said.

She squeezed his cock. He smiled, trying to hide his sadness. It was just as well she couldn't feel his heart.

17 *Le Immagini Incriminante* (Incriminating Images)

The next morning Kiki was standing in the college doorway when Sandro screeched his navy blue and red-striped Fiat to a stop. The *carabiniere* hopped out, waved an admonishing finger at her and opened the car door for Donatella and Francesca.

'I'll see you later,' he said to Donatella. 'Promise me you'll call immediately if you have any trouble. I have to take care of some paperwork down at the station, but I can be here in a couple of minutes.'

'Don't worry, Sandro,' Donatella assured her protector. 'Kiki and I will be together all day, and Francesca will be in the building. We'll be careful.'

Apparently satisfied, Sandro touched his gloved hand to his peak in a half-salute. As he slid back behind the wheel, Kiki felt his gaze rake up and down her body, as if he knew she'd just had sex for the umpteenth time. Her swollen sex lips were testament to her energetic couplings with Gianfranco last night, and she felt the policeman undress her and fuck her with his dark sexy eyes. Then the small police car zoomed off down the narrow Via Pellicceria, startling the few early morning pedestrians.

Donatella watched her lover of the past few days depart. 'He drives like he fucks,' she said with a smile, turning to her friends. 'He's insatiable!'

Kiki couldn't resist teasing Donatella. '*He's* insatiable?' she queried. 'That's not the way I hear it.' She winked at Francesca. 'I hear there's a sex-crazed American professor in town who likes it all ways!'

'You don't think I'm weird, do you?' asked Donatella, as she hitched her briefcase on her shoulder.

Kiki smiled. 'Hey, girl, go for it,' she said. 'You've got a lot of catching up to do. No more polite, ever-so-proper Boston sex, lying flat on your back in the dark and thinking of Harvard. You know me, anything goes in my book. Well,' she added, 'I draw the line at animals.'

Donatella stifled a very unprofessorial giggle and led the way indoors. With a purposeful stride she climbed the stairs and led the way to her office. Few people were around at this early hour. Gina and Sophia's desks were empty.

'Talking about being insatiable,' said Francesca innocently as they walked down the corridor. 'What did you get up to last night, Kiki?'

The little redhead hesitated. 'You won't believe this,' she said.

'Try us,' said Donatella.

'I screwed Gianfranco della Parigi.' Kiki knew she would never be able to keep this news a secret from Francesca. She might as well admit it up front.

'How many times? Where? What's he like?' Francesca was all ears.

Kiki laughed. 'He's pretty good,' she said, 'He's sweet like an angel, but learning to fuck like a devil. I lost count after five times. Once he learned not to come as soon as he put his dick inside, it got real good!'

Francesca hooted with delight and slapped her friend on the shoulder. 'I demand you tell me all about it later,' she said. 'But now I have to get ready for life-drawing class. I'll see you for coffee afterwards.' She walked away and Kiki followed Donatella into her office. Donatella looked as if she wanted to ask her friend more about Gianfranco, but at that moment the two women collided as the professor stooped to pick up a beige envelope from the floor.

'What is it?' asked Kiki curiously, as Donatella extracted the contents.

'Sweet Jesus!' exclaimed Donatella. 'Look at these!'

Kiki found herself staring at three small photographs of Stewart Temple-Clarke having sex with two youngsters. Their faces were turned from the camera, but Kiki could see they were in their mid to late teens. In two photos Temple-Clarke faced the camera, his gaze calm and almost detached as the lens caught him in separate poses; one with his cock deeply embedded in the girl's arse, the second in her pussy. The third photograph didn't show the man's face, but focused on his long cock, poised over the anus of the young man with the fleshy cockhead pushing against the tight hole.

'Who took these?' Kiki said, thinking out loud. 'Are these taken on a timed delay exposure or was someone else there watching?'

'And probably participating,' added Donatella.

'The next question is how did they get here? Who put them under the door?' Kiki automatically looked up and down the corridor, but it was deserted.

Donatella glanced at Kiki. 'Will you find the porter on duty this morning? Ask if anybody was here early before we arrived, and tell him to call that old guy, *il signor* what's-his-name, who locks up at night. Ask if he saw anybody hanging around yesterday evening.'

'*Signor* Vanivitelli,' said Kiki, filling the blank in Donatella's memory. 'He's an old lecher. Used to come barging in on the life-drawing classes "by accident" so he could ogle Francesca's tits. Even she got annoyed after he pulled the stunt two or three times, and one evening she jumped off the podium, walked up to him, yanked his trousers down and pulled his cock out in front of the class. You never saw a cock shrink so fast in your life!' Kiki chuckled at the memory. 'We hardly ever see him now. He just lurks in his little cubbyhole until the students and faculty leave, then goes round and locks up. I doubt if he'll be able to tell us anything, but it's worth a shot. Be right back.'

When Kiki returned a few minutes later, Donatella was standing at the window, examining the images with a magnifying glass in the light of the morning sun.

'No luck,' Kiki reported. 'We're the first ones in this morning, and *il vecchio porco*, the dirty old man, says he saw nobody in the building when he locked up last night. That means it could be someone with a key, or someone just slipped in and out without Vanivitelli seeing him. Or her,' she added.

'Which means it could be one of the faculty,' said Donatella grimly. 'We're going to have to get Sandro and Salvatore to question those bozos.'

Kiki picked up the magnifier and studied one of the photographs. 'I have to admit,' she said, 'for a middle-aged man, Temple-Clarke looks fit. This could be someone ten years younger.' Despite her abhorrence of the man, Kiki couldn't help but admire his long-shafted cock. 'This is a surprise,' she said. 'I didn't think the old bastard had it in him. I never thought of him as someone who got his rocks off like this – especially with boys. Do you think this is some kind of blackmail scam? A jilted lover? Perhaps the person who took these pictures threatened to expose him if he didn't come back, or hand over a bundle of money?'

'Maybe,' Donatella said, seemingly unconvinced by Kiki's argument. 'I rather think they were neatly handed to us to get Temple-Clarke fired on the spot. If I make these public that jerk will never work here again.

The Boston Trustees would get rid of him without a second thought.'

'Then our mysterious postman has done us a big favour,' said Kiki. 'We have what we want. Temple-Clarke's history.'

Donatella shook her head. 'Not really. We want to nail him for fraud and attempted murder, not having sex with teenagers,' she said with quiet determination. 'If these were young kids it would be different, but this boy and girl could be sixteen or even eighteen. Unless the pair come forward there's no case. I want the bastard locked up, not simply dismissed so he can slink off somewhere else.'

Kiki was taken aback by her companion's passion, but she didn't argue. 'OK,' she said. 'What's the next step?'

'I want to see if these photographs can give us any information beyond the obvious. I'm guessing that whoever gave us these wants us simply to take them at face value: here's Temple-Clarke having sex with teenagers. Hence he's a louse and gets fired. It's too pat. After all the effort we've gone to, digging into the affairs of the college without finding any real evidence until yesterday, all of a sudden up pop these dirty pictures. Job done. We can go home.'

'I catch your drift,' said Kiki. 'Could Temple-Clarke himself have sent these to get us off the trail? He knows you're going to get him fired anyway, so he cops this lesser plea of sexual misconduct, resigns and moves away. Case closed. He cuts his losses and gets us off his back.'

'It's certainly worth thinking about, isn't it?' agreed Donatella. She paused and strode back to the window, studying the photos, deep in thought. 'No,' she said, evidently making up her mind about something. 'I'm not going to fall for it. I think someone else is involved. Look at this one.' She held out the image of the man they supposed to be Temple-Clarke pushing his cock into the young boy's arse. 'The other two are standard bedroom shots, but this one's different.' She tapped the photograph. 'It's in a different location. Look. There are racks all along the walls holding lots of objects, and here's something that looks like a piece of heavy equipment. Maybe this is some kind of factory, and he's fucking this lad on his lunch break. Can you scan the images and enlarge them? Maybe we can make something out.'

That early in the morning the computer lab was empty of students. Kiki booted up a Macintosh, scanned the images and imported them into Photoshop. Using the lasso tool, she outlined an area of the background and clicked on "sharpen". The image obligingly jumped into larger, sharper relief. 'What do you make of that?' she asked Donatella, who was looking eagerly over her shoulder. 'It looks like a row of figures, like little sculptures.'

'Can you enlarge them?'

'Not without losing some clarity. I'll try.' A couple of clicks later, the images reformed on the screen, larger and more blurry, but still readable.

'My God!' said Kiki. 'It's a bunch of sculptures with big cocks!'

Donatella clucked in mock annoyance. 'We've got to work on your art history, Kiki,' she scolded. 'Don't you recognise those?'

Kiki shook her head. 'No. I just see lots of little figurines with giant cocks. Sort of like the cast for Aristophanes' *Lysistrata*. Some look more finished than others, though.'

Donatella smiled. 'I see you retain a smattering of classical education,' she said approvingly. 'Yes they are like the characters in that play, human figures with giant penises, but they're not Greek. They're local, from around Arezzo. They closely resemble early Etruscan "Arretine ware", dating from before the Roman Empire. These fertility figures were quite common. The Etruscans must have liked sex a lot.'

'But why's Temple-Clarke fucking this cute boy in front of dozens of these sculptures? Do you think they help him get it up?'

'I don't know what to think, right now,' replied Donatella. 'But look at the different rows. The figures on the middle row don't look quite the same as the ones above. Their shape is the same but they are a slightly different colour. And the ones on the very bottom look more worn and weathered. In fact,' she said, standing up from the screen, 'the ones on the bottom row look very much like specimens you'd see in a museum.'

'You mean these are forgeries?' asked Kiki.

'That's one possibility,' agreed Donatella. 'We might be looking at a sophisticated production line of fakes. Each row could be at a different stage in the process. I doubt if they would fool a serious collector or art expert, but at first glance they look authentic.'

'They could be for the tourist market,' suggested Kiki. 'There are lots of naive foreigners around here who could be easily parted from their money.'

Donatella nodded. 'Yes, but have you seen these on sale around here? With those huge cocks sticking out?'

'You're right. I wouldn't have missed them. Neither would Francesca; she'd have brought one home to play with. Are the real ones very rare?'

'Absolutely. Only major museums have examples. They'd be worth a great deal of money.'

Kiki thought for a moment. 'So these fakes wouldn't be good enough to deceive an expert, but some gullible art tourist, with more money than sense, might think he was getting a real bargain, a special deal on a risqué little item for his private collection back home. Is that possible?'

'Quite possible, I think. But this is all speculation. There might be a completely innocent explanation, though I can't imagine what it might be.' Donatella picked the original photographs off the worktop. 'Save those images on a zip,' she said, 'and we'll lock these away in my filing cabinet. We can look at them again this evening now we have the computer set up back at the villa.'

Kiki grinned. 'Yes, Francesca's bargain with Nico really paid off. We have a brand new Internet access, and Nico got laid. The only person who loses out is Berzitta. But she's such a cow,' Kiki added uncharitably. 'She deserves it.'

18 *Lo Sbaglio* (The Mistake)

The same sunlight that illuminated Donatella's office slid between the shutters of another window and threw a slanting pattern of golds and greys across Anna's naked body. As she stretched across the bed, she lifted her hips as her new lover slid his tongue deep into her, licking her juices and nibbling her. She shivered with lust. She'd do almost anything for a good fuck, and no one fucked her as well as this new lover. Not even her boss.

Anna stretched her hand for the man's cock as he straddled her. His groin filled her gaze; his heavy balls, full of come, hung loose beneath the rigid staff, and his tight anus was visible in the cleft of his arse as his thighs stretched wide on either side of her shoulders. She smelt the fragrance of sandalwood soap mixed with his male musk; he had obviously prepared himself carefully for their siesta of sex.

The scents and sight of his long, hard cock made Anna moan with delight. She reached for it and drew it down to her lips. She could taste his pre-come and raised her head to take the tip in her mouth. His balls brushed her face as she sucked him avidly. Her muscles clenched with desire.

'I want it,' she gasped, releasing his flesh. '*Il tuo cazzo mi fai impazzire!* Your cock is driving me mad. Slide it inside me, please. Now.' She bucked her hips urgently, wanting the full length of it filling her.

The man only laughed, her juices glistening on his lips. 'Not so fast, my little *puttana*. You have some work to do before you get your reward.' He moved to her side and slid two fingers in her wet hole and massaged her clit with his thumb. Anna thought she was going to come on the spot, but her tormentor withdrew his hand as she approached the brink.

'Now suck me, you little slut,' commanded her partner, holding her down on the bed and kneeling over her, his dick pointing at her face. 'Swallow my come and maybe I'll let you get off.'

'Fuck me first,' pleaded Anna, wriggling on the bed, an insatiable desire pent up between her legs. Her only reply was a stinging slap across her thigh, and she obediently grasped his prick and tongued the tip once more, pumping with her hand as she licked the tiny slit.

In less than a minute she felt the first spasm of the man's cock, followed an instant later by a stream of warm, salty spunk. Faster than Anna could swallow, the man came over her tongue until waves spilled over her lips.

'I said swallow it,' growled her partner, and brusquely wiped his jizz from her chin with his fingers, holding them for Anna to lick clean. Only when every drop was accounted for did he relent.

'Good girl, Anna,' he said. 'Very good. Now you can have your reward.' He reached across her body to the bedside table and picked up a long flexible dildo. 'Fit yourself around that, baby,' he crooned.

Anna's pulse quickened. She really wanted warm, live flesh inside her, but the dildo was better than nothing. She splayed her legs wide and let her lover push the fake cock into her pussy. With a small gasp of pleasure she pushed her pelvis towards the make-believe penis, driving it deeper, seeking release.

'Play with yourself, Anna,' ordered the man. 'I want

to watch you make yourself come while I fuck you with my toy.'

Anna needed no second bidding. Her fingers found the familiar button of her clit and she rubbed herself frantically as she felt the man push the dildo fully into her. Her body tensed, her muscles tight around the object, until her fingers brought her blessed relief, and she felt her juices flow and pool on the sheets. Muted waves of joy passed through her slim body, leaving her partially satisfied but wanting more.

'Very good, you sexy little bitch,' murmured her lover, deaf to her desire. He lay down beside her and played absently with her small breasts. 'You've been good today. I won't need to discipline you.' He paused, holding a nipple between the fingers of one hand. 'You're sure nobody saw you go to di'Bianchi's office last night?'

Anna laughed. 'No,' she confirmed. 'I saw Vanivitelli, the night porter, but he didn't see me. He was too busy wanking in his office in front of a computer.' She reached over to stroke her partner's penis. 'His cock is not nearly as nice as yours,' she murmured, fondling the man's balls in her hand and running her nails up the shaft. The flesh began to stiffen at her touch.

The man smiled but then looked serious. He propped himself up on one elbow. 'When you see the boss, I want to make sure you tell him the right thing. Tell him just what we agreed. OK?'

Anna nodded. 'I put the envelope under *professoressa* di'Bianchi's door. It had the photographs in it.'

'If he asks you what was in the photographs, what do you say?'

'That I didn't look. I was too frightened. It wasn't any of my business.'

'Excellent.' The man's fingers circled Anna's nipple, flicking it casually. 'Of course, you did look, didn't you?'

Anna giggled. '*Si. Naturalmente.* After all, I was one of the stars. And I had a great idea. I added another photograph, one I took of Leo getting fucked up the arse. I thought that would get them excited.' The pressure on her nipple turned from pleasure to pain. '*Ahi!* You're hurting me!' she shouted.

A hand came out of nowhere and stung her cheek with a vicious slap. 'You stupid bitch! Why the fuck did you have to meddle? Why couldn't you just do as you were told? Do you realise what you've done? *Raccotami tutto!* Tell me everything!'

Anna winced as the man grasped her shoulders roughly and shook her small body. 'There's nothing more to tell,' she complained. 'I thought it was a good idea, showing something homosexual. It'll grab more attention. Anyway,' she added, trying to minimise her mistake, 'you can't see it's Leo.'

'Bah! That's not the point. It's not *who* it is, but *where* it is! Don't you understand?' The man flung Anna onto the sheet and hurried over to a desk where his mobile phone lay amidst his hastily discarded clothes.

Anna cowered on the bed, listening urgently to one side of the conversation.

'This is Claudio,' said her lover. 'We have a problem. That stupid little bitch Anna fucked up. She put another photograph in the packet for di'Bianchi, one taken in the studio with Leo ... Leo. Yes, I know what it shows. That's the problem ... No, Leo won't be an issue; I'll take care of him ... Anna? The stupid little *pezzo di merda* is here with me. I just found out what she's done.'

Anna watched as Claudio, cell phone clapped to his ear, listened intently. For several minutes he said not a word, then with a brief, '*Si, il mio padrone,*' he replaced the receiver. '*Il nostro padrone* is very angry, little girl,' Claudio said, menacingly. 'He told me there's only one way out of this mess for you. He slapped her across the face. '*Capisce?*'

Recoiling, Anna nodded silently, holding her hand to her cheek.

'If you mess up again, then you're in real trouble! The boss is making some arrangements to cover up your mistake; you don't need to know what. You're getting a second chance, you stupid little bitch, to put things right. But first,' Claudio said as he stroked his cock, which was now back to full strength, 'I'm going to teach you a lesson. Turn around and bend over.'

A hand sticky with lube slathered Anna's anus then, after some probing, Claudio's cock was inside her back passage. Anna bent her body to receive her punishment. She was no fan of anal sex and she knew he was doing this to humiliate her. This is the last time, she thought. After this I get even with you bastards.

19 *La Rivelazione Parziale* (Partial Disclosure)

When Anna was sure she was alone, she picked up the phone and dialled a number from her diary. The instrument at the other end rang briefly before it was picked up.

'*Pronto!*'

'Gina? Hi, this is Anna.'

'*Anna?*' Her older cousin sounded delighted, if somewhat surprised. 'Where are you? I haven't heard from you for ages. Are you in town?'

Anna bit her lip. 'I've been away for a while,' she lied. 'I'm back in Arezzo for a visit. I need to talk to you. Can we meet?'

'Sure.' Anna heard a note of alarm in her cousin's voice. 'Is anything wrong? Are you in trouble?'

'No. Well, yes, sort of. It involves people at the college where you work.'

'*Il Collegio Toscana?*' Gina sounded surprised. 'Whatever has that place got to do with you?' There was a pause and then her cousin's voice came back on the line, higher pitched with growing alarm. 'You're not pregnant are you? Is it a student? One of the faculty?' Anna sensed her cousin's mind racing ahead, full of various sexual dramas.

'No, no. Nothing like that. Don't be worried. I have some information I need to give to the new American professor . . .'

'Donatella?' Another pause. 'Is this something to do

with *il direttor* Temple-Clarke?' Anna could hear growing suspicion in Gina's voice and decided to tell a
limited version of the truth.

'*Sì*. I must talk with *la dottoressa* di'Bianchi as soon
as possible. I have important information about *il
signor* Temple-Clarke.'

'What about Temple-Clarke?' Gina sounded puzzled
and unconvinced.

'I can't talk about it over the phone. Can we meet at
your apartment?

'*Sì...*' Anna could still hear uncertainty in her
cousin's voice.

'*È importante*. Can you set something up for this
evening?'

'OK. Come round at seven. We'll have some wine
and I'll cook supper. I'll call Donatella right away.'

'*Grazie*, Gina! And look, when you speak to her, can
you ask her to come alone? It's personal information. I
don't want other people around. *Molto grazie. Ciao!*'
Anna rang off before Gina could ask for her number.

Turning to her extensive wardrobe, the teenager
selected one of her new dresses to wear to her cousin's
apartment. It was one of her favourites, a floral print
dress with a double-layer ruffle detail and a slender
silhouette. The slim straps suited her delicate frame.
Anna preened in the mirror. The soft blue pastel of
the dress suited her complexion. Her shoes were
delicate, too, and with an elegant slim strap designed
as a snake lacing asymmetrically around her slender
ankle.

As she sat on Gina's bed, just a few minutes after seven,
Anna heard her cousin open the front door. To her
alarm she heard two voices as Gina greeted a pair of
guests.

'*Buona sera, Donatella! E buona sera, Francesca! Mi*

fa molto piacere verderLa. Come sta?' Gina sounded excited.

'Grazie, bene, Gina,' replied a foreign voice, presumably the American professor.

'Come va, Gina? Sono contento di rivederLa,' said the second visitor, who sounded like a young woman with a local Tuscan accent. Anna's tension ebbed a little. Cautious still, she waited for the visitors to get settled. Peeking through the crack in the bedroom door, she saw her cousin bustling around like an over-anxious hostess.

'Avanti! Avanti!' cried Gina, ushering her guests into the small living-room of her apartment and offering them seats on the couch. *'Prego, si accomodi.* Where is Kiki tonight?'

The younger visitor, the Italian, laughed. 'You'll never guess,' she said. 'She's out with Gianfranco della Parigi!'

'Gianfranco? With Kiki? My God! That I thought I'd never see! What's the attraction? What does she see in him?'

The blonde woman pumped her hand in front of her crotch. 'I hear it's a beautiful one,' she said. 'That's a big factor in Kiki's decisions.'

'Oh, be fair,' demurred her older companion. 'He's really rather cute.' The two women grinned at each other.

Anna studied the visitors, noting the older American's elegant clothes, attractive figure and long dark hair. Her beauty was complemented by that of her companion, a luscious ginger-blonde who wore a simple short cotton dress, cut revealingly to show off her breasts. Anna recognised a kindred spirit in the younger woman. With a sigh of relief, she stepped around the door and into the living-room.

Gina jumped up to perform the introductions.

'*Donatella, Francesca, Le presento la mia cugina, Anna. Anna, la dottoressa Donatella di'Bianchi, e la sua amica Francesca Antinori.*'

Anna smiled shyly. '*Salve,*' she greeted them. 'I'm glad you could come.'

Mindful of her duties as hostess Gina offered drinks. '*Che cosa preferisce? Vino? Birra? Coca-cola?*'

Anna sipped a beer to steady her nerves, the others drank wine, and the four women sat around a table for an informal supper of *melone e prosciutto* followed by large helpings of *spaghetti alla carbonara*. After the guests had consumed several glasses of wine, Anna chose her moment carefully.

'*Professoressa* di'Bianchi . . .'

'Donatella, please,' said the American, appearing very relaxed and friendly.

'*Grazie*, Donatella. This is hard for me to begin. Did you know I work for Professor Temple-Clarke?'

The eyebrows of all three older women arched up in surprise. 'What kind of work do you do?' asked Donatella, putting down her napkin and plate.

'I am his whore, his *puttana*, his little sex toy.'

'What are you saying?' cried Gina. 'That lecherous old bastard! He's old enough to be your father! What are you thinking of, Anna? What would your mother say?'

'That old bitch wouldn't care one way or the other,' Anna replied coldly. 'She was glad when I left home. She didn't have to worry about me coming home and catching her on her knees sucking off her latest "boyfriend."'

'You're the girl in the photographs, aren't you? asked Donatella gently.

'What photographs?' demanded Gina, very agitated, 'What's going on?'

Donatella laid a restraining hand on Gina's arm,

urging her to keep her seat and calm down. 'I'll explain what I know later, Gina,' she said. 'You can deal with family matters afterwards. For now, please let Anna talk. I need to hear what she has to say about the director.'

'Yes, it was me,' Anna admitted self-importantly. 'I slipped the photos under your door. I heard you were investigating my boss, and I thought the photos would give you some clues you wanted.' After a pause, the teenager continued, eyes downcast. 'I've had enough,' she said. 'At first it was fun, all the gifts, the clothes, CDs ... and the sex. It's much better having sex with an experienced older man than kids at school.' She flashed a defiant look at her cousin, who glared back.

'What happened to change your mind?' prompted Donatella.

'I got scared. He'd hurt me if I didn't do things exactly the way he wanted. He can be vicious. Look!' Anna stood up and dramatically hoisted her expensive baby-blue dress above her head. She intentionally wore no underwear and her fully exposed body revealed a series of bruises, some old and fading, others recent and vivid, striped across her flesh.

The other three women drew a collective breath as they gazed in shock at the beautiful naked young woman standing shamelessly in front of them, her slender body treated so disgracefully. Slowly Anna let the delicately ruffled garment flutter down to cover her body and sat down, facing Donatella.

'Temple-Clarke sent me here this evening,' she said, ignoring Gina's gasp of surprise. 'He wanted me to tell you a pack of lies about the college and the other faculty, so that you would suspect Professor Ramsey and the others, not him. But I'm not going to do it. He's been fiddling the books at the college for years, taking money out of educational funds and using it on himself

– and on me,' she added. 'But I've had enough. I have some money put aside. I'm leaving town in a couple of days. I never want to see him again!'

'Where will you go?' asked Francesca, urgently. 'I know people in Firenze . . .'

'I haven't made up my mind,' interrupted Anna with a shrug. 'I'm heading north to Milano. Then, who knows? Anywhere, as long as it's away from Temple-Clarke!'

'So he *is* behind all this,' said Donatella, her eyes bright with excitement. 'I knew it!' She looked sharply at Anna. 'Can you get me any proof? I need hard evidence that he's been embezzling money. I've found hints, but nothing conclusive at the college.' The American professor shot the teenager a sharp glance. 'What do you know about Temple-Clarke making art forgeries?'

Anna formed an expression of unknowing innocence. 'I don't know anything about that,' she said.

'But he must have a studio,' persisted Donatella. 'And you must have been there.'

'He does,' said Anna, 'but he never took me there. I don't even know where it is. He's very secretive about it. I do know he has ceramic kilns and all sorts of stuff he bought with college money. I think he makes pottery and sculpture there.' She saw with satisfaction the look of triumph that flashed between the two visitors.

'Proof,' demanded Donatella. 'I must have proof: documents, receipts, records of any kind. Does he keep them at the studio? Or at his house? Do you know? I want enough material to reveal Temple-Clarke for what he is. I want a full exposure of all his criminal activities – everything.'

Anna appeared to think for a moment. 'I don't know about the studio,' she said. 'I can check his house.'

'Can you bring me anything?' asked Donatella eagerly.

'I reckon so. Let me have a look when he's not around tomorrow. I'll meet you in the little church of Santa Croce, outside the walls by the old hospital. It's always very quiet there. No or.e will see us. Make it 8.30 tomorrow evening.'

'Great! This is fantastic!' Donatella was ecstatic, but Anna caught Francesca looking at her oddly.

'Why can't we just meet here?' Francesca asked, a hint of suspicion colouring her question.

Thinking fast, Anna said, 'If anything goes wrong, I don't want my cousin Gina to be involved. Temple-Clarke is not a nice man. He can be dangerous. I don't want him to know Gina has anything to do with this. I'm not trying to trick you,' she added, opening her eyes wide with all the innocence she could muster.

'It'll be OK' said Francesca lightly. 'Our friend Kiki will be with us, and if necessary Salvatore won't be far away.'

'Who's Salvatore?'

'Just a policeman friend of ours.'

Anna's chest heaved with alarm. This was the last thing she wanted. 'No police!' she said. 'I won't come if the police are there!'

'OK, OK,' said Donatella, placatingly. '*Va bene*. We won't bring Salvatore. We'll do it exactly the way you say. Eight thirty at the church; just myself, Francesca and our friend Kiki. OK?' She looked at her watch. 'Speaking of Salvatore, we should call him to come and pick us up. Is that all right?' she asked Anna.

'No,' she said with an angry shake of her head. 'I don't want this Salvatore or the police anywhere near me. Don't call until I've gone – otherwise the deal is off!'

Donatella held up her hands. 'All right. I'll do it later. But I'm worried about you. The police could help . . .'

'Ha! The cops couldn't help each other wank in the dark!' said Anna, dismissively. 'They never helped me before; why should they start now?' She stood up and turned to Gina. 'Thanks a lot, Gina, for doing this,' she said, and bent forward to give her cousin a hug. 'I've got to go now. I'll be in touch. *Ciao!*'

'But you can't walk out on the street like that,' protested Gina. 'You don't have anything on under that dress. Let me find you some panties, at least. And tell me where you're staying.'

'No. I'll be fine. Don't worry.' Enjoying the shock on her cousin's face, Anna grinned and said, 'It won't be the first time I've run around Arezzo without my knickers!' She quickly let herself out of the front door and down the flight of steps to the street before the others could follow, and vanished around the corner.

Despite Anna's bravado, the evening wind was chilly through the thin material of her summer dress, and she hurried through the back streets, heading for her small apartment. Near the corner of her block, a figure detached itself from the shadows and walked towards her. With a flash of alarm Anna turned down a side alley, until a familiar male voice halted her in her tracks.

'It's only me,' the man said. 'Did they believe you?'

Anna swallowed nervously. 'Er . . . yes. They believed everything. Why are you here?' she asked warily.

'I just wanted to check on how it went this evening. I had some business at the college.' His voice hardened. 'You really were stupid to add that extra photograph. It's caused me a lot of trouble.'

'The college isn't in this neighbourhood,' said Anna, her suspicions unabated.

The man laughed. 'Don't be so nervous,' he said.

'Everything's going to be all right. I stopped by his house as well to leave some things where they'll be sure to be found.'

'What things?'

'Nothing you need worry about. Just some papers that the di'Bianchi bitch would love to find. I have, shall we say, edited them carefully. And a few photographs for good measure.'

'Pictures of me?' asked Anna. 'But they already have some.'

'No, not of you,' said her companion impatiently. 'Pictures of something far more damning. Our little Boston professor is no fool, I'll give her that. If I'm not mistaken she'll put together all the information I've left for her in various places, but she'll get exactly the wrong answer.'

Anna was puzzled. 'I don't understand,' she complained. 'What are you trying to do?'

'Just laying false trails,' the tall man said smoothly. Then his voice hardened. 'We wouldn't want any more fuck-ups, would we? We wouldn't want little Anna to say the wrong thing or get ideas above her station.' Anna felt his hard unblinking eyes bore into her. 'You were in your cousin's house a long time,' he added, an accusing tone creeping into his voice. 'Are you sure you just told them what Claudio instructed you to say? You didn't go round embellishing any little details, did you? Or making up little stories?' he repeated harshly.

Anna's apprehension increased. She hadn't expected her actions to be so closely monitored. She wondered if her companion somehow knew what she'd been planning.

'N ... No. Of course not,' she replied. 'How did you know how long I was there? Have you been following me?' she demanded nervously.

'Let's just say I'm keeping an eye on your welfare.

You know I like to take care of the people who work for me.'

Despite the familiar smile that creased the man's features, Anna could not mistake the undertone of menace in his words. 'The American professor doesn't know anything except what I told her,' she said defensively. 'She admitted she hasn't found any conclusive evidence in the college files. She still doesn't have any proof.' But she soon will, the girl thought to herself, and not what you think. Then I'll be out of here!

'Good. Good.' The voice was soothing in its satisfaction. 'Just as I planned. But if you've done your job properly tonight, she'll soon find what she needs, won't she?' He smiled. 'Now come with me. We'll walk back to my place, have a nightcap and relax, that sort of thing. Good idea?'

'I'm really tired,' said Anna, wanting to refuse. 'I was just going home.'

'Nonsense! A drink is just what you need.' A strong arm reached out and took her shoulder, guiding her tense body towards him. 'Come with me. There's a good girl.'

Anna started in alarm but the man's grip tightened. She twisted but couldn't get away, trapped against his chest.

'Why the sudden reluctance, Anna? Don't you want to fuck the boss any more?' Suspicion and anger coloured the man's voice.

'No ... yes. I mean ...' Now Anna was worried.

'Look at me, Anna!' The man held the girl at arm's reach and stared into her eyes. 'Look at me,' he repeated. 'Are you playing straight with me? Are you doing as you are told?'

Anna summoned every ounce of courage and willpower she could. '*Si, il mio padrone*,' she said meekly. 'I have done exactly as you told me, but I'm frightened.

Sometimes you scare me.' She cast down her eyes, the picture of docile submission.

The man's features softened. 'Good girl. I thought you'd be sensible in the end. Are you ready to come home with me now?'

'*Si, il mio padrone.*'

Anna let herself be led away, snuggling compliantly into the crook of the man's arm. Within her chest, her heart was slowing to something approaching its normal rhythm. Once this evening was over, she thought she had about 24 hours to leave Arezzo. To hell with the American professor.

Something in Anna's expression must have betrayed her. A stinging blow caught her across the face, followed by a thumping punch to the jaw. 'Stupid little bitch...' was the last thing she heard as the cobblestones rushed up to meet her.

20 *Le Regazze Scoprono L'Oro!* (Girls Strike Gold!)

Shortly before 8.30 p.m. the next evening, Donatella, Francesca and Kiki walked down the Borgo di Santa Croce towards the small church of the Holy Cross, just beyond the eastern gate in the medieval wall. The small structure sat isolated in a forlorn little park, but to Donatella's expert eye the building retained some residual dignity from the days when it must have been a well-used chapel. A small bell tower stood above the low roof beneath a canopy of tall umbrella pines; as they approached it pealed a desultory half-hour chime.

The park surrounding the small church was deserted. Saturday evening crowds gathered elsewhere in Arezzo, many blocks from this older, almost forgotten part of the city. A feeling of gloom, enhanced by the fading sun, permeated the setting.

Francesca looked around warily. 'If someone was looking for a place to ambush us,' she said, 'this would do pretty well.'

'You think it might be a trap?' asked Donatella.

Francesca nodded. 'Possibly. I don't trust that little minx, Anna,' she said. 'How do we know she was telling the truth?'

'We don't' said Kiki. 'That's why we're here.'

Donatella led the trio through the door of the church. Inside the musty silence was broken only by the sound of their echoing footsteps on the old flagstones. Several candles were lit and the smell of incense pervaded the air. Shafts of low evening sunlight barely penetrated the gloom from tiny windows high above the entrance. Peeling frescoes were dimly visible on the walls around the altar. Donatella was keen to examine them, but Francesca tugged at her arm.

'This is creepy,' she said. 'Let's wait outside in the park.'

The three women paced impatiently as nine o'clock came and went with no sign of Anna.

'I told you we couldn't trust her,' said Francesca. 'What do we do now?'

'I'm due to meet Gianfranco in thirty minutes,' said Kiki with a look at her wristwatch. 'But he'll wait for us.'

'Let's stay until nine fifteen,' said Donatella. 'Anna might just be late.'

At nine thirty, the women left the church and its gloomy little park. 'We'll have a drink with you and Gianfranco,' Donatella said to Kiki. 'Then we can decide what to do.'

'Where do you think Temple-Clarke is now?' asked Kiki as the trio settled around Gianfranco's table at their favourite watering hole in the *Loggia* of the Piazza Grande. 'Anna was going to bring evidence from his house,' she continued. 'Do you think he caught her?'

Donatella was worried about that very thing. 'I'm afraid she might have come to some harm,' she said. 'Look how he has treated her so far. If he got really angry with her there's no telling what he might do.'

'I agree,' said Kiki, downing her vodka and tonic in one go. 'I think we should go by his house right now and check it out.' She stood up. 'What are we waiting for? This might be urgent. Anna could be in danger.' Gianfranco rose beside her.

Donatella and Francesca looked at each other. 'Kiki's right,' said Francesca. 'I think we should go over there.'

'But what if she couldn't get away until later and she shows up at the church and we're not there?' asked Donatella, also rising. 'Kiki, you and Gianfranco go back to the church while Francesca and I look for her at Temple-Clarke's place.'

Gianfranco seemed ready to argue. 'I should accompany you for protection,' he said, but he deferred to Donatella's repeated orders. '*Va bene.* I'll take Kiki home to my place afterwards,' he said. 'We can talk on the phone later.' Kiki made no move to dispute these arrangements and gave her lover's arm a squeeze.

Before the two left, Donatella asked, 'Hold on. Where does Temple-Clarke live? Has anybody been to his house?'

'Not me,' said Kiki. 'He never invites faculty or students to his home as far as I know. I don't even know the address, but it's somewhere in the old part of the city. I thought you knew.'

Donatella shook her head in annoyance. 'I never thought to ask,' she said. 'Fine secret agents we'd make! I didn't find it in the files. We should have asked Anna last night.'

'No problem,' said Francesca, flipping open her cell phone and punching the speed dial button. 'Damn!' she said a few moments later. 'Salvatore isn't answering. It's rolling over to the duty officer. Oh, hi. This is Francesca Antinori, I'm trying to reach Salvatore ... Oh, it's you, Guiseppe! *Come stai? Si, si. Sto bene, grazie.* Listen, I can't reach Salvatore and I need some information. My friend and I are going to meet Salvatore at the Englishman's house – yes, *il signor* Temple-Clarke – but I've lost the address. Do you have it in your file? *Si. Grazie.*' Francesca put her hand over the phone. 'He's looking it up,' she whispered to Donatella.

'Will Salvatore be angry when he finds out?' asked Donatella. 'Is it wise to use his name like that?'

'He'll rant and rave for a while,' replied Francesca, shrugging her shoulders. 'But a bit of cock-worship should quiet him down soon enough. And he can't complain if we stop Temple-Clarke hurting Anna. Besides I get tired of his bossiness sometimes.'

'Interesting,' said Donatella. 'I find that cocky bossiness rather attractive.'

'You do?' queried the Italian with a raised eyebrow as she picked up a pen and scribbled an address and directions on a paper napkin. '*Grazie, Guiseppe, molto grazie. Ciao!*' She closed the phone and turned to her friend. 'It isn't far,' she said, grabbing her backpack. 'Donatella, let's go. Kiki, you run back to the church and we'll talk later.'

The quartet split up, and Donatella and Francesca walked briskly to a tight medieval maze of alleyways behind the cathedral. Francesca looked at her friend quizzically. 'Are you really attracted to Salvatore?' she asked. 'I quite fancy Sandro, myself.' She jabbed Donatella playfully in the ribs. 'Maybe we should have a foursome.'

Donatella didn't have to think about her answer. 'I'd like that!' she said without hesitation, and enjoyed the surprise on the Italian's face.

'Really?'

Donatella nodded. 'Yes, very much actually.'

Francesca grinned. 'Let's do it!' she said.

The two women slowed. 'It must be around here,' said Francesca, reverting to the task in hand and slowly entering a darkened alley. She hesitated then walked on. 'I never knew this *borgo* was back here,' she said with some astonishment. 'I haven't been here before.'

'It's very exclusive,' said Donatella, 'and only a

couple of blocks off the main street. Which one is his? I don't see many house numbers. Nor any lights.'

Francesca consulted her note and took a few steps down another narrow alley. She stopped by a heavy door. 'I think it's this one,' she said and rapped loudly on the wood. There was no answer, nor was there any sound, movement or light to be seen inside. Both women pounded on the door but to no avail. There wasn't even a flicker of response from adjacent houses.

'Maybe he's done a runner,' said Francesca.

'Skipped town?' asked Donatella. 'Weren't the *carabinieri* watching him?'

'They were,' agreed Francesca, 'but they didn't have someone tailing him all the time. He had orders not to leave.'

'There's no sign of him – or Anna,' said Donatella. 'I hope the others find her.'

'Kiki and Gianfranco? If not, they're probably at it in the church by now.'

'Oh!' said Donatella, letting this thought sink in. 'What shall we do now?'

'This is the chance we've been waiting for,' said Francesca. 'We go inside and have a look around.'

Donatella stared in surprise. 'How can we do that?' she asked. 'Everything is locked up and I don't see any open windows.'

Francesca rummaged in her pack. 'Just let me check I have them with me,' she said.

'Have what?' asked Donatella. It was starting to rain.

'Yes! Here they are.' The young Italian held up what appeared to be a bunch of keys. She looked Donatella in the eye. 'How badly do you need this evidence?' she asked. 'Enough to break the law?'

'Why? What are you going to do?' asked Donatella, hedging a bit. 'Break in?'

'Breaking-and-entering was once one of my specialties,' said the young woman without a trace of irony. 'One of those things I learned in prison,' she added flatly.

'Oh,' said Donatella, lost for something suitable to say. The rain was picking up and Donatella stood in the doorway for shelter.

'It was a reward for services rendered,' said Francesca, examining a range of small tools on the key ring.

'What services?' blurted Donatella.

Her Italian friend rolled her amber eyes. 'Use your imagination, Donatella,' she said. 'How do you think young girls survive in a women's prison?'

'Oh,' said Donatella again.

Francesca turned businesslike. 'If this is going to work, you'd better guard the entrance to the alley. Watch that no one's coming,' she said. 'I'll have this door open in five minutes, ten at the outside. Whistle if anybody comes,' Francesca added. 'When I'm in, I'll whistle twice. Then come running. OK?'

Donatella nodded. 'Go for it,' she said and walked quickly to the end of the small lane and looked up and down the street. Apart from some people clustering to enter a bar a block away, all was quiet. She suppressed an urge to giggle: here she was, a tenured full professor from Boston, standing in the rain as the lookout for a convicted burglar!

She watched nervously for several minutes, noting more young men and women gathering at the bar entrance, but none ventured in their direction. Her watchfulness was brought to an end by two low whistles. Hurrying back, she found Francesca holding open the front door.

'I think the house is empty,' said Francesca. 'But we may not have long. Let's get moving.'

The two women quickly combed the house, checking

rooms as they went, making sure that shutters were closed before turning on the lights. On the top floor they swiftly explored a luxurious bedroom, but soon returned to the second floor that housed Temple-Clarke's private workroom, equipped with expensive office equipment and a couple of overstuffed couches.

'Let's focus here,' said Donatella. 'If there's something to be found I bet it's in this room. His studio must be somewhere else. We'll have to look there later when we find it.'

Donatella booted up the computer while Francesca pawed through filing cabinets. 'Don't let it get too chaotic,' said Donatella. 'We'll have to put everything back before we go.' She cursed quietly under her breath. 'He has a slew of passwords. I can't get into his files.'

The pair sat in concentrated silence for several minutes, fingers flicking through papers and across computer keys.

'Eureka!' shouted Francesca. 'Donatella, I've found something. I just played a hunch and looked under "R" for Roma. There's a fat file full of notes and pictures of those figurines that were in one of the photographs pushed under your door.'

'The Arretine Ware?' Donatella looked up excitedly.

'Yeah, exactly. The ones with big cocks,' said Francesca. 'Dating from about 100 BC until the late first century AD, *professoressa*,' she added with a little smirk.

Donatella grinned. 'I was unaware of your extensive knowledge of ancient pottery from central Etruria,' she said.

'I have unplumbed depths,' replied Francesca with an enigmatic smile.

'Let's see,' said Donatella, taking the file and spreading out the papers and pictures. 'Um, yes. Big cocks.' She glanced at Francesca. 'Remind you of anybody?'

'A couple of *carabinieri*, maybe?'

Donatella laughed and turned back to the documents, studying the typed lists and comparing them with the photographs. 'And as far as I can tell,' she said after several minutes, 'these numbers show the dates and quantities of shipments made to a company in Rome. And those...' she pointed to another dense column of numbers, '...show payments received.' She studied the photographs. 'But these were not shot in the studio,' she said, 'not like the one pushed under my door. These are illustrations of finished pieces.'

Francesca shrugged. 'Is that important?' she asked.

'Could be,' replied Donatella. 'I don't know yet.' She studied the images again. 'They really are very good. I'm impressed.' She motioned to her friend. 'Look, let me show you something. Forget the big penises. Do you see the facial features?'

Francesca nodded.

'Look at the smile. Does that remind you of anything?'

The blonde girl thought for a moment. 'It looks a bit like the expressions on the faces of old Greek statues. I've seen them in Kiki's art history books.'

Donatella gave Francesca's arm a squeeze. 'Very good! That's brilliant. You're quite right. It's known as "the Archaic smile," and it's common in Greek sculpture around 600 BC. That haunting expression vanishes from Greek art about one hundred years later, but reappears in Etruscan work around 100 BC. It's one of its defining characteristics. Temple-Clarke really knows his stuff, I'll give him that. He's captured it exactly.'

'Wow! *Càspita*! You know so much, Donatella!'

The art historian smiled at her friend. 'We're a team,' she said. She looked around the well-appointed office. 'There's a photocopier in the corner,' she said. 'I'll make a set for ourselves; then we can study them at our leisure.'

Francesca opened another filing cabinet. Her low whistle alerted her companion. 'Look at these!' she said. 'These *are* like the ones you brought home. Photos of Anna and that young boy.' She handed sheafs of images to Donatella.

The women studied them silently for several minutes. 'Look, here's Claudio!' exclaimed Donatella, setting one aside that showed Kiki's one-time lover having his cock sucked by Anna.

'God!' Francesca said, 'Kiki regrets getting involved with that *bastardo*!'

'It's impossible to identify the man in the others,' said Donatella. 'Do you think it's Temple-Clarke?'

'Who else would it be?' asked Francesca.

Donatella nodded. 'Yes, it all fits. I'll make copies of these, too,' she said, 'including the one with Claudio.' The older woman grinned at her friend. 'You think Kiki might want that as a souvenir?'

Francesca laughed. 'Let's keep it and surprise her,' she said. 'You do the copies, I'll put things away.'

Salvatore and Sandro walked up the staircase from the cells. It had been a long rainy drive from Rome with their prisoner. The *capitano* in particular was in a sour mood.

Guiseppe, the desk officer, called across the lobby. 'Hey, Salvatore! I forgot to tell you. Your girlfriend phoned, looking for you.'

Salvatore was immediately alert. 'When was this? Was anything wrong? What did she want?'

'Just the address of the place you were meeting her.'

'What place? What do you mean?'

'The Englishman's house, *il signor* Temple-Clarke,' Guiseppe said hesitantly, catching sight of the look on his colleague's face. 'I thought ... But you ...' he began, looking perplexedly between Salvatore and the doorway leading down to the cells.

The duty officer had no time to finish the sentence or get answers to his half-formed questions. With a muttered oath Salvatore dashed back into the rain, followed by a puzzled Sandro. Salvatore started the car and shot away from the kerb before Sandro had fully closed his door.

'What's going on? What's the rush?' asked Sandro peevishly.

'Francesca's up to something,' said Salvatore, manoeuvering the Fiat expertly through the narrow streets. 'Why would she go to Temple-Clarke's house? I bet Donatella's with her. They're up to mischief, I know it. That little vixen! I should tie her up and give her a good spanking!' Thoughts of his lover's naked body lifted the policeman's mood. 'She's the sexiest woman I've ever been with,' he said. 'She fucks like the devil herself. Some nights we do it five or six times,' he added boastfully. 'I'm always hard and she's always wet.' He looked over at his colleague. 'How about you and Donatella? Does she still want it all night long?'

It was Sandro's turn to smile. 'I reckon she's as good or better than Francesca,' he said. 'And she can be really kinky, too. Sometimes she likes me to tie her up and be rough.'

'Not violent?' Salvatore was a little alarmed.

'No, just spanking and talking dirty. She's a great fuck!' he added admiringly.

'Does she do it with other men?' asked Salvatore.

'Not as far as I know. Not since that guy in the bar. Why?'

'I'd like to . . .' Salvatore hinted.

The speculation was cut off as they turned a corner. 'Go slowly,' said Sandro. 'We're here.'

In the *borgo* where Temple-Clarke lived, Salvatore parked on a side-street near the Englishman's house.

'What are they doing here anyway?' Sandro said.

'If I were to guess, I'd say little Miss Francesca is back at her old tricks of breaking-and-entering. I bet they're in there right now, looking for evidence. They think they can do the job better than the *carabinieri*!'

'Maybe we should show them who's boss tonight,' Sandro suggested as he got out of the vehicle, slamming the door. 'Come on, Salvatore. Now's our chance. They're at Temple-Clarke's and breaking the law! We'll catch them red-handed. We could even get out the handcuffs. Donatella would like that.' He looked at his colleague. 'Do you really want her?'

Salvatore nodded.

'Well,' mused Sandro, 'once she's tied up, we could both have her. You ever done that?'

'Done what?'

'Had two women at once.'

'Oh, sure. You know how wild Francesca is,' bragged Salvatore.

Sandro laughed. 'Look,' he said, 'if you get to fuck Donatella, I get Francesca.'

'She'd have to agree,' said Salvatore. Already hard, he touched his raised dick through the trousers of his uniform, looked at his watch and made a decision. 'OK, come on. We're off duty in ten minutes. Let's find out what they're doing, Sandro. Act tough about it!'

'I take it that's an order, *sir*?'

'*Assolutmente, il mio compagno.*'

Inside the stone villa, Donatella had nearly finished making several sets of photocopies when she heard a loud hammering on the door downstairs. The two women looked at each other, sharing expressions of alarm and panic. There was nowhere to run.

'Oh, no!' gasped Donatella, sucking in her breath. 'Is that the police? Have we set off an alarm?'

'Oh, shit!' said Francesca. 'I bypassed the one on the door. Maybe there are motion sensors or something. I haven't finished putting these away!'

Another great battery of thumping echoed up the staircase, followed by a familiar voice. 'Open up! *Polizia!*'

'It's Salvatore!' said Francesca. 'Jesus. I'm in for it now!'

'I'd better go down and let him in,' said Donatella. 'You stay up here. Let me handle it. I'll take the blame. You're still on probation. Put everything we've found in that drawer.'

The two policemen burst into the hall as soon as Donatella slipped the lock. They both looked furious. 'Where is she?' demanded Salvatore.

'It isn't her fault. I . . .' she began, but both men raced up the stairs two at a time. Donatella hurried after them.

In the office, Salvatore glared at the two women. The *capitano* strode up and down, slapping one gloved fist into the other.

'I don't know who to yell at first!' He pointed at his girlfriend. 'You, Francesca, for slipping back into your old habits – no, don't deny it,' Salvatore wagged his finger ferociously at her. 'I know you picked the lock to break in here. I should throw you in jail right now!'

He wheeled back to Donatella, licking his lips as he spoke, 'And you, *professoressa*, you should know better. This isn't one of your silly American Nancy Drew mysteries! This is dangerous! You can't go round breaking the law just because it suits you!'

'How do you know about Nancy Drew?' asked Donatella disingenuously.

The policeman brushed away Donatella's enquiry. He swung round to face Francesca again. 'And where is Kiki, our little miss firebrand? Why isn't she here, too, egging you on! The three of you are supposed to stay together!'

'Kiki's with Gianfranco,' said Donatella, trying to stem the flow. 'They're searching for . . .' but she didn't finish.

'So della Parigi is her new boyfriend!' exclaimed Sandro. 'I knew she was seeing someone new. I could tell!'

'Goddammit!' interrupted Salvatore. 'She's always seeing someone. At least it's not some cheap crook like Claudio Pozzi this time!' He turned on the two women and repeated his threat. 'I should bust both of you right now, put you in a cell and throw away the key.'

Donatella tried to intervene but Francesca beat her to it. 'Salvatore,' she said. 'Calm down, sweetheart. Stop acting like some character in a melodrama! This isn't a *film-noir*. I know you're angry with us, but we found some very important material! We came here because we were worried about a young girl who . . . who's involved with Temple-Clarke. She was going to meet us this evening and didn't show up. Kiki and Gianfranco are looking for her now. We thought Temple-Clarke might have harmed her.' She caught hold of her lover's arm. Beneath her thin dress her breasts jostled against him, rubbing and bouncing against his body. 'Shouldn't we show you what we have and then get out of here? Temple-Clarke may be back anytime.'

Donatella saw the policeman's dark eyes lock onto his girlfriend's breasts. She heard him murmur, 'Oh God, those tits of yours get me every time!' He held her tightly.

'Temple-Clarke won't be going anywhere,' said Sandro from the other side of the room.

'What do you mean?' asked Donatella, turning to face her lover. 'Where is he?'

'He's at the police station,' said Sandro. 'We brought him back from Rome and were about to question him when Guiseppe told Salvatore you'd called. We put the bastard into a cell and raced over here. We had no idea what you were up to.'

'What was he doing in Rome?' asked Francesca, stroking Salvatore's leg. 'We thought he couldn't leave town.'

'That's right,' Sandro nodded, moving to Donatella's side. 'We want him here where we can keep an eye on him. But one of our colleagues spotted him getting on the Rome express early yesterday, so we called ahead and the Rome police picked him up at the other end. We drove down and brought him back. But he clammed up tight. Wouldn't say a thing except to swear at us in that smarmy accent of his.'

Under the influence of Francesca's sexy stroking, the police captain's demeanour had softened considerably. 'OK,' he said. 'As we're all here, we might as well look at what you've found. I don't know what the hell we'll do with it, though.' He scowled again. 'It wouldn't be admissible in court as you obtained it by illegal means. Do you realise that?'

His female audience returned his gaze with a mixture of apology and challenge.

'I'll call the station and tell them to hold Temple-Clarke for another few hours,' he said, flipping open his phone and issuing his orders. 'We've got work to do here.' He turned to Sandro, his voice hardening. 'Time for the cuffs, *tenente*!'

Before Donatella knew what was happening her wrists were being held together by the cold metal of Sandro's handcuffs, expertly applied. 'Hey!' she cried. 'What the . . .?'

'You next, Francesca,' said Sandro and quickly pinned the blonde's arms behind her while Salvatore slipped on the metal bands.

'Cut it out, Salvatore,' shouted Francesca. 'This isn't funny!'

The two policemen laughed. 'Oh, I'm sorry,' said Salvatore, 'but yes, it is. It's very funny indeed. You're both under arrest for breaking-and-entering. You're our prisoners, now,' he winked at Sandro, 'and completely at our mercy.'

'What punishment fits the crime?' asked Sandro, returning to Donatella's side and holding her tight as she flailed in his grip.

'First we must strip-search the suspects,' ordered Salvatore, who was similarly restraining the wriggling Francesca. 'We must make sure they have no stolen property hidden about their person, or *inside* their person. We must personally search every possible hiding place – very thoroughly.'

'Perhaps we should check each other's work, too,' suggested Sandro, barely able to keep a straight face.

Donatella's initial alarm dissipated as her captors' plan became clear. Evidently Francesca had come to the same conclusion as she, too, had stopped squirming and protesting.

'You bastards!' the Italian said, but her amber eyes were sparkling with anticipation.

Donatella watched with mounting excitement as Sandro pulled down the jersey summer skirt she was wearing, quickly followed by her thong. Obligingly she stepped out of them. Having dispensed with a bra unless working at the college, her nipples tightened as the policemen's hands unbuttoned her silk shirt and exposed her breasts. Now all she wore was a pair of delicately laced sandals.

Francesca was similarly stripped, standing virtually

naked in front of Salvatore. Both policemen ran their gloved hands over the women's exposed flesh in a parody of police procedure. Donatella's pulse raced when Salvatore came over to her and repeated the process while Sandro fondled Francesca.

'Lie down on the couch, Donatella,' Salvatore ordered, 'and spread your legs. You too, Francesca. Sandro, make sure she does as she's told.'

Both women soon lay spread-eagled on the two couches, naked except for their open shirts bunched around their arms to restrict their movement further. Both officers remained fully dressed and sported huge erections straining their uniform trousers.

'Do your worst, fascist pigs!' hissed Francesca, getting into the spirit of the charade. 'We'll never tell you where it's hidden!'

Donatella's giggle was cut short by Salvatore's finger, encased in a leather glove, entering her pussy. She was so wet, it slid in easily, followed by a second. The texture of the leather inside her made the American gasp with pleasure. She bucked against Salvatore's hand and was thrilled when his thumb circled her clit.

'Just checking,' said Salvatore softly as he withdrew his fingers and examined the juices on the leather. 'Ah,' he said. 'Very wet. I think we need to check more closely,' and he knelt between Donatella's legs and explored her with his lips and tongue.

The brunette glanced across the room and saw Sandro similarly engaged with his face buried in Francesca's pussy. Tingles of pleasure from Donatella's clit announced Salvatore's single-minded devotion to his task.

'Oh, God, Salvatore, do that more. Make me come,' she said, panting, as his face bobbed up and down between her legs, his tongue probing ever deeper into the slick folds.

'Not so fast, Donatella,' said her new lover. 'You wait there. Sandro and I have to get undressed.

The two policemen stood and slowly, tantalisingly, shed their Armani-designed uniforms while Donatella and Francesca gazed impatiently, their hands firmly shackled.

'Jesus!' said Francesca. 'I can't wait for you two!' and she rolled off the couch and crawled over to Donatella. To Donatella's shock and delight, the young woman knelt between her legs and licked her with unerring precision. A whole new wave of sensation flooded through Donatella's body at the woman's touch.

'Oh, Fran!' she cried. 'How do you do that?' She bucked and writhed under her friend's expert technique.

Salvatore and Sandro, now fully naked, hauled Francesca off the panting American. 'That was very bad,' said the senior policeman severely. 'For that you must both receive extra punishment.'

'Oh, please,' cooed Francesca. 'Now.' Both women eyed the two naked cocks that promised them satisfaction. 'God,' said the ginger-blond, 'I want both of them.'

'Bend over the couch,' ordered Sandro. 'Both of you! Hands in front. Bums in the air!'

From her supine position Donatella felt Salvatore's unfamiliar cock slide into her wet tunnel. She gasped with pleasure and looked sideways, where Sandro was fully embedded inside Francesca. Taking her from behind, he was holding Francesca's breasts, moulding them with his hands. With wild and indecorous delight Francesca writhed and squealed Sandro's name over and over.

Salvatore's penis was thrusting hard into Donatella, his fingers probing her anus. She pushed back at him as hard as she could, and was rewarded by a growl and a slap on her arse.

'You sexy bitch!' he said. 'You want some more?'

'Oh, pound me, Salvatore! Pound me!'

The man's balls slapped against the American's arse as he redoubled his efforts. But his efforts were short-lived. 'Oh, God,' he cried. 'I'm coming! I can't stop!'

Donatella felt the captain's dick spurt inside her and moments later heard Sandro's answering yell as he shot his load inside Francesca. Her own release was some way off, and she took matters into her own hands as Salvatore withdrew his slick cock from her tunnel. She stood up and elbowed Salvatore aside, then nudged Sandro with her manacled arms so his softening dick slid out of Francesca.

'Francesca,' she said urgently. 'Lick me. I need to come.'

Francesca giggled. 'Stand back, boys,' she said, 'and watch how it's really done!'

Donatella lay back on the couch once more and Francesca took up position between her widely spread legs. Donatella felt her sex lips open to the woman's talented tongue. She held her girlfriend's face to her crotch with her cuffed hands and smiled at the two men, avidly watching the girl sex and playing with their cocks. 'Just like your fantasies,' she mocked them gently, 'watching two girls get off. Ohhhh! Jesus, Fran. More! More! Oh, God, this is great.' A surge of pleasure washed through her body as Francesca's tongue worked its magic.

Through half-closed eyes, Donatella saw the two policemen were fully hard again, pumping their cocks as they devoured the sight of her orgasm. Francesca gave one last nuzzle to Donatella's clit and stood, her face smeared with her friend's juice.

She held out her wrists to Sandro. 'Here,' she said, 'take these stupid things off and we'll go up to the bedroom. Then it's my turn to have some fun.'

Soon all four were sprawled across Temple-Clarke's large bed. A quick search of the drawers in the bedside chest had revealed a variety of thick viscous lubes. Francesca's eyes sparkled. 'You know where these go?' she asked Salvatore.

'Up your beautiful arse, my dear,' replied her lover.

'Do it then,' she ordered, kneeling in front of him. She gasped as Salvatore slid first one, then two slick fingers past her tight arsehole. 'Now your cock, dammit,' Francesca yelled. 'Slide it in!'

Caught in the wild eroticism of the moment, Donatella squirmed down the bed and positioned herself between Francesca's thighs. From there she had an excellent view as Salvatore, standing on the floor at the foot of the bed, eased his long cock deep into the girl's anus.

'Let me eat you, Fran,' pleaded Donatella, wanting, even as her old lover Sandro caressed her, to return the pleasure she'd received from her girlfriend.

With a sigh of satisfaction, Francesca lowered herself onto Donatella's face, allowing the American to drink the nectar from her slit. For the first time in her life, Donatella tasted another woman and felt a clit between her lips and against her tongue.

'What about me?' complained Sandro, still caressing Donatella.

Francesca giggled, her body shaking from Salvatore's thrusts.

'Donatella's pussy,' she gasped.

Donatella was delighted as the second policeman's hands raised her hips and parted her sex lips. A moment later his cock slid inside, filling her with its familiar bulk. Fingers, smaller than Sandro's, found her clit. Donatella moaned with delight and licked her girlfriend with extra passion as the Italian girl excited her with an expert touch.

Sandro's deep laugh echoed around the room. 'Holy Mother of God!' he swore. 'What a sight!'

For several moments the foursome became one unified sexual entity, nerve endings alight, with sensations sweeping from one body to another. Donatella came first, with Sandro's cock inside her, Francesca's fingers making her clit buzz and the taste of the blonde's sex juice all over her tongue. Urgent motions of the Italian girl writhing against Donatella's face made the older woman pick up the pace and soon she felt the wash of more liquid as Francesca came with a shuddering moan.

Salvatore and Sandro found the spectacle of two orgasmic women too much for their self-control. Almost simultaneously the partners shot their loads deep into the women's bodies, filling Francesca's arse and Donatella's pussy.

Exhausted, the quartet lay back on the renegade Englishman's sheets. Francesca started to smirk, then giggle, and soon all four were laughing at the humour of the policeman's silly games and the crude intensity of their couplings.

'This is like old times,' said Francesca.

Donatella raised an eyebrow, 'How come?

'When I was a kid, we used to break into rich people's houses in Florence for kicks. My boyfriends and I would steal their jewellery to buy drugs. If we had some coke with us, we'd snort several lines and fuck in their beds. It seemed like great fun at the time.'

'And look where it got you,' said Salvatore, suddenly serious.

'You don't miss all that, do you, Fran?' asked Donatella.

Francesca smiled. 'No,' she said. 'I like the friends I have now much better.' She reached over and stroked

Donatella's breast. The professor rolled over and kissed Francesca full on the lips, a deep lingering kiss.

'This may be like old times for you,' she said with a smile, 'but it's all new for me!'

21 *Il Rittorno al Dovere* (Return to Duty)

In the exhausted afterglow Salvatore was the first to refocus on business. He walked unsteadily downstairs and returned with armfuls of miscellaneous clothing, which he tossed casually across the furnishings of the posh bedroom. He slowly pulled on trousers, shrugging off Donatella's attempts to impede his progress. 'It's time to get back to work,' he said as he fastened his belt. He kicked Sandro awake.

Sandro slowly extracted himself from between Francesca's legs, as she made a grab for his dick. 'Give it to me one more time!' she begged.

'Francesca! Get serious for a moment.' said Salvatore. 'Now, all of you, listen!' Once he had the attention of everyone in the group, the senior policeman laid out his plan of action. 'First,' he said, 'none of us must ever speak about this episode. It never happened. Is that absolutely clear? *È chiaro?*'

'*Si, capisco benissimo,*' said Francesca.

Donatella nodded with a little wink.

'Sandro! Back to duty, *tenente!*'

Sandro dropped his hands from Francesca's breasts. '*Si, il mio capitano,*' he said, but he couldn't hide his big Cheshire cat grin, nor his ever-burgeoning erection.

'We have work to do. Francesca. *Café!*' Salvatore ordered.

Francesca jumped up, pulled on her blouse and skirt, and trotted down to the kitchen to make coffee. She saw a look of surprise on Donatella's face, but she didn't mind humouring her lover from time to time. A few minutes later she set a tray of freshly brewed coffee and cups on the desk in Temple-Clarke's office. She looked at her watch. It said 2.30 a.m. 'It's ready!' she yelled up the stairs.

The others joined her, each more or less dressed. Sandro was still trying to smooth out his crumpled uniform. 'Is everything tidy upstairs?' she asked.

Salvatore nodded.

'OK. Now look at these.' Francesca opened the drawer where she and Donatella had stashed the stack of documents and photographs they had discovered a few hours before. 'Look,' she urged the two policemen. 'These figures show the expenses of what appears to be an art forgery business.' She turned to the tall American. 'Tell them, Donatella.'

Taking sips of coffee, the men listened as the professor quickly filled them in about the fake figurines. 'When we cross-reference this information with the irregularities that Kiki and I found in the college budget, we may be able to prove that he was stealing from the college to finance his forgery scam,' she concluded. 'I think we've got him!'

Sandro took that moment to hurry to the bathroom. '*Scusi*,' he said. 'I'll be right back. Lots of sex always makes me pee.'

In his partner's absence Salvatore studied the documents. Despite his disapproval of the women's methods, he looked impressed. 'But . . .,' he began.

Francesca cut him off, waving the photographs in his direction. 'See these, too' she said. 'They show Temple-Clarke having sex with teenagers.'

Salvatore grabbed the photos and studied them. 'How do you know it's Temple-Clarke?' he asked. 'None show his face.'

245

'We have others,' said Francesca, 'in Donatella's office, that reveal it's Temple-Clarke.'

'How did you get them?' asked Salvatore. 'Not another burglary?' He stared pointedly at Francesca.

She stuck out her tongue at him. 'Don't look like that, Salvatore!' she said. 'Someone slipped them under Donatella's door.'

'Who?'

'The girl in the photographs,' said Francesca. 'Her name's Anna. We met her last night. But now she's missing. She told us Temple-Clarke is behind this whole scheme, and we thought at first he himself might have told her to plant the photographs, to distract us from the inquiry.'

'What do you mean?' Salvatore looked puzzled.

'We speculated that he thought we'd be satisfied with a forced resignation, to avoid public scandal. If we closed the case without probing any deeper, it would allow him to escape any criminal prosecution for embezzlement.'

'Hmmm.' Salvatore appeared to consider this. 'Would that have been Miss Kiki Lee's theory, by any chance?' he asked, turning to Donatella with the hint of a smile.

'Yes, actually,' she replied. 'It makes a certain amount of sense, but I'm not convinced.'

'I think this Anna is devious,' said Francesca. 'I don't trust her one iota. How do we know she's telling the truth, even now?'

'What *do* you know about Anna?' asked Salvatore.

'She's a little slut who fucks older men for money,' replied Francesca unthinkingly.

Salvatore's sharp look brought Francesca up short, her expression a mask of contrition. '*Merda!* Don't say it, Sal. I'm sorry. That was cruel of me. I could be talking about myself a few years ago.' The young Italian girl blushed in embarrassment.

Salvatore smiled gently, his severity evaporating. '*Si, la mia cara,*' he said, affectionately petting her golden hair. 'Like when we met. But not now, eh?' The policeman reached out and cuddled his lover to his chest.

Francesca felt a warm rush of affection. She looked up into Salvatore's dark brown eyes. 'No,' she said. 'Certainly not now.' This was deeper than her usual feelings. What would it be like to commit to just one man? What a thought! But it might be worth trying.

Salvatore gave her one last squeeze and then returned to business. 'Sit down everybody and listen closely.' He looked hard at Sandro who had returned to the group, zipping up his dark blue trousers with their broad red stripe. 'What I'm going to suggest involves bending the law. If we are discovered, Sandro, we'll probably be drummed out the force or demoted at least. Does that bother you?'

Sandro shrugged. 'You're the boss,' he said. 'Just make sure we're *not* discovered.'

The *capitano* turned to the two women. 'As you two have already broken the law just by being here, I don't suppose you'd be too squeamish about another little violation?'

'What do you have in mind?' asked Donatella.

'You recall what I said earlier about none of this material being admissible in court because it was obtained illegally?'

The women nodded.

'However,' he said, 'if I were to get a search warrant, return later today and find all the same material, it would be perfectly in order to use as evidence. *Mi capisce?*'

'Do we have enough evidence to go before a judge?' asked Sandro.

His superior nodded. 'I think so. The facts that Temple-Clarke left town suspiciously and won't cooperate by answering questions, combined with the shady finances at the college that Donatella and Kiki discovered quite legally, should be sufficient.' He surveyed his small band. 'Are we all agreed on this?' he asked. 'In my book this is a case of the ends justifying the means. Anybody's scruples get in the way?'

'Not enough to argue with your plan,' said Donatella. 'Go ahead. Nail the bastard.'

'Amen!' said Francesca. 'Just what Kiki would say.' She reached to squeeze Donatella's hand.

'OK,' said Salvatore. 'Here's what we do. Erase as many traces of our presence here as we can. I'll make sure the fingerprint squad does a sloppy job in the morning. If you two accompany us,' he said looking at the women severely, '. . . and touch lots of things "by accident," that should cover up your prints already on papers and surfaces in the villa. It would be more suspicious to wipe surfaces clean than to have lots of different prints.'

'What about the neighbours?' asked Francesca. 'Someone might have seen or heard you come in. You made a lot of noise.'

'We'll say we were responding to a call of suspicious activity in the neighbourhood. I don't think anybody will probe too deeply.'

'And Guiseppe?' continued Francesca. 'He knows we were going to meet you here. That's what I told him when I phoned.' She had the grace to blush at her lie.

Salvatore shook his head. 'He won't be a problem. I've covered for that lazy bastard often enough. He owes me.'

'Right,' said Donatella. 'Let's get on with it.' She picked up the pages of figures. 'These were all in this filing drawer,' she said, slipping them carefully back into place, 'and the photographs . . .' She looked around. 'Where are . . . oh, pass them here, Sandro.'

But Sandro was rooted to the spot. His face suddenly pale. 'Holy Mother of God!' he swore. 'The evil bastard! The stupid, stupid girl!' He whirled towards Donatella, his face a mask of anguish. He brandished a photograph in his American lover's face. 'This is Anna Gentileschi! My niece! Temple-Clarke has made a whore out of my niece! My brother's little girl. I used to play with her when she was a kid. My God, I'll kill that English motherfucker! I'll blow his fucking brains out!'

He crumpled the photograph, hurled it on the floor and lunged for the door, evading Salvatore's restraining arm and sharp orders to stop. He raced down the stairs two at a time, followed closely by Salvatore, still shouting futile commands. Francesca and Donatella followed the two *carabinieri* into the narrow street, only to see Sandro throw himself into the police car and hurtle away.

'*Merda!*' swore Salvatore, and spoke rapidly into his radio. 'Guiseppe! This is urgent. Sandro's on his way. I think he's going to attack the Englishman ... Yes, Temple-Clarke ... Don't ask, I'll explain later. Stop him, *capisce*? Do whatever you have to ... Yes, throw the stupid bugger in a cell if you have to. Just don't let Sandro anywhere near the prisoner. *Capisce? Si*, I'll be right there.'

Salvatore swung back to face Francesca. 'You started this with your foolish little tricks,' he said, angrily. 'Now make sure you finish it. Go back upstairs and make sure *everything* is back in its proper place. When you've finished leave as quietly as you can.'

Francesca nodded meekly, subdued by her lover's anger. She looked around them. Despite the commotion they had made, the alley was still deserted. The thick stone walls and small windows stared back blankly, the night-time hum of the city muffled in the rabbit warren of medieval lanes. They might get away with this.

Her lover broke in on her thoughts. 'You got all that?' he asked.

'*Si, si.*' said Francesca. To her relief Salvatore's expression visibly relented and he pulled her face towards his.

'Don't worry, sweetheart,' he said. 'It will be all right. Sandro will calm down. I'll take care of it. Go home after you've finished here. Stay safe. I'll see you in the morning.' He bent down to kiss her, and Francesca responded fiercely, kissing him hard and crushing him to her body.

'I love you,' she whispered as they drew apart. 'Be careful.'

Around noon, several squad cars pulled up outside Temple-Clarke's house. Salvatore leaped out of the first vehicle. Flaunting the search warrant, he led an assorted team of *carabinieri* officers and technicians accompanied by Donatella and Francesca as 'liaison assistants' between the police probe and the university investigation.

Donatella punched a speed dial button on her *telefonino*. Kiki answered on the other end after several rings. 'We're here,' Donatella informed her assistant. 'Just about to go in the house. Everything all right your end?'

'Oh, yes,' said Kiki. 'Everything's fine.'

'Is Gianfranco there?'

'Yeah, he's here.'

Donatella heard a small sigh escape her friend's lips. 'What are you doing?' she asked suspiciously. An image formed in her mind. 'You're making love again, aren't you?'

'Have you got x-ray eyes?' asked Kiki. 'How did you know?'

'I know you,' said Donatella with a laugh. 'The two of you are inseparable.'

'Yes,' agreed Kiki, with another heavy sigh. 'Ummm. Literally.'

Donatella shook her head. 'Stay where you can answer the phone if we need you,' she ordered. 'I'll call you later and we'll meet at my office.'

'OK. Gianfranco has to go out soon, so I'll go with him. Good luck. *Ciao!*'

The professor rang off and looked around her. Sandro was bustling about giving orders. He looked his normal self, but Donatella could tell he was wound up tight as a spring beneath his official demeanour. Salvatore had given no details, but there had apparently been quite a scene at the police station the previous evening, with Sandro having to be restrained by several fellow officers before he calmed down. Temple-Clarke had by all accounts been terrified and his cynical veneer had crumpled, to be replaced by desperate pleas of his innocence that fell on very deaf ears. The Englishman remained in the cells under close guard.

Following Salvatore's plan, the two women wandered through the rooms in the house, following their path of the night before, trying to look official and useful, but managing to touch doorknobs, drawer pulls, filing cabinets and the like, leaving innocent fingerprints to mask any traces left from their unlawful entry. As the technicians lifted prints from files and photographs, the amateur burglars tried to inveigle themselves into the process but were eventually warned off by the frustrated technicians.

Salvatore pulled the pair to one side. 'That's enough for now,' he said. 'You'll look suspicious if you fiddle with anything else. I think we're covered. Exactly where did you put the photographs with Anna? Sandro would like to make those disappear.'

Donatella opened her briefcase and passed the *capitano* a manila folder. 'They're in here,' she said. 'I lifted them from their hiding place before anybody else got there. This may be a good time for you to take them into "protective custody."'

Salvatore nodded. 'Good work, Donatella. Sandro will be grateful.' He opened the folder and flicked through the images, selecting two and putting them into a briefcase of his own. 'I think I'll keep these as back-up,' he said with a thin smile. 'We wouldn't want Sandro destroying *all* the evidence, would we?'

'There are others in my office,' offered Donatella.

'Excellent. Can you bring them down to the station after we've finished here?' asked Salvatore.

Donatella nodded and the team trooped back downstairs, to find Sandro in the street with a shiny white 5-series BMW. 'This belongs to the Englishman,' Sandro explained. 'It was garaged around the corner. I did manage to get that, and the key, out of the bastard,' he said grimly. 'I'm taking it in for forensic examination. You never know what we might find.'

Salvatore nodded his approval and Sandro sped away. 'Everybody back to the station,' Salvatore ordered his team. He turned to his girlfriend. 'Francesca, will you please go back to the college with Donatella and bring the photographs to me? Then go back to the college or go home.' His eyes embraced the pair. 'You've done your part, ladies.' The *carabiniere* gave Donatella a wink and a smile. 'We'd better play by the book from now on, hadn't we, *dottoressa*?'

Donatella replied in kind. 'Absolutely, *capitano*,' she said, keeping a straight face. 'Let the wheels of justice grind onwards. Who are we to interfere with the majesty of the law?'

Salvatore clicked his heels and snapped a salute. '*Arrivederci, dottoressa*,' he said. Speaking in an aside to his girlfriend, he added. 'Hurry up with the photos, Francesca. We need them as soon as possible.'

'I'll bring them down right away, *il mio caro*.'

Salvatore smiled. 'Thanks, sweetheart,' he said.

The two women walked quickly back to the college, excited by the turn of events.

'Do you really think we have him?' asked Francesca.

'Yes, especially if the police can prove he was behind the hotel break-in and the attack,' said Donatella. 'I hope he'll break down and confess, but something tells me he won't make it that easy.'

At that moment, a familiar figure, head buried in a book, turned the corner and nearly bumped into the pair. 'Oh! *Scusi, signore*, sorry ladies!' he said. He looked up and a smile of pleased recognition lit his face. Donatella could see why Kiki found him so attractive. 'Oh, it's you, *dottoressa* di'Bianchi. Hello, Francesca. I'm sorry, I wasn't paying attention.' Despite his good humour, Gianfranco della Parigi was blushing.

Francesca took his arm and gave him a big kiss. 'Where's Kiki?' she asked.

'I'm meeting her at the bar down the street.'

Just then Kiki appeared with a freshly scooped ice-cream cone. 'Hi, darling,' she said to the tall Italian boy, giving him a *pistacchio*-flavoured kiss. 'I've missed you. It must have been all of ten minutes. Hi, girls,' she added by way of greeting. 'Gianfranco and I tried and tried phoning you two last night. We were worried until we realised that you were probably being well protected by the *carabinieri*! How *is* the life of crime this morning?'

'It has its compensations,' said Francesca.

Kiki raised an eyebrow. 'Anybody going to tell me?' she asked.

'Let's just say Donatella had some new experiences,' she replied, with a smile.

Kiki studied the older American appreciatively. 'I knew she'd be a good student,' she said. 'I don't know that there's much more we can teach her. What do you think, Fran? Should we give her an "A" and let her graduate?'

It was Donatella's turn to blush. 'I'd like a few more lessons first,' she said slyly.

Kiki laughed. 'It's a deal!' She looked at her watch. 'Donatella, you don't need me for a while, do you? We were going for a beer.'

The professor laughed. 'We do have plenty to tell you, but it can wait,' she said. 'Go ahead and enjoy yourselves!'

Donatella's last words were drowned out by a roar and a rattle as a battered van sped along the cobbles of the narrow street. All four pedestrians looked up in alarm. The vehicle showed no signs of slowing. Indeed it seemed to be bearing down on them. Tinted glass and grime hid the driver from view.

Donatella froze on the spot before being knocked to the ground by a large form, the two bodies rolling together into a doorway. The van raced past with a loud snarl and squeal of brakes, tyres spinning mere inches from her face.

Gianfranco stood up quickly and eased Donatella to her feet. 'I'm sorry, *dottoressa*,' he said. 'I hope I didn't hurt you, knocking you down like that. I was afraid you wouldn't get out of the way in time.'

Kiki and Francesca rushed over to their friends. 'Are you OK?' they asked in unison.

Donatella dusted herself down. 'Yes, I think so, thanks to Gianfranco. God, do you think that was deliberate? They could have killed us.' A small crowd was gathering, but Francesca shooed them away. 'It's OK. *Va bene*. My friend just fell down,' she said.

Donatella looked in dismay at the dirty smudges on her recently purchased silk shirt and black cotton chinos. One of the French cuffs on the shirt was torn and her new open-weave leather ankle boots were badly scuffed.

'They were aiming at you,' said Francesca. 'I watched. As we scattered, the driver, whoever it was, seemed to steer straight for you.'

'Damn,' said Donatella. 'This isn't over, is it? I thought we'd won now Temple-Clarke's in jail. Do you think that was Claudio driving the van?'

Kiki winced at the sound of her one-time lover's name. 'Couldn't tell,' she said. 'The windows were too dark. I did notice one thing though. The van had a Rome license plate.'

'Maybe it's the people in Rome who Temple-Clarke does business with,' said Francesca. 'That would make sense. If Donatella was killed, she couldn't testify against Temple-Clarke.'

Donatella looked sombre.

'Who's Claudio?' asked Gianfranco.

Now it was Kiki's turn to go red in the face. 'Let's just say he was a big mistake,' she said.

'He was the last guy she fucked before you, Gianfranco' said Francesca, not mincing words.

'Delicately put,' commented Donatella. 'But if someone just tried to kill me, or us, a discussion about Kiki's sex life has to wait. Don't worry, Gianfranco,' she said with a smile, 'from what I hear Claudio is no match for you. He's history.' Donatella was rewarded with a shy smile and she took the tall youth's hand in hers. 'I sincerely thank you, Gianfranco. You saved my life just now. I want you to know how grateful I am. You could have been hurt yourself.' She looked into the young man's thickly lashed, chocolate brown eyes. They were as deep and attractive as she remembered from that lustful afternoon in her office. She kissed her fingertips and placed them on his lips. 'Thank you.'

Kiki put her arms around Gianfranco's waist from behind, holding him tight. 'You get a special reward,' she said.

'First,' said Donatella, 'we need to go to my office for the photographs so Fran can take them to Salvatore. We can tell him about this hit-and-run attempt as well. After what happened I think we should all stay together. Agreed?'

She received confirming nods and the quartet stepped briskly up the hill to the front door of the college. Gianfranco walked in front, arm-in-arm with Kiki. Francesca nudged Donatella in the ribs. 'Look at them,' she whispered. 'Who would have guessed?'

Once inside her office the first thing Donatella saw was a memo from Ian Ramsey slipped under her door. She examined it impatiently.

'Jesus! I can't deal with that now!' she exclaimed and tossed the paper onto her desk.

'What is it?' asked Kiki.

'Something from Ramsey,' replied Donatella. 'He's still after the director's job. He made a list of all the reasons he should be appointed. I'll handle that later.' She turned to the filing cabinet where she and Kiki had stored the photos, but when she lifted out the file, to her puzzlement and dismay, there were only two images in the folder. The studio shot with the figurines in the background was missing.

'Kiki,' she asked, 'You didn't put it anywhere else, did you?

Kiki gave her professor a withering look.

'Sorry,' apologised Donatella. 'Stupid question. Of course you didn't. But where the hell is it?'

Francesca was examining the metal of the filing cabinet. 'These look like new scratches here,' she said. 'I think someone broke in and took it. They were good,' she added appreciatively, as she moved to examine the door to the room. 'They got through this door and the filing cabinet, leaving hardly a trace.'

Donatella slumped behind her desk. 'How ironic,' she said. 'Tit for tat. But why take just one and leave the other two? And who?'

'Could it be Anna?' asked Kiki. 'Or Claudio? We know it couldn't be Temple-Clarke; he's in custody.'

'This doesn't make sense,' complained Donatella. 'First, Anna delivers the photographs, to help us, she says, but we have only her word for that. Then she disappears. Someone tries to run us down – that couldn't be Anna – and one photograph is stolen back. And all this time Temple-Clarke is either in Rome or in custody.' She turned to Kiki. 'We know Claudio is involved as some kind of accomplice,' she said. 'But does he have the brains to organise something like this?'

'It wasn't his *brain* I was interested in,' Kiki said with a slightly embarrassed moué.

'Claudio could have been driving the van,' said Francesca, thinking out loud. 'And for all we know, he could have been in the Mercedes as well.'

'We saw two people in the Mercedes,' Kiki reminded her. 'The other might have been Temple-Clarke.'

'No,' said Donatella, shaking her head. 'He was seen by faculty at a reception at that time. Remember? But he could have been the other person who attacked *me*,' she added. 'His eyes were in very bad shape the next day, allergies or no allergies.'

'That leaves the vandalism at your hotel and the threatening phone call unaccounted for,' said Kiki.

'And the company in Rome,' added Francesca.

'Ah, yes,' said Donatella. 'The mysterious people from Rome. I wonder if Salvatore knows anything about them. He said he was going to have a colleague down there check the address and ask around. He didn't want to order a full-scale search of their premises until we had more definitive evidence.'

The academic looked around at her younger companions. 'Gianfranco, you'll have to catch up with this as best you can. I'm sure Kiki will fill you in later.' The tall youth and the redhead exchanged smiles. 'One thing we have to decide,' continued Donatella brusquely, 'is whether anyone else is involved. Anyone working in the shadows, unseen.'

'That's a creepy thought,' said Kiki. 'Anybody in mind?'

Donatella spread her hands and shrugged in a very Italian gesture. 'These things are still happening while Temple-Clarke is in jail, which makes me think someone else is involved, and I don't mean Anna and the young boy in the photographs, whoever he is. I'm not comfortable with Claudio being that person. He's not too bright, as far as I can tell.' She looked quizzically at Kiki.

'Sorry,' said Kiki. 'There's nothing I can add. Like I said, I'm no expert on his intellect.' Turning the conversation back a few topics, she added, 'Remember, we do have a digital copy of the missing photograph. I scanned them all into the computer.'

'Of course,' said Donatella. 'We should print it out immediately and get it to Salvatore. And also tell him about the hit-and-run; we should have done that already. They might have been able to catch the van, but I expect it's too late now. Let's print the photo and go down to the police station right now. You coming, Kiki?'

'You and Francesca go on ahead. I thought I should fill Gianfranco in, like you said. I'll catch up with you later.' She couldn't quite keep a straight face as she said this.

Donatella burst into laughter. 'Well,' she said, 'I think Gianfranco deserves a reward for what he did back there, and now is as good a time as any. Just lock the door, OK?'

Francesca picked up the two photographs and followed Donatella to the computer lab. She turned round to close the door behind her and saw Gianfranco's penis was already in Kiki's hand. She blew her roommate a kiss. 'Don't tire him out, Kiki,' she said. 'He might need to save the damsels in distress again later.'

Kiki deftly locked the door behind Francesca and Donatella with one hand, the other keeping a firm hold on Gianfranco's cock, which had sprung magically to life in seconds. She gazed at it in admiration, a full six inches of firm flesh. She never seemed to tire of it and shuddered with delight at the thought of having its bulk fill her up again. I've got it bad, she thought to herself. But it's so good.

'Take your clothes off,' she ordered, but Gianfranco needed no urging. In a moment he was naked and pawing at Kiki's few items of clothing, nearly ripping them from her slim frame in his eagerness.

'I love your body,' he said, with awe in his voice. 'I love your cute little tits and this wonderful forest.' He ran his fingers through Kiki's pubic curls, reaching into the subtle cleft where her clit was already aflame with desire. Without hesitation he dropped to his knees and nuzzled Kiki's groin with his lips, his tongue seeking her sensitive bud.

Together the ardent pair shuffled over to Donatella's desk, where Kiki lay back and spread her thighs in open invitation. Already she was wet and Gianfranco's tongue lapped her juices. 'Lick me here,' she said, rubbing the nub of her clit with one finger. 'Stay there. Don't move.'

Gianfranco was an avid student and a quick learner. Before long he had the young woman trembling on the brink of climax, his tongue and lips working incessantly, his energy entirely focused on his girlfriend's pleasure. He reached up to fondle Kiki's nipples, and the combined sensation pushed her over the edge.

'Oh, God, Gianfranco. That was quick! I've never come so fast in my whole life, and that's saying something. Jesus, you're good.'

'I'll do it again,' said the young Italian with a juicy smile all over his face. 'You taste so good.'

'Oh, twist my arm, baby,' said Kiki. 'Make me come again, then it's your turn.'

Gianfranco duly obliged, this time sliding his fingers deep into Kiki's crevices and finding her G-spot with unerring accuracy. With two fingers crooked inside her and his thumb working her clit, Gianfranco transferred his lips to Kiki's own. Kissing her passionately, the young man allowed his new girlfriend to taste herself as he explored her mouth with his tongue.

Kiki shrieked with delight. 'Jesus, Gianfranco, where's that dick of yours? I want it inside me. Now!' she ordered, and gasped as his hard shaft plunged into her, further opening up her ripe tender flesh.

'Fill me up. Make me come again. Oh, sweet Jesus, harder!' Kiki bucked her hips frantically, adding to the force of Gianfranco's cock thrusting in and out of her wet hole. She locked her legs around her lover, holding him tight, forcing his pubic bone against her clit. Bursts of sensation presaged another orgasm, and she felt him shoot his load in her. Then she came, the orgasm she'd been waiting for, the one that put all others to shame, the one she'd remember for years afterwards. She lay on the desk, limbs splayed out in wanton abandon, panting and trembling with ecstasy.

With his come all spent, Gianfranco fell forward, elbows on the desktop, the weight of his torso upon Kiki's chest. The girl clasped her arms around him, crushing his body to hers, oblivious to everything except the almost unbearable sensations rippling through her body from head to toe.

'Was that all right?' asked Gianfranco hesitantly.

'Christ, silly, that was wonderful. Fabulous. There was only one thing wrong.'

'What?' Gianfranco's face was a picture of alarm.

Kiki laughed. 'I was supposed to give *you* a reward, not the other way round.'

22 *Il Assassino* (The Assassin)

'*Lui era rilasciato su cauzione?*' Francesca's voice was incredulous.

'What?' said Donatella. 'I didn't catch that.'

'The creep got out on bail,' translated Kiki. 'I don't fucking believe it!'

'What?' said Donatella. 'They let Temple-Clarke go?'

Francesca put down the phone. 'That was Salvatore,' she said unnecessarily. 'He said the prosecutor couldn't persuade the judge that Temple-Clarke was a danger to the public, so they let him out on bail, pending the trial. Sal's furious but there's nothing he can do except keep a close watch on the Englishman. Around the clock.'

'But what about the evidence from the house? And our material from the college? Didn't they search his studio as well after they found it?' Donatella's voice was full of anger.

Francesca shrugged. 'Don't blame me!' she said. 'I'm just telling you what happened in court today. They found nothing at his studio relating to forgeries. That was the clincher. If there had been some evidence of criminal activity there, Sal says Temple-Clarke would have been remanded in custody, but without that the judge said this was white-collar crime, and that Temple-Clarke wasn't a danger to the public.'

'But what about the attack on me and the car wreck?' demanded Donatella. 'The hotel break-in and the phone call? Those were dangerous!'

'There's no hard evidence linking Temple-Clarke to

any of those incidents,' said Francesca. 'You have to admit, he's been clever.'

'He must have cleared out the studio, that's all I can think,' said Kiki. 'No one knew where it was until a couple of days ago, when he broke down and told them. He had plenty of time to move stuff out, or get his associates to do it. I wish the *carabinieri* had allowed us to take a look,' she added. 'I still think we might have found something they missed.'

'Ah, yes, his mysterious associates,' mused Donatella. 'We're no further forward in finding out who they are, or even if they exist.'

Despite it being a weekday, the three women were home as the college was on a short break between summer sessions. Donatella sat at the computer composing another report to the Boston trustees, keeping them up to date with events. On the desk were her lecture notes for next week's art history classes. In keeping with her semi-work mode, she was wearing a V-necked silk T-shirt and a short denim skirt, and her legs and feet were bare. Although it was after breakfast she hadn't yet showered, still enjoying Sandro's scent on her body from the previous night. Despite trying to focus on her writing, she felt herself juice up slightly at the memory of their energetic sex.

Donatella understood her lover was worried and preoccupied with finding his niece, but that hadn't stopped him from ravaging Donatella's body every night this week. His lovemaking was even more intense than normal. They were doing it three or even four times a night, and Donatella knew the dark circles under her eyes were from lack of sleep. She closed her eyes momentarily and let her hand slip under her skirt, brushing her clit through the thin material of her panties.

A light kiss on her neck brought her back from her

daydream. 'I thought you were supposed to be working,' murmured Kiki, her hands gently brushing Donatella's nipples as she bent over her friend.

Donatella slipped her finger inside her panties and explored her wetness. 'I was thinking of Sandro,' she admitted. 'But your hands feel so good. Don't stop.'

Kiki gently cupped her breasts in her hands, rolling the older woman's nipples between her fingers through the silk. 'Ummm. I can smell him on you,' she said. 'In your hair and on your skin.'

'He's full of come,' said Donatella dreamily, as her friend's hands sent new shivers of lust though her loins. 'God, we're having so much sex, you think I'd be satisfied, but now I want you, too!'

'That's good,' said Kiki, 'because I've been sitting over there getting horny. I'm the same as you. I get fucked all night long by Gianfranco but, after he leaves, I want more.' She pulled off her shirt and shorts and stood naked, her green eyes glistening with desire. She took Donatella's hand. 'Let's go to bed,' she said.

'Don't forget me,' interrupted Francesca. The other two women looked across the room. Their friend was lying on the couch, skirt up around her waist and her legs apart, openly masturbating. Her fingers slid deep inside her pussy, to emerge glistening with juice. 'Whatever you do, I want some,' she said.

'Boston can wait,' said Donatella, sending the computer to sleep. She was suddenly submerged with desire. Deep down she knew she been waiting for this to happen. It seemed almost inevitable. 'Come into my room,' she invited.

The trio was soon completely naked and lying on Donatella's futon. Francesca had brought a selection of dildos and vibrators from her room, along with some juicy lubes.

'We've never done this before, the three of us, with no men around,' said Kiki. 'Suddenly I feel a bit shy. I don't know where to start. Dicks are helpful,' she added. 'They give you a sense of priorities. Big and hard, you just want to suck them or fuck them.'

'You? Shy?' Francesca was incredulous. 'That's a first. You don't look shy, lying there with your legs wide open. I think I'll start with you!'

The Italian knelt over her friend and plunged her tongue into Kiki's pussy. 'Mmmm. You taste different,' she said. 'It must be all Gianfranco's come inside you.'

'Let me taste,' said Donatella, impatient to get in on the act. Her tongue competed with Francesca's for a taste of Kiki. Soon the pair were kissing each other deeply, transferring Kiki's juice from mouth to mouth. Donatella spread her thighs wide, inviting Kiki to explore her sex. The young woman needed no further invitation, and Donatella gasped with pleasure as Kiki inserted two fingers deep inside the brunette's wet tunnel and rubbed her clit with her thumb. For the second time Donatella enjoyed the sensation of being played with by another woman. She felt it wouldn't be the last.

Francesca selected a long pink vibrator and, slathering the shaft with lube, slid it inside Kiki. Donatella could feel the vibrations as she licked the redhead's clit. Kiki's fingers moved faster and faster inside Donatella in time with her own mounting pleasure, and the professor tasted a fresh flow of nectar from her friend's heightened arousal.

With utter abandon Donatella buried her face in her girlfriend's pussy, taking over the vibrator from Francesca and easing it in and out of Kiki with her fingers. Another hand found its way between her buttocks as Francesca transferred her attentions. With a mixture of apprehension and delight, Donatella felt Francesca's fingers sliding down her crack until they rested on her tight little opening.

'Oh Fran, go easy,' Doratella begged.

The Italian obeyed, teasing Donatella's anus with her lubricated finger, gently testing the resistance and pushing slowly inside. This new sensation was enough. Combined with the insistent rhythm of Kiki's fingers on her clit and the taste of her friend's juices on her lips, Donatella came to her first all-girl climax. She felt her own juice flow out over Kiki's fingers and Francesca's tongue dip down to taste. She let out a low, feral growl of pleasure.

In the throes of her bliss Donatella didn't forget her own responsibilities, and very soon the bucking of Kiki's slim hips beneath her face announced her partner's own orgasm. Donatella slid the vibrator from her friend's pussy and licked it clean, swallowing several inches between her lips. 'Hmm. Not bad,' she said. 'But I don't think I'm ever going to give up cock.'

'Don't forget me,' begged Francesca from behind her. 'I haven't come yet.'

'Don't worry,' laughed Kiki. 'You're next.'

At that moment the phone rang.

'Ignore it,' ordered Francesca as she spread her legs for the attention of her two friends.

But it was Salvatore, and the urgency in his voice on the answering machine dispelled the trio's mood of sexual ecstasy. 'Francesca, this is urgent. Phone me as soon as you get this message. Temple-Clarke has been killed. His car has blown up!'

Francesca was on her feet in a flash and grabbed the handset.

'Salvatore, We're here. What happened?'

She listened intently for several minutes and then put down the receiver. Her face was pale as she turned to her friends, still naked on the bed, but all thoughts of sex banished from their minds.

'It was a bomb,' she said slowly. 'Somebody booby-trapped his car. He and Claudio were blown to pieces. Salvatore wants us down the police station immediately.'

'My God!' said Kiki, alarmed. 'They don't think we had anything to do with it?'

'No. Everybody involved with the case has to make statements. Come on, let's get dressed.'

At the *carabinieri* headquarters the three women gave brief statements confirming their activities and where-abouts, and had their fingerprints taken 'for elimina-tion purposes.' They then besieged Salvatore with questions. Sandro was nowhere to be seen.

'As you know,' said the *capitano*, 'we released Tem-ple-Clarke earlier this morning and he drove his BMW out of the police car park. We followed him to a little house on the edge of town where he picked up Claudio Pozzi...'

'So that definitely tied those two together!' exclaimed Kiki.

Salvatore nodded. 'We wondered whether to arrest Pozzi on the spot – he's wanted, *was* wanted I should say – for the attack on Donatella, but we decided to follow them for a while and see where they went. Anyway, the pair drove off towards Montevarchi on route 69, and near the turn-off to Pergine Valdarno the car exploded in a ball of flame. Sandro was following them a couple of hundred yards behind, and he said they didn't hit anything. There were no other vehicles anywhere near. It wasn't an accident. We think it was a bomb.'

'Where's Sandro now?' asked Donatella.

'At the scene. We have lab technicians crawling all

over the wreckage. Pozzi and Temple-Clarke didn't stand a chance.'

'Ye gods!' said Donatella soberly. 'I despised the man, and Claudio attacked me, so he's no loss as far as I'm concerned, but this is so brutal, so finite. Who do you think could have done it?'

'That's the big question,' agreed Salvatore. 'One theory is that the people in Rome who deal in the forgeries might be behind it. We checked out the company you found in the college files and it doesn't exist. It's a front. The address is just a post office box, where the mail is picked up a couple of times a week. Rome is keeping an eye on it to see if anybody comes by for the post, but so far they've drawn a blank. Even the name and address of the person who rented the box is fictitious.'

'This sounds more and more professional,' said Francesca seriously. 'Not like amateurs.' She glanced at her companions. 'Do you think organised crime might be involved?'

Salvatore nodded. 'You mean the Mafia? Possibly. We don't have any concrete leads that point that way but, as you say, this doesn't seem like the work of amateurs. Maybe forensic will be able to tell us about the bomb. That could give us some insight; it might be the same kind of device used in other assassinations.'

'Do you think Temple-Clarke was killed because somebody was worried he might talk too much?' asked Kiki. 'Was he bumped off before he could implicate other people? Had he confessed to anything?'

Salvatore shook his head. 'Nothing worth a damn. Just a little "creative accounting" at the college.'

Kiki snorted with derision.

A *carabinieri* patrolman poked his head around the door. '*Scusi, il mio capitano, ma il tenente Tirabosco è arrivato.*'

Salvatore nodded. 'I have to go,' he said to the

women. 'I want to hear what Sandro has to say. I suggest you three go home and stay there.' He turned to Francesca. 'I'll get back as soon as I can, darling. See you later.'

Francesca gave her lover a long hug and a kiss. 'Be careful,' she said.

On the drive home the three women were in sombre moods.

'Christ!' said Kiki from the driver's seat. 'Whoever would have thought our little drama would get as scary as the Mafia?'

'Let's not jump to conclusions,' cautioned Donatella. 'Just because we're in Italy doesn't automatically mean it's the Mafia. There could be other possibilities.'

'Like what?' asked Francesca from the back seat.

'Well, who had access to the car?' said Donatella. 'The bomb must have been placed there recently because Sandro impounded it to examine . . .' Donatella couldn't finish the sentence. She stared at Kiki and Francesca in alarm. 'My God! He said he was going to kill Temple-Clarke,' she exclaimed. 'You don't think he really did it, do you?'

'No, it couldn't be,' said Kiki. 'He was simply angry about Anna. He calmed down later.'

'He was more than angry,' argued Donatella. 'He was furious. He's been different all week, tense, full of pent-up emotion.'

'Maybe you underestimate the effect you have on men,' said Francesca, trying to lighten the mood.

Donatella smiled a thin smile. 'Not in this case. It's only been a couple of weeks, but we've had enough sex in that time for me to know what turns him on and how he thinks. I like him. I don't love him, but I do thank him for helping me open up, learning to appreciate sex again. He really is a good lover.'

'I think I love Salvatore,' said Francesca quietly. 'The last time Nico came round I sent him away. I said I was busy. I don't want other men right now. Not if I'm really serious about Sal.' She turned to Kiki. 'How about you and Gianfranco? You've been seeing plenty of each other the past few days.'

'Were you thinking about Salvatore when you were playing with Donatella this morning?' replied the redhead.

'Don't change the subject,' said Francesca. 'That was different. We were just playing this morning. It's not like I have a string of lesbian lovers. You two are special to me. We've broken through the barrier, we're friends and lovers together. That's something to be treasured. We might not have sex like that again for a long time, but I think it would be OK if we did. It wouldn't change how I feel about Salvatore. Anyway,' she said with a pretend pout, 'I didn't get to come this morning, not like the two of you.' Francesca paused as a thought came to her. 'What am I going to do about Marcellino and his blow-job this Saturday?' she asked. 'We still need this little car.'

'Don't look at me,' said Kiki. 'Just like you don't want to cheat on Salvatore, I don't want to cheat on Gianfranco.'

'Ah-hah!' said Francesca. 'I knew it! You have fallen for him!'

'Well, I think that's wonderful,' said Donatella. 'He's a really cute kid ... Hey! Why are you looking at me like that?' she demanded, as her companions stared at her pointedly, big grins on their faces.

'Do you have plans for Saturday morning?' asked Francesca.

'Saturday? You don't mean Marcellino! I couldn't. I mean...'

'You mean that tenured full professors from Boston

don't go round swapping blow-jobs with Italian mechanics for battered old Peugeots?' said Kiki, whose grin stretched even wider.

'No! Yes ... No. I mean ...'

'Sandro says you give great head,' said Francesca. 'He boasted about it to Salvatore.'

Donatella's blush became even more pronounced, but her lips set in firm line. 'OK, dammit. Just to shut you two up, I'll do it. Just the once you understand. Just because we need the car. And Francesca, you have to set it up, introduce us. I can't just walk into his work-shop and say "Pull out your cock. I've come to suck you off!"'

'OK. It's a deal,' said Francesca. 'But I bet you'll go back the next weekend.'

Hell, why not? agreed Donatella, but only to herself.

The matter of the bomb and Sandro's threats was not mentioned further, and the three women soon pulled up in front of their little villa. Francesca started to cook and Kiki closed herself in her room to phone Gianfranco, who came over later and went straight into his lover's bedroom with only the briefest of greetings to the other women. Donatella was left alone with her thoughts. She couldn't shake the memory of Sandro's oath to kill Temple-Clarke from her mind. The explosion of the BMW on a deserted road, when only her police-man lover was nearby, made her wonder if he'd planted a bomb while searching the vehicle and detonated it by remote control where no one else would get hurt. Hours later she was still immersed in the problem when the focus of her speculation walked into her bedroom. She put a shaky smile on her face.

'What's wrong, Donatella?' asked Sandro. 'You look worried.' He started to peel off his uniform and lay it tidily over a chair.

'Oh, it's ... just the shock of Temple-Clarke,' said

Donatella. 'It must have been awful. You saw the whole thing, didn't you?'

Sandro grunted assent. 'I don't really want to talk about it now,' he said, effectively cutting off Donatella's hope that he might, intentionally or unintentionally, shed some light on the matter. 'I want you. I just want to forget today. Get your clothes off.'

'*Si, tenente*,' said Donatella in mock supplication, as she shrugged off her jeans and panties, opening her legs to her lover's hungry gaze. She gently lubricated herself as her man watched, hypnotised by the sight of the woman playing with herself in front of him.

Donatella wanted sex, too. She'd enjoyed her session with the girls that morning, but she wanted to lay down some strictly heterosexual memories over the incident. Her whole sexual persona had changed in the past two weeks, or perhaps, she admitted, it would be more accurate to say it had returned to earlier patterns from her promiscuous youth, before she became wrapped up in the serious world of academia. She was enjoying the fact that her sex drive had blossomed again, and she craved new experiences. But she didn't know if she could handle the full impact of bisexuality right now.

Her hands sought Sandro's hard cock. 'Come here,' she growled. 'No messing about tonight. Just put your dick inside me and fuck!'

It took only five minutes for Sandro's thrusting penis and expert fingers to give Donatella her first orgasm of the evening. She experienced an additional *frisson* as she came, knowing that tonight she might be making love with a murderer. *Un assassino.*

23 *La Posa Piena*
   (Full Exposure)

Early one morning a few days later, at Donatella's request, Kiki was with her in the computer room, busily studying the infamous images of Temple-Clarke. They were hoping to spot a clue to move their probe forward. A new police squad had arrived from Rome to take over the assassination case, a sure sign that senior ranks considered it an organised crime operation. Accordingly, all local investigations had been relegated in importance.

Donatella looked over Kiki's shoulder, seeing the pictures of the man's erect penis for the umpteenth time. 'I think this is a waste of time,' she said dispiritedly. 'If I see that cock one more time my eyes will glaze over.'

'Whose cock? What are you two talking about?' The voice of Jennifer Wrenn announced her unexpected arrival.

'You're early,' said Kiki, surprised. 'I've never seen you in college at this time of the morning before.'

'I've just broken up with that shithead Ian Ramsey,' said the soccer player unexpectedly. 'I thought I'd get straight to work. Try to forget him and his fucking antics.' Her blue eyes widened as she registered Donatella's presence. 'Oh, God, sorry Doctor di'Bianchi. I didn't recognise you there. I thought you were another student.'

'I'll take that as a compliment, Jennifer,' said Donatella

with a laugh, standing and smoothing down her short skirt. 'I have a new fashion adviser,' the professor explained, playfully ruffling Kiki's spiky hair. 'She's trying to overcome my advancing years by making me look like the grad student I was ten years ago.'

'It isn't only the clothes...' began Jennifer. 'It's none of my business ... but you seem different from when you first came here.' The student looked away, embarrassed. 'My God!' she said suddenly, her gaze falling on the computer screen. 'Is that what you were talking about? Is this some class on pornography? Can I take it?'

Kiki laughed. 'No, Jen, sorry to get your hopes up. These are photos of Temple-Clarke, if you can believe it. They're evidence in the case we're trying to tie up for the trustees in Boston. The *carabinieri* have washed their hands of it locally. Now the bugger's dead anyway I don't suppose it matters very much, but Donatella and I want to make sure we have everything accounted for in our report to Boston.'

'Is that really Temple-Clarke?' asked Jennifer, amazed. 'Are they recent?'

'We think so,' said Kiki. 'In the last few weeks.'

'But it can't be him!' exclaimed the graduate student.

'Why not?'

'Because he's impotent. He can't get it up!'

'What?' Suddenly Donatella was all business. 'Are you sure?'

Jennifer looked around, but at this hour they were alone in the computer room. 'Look, I'd rather nobody knew about this. Are you sure it's important?'

'Very,' snapped Donatella. 'You *must* tell me.'

'Well,' began Jennifer, 'I transferred into this college from the University of Kansas last year, from their programme in Siena. I hadn't been doing well there and I thought the change of scene might do me good.

Temple-Clarke interviewed me and it didn't go well. My work wasn't very good then,' she admitted. 'He suggested private lessons to bring my work up to the admission standard.' She rolled her eyes. 'This wasn't my finest hour,' she said, ruefully. 'It was the oldest line in the book, right next to "Come up and see my etchings!"'

Kiki laughed, but Donatella was serious. 'You're saying he seduced you?'

'Yes, I'm sorry to say. Perhaps I'm simply a sucker for an English accent. Look how hard I fell for that bastard Ramsey!'

You're not the only one, thought Donatella, but she said, 'Leave Ian Ramsey out of this for the moment. Temple-Clarke took you to bed but couldn't finish the job? Is that what you're saying?'

'Hell, he couldn't even start it!' exploded Jennifer. 'He was pawing all over me, but when I went to play with his cock it just lay there, like some floppy English sausage! I fondled it, sucked it, almost fucking swallowed it . . . oh, sorry, professor . . .'

'Go on,' said Donatella sharply. 'I understand oral sex. Stop giggling, Kiki! This is important. Finish your story,' she said to Jennifer.

'There's not much more to tell,' admitted the student. 'He broke down and confessed he was impotent. He made me swear never to tell anybody. That was easy; I wanted to forget the whole episode! But I suppose it doesn't matter now,' she added sadly.

Donatella shook her head. 'Oh yes, it does. It matters very much. If these aren't photos of Temple-Clarke, it means that somebody's been leading us a merry dance in exactly the wrong direction. We've been intentionally misled. The question now is by whom.'

Jennifer Wrenn was staring at the photo on the screen, the one where the mystery man was about to push his penis into the arse of the young boy. 'You'll think I'm crazy, but that cock looks familiar.'

'Somebody you know?' asked Kiki.

'I think so,' replied the student. 'Somebody I've sucked off often enough that I can recognize that little dimple on the cockhead.' She pointed at the screen. 'Look there. You see where it curves in more than usual?'

'Christ!' exclaimed Donatella, her brain making the connection. 'You mean it's Ian Ramsey! This is a photograph of Ian Ramsey with Temple Clarke's head substituted! Why didn't we see that?'

'I've never seen him naked,' retorted Kiki. 'You saw him when...' She swallowed her next words just in time.

'That was only twice,' snapped Donatella, unthinkingly.

'Twice?' said Kiki, her eyebrows shooting up. 'You only told us about once! When was the other time?'

Jennifer Wrenn was looking at Donatella oddly. 'You mean you and he ... he never told me he was fucking you as well! Jesus, the bastard!'

Donatella blushed furiously. 'No, Jennifer, you've got it wrong. I didn't have sex with Ian Ramsey. I'm not your rival.'

'But what did you mean...?'

'Look, it's too complicated to go into now. I don't want to talk about it, understand? Just take my word for it. I haven't fucked your precious Ian Ramsey. Subject closed.' Donatella pulled rank as a last resort to avoid the embarrassing disclosure of her voyeurism.

The shock of hearing a senior female professor talk about sex in such a direct fashion stopped Jennifer in her tracks. 'Oh, OK,' she said, but she couldn't take her eyes off the screen. 'He always wanted to do it up the ass,' she said wistfully. 'Eventually I quite liked it.'

That's an understatement, thought Donatella.

Kiki was exasperated. 'Just now you came in here calling Ramsey all the names under the sun,' she said. 'Are you sure you've broken up with the man?'

'Yes, definitely,' replied Jennifer. 'We had a hell of a row early this morning. He got a phone call, on my number, and left the bedroom to take it in the kitchen. That made me suspicious. I thought it might be another woman so I picked up the phone by the bed and listened in. It was some woman all right, speaking in Italian. I couldn't understand it all, but there was something about going to Rome urgently. When I asked him about it he was furious; he said I had no business listening in on his private phone calls. He said it was urgent business and he had given the woman my number in case of emergency. He got really ugly. I haven't seen him like that before.'

She looked at Kiki. 'You remember I asked you about Ian several days ago, said he was acting a bit weird?'

'Sure,' said Kiki.

'Well, it got worse during the week. He's a different person than when I first met him. He frightens me. When he stormed out last night, I thought he was going to hit me.'

'Did he?' asked Donatella.

'No, but I grabbed a big knife from the kitchen, just in case,' replied Jennifer. 'Once he saw that, he left. I can take care of myself,' she added.

Kiki and Donatella exchanged glances. 'If I'm right,' said the older woman, 'he might be a lot more dangerous that you realise. You're well rid of him.'

'Are you thinking what I'm thinking?' Kiki asked Donatella soberly.

'That we've been wrong all along? That it wasn't Temple-Clarke, but Ian Ramsey who was pulling the strings?'

Kiki nodded. 'Yes. But Temple-Clarke must have been in on the deal.'

Jennifer Wrenn was looking baffled. Donatella took pity on her. 'Let's go to my office,' she said. 'I'll give you the *Cliff's Notes* version, so you'll know what we're talking about.'

'Let me call Gianfranco and Francesca,' said Kiki. 'I think they should hear this, too.'

Half an hour later Donatella, Kiki, Francesca, Jennifer Wrenn and Gianfranco were gathered in Donatella's office, looking expectantly at the professor.

'OK,' she said. 'Here's how I think all this fits together.' Her audience sat in rapt attention.

'We know that Temple-Clarke and Ramsey have both been in Tuscany for several years, and that they've known each other for some time. I think Ramsey gradually became the dominant partner, manipulating things in the background while he allowed Temple-Clarke to be the front man. Between them they set up this forgery scam with an outfit in Rome. Who they are and how Ramsey hooked up with them is unclear, but I personally doubt it's a Mafia connection. It simply doesn't seem a big enough deal.'

Francesca shrugged. 'I don't know,' she said. 'They have their fingers in every pie.'

Donatella acknowledged the point. 'You may be right, but that isn't a crucial issue yet. The two Englishmen developed this clever niche market in authentic-looking Arretine ware that went over big in Rome.' She paused, looking intently at Jennifer.

'Carry on,' said Jennifer. 'This is fascinating. To think I was fucking this guy!'

'The accounts we found showed that the business was quite lucrative. As we suspected, the forgeries wouldn't fool an expert but were very convincing for the middle-brow tourist market – something unusual and risqué with a bit of class – but not too expensive.'

'Using Temple-Clarke's influence as director, Ramsey was able to skim off money from the programme to help with their expenses,' added Kiki, 'which increased their profit margin even more.'

'Where do Anna and the boy fit in?' asked Francesca. 'And what about Claudio Pozzi?'

'I think the teenagers did menial tasks around the studio,' replied Donatella. 'If we could discover the whereabouts of the studio, we'd know for sure what went on there. We do know that it's not Temple-Clarke's place. When I went there with Sandro recently it didn't look anything like the space in the photo, the one with the racks of forgeries in the background. There has to be another studio set up somewhere.'

Her audience nodded.

'Anyway,' Donatella continued, warming to her theme, 'we know the kids weren't Temple-Clarke's sex-toys, because of Jennifer's less-than-wonderful experience with the director.'

The student athlete groaned at the memory.

'We think it's Ramsey in the photographs, based again on Jennifer's unique identification,' said Donatella. 'I think they were impoverished kids who Ramsey simply used for his gratification. Anna lied when she said she was Temple-Clarke's whore. I don't know why. To protect Ramsey perhaps? But if we substitute Ramsey for the director, it all makes sense. Ramsey certainly abused her. We saw the bruises. He must have really had her in his thrall for her to want to protect him!'

'But where is she now?' asked Francesca.

'Good question,' interjected Kiki.

'I don't like her or trust her, but I'm worried about her,' Francesca added.

'You've studied the photos again, Fran,' said Kiki.

'You're the other one in this select little group who's had sex with Ramsey. Can you add anything?'

The Italian shook her head. '*Mi dispiace*. Remember, we only did it once, and that was a quickie: doggy-style in the closet in the life-drawing studio. I didn't see much up close. I was going to blow him, but he was just interested in shooting his load.' Francesca shook her head sadly. 'Sometimes I can still be stupid about men,' she said.

Kiki leaned across and squeezed her friend's hand. 'Live and learn,' she said.

'Slowly,' replied Francesca, but she smiled as she said it.

Gianfranco was going red. Kiki smiled at her boy-friend. 'All this talk of sex too much for you?' she teased.

'No, it's just making me horny!' quipped back the young man. 'It's not everyday a guy finds himself at close quarters with four beautiful women, all talking about sex!'

Kiki looked at her boyfriend's crotch, where a defi-nite bulge was forming. Jennifer followed her gaze and Kiki noticed. 'He's not available, Jen,' she said. 'This sexy guy's all mine.'

Jennifer smiled and shrugged. 'Just looking,' she said.

'There are a few more things to put in place,' said Donatella, speaking loudly to recapture her audience. 'Claudio Pozzi is more complicated. He could have been a go-between with the Rome people. I thought for a while that it was simply an odd coincidence that Kiki knew him, but the more I thought about it I wondered whether Ramsey sent him to watch her.' She turned to Kiki. 'Think about it. Who were the student leaders of the protests? You and Jennifer. Ramsey starts up a relationship with Jennifer and sends Claudio to do the same with you. That way he keeps tabs on both of you and leaves Temple-Clarke to brush me off. Except that it didn't work out the way he planned. Temple-Clarke blew it, and Kiki made a fool out of Claudio. That's when things started getting nasty.'

'God,' said Jennifer. 'I got fucked over real good!'

'Donatella, were your hotel break-in and our car accident just warnings?' asked Francesca.

'I think so,' replied Donatella. 'And when that didn't work, they attacked me. I still think it was Temple-Clarke with Claudio that night, but it could have been Ramsey. They're about the same height and build, and I noticed Ramsey was rubbing his eyes the following day. Maybe *he* was the one I caught with the pepper spray.'

'So who planted the bomb?' asked Gianfranco.

'Unless we can get Ramsey to confess, we may never know,' admitted Donatella. 'Sandro could have done it. He had the motive and the opportunity. We heard him threaten to kill Temple-Clarke.'

'He actually threatened to shoot him, not blow him up,' Kiki reminded the group.

'Fair enough,' agreed Donatella, 'but he could have developed another plan after he cooled down. Most *carabinieri* know how to work with explosives. It's in their anti-terrorist training.'

'Did forensics come up with anything definitive on the device?' asked Kiki.

Donatella shook her head. 'Only that it didn't seem like the same type used in recent Mafia hits. But it's not conclusive.'

'There's no evidence that Ramsey knew anything about bombs.' said Kiki. 'That would point to Sandro.'

'That's true,' said Donatella, 'but we all know that these days you can find simple bomb-making instructions on the Internet, so we can't rule him out. He did have a motive: he'd been hiding behind Temple-Clarke all this time. If he thought Temple-Clarke was going to crack, Ramsey could have killed him before he could say anything. Remember, Temple-Clarke had just been released; it was the first chance Ramsey had. Killing Claudio might have been a bonus.'

'If Ramsey killed those two, it doesn't augur well for Anna and the boy,' said Kiki.

'No, it doesn't,' agreed Donatella. 'I fear we might hear a news item one day that two young bodies have been discovered somewhere.'

'Jesus,' gasped Jennifer. 'That would be four people he's killed.'

'We don't know if he's killed anybody,' cautioned Donatella. 'This is purely supposition. The kids could just have run away. And Sandro could have planted that bomb.'

Francesca looked at Jennifer and Donatella. 'Well,' she said, 'at least one of you has fucked a murderer; possibly both. That's a strange sisterhood.'

Both women in question frowned. 'Not a pleasant thought,' Donatella said, but she remembered with a pang of guilt the extra thrill she got from fucking Sandro during the past few days.

A pensive silence descended on the group, broken eventually by Francesca. 'So, what's next? Should we call Salvatore, let him deal with it?'

Donatella demurred. 'What would we tell the *carabinieri*? That we think this man is the criminal, but to make sure we need to check out his cock? They'll think we're crazy.'

'I think you're crazy,' said Gianfranco, 'But I'll help you.'

'Me, too,' said Jennifer, grimly.

'OK,' said Donatella. 'That makes five of us to one of him. If we can take him by surprise those should be good enough odds.'

'But how do we do that?' asked Gianfranco.

'I do have an idea,' said Donatella.

'Go, Nancy Drew!' said Kiki, *sotto voce*.

Donatella tried to swat her friend playfully, but Kiki ducked. 'No, I'm serious,' said Donatella. 'Ramsey has been badgering me about the directorship. He thinks it should go to him. I've rebuffed him a couple times, but I could let him think I'm reconsidering if, say, the terms and conditions were right.'

'You mean, let him think he could fuck you for the job?' Francesca cut to the chase.

Donatella grinned. 'As direct as always, Fran,' she said. 'But, yes. That's what I mean. Listen, this is what I thought we could do ...'

The next day a smiling Ian Ramsey knocked on the door of the house in Bucine. Donatella, dressed casually in T-shirt and short skirt, let him in and led him to the main living-room. Except for their footsteps, all was quiet.

'Anyone else at home?' inquired Ramsey, innocently.

'No,' said Donatella. 'I thought our ... negotiations would best be carried out in private. Do you agree?'

'Absolutely.' Ramsey settled himself in an easy chair. 'Your move, I think, *dottoressa*. Your note said you had a proposition about the directorship. I'm interested. It has been a strange time for the college recently. I still can't believe what's happened to Stewart. Still, life must move on. It doesn't affect the fact that we still have to pursue our careers and lives.'

Donatella tried to stay calm. She had to get this right. 'I've been reviewing your qualifications,' she began. 'In conversation with the Trustees, they and I have agreed that it would be in the best interests of the college if a change of leadership could be effected with the minimum of disruption. In fact, they stressed that

283

continuity might be advantageous in the light of the recent tragedy.'

Ramsey bowed his head in acquiescence to this idea.

'That is, if a suitable candidate presents himself or herself,' added Donatella.

'And is there one – in your opinion, that is?' asked Ramsey.

'There might be,' admitted Donatella. 'But there needs to be a special ... interview procedure shall we say, before any appointment could be recommended.'

Ramsey merely raised an eyebrow.

Donatella casually crossed her legs, making sure that Ramsey got an unmistakable view up her skirt. She was not wearing panties, and she hoped he could see right up to her pussy. Despite her distaste for the Englishman, she felt a trickle of arousal. I might already have fucked one murderer, she thought. Why not two?

The glint in her adversary's eyes confirmed Donatella's hopes. A small smile of anticipation played at the corners of Ramsey's mouth.

'I like your interview technique,' he said, archly.

'It gets better,' said Donatella, not to be outdone in the irony stakes.

'I can't wait.'

'You don't have to,' said Donatella. 'Here's the deal. I've wanted to fuck you ever since I saw you that first day in the office.' Well, that much was true. 'I want you to fuck me now. How much pleasure you give me will affect my recommendation.' She stood up and walked to Ramsey, raising her skirt so that her pubic curls were fully exposed, almost at the level of his face. She slid the tip of one finger into her moist lips and traced a trail of juice along Ramsey's jaw to his mouth. 'You want more?' she asked.

Ramsey's erection was at full bore, tenting his trousers as he sat in the chair. He quickly opened his fly and prised his cock free from its constraints. 'I think *you* want some,' he said. 'I thought you were a cock-hungry slut the moment I saw you.'

Donatella dropped to her knees and examined the penis up close. She stroked the shaft and ran her finger around the ridge of the Englishman's cockhead. The little curved dimple in the tip was very pronounced. 'Oh, yes.' Donatella murmured. 'This is exactly what I want.'

'Sit on it, professor, and I'll give you the ride of your life.'

Donatella undid Ramsey's belt buckle and teased his trousers down around his ankles, effectively hobbling the man. All the time she held on to his cock with one hand. Now the other one fondled his balls. 'My, my,' she said. 'I bet these beauties are full of come.'

On that precise cue the door burst open, and in rushed Gianfranco and the three women. Ramsey struggled to rise but fell over, trousers shackling his ankles.

Kiki hauled Ramsey's face off the floor and chopped him hard across the bridge of his nose with her fist. The man screamed in pain. So she did it again for good measure.

Gianfranco quickly looped nylon cord around the hapless Englishman and trussed his arms to his sides, pulling the cord tight and tying a series of knots. Francesca stood by with a can of pepper spray, looking keen to use it, and Jennifer Wrenn hovered behind with another long kitchen knife, her weapon of choice. In only a moment Ramsey was trussed up and helpless on a couch, his trousers down and his dick limp and floppy on his thigh.

'You fucking bitches!' he screamed. 'What the fuck do you think you're playing at? Jennifer, put that knife down! I didn't mean what I said.'

His former protégé stood next to the couch, tracing a line down his thigh with the point of her knife. Ramsey flinched. 'Jesus,' he whispered.

'Put that away,' ordered Donatella. 'You might hurt him.'

'That's the general idea,' snarled Jennifer. 'You asshole!' she hissed at the recumbent Ramsey. 'I should cut this fucking prick off, right now!' She picked up Ramsey's penis in her fingers and gently touched it with her knife. Ramsey screamed.

'Don't cut it off,' said Kiki urgently. 'It's evidence!'

'Oh, don't worry, I'm going to make it full and hard first,' said Jennifer and, letting go the knife, dropped her face to Ramsey's groin, taking his detumescent penis in her mouth. 'Come on, Ian,' she cooed, after sucking it for a few moments. 'Get your lovely prick hard for Jennifer. You know how to do that, don't you?'

Ramsey screwed his eyes shut. 'Fuck off, you crazy bitch,' he sobbed. But Jennifer's expert technique was too much for his self-control. Before long his dick was standing straight up as his former girlfriend pumped his shaft and suckled the tip, running her tongue down the shaft.

'That's fine, Jennifer,' said Donatella, skirt smoothed down and camera in hand. 'Good job! Lean back out of the picture.'

Several flashes of the digital camera recorded Ramsey's erection for posterity. 'Gotcha!' said Donatella, triumphantly.

With Ramsey slumped on the couch, Donatella pulled up a chair. 'Time for your interview, Professor Ramsey,' she said sardonically. 'I have a few questions for you.'

Ramsey glared back defiantly.

'Did you doctor those photographs?'

'Which photographs?'

'You know very well. The ones with Temple-Clarke's head on your body.'

'Yes.'

'Why?'

'I wanted to make sure the guy was caught! You weren't getting anywhere with your precious investigation. I thought they would give you some help.'

This gave Donatella pause. That could just be true.

'Who put them under my door?' she asked.

'I did.'

'You? Not Anna?'

'Anna who?'

'You know who. Anna Gentileschi.'

'Never heard of her,' he insisted.

'Where is she?'

'I don't know the girl.'

'Who is the boy?'

'What boy?'

'The one sucking your cock in the photograph.'

'Just a friend.'

'He's a very young friend.'

'He's over the age of consent. Are you my moral guardian?'

'Where is he?' Donatella ignored his question.

'He left town.'

'Where'd he go?'

'He didn't say.'

'Do you expect me to believe that?'

'Believe what you want, bitch!'

Donatella was unfazed by Ramsey's venom. 'Do you know Claudio?'

'Who's that?'

'Claudio Pozzi. Temple-Clarke's associate.'

'No.'

'Never met him?'

'No.'

'What do you know about the forgeries?'

'What forgeries?'

'The ones you and Temple-Clarke made for the people in Rome.'

'I don't know any people in Rome.'

Donatella stood up in disgust. 'This is useless,' she said. 'Francesca, call Salvatore. Tell him we've got a prisoner. Let the *carabinieri* have a go at him.'

Before her friend could comply, the house phone rang on a nearby table. Donatella snatched it up. '*Pronto!*'

'Donatella, it's Salvatore.'

'Oh, Salvatore, I was just . . .'

The policeman interrupted her. 'Listen, Donatella, this is important. We've found the apartment where Anna lived with a kid named Leo; probably the boy in the photographs. And guess who it's owned by.'

'Ian Ramsey?'

There was silence on the other end. 'How did you know?' asked Salvatore, sounding rather deflated. 'It took us ages to trace it through a bogus company.'

'I didn't,' admitted Donatella. 'But it was a pretty easy guess. Ramsey's right here. We found out that those photographs are really of him; he digitally superimposed Temple-Clarke's head on his body.'

Salvatore's voice was suddenly full of alarm. 'Ramsey's there, did you say?'

'Don't worry, Salvatore, we're all here, and we have him tied up. He isn't going anywhere.'

The tension in Salvatore's voice was unabated. 'Don't move,' he commanded. 'And don't untie Ramsey, whatever you do. I'll be right over.' He paused. 'We've found Anna,' he said. 'Sandro traced her to an uncle's house in Milan. She's OK, but very frightened. She told Sandro that Ramsey treated her pretty badly. He plays rough, that *bastardo Inglese*. Be careful!'

* * *

The two *carabinieri* left their police car running and raced into the house. They quickly took charge, untying Ramsey so he could get dressed.

'Will you explain to me what the hell's been going on?' Salvatore asked Donatella in an exasperated undertone. 'Why is he half naked?'

Donatella didn't feel up to laying out the whole case they had constructed against the Englishman. 'Can this wait?' she pleaded. 'At least until he's in the cells, then we can tell you all about it at our leisure. It's rather complicated.'

'OK,' agreed Salvatore, reluctantly. 'Let's go,' he said to Sandro. 'Get the cuffs on him.'

At that moment Ramsey lunged sideways and grabbed the knife that Jennifer had laid on a side table. Before anybody could stop him he raced for the door, grasping Kiki in a headlock and pulling her slight frame with him. In a flash Sandro's automatic was in his fist but he hesitated to fire. Ramsey had the knife at Kiki's throat.

'That's right, *tenente*,' said Ramsey. 'Don't shoot. If you do, this little slut gets her throat cut! Sorry to sound like an old western movie, folks,' he added in a mocking tone, 'but put your guns down on the floor and kick them over to me. That's right. Both of you. Very good!'

'Put her down, Professor Ramsey,' said a quiet voice. 'Put her down, please. Take me instead.'

All heads turned to Gianfranco, who was advancing with his arms behind his head. 'Stay back, boy!' shouted Salvatore.

'No. I mean it.' Gianfranco was not deflected by the policeman's command. 'Let Kiki go,' he said. 'I'll be your hostage.'

'No, Gianfra—!' Kiki's scream was cut off by Ramsey's savage grip on her windpipe.

'Nice try, kid,' said Ramsey, with a sneer. '*Molto galante*. Now back up, all of you!'

Gianfranco reluctantly retreated, his chocolate eyes never leaving his girlfriend's face or the knifepoint just millimetres from the pulsing artery in her throat. Ramsey bent to scoop up the two automatics, but in doing so he had to release his grip on Kiki slightly. She took her chance, twisting out of his grasp and slamming her elbow into Ramsey's stomach. The Englishman retched and dropped the knife but held on to the guns. Kiki's grab for the knife was foiled by a steel gun barrel jammed in her face.

'Back up, bitch!' hissed Ramsey, his breath coming in gasps from the force of Kiki's blow. 'I should kill you right here and now!'

'Then I'd kill you,' announced Gianfranco with deadly calm. 'You wouldn't get out of this room alive. There are too many of us.'

'The boy's right, Ramsey,' said Sandro. 'If he doesn't, I will. You hurt my niece and shamed my family. It will be a pleasure to break your neck.'

Ramsey backed quickly to the doorway, a gun in each hand. 'Oh no, me bonny lads,' he said, the tension in his voice bringing out his Geordie accent. 'Not so fast. You!' He motioned to Donatella. 'You come with me and open the front door.' He directed his maddened gaze towards the others. 'If anyone else comes into the hallway I'll blow the bitch's brains out. Understand?'

Donatella walked unsteadily with Ramsey until the pair reached the front door. She obediently opened it. The blue and red police car was standing at the bottom of the steps, its motor running.

'Taxi's here, I see,' said Ramsey, and bounded down the steps three at a time. Donatella dropped to the floor and rolled behind the door. Three shots sliced the air above her where she had been standing a second before.

Ramsey screeched the police car around in a circle, firing out the window as the *carabinieri* appeared in the doorway. They, too, dived for cover. The shots went wide. Ramsey was around the corner and out of their sight before they could do anything to stop him.

'Damn!' swore Salvatore. 'There'll be hell to pay for this! Are you all right Donatella?' He helped the shaken professor to her feet.

'Yes,' she said hesitantly. 'Is anybody hurt?'

'No, thank God,' said Kiki, coming to the front door hand-in-hand with Gianfranco.

Sandro and Salvatore were speaking as fast as they could into their *telephonini*, trying to explain themselves and organise road blocks at the same time. 'Don't worry,' said Sandro. 'He won't get far.'

24 *Gli Amici e gli Amanti* (Friends and Lovers)

The next two weeks passed in a frenetic haze as Donatella worked like a whirlwind to keep the *Collegio Toscana* from collapse. Several of the faculty were so shocked by the tragic events they barely went through the motions of teaching. Donatella supported the ones she thought worthy of retaining and ruthlessly chopped the dead wood, arranging for them to be paid until the end of the summer term but asking them to leave immediately.

'It's better they go now, rather than hang around dragging the place down,' the acting-director said to her graduate assistants Kiki Lee and Jennifer Wrenn, as the threesome sipped glasses of Chianti at the end of a particularly hectic day.

'Are you two sure you can handle the undergraduate classes in photography and painting, see them through the end of the summer session?' she asked.

The two young women nodded, pleased with the responsibility and the older woman's trust in them. 'How about you?' asked Kiki, who had changed her look radically from the way she appeared when Donatella first met her. Today her slipdress was fastened at the top of the bodice and the drape of the fluid matte jersey slid over her figure seductively. Her form was sleek but defined. 'At last count you were teaching life drawing and art history, and supervising several graduate independent studies.'

'It's quite fun, actually,' said Donatella. She sipped her wine and rolled her head from side to side, stretching her neck muscles. Today the tall American wore a stretch silk wrap top with a fitted, cropped shape that followed every curve. The café-espresso hue matched the colour of her hair, which she wore cascading over her shoulders. 'It's OK,' she said. 'Hectic, but I think the students are getting a better education than previously. God knows how those half-brains on the faculty ever got hired.' She crossed her legs, showing off her tan. 'Was it just that Ramsey and Temple-Clarke wanted the college staffed with idiots so that no one would comprehend that they were ripping off the college *and* the students?'

The two younger women nodded in agreement. 'That's what we think,' said Jennifer, who was still dressed like a 'girl-jock' but more stylishly this day. Her silky soft navy running shorts looked attractive with her micropoly bra top in a matching print. 'Some of them were lousy teachers,' she added, adjusting the laces on her new navy and red canvas sneakers. 'What news do you have of Ian Ramsey, by the way?' she asked. 'Any word from Salvatore?'

Donatella shook her head. 'No change since yesterday or the day before that or the day before that,' she said, pouring some more wine. 'The *carabinieri* use a different expression each day – "arrest expected shortly," or "pursuing several new leads" – to disguise the fact that they don't know where he is. Salvatore is as mad as hell. He's getting the blame, but it was really the fault of the *carabinieri* at the road block near Capannole. They were told to look out for a police car, but Ramsey was wearing Sandro's peaked cap that he'd left on the back seat, and had the lights and siren going full blast. The guards didn't realise it wasn't a real policeman until too late.'

Kiki nodded in commiseration. She and Francesca had heard Salvatore's bitter explanations many times during the last several days. Ramsey's escape car had been found near San Gimignano, but the fugitive Englishman had vanished without a trace. 'Have you heard from Sandro, since he was transferred?' the redhead asked Donatella.

'Once. He doesn't like Sicily. Says it's the back of beyond compared to his beloved Tuscany. Ostensibly his transfer is a promotion, but he's convinced he's being shunted sideways into obscurity because of Ramsey's escape.' Donatella smiled grimly. 'I think he'll be OK once he finds a nice Sicilian girl to fuck.'

Donatella didn't add that, privately, she considered her former lover a prime suspect in the bombing of Temple-Clarke's BMW. Or that she thought his transfer to an anti-terrorist squad in a distant part of Italy might be a bureaucratic way of making sure that possibility was never discussed; the *carabinieri* taking care of their own with a minimum of fuss.

'It's all over with him, then?' asked Jennifer.

Donatella nodded. 'Yes. It was great fun while it lasted, but I'm not particularly sad about its ending. There was never any deep emotional attachment between us; simply carnal craving. We loved the sex. It would have ended of its own accord sooner or later.'

'Anybody new on the horizon?' asked the graduate student.

'Only Marcellino,' chimed in Kiki cheekily. 'I hear he's raised his prices.'

Donatella made a very unprofessorial face. 'Yeah. That's the market economy for you. A simple blow-job doesn't pay the rent on the car any more,' she said with a smile.

Jennifer couldn't resist asking. 'What does he charge?'

'Guess.'

'Oh, the works, right? All the way?'

Donatella smiled again. 'He's not a bad fellow, actually,' she said. 'He has a nice kid, a young boy from a previous marriage. His wife ran off with a racing car driver. It's a pleasant way to spend a Saturday morning.' Very pleasant indeed, remembered Donatella. During her last visit she'd been stripped naked and splayed across the bonnet of a red Ferrari, feeling the mechanic's penis thrust deep inside her. But she wasn't going to recount all her lustful activities to her friends. Now she had a college to run for real – she expected confirmation from Boston of her permanent appointment any day now – such brazen confidences and informality were not always appropriate.

'And Friday night, and last Wednesday, if I'm not mistaken,' added Kiki, teasing her friend, pricking her fragile bubble of propriety.

Donatella raised her hands in surrender. 'OK. OK. I thought we might improve our transport situation. Move upmarket a bit. That old Peugeot has so many rattles. I have my eye on a nice little second-hand Rover. Some students from North Carolina dented it last month and Marcellino's been repairing it. We're just . . . negotiating the price, you might say.'

Kiki laughed and Jennifer joined in, a little perplexed. Donatella smiled at her new assistant's uncertainty. She was probably not used to senior professors talking about providing delicious sex in return for a new car, she thought. To herself it seemed a perfectly good deal, mutually satisfactory to both parties.

The trio's conversation was interrupted by Francesca, who burst in, holding an airmail express package.

'Look! This just arrived for you, Donatella,' she said, throwing herself down in a chair. 'It's from McGraw-Hill in New York. Looks important. God, give me some wine, quick. I'm exhausted,' she continued, talking fast. 'That was a wretched pose you had me take for that last life-drawing class, Donatella.'

'I thought you looked very sexy,' said Donatella. 'An opinion shared, I might say, by many of the students, judging by their shaky line quality.' Her fingers tore open the cardboard envelope and extracted a sheaf of papers.

'What is it?' demanded Kiki.

'It's a contract,' said Donatella slowly, skim-reading the cover letter and the first few pages. 'My publishers want a new book on Caravaggio, one concerned exclusively with his paintings in Rome. Wow!'

'What?'

'There's a $10,000 advance when I sign this contract. This is fabulous!'

'When do they want the manuscript?' Kiki asked.

'Next summer,' replied Donatella. 'That means I could spend time in Rome during the fall – I know all the paintings already, so there isn't too much research there – and get to know more of the background, all the personalities involved. I could tell the story of the paintings, explain some of their characteristics.' The professor thought for a moment. 'I have a lot of material in my other book. I just need to give a fresh slant to it, perhaps discuss Caravaggio's use of optical aids, like David Hockney mentions in his recent book.' She beamed at her companions. 'This is going to be fun!' she said.

'David who?' asked Francesca.

'Another bloody Englishman!' said Kiki with a big grin.

Three weeks later Donatella, Kiki and Francesca gazed over Bucine from the rear porch of the small villa that had become their permanent home. In the kitchen

Salvatore and Gianfranco were washing up after an excellent supper. School was over for the summer, the students off on their travels, and several new part-time faculty short-listed for interview, to fill in during the fall term until full-time replacements could be hired. This evening was in the nature of a celebration: for tasks well done and trials and tribulations survived.

Reaching out in a gesture of complete intimacy, Donatella took her two companions' hands in hers, gently stroking their fingers. The trio watched in silence as bats swooped round the nearby alleyway light. To the older woman's pleasure, her two promiscuous young friends seemed to be forming serious relationships. Kiki and Gianfranco were acting like a newly married couple; and even Francesca had settled for a sort of modified monogamy with Salvatore.

She turned to her friends. 'I'll miss you while I'm working in Rome,' she said.

'Likewise,' said Kiki, affectionately. 'It won't be the same without you around.' She looked at Donatella, blinking her deep green eyes. 'You're very special to us, to me and Fran,' she said seriously. 'You're much more than a friend. I don't know how to say it, other than ... we love you. Oh, I don't just mean the sex when we romped around in bed, although that *is* fun. It's something deeper. You've changed our lives.'

Donatella looked away so that her friend wouldn't see the tears that were forming. 'I love you too, Kiki. And you, Francesca.' She gripped both friends' hands fiercely. 'I owe you both a tremendous amount. It's you who have changed *my* life. I feel so much more stable now; more in control of my life. When I came here I was only half a person; good at my career but undeveloped as a woman. You know,' she laughed at the thought, 'if Ian Ramsey walked in here tonight, I could handle him. With the self-defence you've taught me,

Kiki, and the fact that I'm a different, stronger person, he doesn't scare me any more, for all his bluster. In fact, I almost wish I *could* meet him one more time and finish him for good!'

'Ugh!' said Francesca. 'Don't say his name! He's evil! Don't spoil a great evening.'

'You're right,' said Donatella. 'Silly of me. It *is* a great evening.'

'There's more to come,' said Kiki, mysteriously.

'Let's go inside,' said Francesca, right on cue. 'It's getting a bit chilly.'

All was quiet in the house. Of Gianfranco and Salvatore there was no sign.

'We got you a going away present,' said Kiki.

Donatella was charmed. 'Oh, how lovely!' she said. 'But you shouldn't have gone to any trouble. I'll only be gone a few weeks.' The professor looked around the room but saw nothing that resembled a gift.

'Oh, it was no trouble,' said Kiki. 'Come on, it's in your bedroom.'

Donatella's mind immediately filled with thoughts of some erotic item, a new vibrator or a special dildo for her lonely nights in the Rome hotel. But she was completely unprepared for the sight that met her eyes as she entered her bedroom. On her bed was Gianfranco della Parigi in all his glory, naked and playing with his long thick cock. The young man smiled shyly at the American professor as she stood in the doorway and continued to fondle his shaft seductively, displaying it for her delectation.

Donatella was mesmerised by the young Italian's wonderful penis. She'd heard so much about it from Kiki, but here it was in full, fleshy reality. She turned to her friend. 'Oh, no, I couldn't! I mean, you and he ... you're ...'

'He wants to be your gift for the evening, Donatella,'

Kiki said with a sexy grin. 'Just get naked and enjoy him, all night long.' Anticipating Donatella's objection she added, 'It's fine. Gianfranco and I have talked about this a lot. I'm very happy with the idea. I think he still has wet dreams about you when I'm not around,' she teased. 'But seriously, he's had a crush on you ever since that first day when he burst into your office by mistake. Believe me, you'd be doing him, and me, a favour! Then he'll know for real what he's only been imagining for the last couple of months: what it would be like to fuck *dottoressa* Donatella di'Bianchi!'

'Well,' said Donatella, 'if you put it like that . . .' She already had her sandals off and paused. 'But what will you do?'

'She'll be OK,' said Francesca, who'd been watching from the doorway. 'She's coming with me and Salvatore. Lucky Sal gets to act out a few fantasies tonight, having his cock devoured by two insatiable horny women!'

'So everybody wins,' said Donatella with a smile. She looked at Gianfranco and enjoyed the dark, handsome eyes and the long shapely hands that had so nearly undone her many weeks before.

'Especially me,' said Gianfranco. 'I never believed I'd have the chance to do this.' He glanced sideways at Kiki. 'But then I never thought I'd fall in love with the sexiest girl in Tuscany,' he said.

Kiki came forward and kissed Gianfranco and Donatella. 'I love you both,' she said. 'I've had both of you, so I know you'll be great together! Now if you'll excuse me, I have to visit a horny policeman and his girl-friend!' She slipped out of the room with Francesca, leaving Donatella alone with Gianfranco.

Shutting the door, Donatella joined Gianfranco on the bed and took one of his hands and placed it on her breast. His fingers gently fondled and squeezed her nipple. 'I wanted you to do that, that first afternoon,' she breathed, huskily.

'Me, too,' said Gianfranco.

'Kiki's really something, Gianfranco, isn't she?' said Donatella.

'She is,' said the young Italian admiringly. 'But so are you, *professoressa*.' He looked deep into her eyes, all traces of shyness banished from his expression. 'Would you like to suck my cock?'

Epilogue

On another balcony, high above another piazza, a lone man peered over the city of Rome at night. His light brown hair was darker now and cropped short. Six months' growth of well-trimmed beard masked his chin, and contact lenses changed his eyes from hazel to dark brown. He knew how to cover his tracks well and had vanished from his former life with barely a trace, despite the police searches. Several months and several identities had passed into history since he abandoned the police car near San Gimignano. From there a series of favours, called in from former lovers and associates, had helped him disappear. New papers and a new persona had cost him all his savings, but he'd recently begun to feel secure from prying eyes.

Until today.

Tonight his mind was churning, reminding him of the day, months ago, when he first heard of the arrival of the American bitch who was to turn his finely crafted world upside down. Earlier today, while sitting quietly in the church of San Luigi dei Francesi and contemplating the great Caravaggio masterpiece *The Calling of Saint Matthew*, he recognised with a shock the woman who'd never been far from his thoughts since fleeing Arezzo. He'd tried to follow her as she left the church, but lost her in the crowds of Christmas tourists and pilgrims.

Or had *she* lost him? Had she seen him? Did she know he was hiding here in Rome? Was she toying with him, flaunting herself to entrap him, luring him to a place from which he could not escape? Why did she come to that particular church, right when he was sitting there? Was she – or the *carabinieri* – watching him now? He stepped back from the railing.

Tonight, despite his fear, his mind filled with the image of her body, and the smell of her sex from that last fateful day. He unzipped his fly and slowly stroked himself. Part of his mind still lusted for her now, just as he had lusted for her then, with a mixture of desire and hate. After all this time, that woman – the di'Bianchi bitch – was back.

Was he the hunter or the hunted? Tomorrow he would begin the search, watching from the shadows. And watching his back.

Visit the Black Lace website at
www.blacklace-books.co.uk

LOOK OUT FOR THE ALL-NEW BLACK LACE BOOKS – AVAILABLE NOW!

All books priced £6.99 in the UK. Please note publication dates apply to the UK only. For other territories, please contact your retailer.

succumbing to his charms, is Annie stepping into territory too dangerous even for her? **By popular demand, this is a special reprint of a free-wheeling story of lust and trouble in a fast world.**

Coming in June

WICKED WORDS 6
A Black Lace short story collection
ISBN 0 352 33590 0

Deliciously daring and hugely popular, the *Wicked Words* collections are the freshest and most entertaining volumes of women's erotica to be found anywhere in the world. The diversity of themes and styles reflects the multi-faceted nature of the female sexual imagination. Combining humour, warmth and attitude with fun, filthy, imaginative writing, these stories sizzle with horny action. Only the most arousing fiction makes it into a *Wicked Words* volume. **This is the best in fun, cutting-edge erotica from the UK and USA.**

MANHATTAN PASSION
Antoinette Powell
ISBN 0 352 33691 9

Julia is an art conservator at a prestigious museum in New York. She lives a life of designer luxury with her Wall Street millionaire husband until, that is, she discovers the dark and criminal side to his twilight activities – and storms out, leaving her high-fashion wardrobe behind her. Staying with her best friends Zoë and Jack, Julia is initiated into a hedonist circle of New York's most beautiful and sexually interesting people. Meanwhile, David, her husband, has disappeared with all their wealth. What transpires is a high-octane manhunt – from loft apartments to sleazy drinking holes; from the trendiest nightclubs to the criminal underworld. **A stunning debut from an author who knows how to entertain her audience.**

HARD CORPS
Claire Thompson
ISBN 0 352 33491 6

This is the story of Remy Harris, a bright young woman starting out as an army cadet at military college in the US. Enduring all the usual trials of boot-camp discipline and rigorous exercise, she's ready for any challenge – that is until she meets Jacob, who recognises her true sexuality. Initiated into the Hard Corps – a secret society within the barracks – Remy soon becomes absorbed by this clandestine world of ritual punishment. It's only when Jacob takes things too far that she rebels, and begins to plot her revenge. **Strict sergeants and rebellious cadets come together in this unusual and highly entertaining story of military discipline with a twist.**

Coming in July

CABIN FEVER
Emma Donaldson
ISBN 0 352 33692 7

Young beautician Laura works in the exclusive Shangri-La beauty salon aboard the cruise ship *Jannina*. Although she has a super-sensual time with her boyfriend, Steve – who works the ship's bar – there are plenty of nice young men in uniform who want a piece of her action. Laura's cabin mate is the shy, eighteen-year-old Fiona, whose sexuality is a mystery, especially as there are rumours that the stern Elinor Brookes, the matriarch of the beauty salon, has been seen doing some very curious things with the young Fiona. **Saucy story of clandestine goings-on aboard a luxury liner.**

WOLF AT THE DOOR
Savannah Smythe
ISBN O 352 33693 5

Thirty-year-old Pagan Warner is marrying Greg – a debonair and
seemingly dull Englishman – in an effort to erase her turbulent past. All
she wants is a peaceful life in rural New Jersey but her past catches up
with her in the form of bad boy 'Wolf' Mancini, the man who seduced
her as a teenager. Tempted into rekindling their intensely sexual affair
while making her wedding preparations, she intends to break off the
illicit liaison once she is married. However, Pagan has underestimated
the Wolf's obsessions. Mancini has spotted Greg's own weaknesses and
intends to exploit them to the full, undermining him in his professional
life. When he sends the slinky, raven-haired Renate in to do his dirty
work, the course is set for a descent into depravity. **Fabulous nasty
characters, dirty double dealing and forbidden lusts abound!**

THE CAPTIVE FLESH
Cleo Cordell
ISBN O 352 32872 X

Eighteenth-century French covent girls Marietta and Claudine learn that
their stay at the opulent Algerian home of their handsome and powerful
host, Kasim, requires something in return: their complete surrender to
the ecstasy of pleasure in pain. Kasim's decadent orgies also require the
services of Gabriel, whose exquisite longing for Marietta's awakened lust
cannot be contained – not even by the shackles that bind his tortured
flesh. **This is a reprint of one of the first Black Lace books ever published.
A classic piece of blockbusting historical erotica.**

Black Lace Booklist

Information is correct at time of printing. To avoid disappointment
check availability before ordering. Go to www.blacklace-books.co.uk.
All books are priced £6.99 unless another price is given.

BLACK LACE BOOKS WITH A CONTEMPORARY SETTING

☐ THE TOP OF HER GAME Emma Holly	ISBN 0 352 33337 5	£5.99
☐ IN THE FLESH Emma Holly	ISBN 0 352 33498 3	£5.99
☐ A PRIVATE VIEW Crystalle Valentino	ISBN 0 352 33308 1	£5.99
☐ SHAMELESS Stella Black	ISBN 0 352 33485 1	£5.99
☐ INTENSE BLUE Lyn Wood	ISBN 0 352 33496 7	£5.99
☐ THE NAKED TRUTH Natasha Rostova	ISBN 0 352 33497 5	£5.99
☐ ANIMAL PASSIONS Martine Marquand	ISBN 0 352 33499 1	£5.99
☐ A SPORTING CHANCE Susie Raymond	ISBN 0 352 33501 7	£5.99
☐ TAKING LIBERTIES Susie Raymond	ISBN 0 352 33357 X	£5.99
☐ A SCANDALOUS AFFAIR Holly Graham	ISBN 0 352 33523 8	£5.99
☐ THE NAKED FLAME Crystalle Valentino	ISBN 0 352 33528 9	£5.99
☐ CRASH COURSE Juliet Hastings	ISBN 0 352 33018 X	£5.99
☐ ON THE EDGE Laura Hamilton	ISBN 0 352 33534 3	£5.99
☐ LURED BY LUST Tania Picarda	ISBN 0 352 33533 5	£5.99
☐ THE HOTTEST PLACE Tabitha Flyte	ISBN 0 352 33536 X	£5.99
☐ THE NINETY DAYS OF GENEVIEVE Lucinda Carrington	ISBN 0 352 33070 8	£5.99
☐ EARTHY DELIGHTS Tesni Morgan	ISBN 0 352 33548 3	£5.99
☐ MAN HUNT Cathleen Ross	ISBN 0 352 33583 1	
☐ MÉNAGE Emma Holly	ISBN 0 352 33231 X	
☐ DREAMING SPIRES Juliet Hastings	ISBN 0 352 33584 X	
☐ THE TRANSFORMATION Natasha Rostova	ISBN 0 352 33311 1	
☐ STELLA DOES HOLLYWOOD Stella Black	ISBN 0 352 33588 2	
☐ SIN.NET Helena Ravenscroft	ISBN 0 352 33598 X	
☐ HOTBED Portia Da Costa	ISBN 0 352 33614 5	
☐ TWO WEEKS IN TANGIER Annabel Lee	ISBN 0 352 33599 8	
☐ HIGHLAND FLING Jane Justine	ISBN 0 352 33616 1	

- [ ] PLAYING HARD Tina Troy — ISBN 0 352 33617 X
- [ ] SYMPHONY X Jasmine Stone — ISBN 0 352 33629 3
- [ ] STRICTLY CONFIDENTIAL Alison Tyler — ISBN 0 352 33624 2
- [ ] SUMMER FEVER Anna Ricci — ISBN 0 352 33625 0
- [ ] CONTINUUM Portia Da Costa — ISBN 0 352 33120 8
- [ ] OPENING ACTS Suki Cunningham — ISBN 0 352 33630 7
- [ ] FULL STEAM AHEAD Tabitha Flyte — ISBN 0 352 33637 4
- [ ] A SECRET PLACE Ella Broussard — ISBN 0 352 33307 3
- [ ] GAME FOR ANYTHING Lyn Wood — ISBN 0 352 33639 0
- [ ] FORBIDDEN FRUIT Susie Raymond — ISBN 0 352 33306 5
- [ ] CHEAP TRICK Astrid Fox — ISBN 0 352 33640 4
- [ ] THE ORDER Dee Kelly — ISBN 0 352 33652 8
- [ ] ALL THE TRIMMINGS Tesni Morgan — ISBN 0 352 33641 3
- [ ] PLAYING WITH STARS Jan Hunter — ISBN 0 352 33653 6
- [ ] THE GIFT OF SHAME Sara Hope-Walker — ISBN 0 352 32935 1
- [ ] COMING UP ROSES Crystalle Valentino — ISBN 0 352 33658 7
- [ ] GOING TOO FAR Laura Hamilton — ISBN 0 352 33657 9
- [ ] THE STALLION Georgina Brown — ISBN 0 352 33005 8
- [ ] DOWN UNDER Juliet Hastings — ISBN 0 352 33663 3
- [ ] THE BITCH AND THE BASTARD Wendy Harris — ISBN 0 352 33664 1
- [ ] ODALISQUE Fleur Reynolds — ISBN 0 352 32887 8
- [ ] GONE WILD Maria Eppie — ISBN 0 352 33670 6
- [ ] SWEET THING Alison Tyler — ISBN 0 352 33682 X
- [ ] TIGER LILY Kimberley Dean — ISBN 0 352 33685 4
- [ ] COOKING UP A STORM Emma Holly — ISBN 0 352 33686 2
- [ ] RELEASE ME Suki Cunningham — ISBN 0 352 33671 4
- [ ] KING'S PAWN Ruth Fox — ISBN 0 352 33684 6
- [ ] SLAVE TO SUCCESS Kimberley Raines — ISBN 0 352 33687 0
- [ ] STRIPPED TO THE BONE Jasmine Stone — ISBN 0 352 33463 0

BLACK LACE BOOKS WITH AN HISTORICAL SETTING

- [ ] PRIMAL SKIN Leona Benkt Rhys — ISBN 0 352 33500 9 £5.99
- [ ] DEVIL'S FIRE Melissa MacNeal — ISBN 0 352 33527 0 £5.99
- [ ] WILD KINGDOM Deanna Ashford — ISBN 0 352 33549 1 £5.99
- [ ] DARKER THAN LOVE Kristina Lloyd — ISBN 0 352 33279 4
- [ ] STAND AND DELIVER Helena Ravenscroft — ISBN 0 352 33340 5 £5.99

To find out the latest information about Black Lace titles, check out the
website: www.blacklace-books.co.uk or send for a booklist with
complete synopses by writing to:

> Black Lace Booklist, Virgin Books Ltd
> Thames Wharf Studios
> Rainville Road
> London W6 9HA

Please include an SAE of decent size. Please note only British stamps
are valid.

Our privacy policy
We will not disclose information you supply us to any other parties.
We will not disclose any information which identifies you personally to
any person without your express consent.

From time to time we may send out information about Black Lace
books and special offers. Please tick here if you do <u>not</u> wish to
receive Black Lace information.   ☐

Please send me the books I have ticked above.

Name ....

Address ....

....

....

....

Post Code ....

Send to: Cash Sales, Black Lace Books, Thames Wharf Studios, Rainville Road, London W6 9HA.

US customers: for prices and details of how to order books for delivery by mail, call 1-800-343-4499.

Please enclose a cheque or postal order, made payable to Virgin Books Ltd, to the value of the books you have ordered plus postage and packing costs as follows:

UK and BFPO – £1.00 for the first book, 50p for each subsequent book.

Overseas (including Republic of Ireland) – £2.00 for the first book, £1.00 for each subsequent book.

If you would prefer to pay by VISA, ACCESS/MASTERCARD, DINERS CLUB, AMEX or SWITCH, please write your card number and expiry date here:

....

Signature ....

Please allow up to 28 days for delivery.